Praise for

BALLOON DOG

"When you think of art heists, it's often centuries-old paintings or sculptures that come to mind. Daniel Paisner's *Balloon Dog* demonstrates just how thrilling it can be to put a contemporary work of art into a narrative—and a massive maximalist sculpture, at that. And that's without touching on Paisner's incisive riffs on suburban ennui throughout the book. Imagine a literary mash-up of *The Hot Rock* and *A Serious Man* and you have a sense of where this novel is coming from—but not of the surprises it has in store."

—TOBIAS CARROLL
Author of *Reel* and *Ex-Members*

"Opportunity looks different in middle age than it does in youth—especially in Daniel Paisner's *Balloon Dog*. Slightly lost, deeply frustrated, and desperate to know if there's still life to be had in the back half of the game, Paisner's characters handle marriage and divorce and aging parents and money problems with a lack of grace that provides a plot full of comedy and pathos. Darkly funny and painfully true, *Balloon Dog* proves that the unknowable road of life is best handled by experienced drivers: those who know only that twists are coming and trust they'll be able to navigate them in their own imperfect way when they do."

—LAURA ZIGMAN
Author of *Separation Anxiety*

"Daniel Paisner has a winner on his hands—actually, we all win here. How often is a book this funny, intense, exciting, and intensely stylish, all at once? Paisner does a masterful job—well plotted, fast-paced, and a hell of a read."

—DARIN STRAUSS
Author of *The Queen of Tuesday* and *Chang and Eng*

"Daniel Paisner's *Balloon Dog* is a little bit of everything—rumination on life, desire, regret for the paths we choose and those we've walked and to which we can no longer return. It's also a heist novel and a psychological thriller, what might result if Philip Roth and Elmore Leonard wrote a book together. In the end, *Balloon Dog* is a magnificent and magnificently written rendering of life on all sorts of margins, and one you won't want to miss!"

—TED FLANAGAN
Author of *Every Hidden Thing*

"Funny, smart, and populated with empathetic, unforgettable characters you wouldn't mind teaming up with for an art heist. Daniel Paisner's fiction pen hasn't lost an ounce of ink. A yarn you're not going to want to put down."

—DANIEL FORD
Author of *Black Coffee* and host of the *Writer's Bone* podcast

"*Balloon Dog* is my favorite kind of novel—darkly comic, great characters, and snappy dialogue, and not afraid to go to wild places with its plot. I loved it. Kudos to Daniel Paisner!"

—ANNIE HARTNETT
Author of *Rabbit Cake* and *Unlikely Animals*

"*Balloon Dog* is great company, and full of surprises—at once an art heist and domestic drama, an astute reflection on value, and a poignant meditation on middle age. This novel is a breath of fresh air."

—Lydia Kiesling
Author of *The Golden State*

"Funny, insightful, and original, *Balloon Dog* delighted me on every page. Daniel Paisner writes with gusto, intelligence, and a voice so fresh I was entirely enchanted. What a joy to read!"

—ELLEN MEISTER
Author of *Farewell, Dorothy Parker* and *Take My Husband*

"*Balloon Dog* beautifully captures the inner lives of its characters, their disappointments, regrets, and hopes, the joys and absurdities of our modern world. An art theft, midlife crises, marriage, divorce, intimacy, parenthood, caring for an aging parent, and the lures of money and social media all converge in Daniel Paisner's wonderfully funny, inventive, and insightful novel."

—RONNA WINEBERG
Author of *Artifacts and Other Stories*

Balloon Dog

By Daniel Paisner

ISBN 978-1-64663-699-0

Cover design and illustration by Skyler Kratofil.

Published by

köehlerbooks™

3705 Shore Drive
Virginia Beach, VA 23455
800–435–4811
www.koehlerbooks.com

BALLOON DOG

DANIEL PAISNER

VIRGINIA BEACH
CAPE CHARLES

For Sal

TABLE OF CONTENTS

SPRING

FALL

Abstraction and luxury are the guard dogs of the upper class.
—*Jeff Koons*

SPRING

1.

FIRST THERE IS A MOUNTAIN

LEM DEVLIN

MAKES NO SENSE, hauling this giant sculpture up and down this mountain. Eight, nine guys on the crew. Sixty man-hours, easy, plus how long it takes to clean and crate the thing back at the warehouse. Two flatbeds, a crane, whatever else their asshole boss tells them to bring to the site. Guy walks around with a clipboard, a whistle—a whistle!—a double-walled, sixty-four-ounce Hydro Flask thermos. Shit-kicker work boots looking fresh from the box—like, always. What, he steps into a new pair every morning?

Been a couple years on this job and Lem doesn't get it. The things people with money do with their money. What they get people to do for their money. The ways people with money actually *get* their money. Man. Like, okay, this house with the sculpture, some water balloon-looking shit.

Every year, same deal. The snow disappears—May, June—they take the crates from the warehouse in Bountiful and cart the works back up to Park City for the summer. Those killer homes they've got up there? Promontory. Jeremy Ranch. Tuhaye. And this one, The Colony. Ten, twenty thousand square feet. State of the art everything. The finest materials. Flown in, trucked in from all over. Lebanese cedar. Italian marble. Picture windows making it look like nothing separates the inside of the house from the outside, from some angles. Each home set so you can't see your neighbors, people pretending the whole damn mountain belongs to them. Places sit empty, what, three hundred nights of the year. More, maybe. Dude with the water balloon, he worries the snow, the ice, the cold temperatures will fuck with his sculpture, so he takes the thing apart before the snow flies each winter and has it shipped to this warehouse.

Bountiful. It gets to Lem, how they put this warehouse in this nothing-special town, just outside the city. The shit they store, the clients they serve . . . amazing how these people have run out of room for all their stuff and now they have to store it in these secure, climate-controlled buildings, the whole place alarmed and rigged up with cameras like it's Fort Fucking Knox. Art storage, they call it, there's a whole industry, and if you studied the business models of some of these companies, you'd think art is meant to be locked away, out of the reach of humidity and sunlight and extreme cold, where no one can even see it. Also amazing: how it just works out that the top storage place in the Midwest for these expensive works is in a town with a name that reminds these fuckers what they have, this uncontainable bounty. This is how Lem has come to think of it. These people, they're, like, too rich for their own homes. They've got too much stuff for the wide-open spaces they occupy. How about *that*, motherfuckers? Artwork, antique cars, furniture—jewelry, even. Lem rides shotgun on some of these armored truck calls and he can't imagine how much money he'd have to have before he couldn't find room in his house for his fucking jewelry. And here's this guy, his boss—calls himself Artemis—he sets up this business, makes like he's got all these fine art degrees from all these big deal schools. Maybe he does, what the hell does Lem know? Only, he knows the guy's name isn't Artemis. Shit, his wife calls him Arty. She comes by the office, doesn't make it any kind of mystery. And he doesn't look like no Artemis—although, truth, Lem wouldn't know an Artemis from a Bartholomew.

Either way, Lem's seen the paperwork on the trucks his boss runs in his Fine Artemis fleet, and they're all registered to Arthur Hammond. *Fine Artemis*—can you beat that? Boss gets himself bonded and insured and opens this warehouse in Bountiful. That's the actual fucking name of the town. It's like a suburb of Salt Lake, and Lem wonders if Arty got himself a deal on the space or if he's making some kind of statement.

Whatever. It's a job, right? Pay is decent. Work is steady. Benefits—for Lem, anyway. Some days, the work is even a little interesting—the places he's sent, the shit he hauls. The back-and-forth on this one sculpture, it's been something to notice, that's all. That's how it is with Lem Devlin— just short of forty, just shy of getting out in front of his bills. He picks up on things. Other people, they take things as they come, but Lem looks for patterns. What makes sense, what doesn't make sense. He looks for ways to fit himself into the spaces between—opportunities, which most times aren't really opportunities at all.

Possibilities, you know.

Lem gets to thinking this way because he sees the job on the schedule. This is how it starts, like a puzzle he works in his head. Every year, he gets to thinking in the same way. First puzzle piece is the weather-watch on the warehouse calendar. If the temps stay warm, and the snowmelt finishes doing its thing, a Fine Artemis crew will be carting that giant balloon sculpture back up the mountain before too, too long. Up and down, back and forth, over and over. . . makes no fucking sense to Lem, but here it is, something to think about, and as he settles into his thinking, Lem wonders again if there's maybe something in it for him, this famous piece of art, nobody really knowing whether it's supposed to be parked on the side of a mountain in Park City or tucked away in some art storage facility outside of Salt Lake City.

Somewhere in there, Lem gets to thinking the only way to ever get ahead in this world, *truly* ahead, is to grab at what you want. He's tired of walking through life with his hand out, waiting for good things to come his way. Been that way forever. Everyone he knows, same deal. They're all waiting, waiting, waiting for their turn to show up on the calendar. Waiting for the snow to melt and the flowers to bloom and the sun to finally shine on a way forward. Everyone he knows, they want to walk in that fresh sunlight—it's just, it never seems to shine on them. He's tired of standing with everyone else, on the margins, shit out of luck, always, so that's where he gets to thinking about this sculpture. That's the second piece of the puzzle.

Last time he was thinking this way, probably when they reclaimed the balloon from the mountain last fall, Lem read somewhere that a much smaller piece by the same artist had just sold for over ninety million dollars. Article said it was a record auction price for a work by a living artist. A stainless-steel rabbit, about two feet high, looking like something Lem would find in the close-out bin at Costco, week after Christmas. Like a toy. But this artist, Koons, he's stepped in some sweet shit. Got all these billionaires thinking his art is speaking to them in a meaningful way—and, who knows, maybe it is. What the fuck it's saying, this balloon-animal-looking shit, Lem's got no idea. He doesn't *do* insight or introspection, wouldn't recognize that shit if it bit him on the dick, but he knows this artist must be saying. . . *something*. Something about a return to simplicity and basic human decency, or having it all, or finding beauty or magic or wonder in the stuff we already have laying around. A bunch of bullshit, you ask Lem, but someone pays you ninety million dollars, you tell him what he wants to hear, and when that someone is an outrageously rich banker who happens to be the father of the outrageously rich banker who happens to be Donald Fucking Trump's Treasury secretary . . . well, that's when you know that sweet shit is good and stuck in the treads of your shoes.

Another something to notice, you know. Another piece of the puzzle.

This sculpture they're dismantling and reassembling every year, it's bright red, meant to look like a balloon animal. It's right there in the name of the piece: *Balloon Dog #17 (Red)*. And there it is on the calendar, in nickname: *Woof Woof*. That's how Fine Arty writes it down, with a bright red marker, in block letters. Like it's all one big fucking joke. To Lem, the sculpture looks more like a giant pile of stringed sausages, or maybe one of Princess Leia's buns, dipped in blood and set on its side—but maybe that's because he's used to seeing it in pieces, disassembled, draped in drop cloths, away from its natural habitat.

To look at this sculpture assembled, you get the feeling it might fly away. That's probably because it's got this light and airy feel to it, but it looks to Lem like a whole bunch of nothing at all. Meaningless. Artless. It weights a shit-ton, but it's like there's no weight to it at all. The guys on the crew, they set the thing up, Arty on hand to make sure everything is just right, and at some point, they step back and wonder what the fuck they're looking at—thinking, you know, where's the art? What is this thing supposed to even *mean*? Lem's watched them over the years, and to a man every damn hauler and trucker assigned to the job takes a moment to step back and wonder what they're doing on the top of this mountain, assembling or disassembling a giant red balloon dog. It's like someone is fucking with them. Each link of the balloon sausage is fixed in some way to an enormous steel rod that stands in the middle. The rod only stands when it's balanced by the weight of all these balloon pieces, which seem to float and sway when everything is fitted into place. Structurally, it's a pretty ingenious design, the way this Koons guy has distributed the weight among all these connecting parts. The way it moves—dances, almost—against a big wind. Lem doesn't think the sculpture was meant to be taken apart and put back together every couple months, but that's what happens when you sell your shit to the highest bidder. Probably, it wasn't meant to be displayed outdoors—especially in the great outdoors of these mountains, middle of winter. Wasn't anything close to that ninety-million-dollar rabbit, but Lem guesses the sculpture is worth about ten million. Tough to tell, because it's changed hands a bunch of times and landed at this house in Park City through a private sale. But Koons is a hot, talked-about artist and his big, industrial-type sculptures have been selling for big, industrial-type dollars . . . so, yeah, ten million.

That's the number, the final piece of the puzzle. For now.

Lem knows all of this because of the ways he's been thinking. Because no one's ever in the mammoth house on the mountain every time he breaks the piece down and sets it back up. Because pretty much *all* of those houses sit empty most of the time. Because even the moose and elk and deer are nowhere to be seen when they pull up with their crane and those flatbeds.

Because it would just be too fucking easy.

————————

So. He brings his buddy Duck into it. What Lem's thinking, hijacking the Koons balloon sculpture, it isn't something he can do on his own. What he's thinking is maybe Duck and a couple other guys they know can borrow some trucks and head up to Park City, break the thing down, haul it away. The idea is to do it smooth, professional, like they've been doing it at Fine Artemis past couple years.

Like they belong, you know.

"You shittin' me, right?" Duck says, after Lem lays it all out for him over beers. They're at this place, Beer Bar, in downtown Salt Lake City. Lem likes it because it's no frills, busy. It tells you what it is right on the sign. Every damn beer you can think of, every damn beer you've never even heard of, they've got it there.

"I'm tellin' you," Lem says, sipping at a Moody Tongue Shaved Black Truffle Pilsner—because, hey, how often do you see a shaved black truffle pilsner? "It's, like, asking to be stolen."

"Not asking *me*," Duck says, behind the neck of his Coors Light.

"No," Lem says. "*I'm* asking you. Should be thanking me, bringing you in."

"You're out of your fuckin' head," Duck says. "Said yourself, thing weighs a ton. Can't exactly sneak a crane past the neighbors. All those trucks. C'mon."

"Me, I'm out of my head," Lem says, pointing to Duck's beer with the neck of his own. "You're the one sipping piss. They've got a thousand beers. The fuck is wrong with you?"

"The fuck is wrong with me is my circle of friends," Duck says, tipping the neck of his beer toward Lem.

Lem knows this dance with Duck. His thing is to go negative, you know. One of those glass-half-empty types. He sees what's on the surface instead of what's below. Anyway, he's not seeing what Lem is seeing, so Lem lays it out for him again, how they've been handling this sculpture for years at work, how he knows the drill, knows the owner's routines, how the legit job is already on the schedule. "We print up some shirts, make sure we're all wearing the same thing, maybe put a sign on our vehicles, make it look legit," he says. "Like we're supposed to be there, carting away this ten-million-dollar balloon."

"Like hiding in plain sight?" Duck says. He's just watched this movie with his girl, a bank heist, and that was the hook of the whole story, the bad guys being right out in the open with what they were doing. Like they were entitled.

"Exactly," Lem says. "Set-up is next week. Take-down is September, last week or two, but the client is always gone by Labor Day. House is empty. It's shoulder season, whole side of the mountain is empty."

"The neighbors," Duck says. "Tell me how they don't see what we're up to."

"Shoulder season for them, too," Lem says.

"Meaning?" Duck says.

"Meaning, no neighbors," Lem says. "Meaning, everybody clears out. It's like a ghost town up there, I hear. A private fucking wilderness. And even if someone sees us, they know this balloon dog sculpture. They know it comes and goes every summer. It's like a local landmark. Thing is fucking huge, you'll see. It's in every aerial photo ever taken, that side of the mountain, that time of year. Check Google Maps. You can see it for miles."

He pauses and his face lights in the small smile that finds him when he thinks of something that strikes him funny. "Birds know it, too," he says—struck, continuing. "Sometimes, we get there, the thing is splattered with hawk shit, eagle shit, whatever. Like target practice."

"Damn," Duck says—what he usually says when there's nothing else to say.

"Someone'd have to be crazy," Lem says, "try to make off with something like that, broad fucking daylight."

Lem takes a meaty swig of his beer and slaps the bottle on the wooden table. Then he leans in and makes his eyes go big and wide, and points his finger at his own head, in a way meant to indicate crazy.

"Tell me the Labor Day part," Duck says. "How you know he'll be gone."

"How I know he'll be gone is he and his wife host a famous party every year at their beach house in Malibu," Lem says. "Every Labor Day. It's on the news. A *white party*."

"A *white party*, like, for white people?" Duck says.

"A *white party*, like, for what you're supposed to wear," Lem says.

Duck downs the last of his beer and signals the waitress for another.

"Mix it up," Lem says, meaning the beer. "Try something new."

"I like what I like," Duck says. He places his hands at the edge of table directly in front of him and presses down. He lowers his head, and Lem gets that this is how he thinks things through. This is Duck, going over every detail Lem has set out for him, thinking how it can all go wrong, how it can all go right—just, you know, thinking.

Lem knows not to bother Duck when he's thinking, so he hangs back, lets the job register—what's involved, what it might mean. It's taken him years to talk himself into believing he can pull off a job like this, so he knows to hang back and give Duck some time to wrap his head around the idea in the same way.

After a while, Duck looks up from his thinking and starts back in. "Say we do this," he says. "Say we get all the red balloon pieces loaded onto our trucks, not a scratch. Say we make it down the mountain and get to someplace safe. Say we pull it off. Then what?"

2.

WHAT IT IS AIN'T EXACTLY CLEAR

HARRISON KLOTT

NOT A PRETTY PICTURE: Harrison Klott, pants unbuttoned, left hand on junk, right hand on keyboard. Ready position.

Ready for *what*—well, it's hard to say. Default position would be more like it because this is how things usually go when they go in just this way, how his hands usually fall.

The house is quiet, for the moment. Kids at school. Wife at work. Housecleaner through with her idea of housecleaning.

Also not a pretty picture: Klott himself. At fifty-one, he's gone round at the middle. Relatedly, he's committed to riding his pants just below his belly, but the way things are going in that area he might have to rethink his strategy and take it up top. Also relatedly, there are hairs clumped in the *c* of his inner ear. Too, his jawline has been swallowed up by his ears—an unfortunate aspect of his senescence his one and only client the plastic surgeon has been after him to do something about. But it doesn't end there. Whatever youthful enthusiasm and boyish good looks that may have once attached to Harrison Klott have by now left the building, the town, the state. These days, his resting expression is one part stroke victim, one part guy strap-hanging next to you on the subway who's been going to the same place for lunch every day for the past seventeen years. Each time he passes a mirror, Klott can't shake thinking he's looking more and more like his father—a man who, at eighty-one, looks less and less like Klott's father every time Klott visits. They still have their hair, though— father and son, both. Say what you will about Harrison Klott—the man's got a decent head of hair. Steve Bannon hair, his wife Marjorie pointed out, when the guy was all over the news. Long, wavy, thick . . . No doubt Marjorie Klott was looking to make lemonade from the sack of turned lemons her husband was fast becoming, but Klott took her point.

It would be easy to get the wrong idea about Harrison Klott, who is not the sort of man who spends his weekday afternoons, pants at his ankles, looking at porn. He is not even the sort of man who spends his precious half hours in just this way. He is, however, the sort of Internet troll who follows the endless stream of links teasing a glimpse of Kardashian ass-cleavage, a wisp of Rihanna side boob. Sex tapes, outtakes, topless vacation pics . . . he'll seek it all out, only to be endlessly frustrated when the promised footage is no longer available, or his browser is deemed unworthy, outmoded. He's like a puppy, willing to be fooled each time out.

Regrettably—and, perhaps, inevitably—this tic of Klott's online personality runs to fully clothed indecency as well, of every size and stripe, including but not limited to unflattering celebrity mug shots, beheadings, security camera transgressions. And so, Harrison Klott appears to be a stuck, restless, middle-aged man with a little too much time on his hands, a little too much flab at the belt, a little too much wattle at the neck, a little too much imagination for his own good. But then, just beneath the surface, at which depths there are aspects of character Klott himself cannot always recognize, there is as well the congealing truth of a man plopped down on the moving sidewalk of his life, progressing slowly in the very direction he'd set out for in the first place but not really digging the thought of where he is headed.

What gets Harrison Klott going, after all, most of all, is the trace evidence of lives more fully, more purposefully, more lustily lived than the one he has consigned himself to living.

"There's something happenin' here," he sometimes mouths to himself, half-singing, bending that old Buffalo Springfield song so that it underlines these moments of prurient surprise instead of the counterculture unrest that preceded his growing up. He even drops the *g*, like he's Stephen Stills.

It's one of his things, to attach a snatch of lyric to whatever's going on in his life, to whatever's not going on, only with Harrison Klott it's not like he slaps the words on a scene like a thought-bubble. No, he actually *hears* the line, in full, the way it's been drilled into him—the soundtrack of his life and times, punctuating his moods.

This Internet trolling business started out an innocent obsession, and Klott can make the argument that there it remains. However, he can appreciate the other side of the argument as well. *Obsession*, yes, *innocent*, hardly. You see, around the time copies of his first (and only) novel disappeared from bookstores the moment they hit the shelves (out the back door, mind you, re-boxed in the same cartons in which they'd arrived, and not out the front, gift-wrapped or stuffed into one of those bookstore shopping bags with the line-drawn portraits of Shakespeare, Dickinson, Patterson); around the time Marjorie stopped reaching for him in the middle of the night and went from occasionally initiating sex to somewhat less than occasionally acquiescing to it; around the time the boiler hit its rated life expectancy and marked the occasion by dumping its rusted sludge water onto the basement floor; around the time young waitresses ceased flirting with him to lubricate their tip lines and instead determined he wasn't even worth the trouble; around the time the doctor found that suspicious lump on the back of the neck of his oldest, Joanna (it turned out to be nothing, but still…); around the time he started realizing he no longer had anything to actually *say* in the subsequent novels he was never quite able to write (and, had he written them, would have never been able to publish); around the time the weight of his worries (taxes, mortgage payments, the lackluster, lack *anything* reviews of his book) began to press the air from his lungs and leave him gasping, scrambling for a hold on his days; around the time he started working for his one and only client (the head of a local plastic surgery group who needed help editing and preparing and overthinking a never-ending output of articles, position papers, blog posts, and pamphlets, most of them concerning the esteem-building benefits of liposuction and breast augmentation); around the time a countdown clock began to hover over his head like a drone, reminding him of his own mortality… well, it was in and around and through *these* times that he began to look at Facebook and Instagram with his dick in his hand.

To be fair—and, to place this behavior in context—Harrison Klott's hands have been in his pants since he can remember. Nursery school, probably. Grade school, certainly. High school, alarmingly. To this day, he holds a vivid memory of a particularly heated AP Lit class discussion on *Heart of Darkness* and the latent homosexuality of Conrad's main characters, seated behind the particularly long-haired and sweet-smelling Marybeth Fitzsimmons. There—surreptitiously, it is now hoped—Klott slipped his right hand beneath the button fly of his crisp Wranglers and started playing with himself. Not *jerking off*—playing with himself. The difference was and remains key. Since he first heard the term, he's moved about the planet thinking this elemental euphemism was somehow coined with him in mind because it was never *really* about sexual pleasure for Harrison Klott, this hands in the pants business, so much as it was something to do, a way to separate himself from the world around. There was no end game to it, no thought behind it, other than the extra efforts he took to keep from being found out—but even those thoughts fell away in time, with all that practice. By the age of twelve, Harrison Klott was fairly expert at finding ways to touch, rub, cup or otherwise apply a pleasing bit of friction to himself without anyone suspecting what it was he was up to. A forearm placed stiffly across his lap as he sat in the cafeteria. A fist in the pocket, sent looking for loose change or a crumpled-up note, only to linger a too long while as he worked his fingers against his dick through the fabric. The constant tucking and untucking of his shirt, for the sole purpose of thrusting his hands into the front of his pants in a socially acceptable way.

If, in an alternate universe, the subtle tugging and rubbing of post-adolescent private parts had been elevated to the level of sport, Harrison Klott would have certainly made varsity.

And now here he sits, all these years later, clicking the iconic Facebook *f*, his eyes drawn to the distinctive Klavika font as if by suction, pulling back the curtain on all these lives, all around. It happens for Klott without a thought: the unzippering of his pants, the disheartening realization that there are no new friend requests awaiting him, no direct messages requiring his attention, nothing to indicate that he had been this way before or to explain how it is that he's managed to assemble a network of 643 friends (even acknowledging that a good percentage had been culled from the plastic surgery conventions his one and only client insists he attend), not a single one of them likely to notice if he fell off the "Face" of this "book." Harrison Klott goes through these motions and emotions like nothing at all—because, hey, they are like nothing at all. To call them second nature would be to suggest that there is something natural about the choreography of connecting to all these loosely connected people in such a disconnected way.

In Klott's mind, the position we find him in doesn't mean much at all—and yet, here it is. Here *he* is, alighting on the weekend adventure photos of a girl he knew only vaguely in college who has now taken up bird watching. These days she appears to be married, or at least ineluctably joined, to a bespectacled man who wears many-pocketed safari vests and floppy sun-shielding hats, with a collection of like-minded and like-attired friends in her traveling party who seem inclined to post pictures of ruby-throated sparrows—although, frankly, Klott couldn't pick one of *these* out of a lineup, only knows the name from the song.

Scrolling, he comes across a landscape photo with the legend "When you can't sleep at night, it's because you're awake in someone else's dream"—a curious sentiment to Klott, who tends to fall off as soon as he hits the pillow.

Next, he pauses on an album of photos shared by one of his neighbors. The woman has got to be in her late seventies but, judging from her photos, it looks like she's won some sort of aging lottery. That, or she's found a way to incorporate formaldehyde into her beauty regimen. Here she appears to be touring the vineyards of Napa with a collection of similarly well-preserved older women, one in particular who is surely the first person in her cohort to own a selfie stick—said stick apparently coming into her possession without the requisite set of instructions, because the woman is unable to keep herself or her companions in frame.

The time fairly flies. Someone's kid lost a tooth. Another someone visited his parents in Florida and took them to a nice dinner. Another someone wants him to "like" his page—a minimalist effort featuring a collection of bereavement poems for beloved household pets. And still another someone has thought to rage against this very platform. Really, there's no end to what Harrison Klott's Facepeople find interesting, memorable, suitable for public consumption. They are a race of his own making, and he is here to touch himself and sit in judgment and bemusement of them all.

What's this? A list of uncommon uses for pomegranates? A video link to one of last night's ball games, where something unusual/unlikely/unbelievable happened? A carefully considered think-paragraph on the courage of Caitlyn Jenner? There was a time when Klott would have lingered on many of these posts, the same way he used to read the hell out of the bathroom graffiti at school, but he's gotten to where he no longer gives a shit what some of these people think, only that they are thinking to put these thoughts on display for his consideration so he can eavesdrop on their conversations and imagine himself as someone who matters to them in the fundamental ways that seem just beyond the purview of Mark Zuckerberg's business plan.

And then, at last, there is this: an album of sun-splashed family photos posted by Shari Braverman, a woman Klott met at a local bookstore event he was not participating in but felt he should nevertheless attend, having once been the sort of person for whom a local bookstore event might have meant something. Shari Braverman—she of the lustrous dirty blonde hair, the fit and fetching and apparently unattached mom-bod, unfailingly sheathed in an assortment of brightly-colored Lululemon leggings and sports bras . . . a stunning creature for whom the conventions of social media networking seemed to have evolved.

Here is what Harrison Klott has gleaned about Shari Braverman in their months-long Facebook friendship:

She is the single mother of two—a boy, Jaxon, who appears from his mother's posts to be about thirteen; and a girl, Jana, probably seven or eight. Both children have very good teeth.

She is divorced or separated from an heir (or, at least, a cousin) to the Braverman snack food fortune—the makers, most famously, of off-brand cheese curls. This is made clear to Klott by the very many photos of Jaxon and Jana sporting the Braverman logo in its distinctive Pickwick font on various T-shirts, hats, and hoodies. Also, there is occasional note and comment in the threads beneath her posts about the suspect health effects of Braverman products, and the processed cheese dust that can't help but stick to your fingers after enjoying the family fare. Also, the boy goes by "Jax," spun from the name of the company's signature non-doodle snack, "Double Jax," which in turn had been spun from yet another non-doodle brand.

She is an interior designer, freelance, working on the fine homes of the moneyed class—in the Hamptons, in the Berkshires, on the Upper East Side. She has an eye for big leather furniture and natural woods. Last summer, she attended a design conference where she posed for a picture with Robert Redford in a high-ceilinged ski lodge decorated in a similar manner, and after she'd posted it, Klott spent the next couple hours trying to craft the perfect off-the-cuff quip to add to the comment thread that had quickly filled with *oooh*s and *aaah*s and *lucky girl*s beneath the photo, most of them followed by multiple exclamation points. Of course, the head-scratching and obsession ran somewhat counter to the spontaneous tone he was seeking, but it was important to him to get it right. He even consulted Wikipedia for a list of Robert Redford movies, hoping to come up with a clever play on words that might stand in for the quick wit that had always eluded him, finally settling on a lame-ass place-holder comment Klott immediately regretted posting: *the way you were?* Still, the lucky girl took the time to "like" Klott's comment, and so did two of her friends, so he was able to put the sorry business in the plus column.

She enjoys a good glass of wine, a nice piece of chocolate, and fresh flowers.

She does not know Harrison Klott to say hello when he passes her in the spice aisle at the local Whole Foods—but then, Klott doesn't greet her either, only he has to think that her reasons for looking straight past him have nothing to do with a fear of stammering, a fear of not having just the right thing to say, a fear of coming across as somehow pathetic or loserly or *less than.*

She is not a fan of excessive make-up, although she surely keeps a good supply of gloss in the Brighton tote she seems to favor, because her lips are always shimmering.

She spends most of her free weekends, when Jax and Jana are with their father, in the company of a good group of mostly women friends, some of whom Klott is able to recognize in the pictures she shares as they hike, bike, and otherwise empower each other, many of them presumably on the same joint custody schedule with their own ex-husbands.

Also, this: these women have banded together in such a way that they've taken to calling themselves the Joint Custody Club and dressing in uniform—specifically, in hats and T-shirts decorated with the letters *JCC,* which no one seems to want to acknowledge should rightfully suggest an affiliation with the local Jewish Community Center.

And speaking of the JCC, she belongs to the same synagogue as Harrison and Marjorie Klott. Once, on one of the Lesser Holidays (*Shemeni Atzeret,* he thinks), Shari Braverman sat across the aisle from Klott, two rows in front, and she did not appear to notice him.

She looks altogether sensational in a one-piece racing suit, emerging wet from some lake where a friend has a log home, the interior of which suggests she had a hand in the decorating.

She also looks good in hats, on horseback, and in repose.

She is not the type to sit still—however, when she does choose to spend an evening at home, it is often accompanied by a joyful announcement on her message board, together with a picture of a fireplace, an extravagantly home-cooked meal, a dust jacket of the book she's reading, a link to a trailer of the show she's binge-watching. Her reading tastes lean away from book clubbish bestsellers, in favor of second-tier works of great writers. (She was last seen reading Isak Dinesen's *Gengaeldelsons veje*—"The Angelic Avengers"—in translation.)

She went to see the Stones when they played in Brooklyn.

She is not ready to start dating again because she wants to be fully present for her children. However, there seems to be a long line of jewelry-wearing men who press close to her in group photos taken at the many bar and bat mitzvah celebrations she has lately been attending. (Like Klott's twins, Jax seems to be on the circuit.)

Klott guesses that when she is ready to start dating again, these men will be the first to know. However, by the time word gets around to Harrison Klott, he fears it might be too late. Too late for *what*... well, this too is not entirely clear. Really, he can't begin to fathom.

———

He is awakened from his Facebook reverie by the bleat of phone—his landline. He answers on the third ring.

"Hey," he says.

"Hey back," he hears. He recognizes the voice—his preternaturally insufferable college roommate, Teddy, who in his own take on mid-life crisis has started introducing himself as Theo.

Teddy Pluscht went into his family's conveniently named plush toy business immediately after graduation, which just happened to coincide with the slow realization that none of the nation's top law schools were inclined to accept him and that even the middle-tier schools were not all that interested. It was just as well, because Teddy arrived on the scene just in time to help Pluscht Toys ride the last wave of the Beanie Baby craze with its own line of knockoffs, making the kind of money Teddy would start referring to as "generational wealth" and giving the lie to Teddy Sr.'s not-so-closely-held belief that his son would never amount to anything.

"You book your flights?" Teddy says.

His flights. Klott has been dragging on this—Teddy's annual gathering of college friends and acquaintance-type pals of more recent vintage. It started out, Teddy rented a ski house in Vermont one winter, and he invited an assortment of friends for a boys' weekend. There was drinking and merrymaking of the kind that seemed to grow more meaningful in the minds of the participants over time than Klott had been able to note when he was in its middle. In moments of self-awareness, Klott might have acknowledged that one of the reasons the others seemed to enjoy the weekend more than him was because they all seemed to *have* more than him. More money, success, fulfillment, security. . . more of everything, really. They were plastic surgeons, divorce attorneys, investment bankers, reality show producers, plush toy magnates, and as they sat around Teddy's great stone fireplace sipping the kind of single malt scotch Klott could never afford and could hardly appreciate, it occurred to Klott that he had somehow failed to have been swept up in the same currents that move the rest of the world—the rest of *this* world, anyway.

But Teddy kept inviting him—back to Vermont the next year, and then to a fabulous resort in the Dominican Republic, a fabulous penthouse in Miami, a fabulous beach house in Malibu. Each year, the *fabulousness* was amped up a couple notches. And Klott kept going, in large part because Marjorie insisted it would be good for him to get out of the house and be with his "friends." Teddy was determined to one-up himself each time out, and after those first couple years he was helped along in this by the fact that his sister had married well. The Vermont place was just a rental, and Teddy found the Punta Cana resort on VRBO, but the Miami and Malibu digs belonged to his sister, whose husband had parlayed early-stage investments in Google and other Silicon Valley start-ups into a billion-dollar portfolio. In self-satisfied moments, Klott contented himself that his insufferable college pal who had merely earned tens of millions in the plush toy business had somehow been consigned to the kiddie table in his father's estimation, and that his kid sister was the one with her name on hospital wings.

Funny, the shit life throws at you. In any other family, in any other circumstance, at any other time in our history, Teddy Pluscht would have been a kind of golden child, a favorite son, the keeper of the flame. In his own family, however, at just this time, his kid sister Robin was the game-changer—little Robin Pluscht, who'd had to be bribed with a new BMW convertible before agreeing to go to college, where she had the good fortune of meeting a budding tech investor. The irony was not talked about among Teddy's friends, but it was hard not to notice, and Teddy was only too happy to take good and full advantage of his sister's good fortune. He had an open invitation to her homes in Miami, Malibu, Park City, and Paris, and he wasn't shy about using them. It was his sister, after all.

"Was kinda hoping Robin would send her plane," Klott says.

"We're roughing it this trip," Teddy says—meaning, they will have to fly commercial.

Teddy was billing this gathering as a golf and fly-fishing getaway among his crowd. In the subject line to the group email he sent around to alert his friends to the dates and planned activities, he wrote, "A Water-Hazard Runs Through It" and thought it clever.

Before Klott can weigh in with his travel plans, the kitchen door bursts open. His kids, Sydney and Stewart. Twins, it should be noted. They sprang from Marjorie's womb as in a cliché, one of seventeen sets of fraternals in their middle school class of 149, and here they spring across the threshold into the butt-end of Klott's day with the same whiff of predictability. It does not do for these Klott twins to simply enter the front door after having been deposited down the street by the school bus. No, they must bound and burst and bluster forth, making their presence well and truly known—this despite the beseeching of their only somewhat put-upon father to keep in mind that his small study off the kitchen is also a place of business. And yet even his own children cannot seem to stifle a small smile at the incongruity of this phrase. *A place of business . . .* Indeed, it appears that Harrison Klott has reached for it a time too many, and now he has only to look about his modest workspace, carved from an alcove that had once been a windowed pantry, to see how it is he must appear to these bounding, bursting, blustering children.

Absurd. Reduced. Inconsequential.

He whisper-shouts in the direction of the twins' commotion: "I'm on the phone."

Teddy hears this on his end and says, "Fuck that, Klott. Put me on speaker."

This he does, and says, "You're on speaker."

"Hey, kids," Teddy says. "It's your Uncle Theo."

"Teddy!" Stewart says, genuinely happy to hear his voice—almost as happy as Klott at the way his children refuse to indulge this *Theo* business.

Klott, back to Teddy: "It's witching hour 'round here. Let me say hello to my beloved children and call you later."

"Yessir," Teddy says, still on speaker. "You kids be nice to your father. Don't do drugs. Stay in school."

Klott cuts the call and turns to the twins. "Hello to my beloved children," he says.

As if by some strange combination of instinct and suction, he moves toward the energy of these twins. It is an amazing thing, this energy. He is drawn to it, powered by it. Always, he finds himself lifted by this great force field that surrounds Sydney and Stewart, transported from the plain sameness of his days into the swirl of their comings and goings, but at the same time he can feel it pressing down upon him, to where he might collapse beneath the weight of that plain sameness. Does this make sense? It is a weight and a buoy, both. A jolt and a salve. Their sister Joanna is off in her high school swirl, busy most days from sunup to way, way past sundown, so the force field has lately been limited to the energy that flows from these two.

"One plus one?" Klott asks—an open question meant for either twin-child. It is an end-of-day game Klott jumpstarted with Joanna after her very first day of kindergarten, to stand in place of the standard "What did you do in school today?" line of questioning that passes for attentive parenting in these parts, and continued with Sydney and Stewart, and the punchline all these years later is that he's never moved his pop-quizzing beyond that curriculum.

"Seventeen," Stewart says, throwing a punchline of his own.

Klott wishes he could tousle the boy's hair but turns instead to Sydney. "Capital of Oregon?" he asks.

"O," she says, monotone.

They are barely amusing themselves, these kids, but this is one of their routines, and they toss their backpacks onto the kitchen counter in their usual spots and start rummaging through the fridge and snack cabinet. It is as if they've pulled in at a pit stop at the Indy 500 and need to top off their tanks and rotate their tires. Together, they move about the small kitchen to a choreography Klott can no longer remember taking shape: Sydney ducks to remove a still-warm ice cream bowl from the dishwasher, just beneath her brother's outstretched arm as he reaches for a plastic tumbler he means to now fill with a half gallon or so of Newman's Own iced tea; Stewart tugs slightly on the utensil drawer so that it rolls open just enough for his sister to pull two soup spoons from their cradle and to fork over one of them to her brother as he leans into the freezer for the working pint of Breyer's French Vanilla Swirl.

Klott has learned from experience that there is not much to be said during these after-school dances in his kitchen. His family therapist friend Alan tells him it is enough that he is present, in the twins' midst. If they need something of him, they will ask for it. If their sister needs something, she will ask for it. Or, not. Here Klott has made his presence known and leaves it to Sydney and Stewart to let it be known if more is needed from him. At this moment, the twins seem to have things covered, although there is a small piece of parenting requiring his attention. Stewart turns to his father and says, "One sec," and pulls a loose permission slip from the bowels of his backpack that appears to have been bunched into a paper ball and then un-bunched and flattened. He crosses with it to the threshold of his father's pantry-office and hands it to him.

"Some Hebrew school bullshit," Stewart says. "You need to sign and return."

"Thought Hebrew school was pretty much done," Klott says. "It's almost June."

"It's for next year," Stewart says. "Some new policy."

At this, Sydney starts in with some backpack disemboweling of her own, unzippering her Jansport camo tote to where the thing looks as if it has been flayed. "Me too," she says, mostly to herself as she rifles through the mess of papers she's tucked away in there. "Me too, me too, me too, me too . . . "Her voice drifts off, as in a refrain. After a couple beats, she pulls a folder from the wreckage, and from the folder an already flattened piece of paper, not in need of any un-bunching. She walks it over to her father.

"Me too," she says again.

"Stop saying that," Klott says. "Phrase is starting to creep me out."

"Me too," Stewart says—agreeing, needling.

Harrison Klott reads the less tossed-about copy. Usually, he just signs these things and moves on, but it is clear that these permission slips contain a lot of information. There is writing, single-spaced, on both sides of the document, with bulleted items and numbered paragraphs. Something above and beyond the usual Hebrew school bullshit.

"What am I signing?" he says, to whichever twin cares to answer. "Help a brother out."

"Permission slip," Stewart says.

"Funny," Klott says.

"New policy," Sydney says. "They told us about it."

"And?"

"And what?" Sydney says.

"What did they tell you?" Klott says, on his way to exasperation.

Turns out the change in policy has to do with parent involvement for the coming year—a change that conflicts with the internal policy Harrison and Marjorie Klott have put in place on their end. Early on, the two agreed that the sort of community parenting required by affiliating with a local synagogue would run counter to their notions of keeping to themselves. Oh, they are good and attentive parents, but they define their good attentiveness on their own terms. They are the ones who stay in the car on the carpool line after Hebrew school, while the others, mostly moms, step from their queued cars and trade gossip and esteem-building strategies. The ones who sit in the bleachers with the Sunday *Times*, while the other parents, mostly dads, run around on the field or the diamond or the court and go out of their way to remind each other they could have played college ball if it hadn't been for, you know, the time commitment.

The new policy, apparently, is that parents of *b'nai mitzvot* are now expected to make an appearance during Shabbat services the week *before* their blessed offspring's ceremonial turns. And not just a pop-in-type appearance—a full-on shift, stretching from a half hour before services are scheduled to begin, until the Torah is tucked safely back in the ark and the sanctuary cleared. Klott has no recollection of this policy from when Joanna was in Hebrew School, although it's possible he and Marjorie had an easier time ignoring it when it was just the one kid going through these motions. Either way, it seems the synagogue board has had a bitch of a time recruiting volunteer ushers on Saturday mornings—and so now Klott will have to log an interminable shift at the back of the sanctuary, hushing a gaggle of giggling middle schoolers whose names he should probably know and reminding them of the solemnity of the sabbath.

A gaggle of middle schoolers? Klott wonders what the collective noun might be for a cluster of *b'nai mitzvot*. A swarm? A clutch? A bellowing? Ah, he's got it: a *kvell*—as in, "Aw, fuck, Marjorie. Why do I have to be the one to have to deal with that *kvell of b'nai mitzvot*?" It gently amuses him, this turn of phrase, but he's interrupted from his little revelry by Stewart's snapping fingers, which have been placed about an inch in front of Klott's face.

"Hello?" Klott hears, as in a question. "Earth to Dad."

Klott swats at the air in front of him like he's shooing a cloud of gnats. "You're, like, my least favorite child," he says.

Sydney pretends at offense. "Hey," she says. "What about me?"

"Fine," Klott says. "You're both my least favorite."

3.

ONE AND ONE AND ONE IS THREE

LEM DEVLIN

THERE'S A LOT TO CONSIDER.

Like, for one, how many guys to bring in on this with him and Duck. Too many guys, it cuts into whatever they hope to make. Not enough guys, it cuts into their ability to do the job clean. Lem runs it this way and that. There's a *just right* way to hit it, he knows. Not too hot, not too cold—*just right*, like the three fucking bears.

One of the things he's thinking is making like he's legit and not even telling his crew the full deal. He knows enough people in construction, road maintenance, and moving and storage, it shouldn't be a problem getting a team together. They'd be happy for the work, would be no reason for them to even think to ask questions. They know how to look the other way.

Duck is with him on this, but he only sees the money part. With Duck, it's the size of the pie and how many ways they'll have to slice it. With Lem, it's how many guys need to be in on it with them, how many moving parts. The guys he might reach out to on this to make up his crew, they'll have his back, but at the same time he worries how people talk, and all the ways this thing can go wrong. There are enough variables to this job as it is, so he wants to play it tight, close.

Just right. That's how he sets out to play it, but the job pushes back. More and more, it comes to him that this job has its own ideas on how to get done. He can play it safe or take some risks. He can move on it first thing on a weekend morning or late one weekend afternoon. He works it over and over in his mind. One thing Lem knows is not to leave any kind of trail. A thing like this, making off with an industrial-size sculpture by one of America's leading artists, in broad daylight, it'll make some noise when it happens, and he wants to do what he can to keep it to a dull hum. Nothing he can do about his connection to Fine Artemis or the mess of paperwork connecting the company to this one client and this one sculpture, but you can say the same about a dozen other guys, a dozen other clients over the years who've had shit go missing. No reason to think the finger will point to him, any more than it will point to Arty Hammond himself. Plus, you know, maybe it's a good thing, Lem being on the inside the way he is. He's got what he's heard people call portfolio—meaning, a reason to poke around. He *belongs*, in a sidelong way, so he limits his online research to one of the warehouse computers. An art theft like the one he's planning, they'll probably seize Arty's computer, so he might as well fill it with a search history. Might as well learn what he can about Jeff Koons and study his recent sales on a computer where you'd expect people to be sniffing around in this way.

Lem makes himself a Jeff Koons expert, basically, and what he gets is that critics either love this guy or they hate him. Not a whole lot of in-between. Collectors, though . . . they swallow this shit whole, so Lem tells himself it'll be no problem to move this piece later on. Might have to sit on it a while, but one thing he's got is time. Truth is, he knows shit about how to sell a massive sculpture that could probably fill the front lobby of the Salt Lake Tabernacle in Temple Square—a sculpture that made headlines the first couple times it sold. He understands there's a black market in high-end art, but he's not exactly sure how to tap it only that he's not about to start in on the tapping until he knows all there is to know about what he may or may not be able to do. Only thing he knows right now is he'll have to take a hit on the price—that's, like, a given. In his head, he's going with ten-million dollars for what this balloon dog might be worth, but it could be twice that, easy. Whatever it is, he'll probably have to cut that number in half, so he sets it up that he's looking to clear five million. That's the price he uses to calculate his cut, to figure Duck's share, to justify the expenses he knows he'll have to carry into the job.

Takes money to make money, that's what people say, and here Lem guesses it'll run him three to four hundred bucks a man, for five or six hours of work—enough to attract a decent group, but not too much to invite suspicion. The trucks, he can borrow. The crane, he can rent. He knows a couple places he can call, thinks it'll set him back about twelve hundred for a full-day rental, a couple grand if he needs the crane overnight. Also, he'll need someplace safe to off-load the sculpture. No way he can lease out space in a traditional warehouse, even outside the city, because every urban facility will be wired with security cameras and those will probably be the first places investigators look, assuming the missing Koons makes the kind of headlines that warrant a full-scale investigation. Everything falls the right way, he might have a running start, maybe a week, before the sculpture is reported missing—time enough to get it situated and figure his next moves. He's thinking he needs to find some tucked-away barn or some ranch with an out-building he can repurpose on the cheap for his short-term storage needs. Or maybe it'll turn out he needs a place long-term. No way to know how to price that kind of space, or how long he'll even need it, so he leaves it blank on his expense ledger.

He's filled three yellow legal pads with numbers and sketches and every risk/reward equation he can imagine. There's a punch-list of things to worry about, a timeline for a dozen different scenarios, names of movers and haulers he's planning to call. At the top of each page, he's written the words *SITE VISIT*, in all caps. On some pages, he's underlined the words, two or three times. On others, he's followed them with exclamation points. So here he is now, making the drive from his place in Sugar House to Park City—about a half hour, not counting for traffic. This time of year, early June, midweek traffic's never an issue, but he wants to be prepared for anything, everything. His idea is to make several trips over the next few weeks, different times of day, different days of the week, and see what there is to see.

The Fine Artemis crew has just been to the house the week before, returning the Koons to its perch on a sixteen-foot by nineteen-foot concrete slab, halfway up the Canyons side of Park City Mountain Resort. Lem marks that delivery as the unofficial start date on this side job. Up until now, everything has been theoretical . . . hypothetical . . . pie-in-the-fucking-sky. With the Koons back in place, he kicks things onto a whole other level, and as he spills off I-80 onto State Route 224, he begins to pay good and close attention. First thing he notices is there's a mess of construction in Kimball Junction, the sprawling network of malls and office parks and residential developments on the fringes of Park City. The sprawl stretches all the way to the access road to Canyons Village. Lem considers this a good and welcome thing. The more trucks and haulers and cranes they've got coming and going in the area, the easier it'll be for his men to blend into the scenery.

There are construction sites all the way up the access road to the base of the ski resort, and from there he's thrown onto an unmarked, unnamed road that climbs the mountain beneath the Timberline chairlift. The construction fencing has faded in his rear-view to where there no longer seems to be anybody on this road but him. The transformation is sudden and complete—also a good and welcome thing, he thinks.

Another detail: the homes in this area are set into the mountain in such a way that homeowners are unable to see any neighboring homes, but Lem knows this will not guarantee that his efforts in removing the sculpture at the end of the summer will go unnoticed. The reason for this, he notes on his legal pad beneath the heading *SKI-IN/SKI-OUT*, is that the homes are meant to be accessed from the network of public ski and mountain bike trails that have been cut into to the terrain. Lem doesn't ski or mountain bike, but he gets the idea. He gets that privacy matters to these particular homeowners in this particular setting, but he also gets how important it is for them to fool themselves into thinking this mountain playground belongs only to them and their invited guests. He thinks this must be what it's like to live at the beach, behind some elaborate security system that somehow only protects the home from the street. On the ocean, any asshole with a dog can step to your property and pee on your prized African lilies—and here at nine thousand feet it's possible for any asshole with a decent pair of hiking boots to step over the knee-high stone walls that rim each meticulously-sited home and pee in your hot tub.

Something to be said for the honor system, he thinks.

Lem pulls onto a graveled shoulder of mountain road and gets out of his car. He was careful to grab one of Arty's uniform shirts before heading out, for cover. If anybody spots him or questions what he's doing, he can point to the name on his shirt and say he's doing a follow-up inspection. If it gets back to Arty, he can always say he lost something—a set of keys, say—and he'd gone back to look for it. Anyway, he moves about as if he belongs. He carries a clipboard with him, to complete the picture, but these precautions do not seem necessary. There is no one around. No hikers, no bikers. No homeowners, no property managers. There is only a small deer grazing in some tall grass a hundred yards or so up the trail, alongside a copper statue that appears to be in the shape of a somewhat larger deer.

The sky is like something from a brochure, the blue moving from dark to light as if on a color wheel. There are cloud puffs every here and there that seem almost strategically placed, as in a repeating pattern on a roll of wallpaper. To Lem, it seems almost unnatural, all of this natural beauty, all around. It is too, too perfect, as if this sky does not belong here, in real life.

He circles the home looking for security cameras. He knows from last week's install that the sculpture itself is not alarmed. It's secured to its base by a network of bolts driven into the concrete, but the balloon pile does not sit behind reinforced Lucite panels or any type of discrete fencing. It is open to the elements, naked to the world, a thing to behold. The effect, Lem sees now, with perspective, is of a playfully shaped red balloon that seems to have magically fallen from the mountain sky and come to rest here in this unlikely way, in this unlikely place.

Best Lem can tell is that the home itself is only secured by the knee-high stone wall rimming the property, although there is a double-wide gate at the mouth of the driveway. There is a camera mounted to the base of one of the gates, facing away from the sculpture. The gate may or may not be a problem, Lem is realizing. There is perhaps enough room in the narrow approach road to pull two flatbeds alongside the property line, and he might be able to park the crane there as well, depending on the reach of the boom. He returns to his car and grabs the tape measure in the glove compartment through the open front passenger window, then he walks back with it to calculate the distance between the stone wall and the balloon dog. Then he measures the width of the road. He is unlucky enough as it is—last thing he wants is to set up the job just right and fill his legal pad with every imaginable contingency and mess up this one small detail. The key is to be able to leave enough space for other vehicles to pass, because Lem's crew will be at it for a couple hours and he doesn't want to call any more attention to what he's doing by causing a small traffic jam. He makes a note on the legal pad fixed to his clipboard prop to determine the dimensions of the trucks and the crane.

As he walks the property a final time, Lem notices that the house has been built alongside a ski trail named *Oops*.

Yep, he thinks. Oops. Oopsy fucking daisy.

He takes out a pen and writes the word *OOPS* on his pad. Then he copies down the models and license plate numbers of the three cars parked in the driveway: a Land Rover, a Tesla, and a Ford King Ranch truck, all sparkling in a cherry red to match the Koons.

Lem steps back to take in the scene—the house, the cars, the sculpture, the mountain—and it looks to him like it's been staged or set-designed. The color-coordinated splashes of red, the snug-fitting stone wall, the electric blue sky . . . it's all just a little too perfect, you know.

"You come up with those names for me?" Lem asks Duck. He's stopped at a 7-Eleven in Kimball Junction to grab a coffee and noticed the pay phone, thinks to check in.

"Got guys who can do the job," Duck says. "What I don't got is guys we can trust."

"Thought you said you had a buddy in moving and storage in New Mexico," Lem says.

"Haven't sat with him yet," Duck says. "Staying off the cell, like you said."

"The fuck you waiting for?" Lem says, pissed.

"He's headed up here next week," Duck says. "Visiting his mother or some shit."

"I'm up here now," Lem says. "*Here* here. Park City."

"What for?"

"Recon."

"And?"

"And, I need you to get me some specs on that flatbed you mentioned. Load specs. How wide, wheel-well to wheel-well. Front to back too, probably." He explains about the gated driveway, says it's probably not a problem, they can stage their vehicles alongside, but he wants to make double-sure the trucks and the crane don't block the narrow road.

"On it, boss," Duck says.

"Fuck that *boss* shit, Duck," Lem says. "This goes bad, it goes bad for us both."

"Yes, boss," Duck says.

"Fuck you," Lem says, cutting the call. He steps inside for the coffee, which he chases with an individually wrapped serving of Hostess Apple Pie. He can't remember the last time he ate an actual meal. He's been running on convenience store snacks and momentum since he started working this plan. Thing is, he's not dragging. He's feeling pumped, dialed in. Like he's in the middle of it. At fucking last.

4.

BET YOU'RE WOND'RING HOW I KNEW

SHARI BRAVERMAN

OKAY, SO THE FIRST THING that needs doing is nothing. That's all. Just lay here a while longer, maybe try not to move. Keep totally still. *Let the day find you*—that's the phrase she runs through her mind.

Shari Braverman figures this is something she can handle. It's like she's left herself no other choice. *Jana* has left her no other choice. Shari can't even remember Jana crawling into bed with her, but here she is, this child, splayed across the body pillow they've apparently been sharing. Jana has always been a restless sleeper, so Shari is careful not to wake her. *Rest with intention*, she tells herself. Shouldn't be too, too hard, right? And yet, move a muscle, breathe too loudly, get up to pee and the day will run away from Shari Braverman, just as all the days now run away from her.

Basically, she wants to keep the world from spinning. To be good and ready when the day comes looking.

There's a fine fur of soft down on Jana's arms that seems to Shari to
have been windswept across her daughter's skin in a perfect pattern. Look
carefully or you might miss it. There . . . there it is. Shari looks on and
wonders at the confluence of DNA at play in this child that leaves her
sprouting these perfect puffs of arm hair, breathing these short, rhythmic
breaths that leak from her sweetly pursed lips like a half-remembered
lullaby. With Jaxon, when Shari watches him sleep, her thoughts run to
the bundle of energy he is in his waking moments, in much the same way
she might marvel at the tiny Bose speaker she just bought with the credit
card she once shared with her husband, wireless, which when idle gives
off nothing of the deep wall of vibrant sound it is capable of creating. It
is as if the one thing has nothing to do with the other, beyond the thing
itself. It is what it is until it asks to be something else. And yet with Jana
she can lose herself in the quiet miracle of creation. Who is this child?
Shari wonders. What am I to this child? Where are we going, together?

In therapy, and among her growing collection of divorced or otherwise
unattached friends, there is a lot of talk about the ways we travel through
this life in the arms of our children. Beyond the sanctuary of her bedroom,
the phrase sounds like it fell from the back of a greeting card truck. But
here, now, it strikes her as meaningful, insightful, and Shari Braverman
wonders if this is so among the freshly single men in her acquaintance, if
they define themselves as they are defined by their children. Probably not,
she's betting. Probably, none of them are lying awake, a little too careful
not to rouse a sleeping child next to them, a little too mindful of what
the day might hold, a little too desperate to remain in a moment such as
this one for longer than the moment might require. They might be good
dads, some of them, but they're not wired in quite this way. Her Brian
certainly wasn't.

Isn't.

Whatever.

That's another thing, comes up all the time with her therapist. The
way Shari tends to speak of Brian in the past tense, as if he's no longer here.
He is and he isn't, of course. What she means is that he's not, you know,

dead or anything. But he might as well be. Married fifteen years, together three or four before that, and she finds him in the garage one Saturday afternoon sucking off their neighbor, Fred. That's the phrase she always uses when people ask what could have possibly happened. *Sucking off our neighbor, Fred.* Like in speaking bluntly she might dull the pain of the moment, maybe take back some of what was taken from her. Oh, you can't imagine. People write *New York* magazine cover stories about such as this. There are movies, television shows, *60 Minutes* segments . . . it's become a cliché, the long-suffering, ill-married husband who can't seem to find the courage to take it up the ass the way he was meant to all along. Until one day a sweet, dolled-up drag queen named Epiphany or Courage or Truth comes along and tears him a new one. Oh yes, oh yes, it's become a *thing*.

And yet Shari Braverman can't shake thinking she loses a piece of herself, a piece of whatever it was she had with Brian, whatever they were building with Jaxon and Jana, whatever future they meant to share, every time she scrolls through her Netflix options and tries to ignore the Jane Fonda-Lily Tomlin series that seems to always taunt her in her "Recommended for You" queue—*Grace and Frankie*—about the wives of two law partners who find themselves in just about the same situation. But here's the thing: these ridiculous comings out crafted for our mass entertainment do not get at the essence of how Shari's life now seems to her. They make it like they know, the writers of these shows, but they cannot know. They can only imagine . . . and this, too, is a thing. Imagining what it must be like, on the inside of such as this. Lately, Shari's been on the receiving end of so many concerned looks from her presumably well-meaning friends and acquaintances, she can see them coming. There's a pattern to them, she's now realizing. She's made a study of it, determined there are notches on the familiar tilt of the head that finds her in greeting as she moves about in public. Each notch is somehow aligned with a measure of concern. There's the first-level tilt when Shari sees someone who knows only the broad strokes of her story, that she and Brian are divorcing. There's the next-level tilt, with the ear now approaching the corresponding shoulder, meant to show even deeper concern. This is how it almost always happens, as the details of her divorce come clear, as the size and shape of Brian's transgression begin to form, each notch a further indication of her perceived state of suffering—until, eventually, she'll be made to consider the ultimate-level tilt, as the angle widens and the troubled head snaps from its base and tumbles to the floor.

Oh, she is not shy about sharing. Up until the Fred-suck, as she has taken to calling it, Shari was a fairly private person. Her business was her business. *Their* business was their business. She wasn't one to talk about her personal life, even with her good girlfriends, even in the way women sometimes do when they get together around a couple bottles of better-than-decent wine and start talking about the guys they dated in college who could get them off just by looking at them. And yet here she is, now, spilling the intimate details of Brian's latent homosexuality like she doesn't give a plain shit—as, indeed, she does not. *Let Brian deal with the mess he's made*, she thinks. *Let him be embarrassed, make repairs with his children, whatever.*

And Fred? Fuck Fred. Let him sink under the weight of all those therapy bills that will surely come his way once *his* wife and kids are met with the full force of Shari Braverman's blowback.

The Fred-suck, she has come to believe, was an especially cruel and exponential betrayal, because in pressing his lips to their neighbor's penis her chickenshit husband didn't just step outside their marriage. He also took a pickaxe to the very foundation of that marriage, to Shari's sense of self, to her underlying worldview. Jesus, the whole time they were together, the bastard wouldn't even kiss her after she swallowed his cum, the one intimacy apparently too much for him to take on the back of the other, and like an idiot Shari Braverman had simply assumed this was a kind of knee-jerk homophobia on Brian's part. Like an idiot, she continued to love him and blow him and make a life with him.

She hates how her sudden and surprising hatred of this man with whom she once believed she'd been necessarily joined must now cast her as homophobic herself, although she'll argue the point. She doesn't have anything against homosexuals in general, just this one in particular—the one

her good friend Tania dubbed the Cheese Puff, after a deservedly long night
of better-than-decent wine drinking that had been accompanied by two bags
of Braverman's Double Jax, pinched from the family's bottomless cache.

(For the record, there's not a grape on this here earth that pairs well
with a mouthful of processed cheese dust.)

In the space where this man had once been in Shari Braverman's life
there is now a kind of oppressive sadness, a feeling like her life has been
wasted—worse, like it hasn't even been *lived*. She has been left feeling
taken, duped—and yes, there are these lovely parting gifts in the form of
her two beautiful children, but still . . .

She reaches for the fine hairs on her daughter's forearm and begins to
trace them absentmindedly with the tippy-tip of her fingernail, but even
this soft touch is too much for Jana to endure in sleep. She is startled
awake, rubs the dreams from her eyes, sighs theatrically, buries her face
in her mother's body pillow and says, "Good god, woman. What do you
want from me?"

———————

Breakfast.

Kind of a big deal around here—one of Brian's influences. He was
always into a full-on morning meal. Eggs. Bacon. Fresh-squeezed orange
juice. Toast, lightly browned. *Toad-in-the-hole.* Even on a busy school day,
meetings and closings lining up at work, he'd be up and at it in time to
whip up a stack of pancakes, or whatever he felt inspired to make. And
there *was* inspiration here, of a kind. Shari would alight in the kitchen
and relish in the loopy swirl of the life she and Brian had made. All these
moving parts, coming together. These sleepy-headed children, gathering
fuel. Brian appeared to her then as a kind of maypole, everybody circling
around him, and for the longest time following the Fred-suck Shari
worried if she'd ever be able to take on that kind of role. And, indeed, for
the longest time she didn't—couldn't. What was left of her little family
spun wildly out of control. The kids fisted cereal from boxes, drank juice
from the carton, pinched toaster-hot French toast sticks or Pop Tarts or

whatever processed foodstuffs she'd managed to stock as they made for the door, and as they were swallowed up by the school bus she would sit in her too-quiet kitchen and weigh what her life had become.

She was going through the motions, just.

Things went on in this dispiriting way for three or four months, maybe longer, until one morning during Passover Shari woke early and did what she could with her grandmother's *matzo brei* recipe. Cinnamon, raspberry jelly, a sprinkling of sugar after serving. And it wasn't that she felt her kids were missing out or sent to school each day somehow wanting, as far as the USDA dietary guidelines were concerned. Wasn't any kind of breakthrough. Wasn't even that it was Passover. No, it had more to do with the fact that she herself had a taste for her grandmother's *matzo brei*, and Brian wasn't around to make it for her anymore, and if this was something she wanted she would just have to reach for it herself, even if it meant making do with an unopened box of matzahs from the previous Passover.

Jaxon, bless his hungry heart, cleaned his plate in what might have been one deep inhale, without a word, but Jana lingered over her portion, staring at her mother as if trying to place her.

Finally, a couple mouthfuls in, she caught her mother's eye, raised her fork in semi-salute and said, "About fucking time."

And it was.

However long it took for Shari to get her act together in this way, it was nothing alongside the perfidy of her now-gay husband—*perfidy* having lately become one of her favorite words, for the way it body-slammed her ex for his transgressions while at the same time put it out there that the woman he reverse-cuckholded knew how to work a thesaurus to advantage.

So now, another few months on, breakfast is once again a big deal. No, she can never match Brian's inventiveness in the kitchen, but she can at least go through these homemaking motions and restore some of the equilibrium that had been sucked from their lives—*sucked*, as in allowed to have been forcibly removed, as if by a vacuum. (Or, *sucked*, as in drawn into Brian's mouth through their neighbor's penis.)

On this particular Saturday morning, after a night's sleep truncated—
and, just as accurately, highlighted—by Jana's wee hours visit, Shari is back
into *whatever* mode. There is no school bus to catch, no meeting to attend,
no housekeeper to direct or admonish, no soccer game to get to, and so
she leaves her kids to feed themselves. A certain measure of independence,
Shari Braverman has come to believe, is a good and necessary thing, and
in this one small way she likes to think she is pushing her children in the
direction of self-reliance.

Jaxon, down first for breakfast (ahead of Shari, even), appears to be
waiting for a plate of food to appear in front of him, his head resting on
the table on the pillow of his arms, as if the very weight of it is too, too
much for him to carry at this moment. Shari cannot guess how long the
boy has been sitting like this, cannot at first think what to say to him in
greeting.

"Morning," she says.

"Morning," she hears back, muffled through the fleece knit sweatshirt
he's wearing, neon green, a couple sizes too big, with the words *I Survived
Jordie's Jew-asic World* silk-screened to the back, in a typeface and style
meant to evoke the *Jurassic World* movie poster—a bar mitzvah giveaway
Jaxon seems to have plucked from the ever-growing pile of hoodies, pajama
bottoms, and long sleeve T-shirts he's collected from the weekly rites-of-
passage-fests that have lately filled his calendar. Don't get her started on
these relentless comings of age, commemorated by these brightly colored
souvenir garments that will just as likely as not wind up on the backs of
area landscapers and housecleaners, owing to the misplaced kindnesses of
their clueless clients eager to clean out their kids' closets to make way for
the next batch of swag.

There is no end to these celebrations these days—and, more and more,
no point as well. It's gotten so Jaxon and his friends have taken to judging
each event based on the goodies they get to take home, the name-brand
rappers hired to freestyle with the guest of honor, the arcade games trucked
in to distract the children from the misbehaving adults in attendance. On
some weekends, Shari is made to shuttle Jaxon back-and-forth to two or

three parties, each one more over-the-top and devoid of spiritual meaning than the last, some of them running on past one o'clock in the morning, and all of them costing more money than her first apartment.

Once, in an elaborate show of kindness and preparedness, emphasis on the *show*, she pulled up in the parking circle of a nearby golf club that had until the financial crisis of 2008 been disinclined to admit Jews as members—*disinclined*, as in *had absolutely no fucking interest in doing so*—and was greeted by a team of lovely female valets offering hot chocolate and warmed Cronuts, indicating to Shari that she was meant to enjoy these seasonal treats in the comfort of her car while she waited for the party to end. That it was the week before Christmas and these lovely valets were dressed suspiciously like Santa's elves only added to the solemnity of the moment.

Shari's friends tell her she's crazy to drive her kids back and forth to these events, reminding her there's usually a subset of Jaxon's friend's parents already in attendance as invited guests who are happy to offer a ride—like she'd ever put him in a car driven by some drunken dad whose idea of a good time is to day-drink with his fellow masters of the universe and circle the dance floor ogling the inappropriately dressed middle school girls who trade turns bumping and grinding and lasciviously mimicking the also-inappropriate moves of their favorite music videos.

And the thing of it is, these day-drinking louts had been Brian's friends, *their* friends, until Brian went and sucked off their neighbor Fred. So now Shari is made to take in these proceedings in a once-removed way, having been *once-removed* from a few too many guestlists she might have expected to be on, had she and Brian still been together. She tells herself this is no big deal. She tells herself the last thing she wants is to spend a Saturday afternoon on the receiving end of so many increasingly angled head tilts—the knowing, pitying glances tossed her way by the distaff halves of her couple friends who seem to Shari to want to feel a little better about the fallings short in their own marriages by *tsk-tsking* at the falling apart of hers.

Jaxon's own bar mitzvah is coming up on the calendar, and this too has been weighing on Shari Braverman, reaching back to those first mornings in her quiet kitchen after she'd asked Brian to move out. The date had been assigned by the synagogue when Jaxon was ten years old, along with a three-page explainer detailing the policy for switching dates with another family, outlining the community's *expectations* of *b'nai mitzvah* families, and answering every conceivable question that might arise with regard to the same. Shari wonders if she bothered to keep the document but guesses the synagogue's ritual committee didn't think to address the appropriate etiquette for when the father of the bar mitzvah has been caught sucking off his neighbor Fred.

Is she meant to stand on the *bima* with her ex-husband and expect those in the know to refrain from imagining him on his knees sucking off their neighbor Fred?

Is she meant to address her former in-laws and the rest of Brian's extended family with good cheer and expect them to refrain from imagining their brother/cousin/uncle/whatever on his knees sucking off their neighbor Fred?

Is she meant to assume that the whispering and tittering that will surely pass among Jaxon's little friends, seated in the back rows of the synagogue and plugged into the world around through social media and their own gossiping parents, will have nothing to do with the ways they will surely be imagining Jaxon's father on his knees sucking off their neighbor Fred?

And what about their neighbor Fred? Do he and Mrs. Fred rate an invitation? There had been a time, not too very long ago, when they would have been near the top of their guest list—a wistful thought that now leaves Shari wondering crudely if he was the top in this relationship with Brian, or how that even works.

The sight of Jaxon in his fleece sweatshirt fills Shari with anxiety— only, when she goes to "unpack" her emotions, in the language of her therapist, she realizes that what she's anxious about is not the bar mitzvah itself, or the many details relating to it requiring her attention, but the fact that she will have to share the day with Brian and his family. On a kind of public stage. The thought leaves her stomach doing flips, but she has learned over these past months to power past her own anxieties and turn her attention to the care and feeding of her two children.

"You hungry?" she says to the spot on the table where her son's head has come to rest.

In response, Shari Braverman thinks she detects a shrug coming from the mass of wildly indifferent flesh beneath the bunched-up hoodie that may or may not correspond to Jaxon's shoulders. It's a wonder she happens to be looking her son's way when he just happens to be shrugging.

"That a yes?" she says, trying again.

There follows another apparent shrug—and this one, Shari chooses to ignore. She figures a cup of coffee will fill the time between the proffered breakfast and the actual preparation that might go into it, so she reaches for one of the unmarked Nespresso coffee capsules she keeps in a Lucite rack on her kitchen counter. Not incidentally, these unmarked capsules have become one of the small frustrations that color her days, for the way she is made to guess at what's inside. More and more, she has had less and less patience for these small frustrations. Her aggravation is plain: the capsules are color-coded to correspond to descriptions on the package sleeve, but once she's removed them from the box, she's got no way to know if she's making herself a cup of *Melozio* or *Elvazio* or *Voltesso*, with its distinctly sweet aroma and surprising biscuit notes.

She's flying blind, and as she brews her single cup, she wonders if this is some sort of metaphor for the life she is now living. If she has been reduced to someone who is meant to move about the planet like she remembers the color codes to connect the life she imagined to the one now at hand.

5.

AH, BUT I WAS SO MUCH OLDER THEN

HARRISON KLOTT

THERE ARE OF LATE two states of being in and around the Klott household, two prevailing moods: there is motion and melancholy. There is the hum and energy that attach to those moments before and after school—when the twins are going and coming, when Joanna is stressing over some extra-curricular something, and when Marjorie is quarterbacking their shared lives—when the minutes fly. And then there is the slow creep of nothing doing that finds Harrison Klott when the digital clock on the microwave oven seems locked as if in freeze-frame and the quiet of his empty prospects appears before him as a killing, wearying thing.

This is one of those moments. This is *always* one of those moments. This is the moment Harrison Klott stands from his familiar seat at the far end of the repurposed barn door that functions as the family's kitchen table and sweeps the stray muffin crumbs from the spot where his son had been breakfasting into his cupped left hand and walks the small mess to the other small messes that have been congealing in the sink-trap to the garbage disposal. This is the moment he rubs his hands together over the sink to chase the last of the crumbs and dries his palms against the thighs of his jeans and in so doing catches his reflection in the picture window overlooking the hardly manicured side yard where a Little Tykes play set has sat untouched for six or seven years, the primary colors of its plastic frame faded by sun and disinterest. What he sees is startling: a middle-aged man, stooped awkwardly, mired in the sameness of a life he never imagined.

Nothing doing.

Also, *Stasis*—the band name he'll never get around to using for the group of middling middle-aged musician pals he'll never get around to assembling, to accompany him on the refurbished Gibson guitar he'll never get around to *really* playing.

Alas, Harrison Klott is practiced enough at the fine art of not writing to recognize that the sudden taking in of a self-image that appears as wholly *other* than the more familiar, more welcome picture he somehow still carries in his mind's eye is but a hackneyed trope of the *not-writer*. Yeah, yeah . . . he gets it. He is not what he was.

He moves to adjust. He stands ramrod straight, smooths what there is of his hair, sucks in his middle. He wills his reflection whole, but it's like he's looking at someone else, and for a moment he imagines himself in a relatedly hackneyed bit from a hundred movies he has seen a few times too many. The protagonist stares into a mirror and is himself momentarily startled when his gestures aren't copied by his reflection. There is something off, out of sync. The scene typically follows a not-unrelated sequence of scenes, perhaps offered in montage, wherein the protagonist slowly realizes his life has somehow careened out of his control, together with the conjoined realization that if he is unable to master his own movements as they bounce back to him in the mirror he can never hope to control his own destiny. Typically, there'll be a *Big Chill*-type soundtrack to underscore this familiar epiphany.

Cue Dylan's "My Back Pages." Fire up the Gibson. And . . . fade.

And so here he is, Harrison Klott, fleetingly accomplished writer of introspective fiction, barely accomplished "writer" of press releases and social media snippets and seasonal restaurant menus—a man for whom the irony of air quotes inevitably attaches to descriptions of what he does for a living—held by his own reflection in the picture window over his kitchen sink to where he cannot shake thinking there is something missing in his life and work, the kind of something that might explain the dull ache that seems to have filled the places where his hopes and dreams used to be.

Woe is him. Woe. The. Fuck. Is. Him.

(This, the dicing of an already short sentence into a staccato string of even shorter single-word sentences, punctuated by a stand-alone guttural expletive, alights in the sluggish mind of Harrison Klott as still another hackneyed trope—one he'd managed to avoid in the writing of his first novel, and look where that got him.)

He returns to the kitchen sink and runs the tap into his half-empty coffee cup. This is the drill since Marjorie's been on him to cut back on caffeine. He starts his day with a cup of Stop 'n Shop instant, nuked for two minutes in the microwave, and then he sips at it absentmindedly until he realizes the coffee has gone cold. Then he adds water and reheats. He does this five or six or ten times each morning, weakening the mix until what he's drinking can be more accurately described as coffee-flavored water. In this way, he spends his mornings nursing his first (and only!) cup of coffee. It is something to do, a way to procrastinate, fill the time. It is also about what he deserves, given the way he keeps diluting the work that may have once been at something resembling full strength. It occurs to him, this half-realized truth, but he does not give it voice, believing that in suppressing it he will in some way preserve the delusion that he is still, at bottom, a writer.

Coffee. Or, at least, the essence of coffee, to be consumed in diminishingly robust portions by the essence of Harrison Klott, a so-called writer who was once encouraged to believe a promising literary career lay in wait. To be clear, the encouragement was mostly self-induced, but it would not have been laughable to suggest that he was looking ahead to a writing life, that his second book might have flowed from his first, and then another from that, and on and on from there. Over time, he imagined, he would have developed a following, and filled a closet with worn sports coats with leather patches at the elbows, only he found himself stuck instead, with nothing at all to say and all the time in the world in which to not say it—the limbo where would-be writers often find themselves in the wake of a modest success.

Woe indeed.

He is awakened from his morning routine by the bleat of the phone. He answers on the second ring.

"Klott," he says, stating the obvious.

"Hey!" he hears. "You blow us off, or what?" It is the voice of one of the underlings from his one and only client's social media firm.

"Hey!" he says back, having long ago learned that if you want to get along, you have to get along. "My bad. My very bad."

As soon as he says this last part, he wants to take it back. *My very bad.*

"Eight-thirty, old man," the kid says. "Rise and fucking shine."

These social media phenoms—Klott knows their names as Jess and Avery, but he can't tell you which is which, who is who. One male, one female . . . he knows that much. Also, he knows this Jess and Avery are good at setting up accounts on Instagram, Facebook, and Twitter, but that's about the limit to their strengths. Analytics, click-through rates, geo-tagging . . . Jess and Avery don't seem to have the first clue. They'd rather talk to Klott about "punching up" his tweets, "dressing up" his Instagram posts, "dialing up" his Facebook activity. Everything is up, up, up with these two.

"You're a writer, man," Jess or Avery says, whenever they run out of ways to describe what they're looking for from Klott. "So, hey, what can I tell ya? *Write.*"

The incongruity of hearing just these words, voiced in just this way, by just these young people is never lost on Harrison Klott, who stopped thinking of himself as a writer around the time the ejaculate of the soon-to-be-disgraced president began to cling patriotically to the blue dress of his White House intern. Yes, it's been a while. To this day, he'll hear Marjorie describing him in writerly terms to a new acquaintance, and he'll have to choke down a correction. Him? A *writer*? No, these days he considers himself an *editorial consultant*—the sum of his way with words. And Marjorie, for her part, will hear Klott introduce himself in this way on those rare occasions when he is the one making a new acquaintance, and she'll be the one biting her lip, trying not to gently correct *him*, for it is one of the things she's always loved about him, his writing. Afterward, on the car ride home from wherever it was they'd made their new acquaintances, she'll say something like, "But Harry, your book. You're absolutely a writer."

(She calls him *Harry* in the sweet moments they still share—a name he'd always hated as a kid but doesn't seem to mind too terribly much from the lips of the woman with whom he'd determined to build a life.)

At this point, he'll usually say something like, "Maybe once," and there the conversation will reach a full stop, the words hanging between them until the suffocating truth of what he'd set out to be bumps against the reality of what it was he has become and they drive on in silence, neither one of them knowing what to say for the next while.

Back to Jess and Avery and his one and only client, who now seems to want Klott to supply current and prospective patients with a steady stream of before-and-after photos, ideas for cosmetic enhancement, links to helpful articles.

"Where am I supposed to get this content?" Klott quite reasonably wants to know.

"Oh, don't worry about that." Jess or Avery says.

"Kind of important," Klott says.

"Let's build the frame first," the other one says.

Klott does not know what this means, but he knows to let these young people talk. At some point, he will sit with his one and only client and his *editorial consultancy* will turn its focus back to some speech, some article, some pamphlet that allows him the use of more than 280 characters.

(It should be mentioned here that in addition to the plastic surgery-based content he is meant to create for his one and only client, he has lately been tasked with the writing of the seasonal menus for the small chain of American fusion restaurants his one and only client has opened on Long Island—an assignment Klott has so far placed in the minus column on his list of career accomplishments because he has been unable to convince his one and only client to stop using the term *American fusion* to describe his cuisine. "A fusion of what and what?" Klott kept asking, the first time they sat for a strategy session to develop the menu palette—a term pushed by the same restaurant branding expert who'd also been pushing the *American fusion* label. "Last I checked, a fusion of hamburger and hamburger is a fucking Big Mac.")

After a while, Jess and Avery run out of things to say. There is a course of action in place, they believe, only Klott cannot begin to guess what it might be, and as they make their congenial goodbyes, he hears footsteps on the front hall stairs. Klott hadn't realized anyone was home, but it turns out Joanna had been sleeping in. Oh, right, *her...* How the hell could he forget Joanna? You'd think, this deep into the new school year, he'd have figured a couple things out, but he can't seem to track her schedule. For years, school mornings were pretty much set, but now that Joanna is in high school and her friends are driving, her goings and comings are a little less predictable. Like today. As soon as he hears her barreling down the staircase, Klott realizes it must be one of those mornings when she doesn't have a first period class and she's made arrangements with one of her friends to drive her, after stopping at the local Starbucks on the way for a double-spiced grande latte whatever.

"You're still here," he says as she fills the kitchen with her cultivated presence. Every day with this one is a Snapchat Story waiting to be told, and it often appears that the telling is being staged by a costume director and stylist, set to a soundtrack curated by an electronic house music DJ who seems to think the world can only move to the throbbing pulse of a Vegas nightclub soaked in chintz and neon and cheap champagne. Klott looks on at his much-earringed daughter, at her put-together outfits and rakish caps tilted just so, and he tries to guess at the number of hours she spends in front of her mirror each morning before settling on her look for the day.

"I'm still here," Joanna says, agreeing with her father in a way that manages to also come across as disagreeable.

She is wearing a pair of faded jeans that look as if they had been left in a small cage with a family of bobcats. The jeans aren't torn so much as ripped to shreds—she's showing more skin than denim. Klott knows enough not to say anything. There was that time, only last month, when he committed the unpardonable sin of just happening to mention that a Betsey Johnson top Joanna was wearing made her look like a slut. Of course, Klott didn't know Betsey from Lady Bird, but he learned soon enough that he could take his entire family to Benihana and order the *Splash 'n Meadow* dinner for everyone for less than it cost to drape his eldest child in one of her "fun" tops. Klott hadn't meant to use such forceful language to express his disapproval, but when his initial cry of "You have got to be kidding me" was met with a little pushback, he felt boxed in. Joanna gave him the cold shoulder for the next several weeks, which worked out well considering the tops she wore to school during that period left her cold shoulders on full display.

And yet for all of Joanna's public displays of disaffection, she is a good and attentive student, a devoted older sister, a thinking, caring soul. You'd never know it to look at her, Klott has caught himself saying, perhaps in whispered apology. And, blessedly, there's a bond between Klott and his oldest daughter that can somehow survive two weeks of cold shoulder. Really, at any time during those two weeks, Klott could have sidled up to Joanna while she was at her desk in her room or laying out on the deck reading one of the graphic novels she has come to favor (another slap to Klott's hardly apparent skill set, where the words on the page have somehow ceded prominence to the illustrations) and found a way to make her smile. He knows this. Joanna knows this. Underneath these abundant shows of teenage rebellion, Joanna is still very much a daddy's girl, and he is very much a clump of warm putty, willing to contort himself every which way in order to brighten her day. And so the tension that has lately found the two of them in these moments is in many ways a false tension, because each knows it can be gotten past, and yet they continue to move about in this curious détente as if in slow motion, on tenterhooks—a fitting idiom, he now believes, for the way it brushes against the clothes his daughter so provocatively wears, over which Harrison Klott has hung himself out to dry.

There is also the tinny sound of electronic house music seeping from the dangling earbud that hangs from Joanna's right shoulder. Presumably, she is getting enough of the stuff pumped into the bud she keeps fitted into her left ear to get the idea of the music, her skeletal system sufficiently rattled, while taking in enough of the real-world noises that manage to find her on the other side of her head. Klott wonders at the senses his child is dulling with the constant wall of sound she attaches to her days. He and Marjorie have discussed this, how their firstborn child chooses to interact with the human race, half listening, and together they have agreed that the best way to address this apparent failing in their parenting is to gently remind Joanna that they expect to be able to address her without the distraction of electronic house music thumping into one of her ears, in hopes that Joanna, on her own, will perhaps take up the reminder when addressing the other adults who might happen to cross her path throughout the day—like, say, her teachers.

Klott puts himself in Joanna's line of sight and points to his own left ear, to indicate his desire to address his daughter in stereo. At this, Joanna manages to roll her eyes and loll her head to one side in a practiced gesture meant to show equal parts disrespect and respect. There follows a second, not-unrelated gesture, wherein she unplugs the earbud from her left ear and lets it fall to her collarbone, and in so doing she lolls her head back to the other side and flashes her father a look to let him know that whatever it is he is about to say to her had better be good.

"Need a ride?" he says, as on a hundred other mornings, wondering if Joanna will find this line of conversation meaningful enough to have merited her full attention.

"I'm good," she says.

"Hungry?" he says.

"I'm good," she says.

"Good, as in, 'Yes, father dear, I would so enjoy a bowl of your famous overnight steel cut oatmeal?'" he tries.

"Good, as in, 'I'm good.' I'll get a scone or something at Starbucks."

In the history of teachable moments, this last suddenly appears to Klott as an opportunity to throw down with his eldest child on the value of a dollar. That this might not be the time for such as this doesn't even occur to him, as he does the math behind Joanna's morning ritual and becomes apoplectic—or, at least, as close as he can comfortably manage without giving himself away. He figures a scone and a double-spiced grande latte whatever has got to run seven dollars, easy, and he says as much. He says, "You go there every day, all school year, that's like a thousand dollars, right there."

"You're forgetting the tip, father dear," Joanna says back. Like she's baiting him.

Yes, he supposes he is. He supposes, too, that he has somehow failed to make his point, and that whatever friction there might have been between him and Joanna has by now been rubbed raw, but he cannot stop himself, believes it to be the collateral damage to this particular piece of parenting.

He says, "I'm serious, Jo-Jo."

She says, "I know."

He says, "And?"

She says, "And what?" Baiting, still.

She reaches for the dangling left earbud and rolls it between the pinched fingers of her right hand, as if she's threatening to restore it to its rightful place—in this way, placing quite a lot of pressure on her father, who is once again made to realize that there's a whole lot riding on whatever he chooses to say next.

"And what do you plan to do about it?" he says.

At this, Joanna lets go of the earbud and reaches into the too-tight pockets of her shredded pants and fists out a crumpled ten-dollar bill, which she drops on the kitchen floor in front of her father in a grand show of indifference—a gesture her father believes is meant to demonstrate independence.

Klott, feeling near as faded as what's left of his daughter's jeans, stoops to pick up the crumpled bill—a small indignity he'd never imagined suffering when he got out of bed this morning—and carries it to the kitchen table, where he attempts to smooth it against the wood of the old barn door. Satisfied, he picks up the flattened bill, a thumb and forefinger pinched at each upper corner, and snaps the thing open a time or two, as if in emphasis.

He says, "It's not like you have a job or anything."

His intention, he supposes, is to remind Joanna that she has certain responsibilities when it comes to the care and spending of the family dollar, and that a simple scone and coffee order can metastasize over time, and that the mere fact that she can produce a crumpled ten-dollar bill from the too-tight pockets of her too-torn jeans doesn't mean she had a thing to do with earning it. It doesn't even mean she took particular care in not spending it in the first place, only that she hadn't gotten to it just yet. Even so, the effect of this flattening-snapping gesture is to make Klott appear to his daughter as a bit of a dick, and in response she spins on her heels, throws a dickish tell-it-to-the-hand gesture of her own, returns both buds to her ears to signal that she is, like, so done with this conversation. She makes for the kitchen door and says, "Whatever."

"Joanna," he says, calling after her.

She turns and faces him, throws up her shoulders in a half shrug, as if to say, *What?*

Klott doesn't say anything, but he holds her gaze with his own. One of the ways he's always been able to pierce his daughter's many moods has been to challenge her to a staring contest, and it appears one such standoff has now taken shape on its own.

Joanna, indignant, has been the last to engage, and she hardens her gaze in a way that lets her father know the next move is his.

Klott, frustrated, but now also amused, returns a hard gaze of his own, to let his daughter know he's dug in.

They stare each other down in this way for the longest time—twenty seconds, at least— before either one of them notices they are deep into it, and another twenty seconds before they start to think of their exit strategies.

Finally, after about a full minute, Klott breaks the tension by sticking out his tongue.

Joanna smiles. Of course, she smiles—and, at first, she hates that she's smiling. She hates that her father still treats her like a little girl, even though she also kind of doesn't. At least, that's Klott's read on the situation. Joanna might be hard on the outside, but there's still a sweet softness to her, deep down.

She's still a little goofball—*his* little goofball.

"You're such an asshole," she says, smiling, trying not to laugh.

"Yes, I am," he says, leaning over and swinging his right arm to the side like he's taking a deep bow on stage. "You're welcome."

"Okay, so this has been fun," she says, in a tone meant to suggest that it's only been a little bit fun.

"We should do it again sometime," Klott says, up from his bow, in a tone meant to suggest that whatever tensions there might be between them will be behind them soon enough.

"Gotta go," Joanna says, turning for the door.

As she leaves, trailing the scent of something called I Hate Perfume, which Marjorie tells him is what all the resentful young women are wearing these days, at about a hundred bucks for a three-ounce bottle, Klott allows himself the kind of small sigh he used to give off in exaggeration, for someone's benefit other than his own—only here he hadn't realized he'd been kind of holding his breath the entire time Joanna was in the kitchen with him, like he'd been waiting for some other shoe to drop.

The rest of Klott's morning is upended by a call from his father's assisted living facility in Florida. Klott the Elder—Hymie, to friends and family and the Fronton Center Irregulars at Dania Jai Alia—had been living at the High Meadow Residences in Del Ray for three or four months, during which time Klott the Younger had been to visit only once, remarking to Marjorie on the phone afterward that the place was just two blocks from the beach and most decidedly at sea level and that there was not a meadow to be found.

"Why not The Sandy Rest?" Klott had said to his long-suffering wife, continuing his steady pursuit of truth in advertising—or, at least, plausible deniability. "Distant Shores?"

"Hymie," Marjorie had said, trying to keep her husband focused. "How is he?"

"You know my father," Klott had said.

This was precisely why Marjorie was asking. How Hymie Klott had been was recalcitrant, as ever, unwilling to be bathed, dressed, fed, or soothed. The good people of High Meadow had assured Harrison Klott they would be able to care for his father, just as the good people at Sunrise Heights and Del Ray Gardens had assured him of the same, and now here is a supervisor named Lurlene on the other end of Klott's phone telling him she believes his father has become a danger to the other residents.

Right away, Klott sees where this is going. "A danger how?" he says.

"He's hitting them with a cane."

"A cane?" Klott says. Last he checked his father wasn't in need of a cane.

"It's not *his* cane," this Lurlene says, clarifying. "He pulls the cane from another resident and starts swinging. Just now he hit Mrs. Raccannelli in Nine West. With her *walker*."

Klott takes a moment to picture his father on his old-man rampage. In that same moment, he allows himself to think, *Well, at least he has friends*.

It is determined, in the course of this call, that the best thing for the family of the regrettably named Hyman Klott is to make other arrangements for placement. This is the phrase that seeps from the practiced lips of this Lurlene, who is apparently more proficient in the art of slick-packaging what she means to say in such a way that the person on the receiving end of her disappointing news is inclined to thank her for her kindness than a veteran writer like Harrison Klott seems to be at selling unnecessary products and services to the coddled and collagen-ed patients of his one and only client.

"How soon?" Klott says.

"Would this weekend be convenient?" this Lurlene says, knowing that it would not.

"Like, tomorrow?" he says, making her work for it.

"Shall we say noon?" he gets back. "That should give you plenty of time to travel in the morning."

Klott, recognizing that this Lurlene's notion of time might be somewhat at odds with his own, cannot think what to say in response, and so he says nothing. For the longest time, he says nothing, to where the patient advocate attempts to do what she can to move the conversation along, as if reading from a playbook.

"We can make some recommendations for other facilities, if you'd like," she says.

"Yes, I'd like," Klott says, not meaning to agree to this woman's timeline, or to succumb to the sunny pleasantness in her voice, or to remind her that his father had already been to most of the other facilities in and around Del Ray but recognizing that he is overmatched.

"Our staff will see to your father's things ahead of your arrival," she says.

As he hangs up, Klott tries to understand what just happened, the ways he has been played. One moment, he's arguing with his daughter about the cost of scones and double-spiced grande lattes, and in the next he's being summoned to Florida to see about his father.

Would this weekend be convenient?

He wants to pluck the handset from its perch on the kitchen wall and slither through the phone lines, all the way to Florida, where he might emerge from the earpiece of this supervisor's phone to give her what for.

Someone should tell her that when you make it your business to attend to the care and feeding of the elderly, there is bound to be some stickiness to the transaction. Someone should tell her she and her colleagues are to expect the unexpected in this line of work. Someone should remind her that her clients' families have commitments that do not always allow them to put their lives on pause and hop the next flight to Florida to clean up the messes that, by contract, should be theirs. Someone should point out that an enfeebled older gentleman who is no longer able to feed himself, or dress himself, should be able to be coaxed, cajoled, or even canoodled into something resembling compliance, so that he, Klott, can go about his business and be somewhat assured that his father's needs are being professionally and amiably met. Someone should maybe call the family of this Raccannelli woman to see if there was perhaps something in her past or in her nature that might have incited a harmless coot like Hymie Klott to start swatting at her legs with her walker.

But that someone will not be Harrison Klott. Not today. Not any time soon. He doesn't have it in him to rail over such as this, only to stare into the phone and imagine the things he might have said to this supervisor Lurlene, who in the name of patient care seems to have placed the interests of the assisted living facility ahead of his father's.

Where is the patient care in that? Klott wonders. Someone should tell him. Please.

6.

YOU GOT ME SO I DON'T KNOW WHAT I'M DOING

LEM DEVLIN

ANOTHER RECON MISSION—this time to check out a barn in Morgan County, northwestern part of the state, this time with Duck in tow. It's a straight shot east on I-80, another straight shot west on I-84 toward Ogden. Middle of fucking nowhere, but close enough to make a couple roundtrips without thinking about it.

Place showed up on a flyer tacked to the bulletin board at Smith's—one of those sheets with the fringes on the bottom, telling you to take the phone number. Lem had stopped in to grab a couple frozen pizzas for dinner and a sixer of whatever local craft brew might be on sale and paused on the way out in front of the bulletin board. He'd gotten in the habit since that time he found someone peddling a vintage KLH turntable with a new stylus for just twenty-five bucks, and that other time he came across someone giving away a complete set of the Harvard Classics in relatively good condition, so now he makes it a point to give the thing a good look—Lem's idea of self-improvement, taking other people's crap and putting it to work for you. You never know what you'll find, where it might take you. Plus, it's the closest thing there is to a town square in these parts, this little vestibuleish breezeway at the front of the store, where they keep the fitted-together carts and the local real estate magazines and bundled firewood and coupon circulars—a way to feel connected, you know.

Whoever put up this *LAND FOR LEASE* flyer hadn't even bothered to precut the fringes, so Lem had to tear one of the sections from the bottom and pocket the phone number. In the description, it said the land measured just over five acres, secluded, with off-road access, an oversized barn with a new roof, and several additional outbuildings—what he was looking for, before he even knew what he was looking for.

He'd called from the car.

"That land still available?" he said, when a male voice answered.

"What land?" the male voice said. Not being cagey or anything—just, you know, caught thinking of something else.

"That flyer you put up. Five acres, with a barn," Lem said. "*That* land."

"Far as I know."

"Far as you know?" Lem couldn't understand the response. Either it was still available, or it wasn't. He rethought the cagey part—sounded more like strategy or posturing than surprise.

"Depends. Who's asking?" the voice said.

"Me," Lem said. "I'm asking."

"And who are you?"

"Name's Clem," Lem said, not quick enough to shield his identity with anything more than a single letter.

"And?"

"And, got some construction equipment I need to store. Some building materials. Short-term, long-term, not really sure. Could probably do first month and security in cash, if that helps."

There was a long pause, and as it played out Lem couldn't tell if he was meant to keep talking or if it was the other guy's turn. "Tell me," he finally said. "Who'm I talking to?"

"Pete Charles," the voice said. "My father's land, actually. Just helping him out."

"And?" Lem said—his turn to tease out the rest of it.

"And, yeah. Still available."

"Pete Charles?" Lem said, switching things up. "That a full name, or a first and middle?"

"Some people call me PC," he heard back.

Lem heard that and thought, So fuckin' weird. Job is in Park City. PC. It's, like, fate, destiny . . . whatever.

They didn't talk price, but the two men agreed on a time for Lem/Clem to drive out to inspect the property, and now here he is, barreling through the town of Coalville, wondering how in the fuck people live all the way out here and what they do when they get home and realize they're out of milk or toilet paper.

"There's, like, not even a place to eat," he says to Duck.

"Thought you just ate," Duck says.

"Just sayin'," Lem just says.

"Not like we're moving here or anything," Duck says.

"No," Lem says. "Not like."

The two men drive on in silence, hugging the Weber River, until they approach a marker by the side of the road announcing a scenic overlook. "I could pee," Duck says, nodding in the direction of the approaching rest stop.

Lem knows not to go against Duck when he expresses a basic need, so he eases the rented Kia onto the exit ramp and into the sliver of parking lot, and as he throws the car into park, he notices the vista and the sign announcing the Devil's Slide landmark. He's been living in Salt Lake a half dozen years, and he's heard about this place but never been. Shit, he's hardly explored the area at all, beyond whatever job he's running for Fine Artemis. What he sees out the truck window is what he takes in, hasn't had the head or the time for any of that tourist shit. It's all kind of wasted on him, Utah. All these fuckin' national parks and monuments, these famous moonscapes, desertscapes, mountainscapes, whatever. His eyes are drawn to this heaving mass of limestone or some shit, looking like it's been form-fitted to the side of the road by a Hollywood set director.

"The fuck is that?" he says.

"Read the fucking sign," Duck says.

"No, I mean, what the fuck is that?" Lem says. "Like nothing there is in nature." What's especially jarring is the way the ridges come together to form a dark, gravelly peak, which seems to grab at the deep, brilliant blue of the sky like it wants to shake some sense into it.

"Shit is crazy," Duck says, apparently in agreement.

Yes, Lem thinks. Yes, it is. Crazy how these two giant limestone ridges run from the parking lot up a couple hundred feet to the top of the mountain, side by side, like in some grand design. Crazy how such a mighty rock formation can rise from this riverbed like nothing at all. Just, crazy. Lem can't stop staring at this hard-to-figure slide, wondering how it formed in just this way, on just this spot, and how it is he's come upon it at just this moment. The limestone ridges look to Lem like a bobsled run—better, like that vodka ice luge they had at the bar at his sister's first wedding, the people lined up ten, twenty deep to put their lips on the thing and suck back a chilled shot of Tito's.

One ridge, one column, one whatever the fuck it is . . . Lem can maybe get his head around something like that. A freak of nature kind of thing. What's that word, for when a thing appears out of nowhere, looking like nothing that's ever appeared in quite the same way before? An aberration? But two mirror-image aberrations, running parallel like this . . . what's the word for *that*? Whatever. It's freaky, other-worldly. Also, like they're meant to be together. He thinks this must be what people mean when they say something is breathtaking.

"You ever see something like this?" he says to Duck.

Duck, peeing into the front passenger wheel-well, the open door guarding his business, looks over his shoulder and tries to see what's got Lem so excited.

"Devil's Slide, man," Duck says. "Thing is famous."

Lem guesses it is.

"There's a plaque and everything," Duck says, nodding in the direction of a large stone with a bronze sign bolted into its center.

He's big into nodding at what he wants, Duck. What he means to share.

Lem crosses the lot to the sign to see if maybe it might explain what he is seeing and learns that 180 million years ago this place was covered by water, and that these massive ridges are made up of left-behind sediments of limestone and sandstone. He thinks about this for a beat, how it is that he's standing on a spot in the middle of this big-ass continent and he's only now learning it is in the middle of some dried-up ocean. He doesn't understand the science of it, the geology of it, but he's struck by the history—awed, really. He tries to get his head around the idea of such an unknowable stretch of time, and the possibly related idea that by stepping from the car and across the parking lot to consider this weird-ass rock formation, he has drawn a line between how things were 180 million years ago to how they are today—another way to feel connected, you know.

He looks across the parking lot to Duck, who's finished his business and has now fitted himself into the V between the open passenger door and the front seat. Duck stands looking over the hood of the car at Lem, looking at the slide, looking at the clear blue sky, taking it all in, but then he turns from the imposing scenery and looks at his watch, takes out his cell phone. Lem wants to bring Duck in on what he's feeling, but Duck seems happy to stay right where he is, stuck in this time and place and the shit they've set out to do.

"Says here this used to be the middle of the fucking ocean," Lem hollers across the parking lot to his friend. "A hundred and eighty million years ago."

"Surf's not exactly up," Duck hollers back. Then, suddenly impatient, he points to his watch and says, "Don't want to keep Sonny Boy waiting." Meaning this Pete Charles character, running this land lease deal for his father. Meaning Duck is done with this sightseeing business and ready to move on. "This balloon dog, not gonna store itself," he says.

"You're a sorry sack of shit," Lem says, walking back to the car. "Ever heard of the wonders of nature?"

"What's to wonder?" Duck says, the two of them back now in the cab of the car. "Here we fuckin' are. In another hundred million years, there'll be two different assholes standing in this same spot, and here they'll fuckin' be."

Lem shuts the driver door, turns the ignition, thinks maybe Duck has got it right. No point being thunderstruck by these breathtaking rock formations or what they represent, where they come from, when they've got this mission taking shape right in front of them. No point looking back to the beginning of time when what's about to up and happen might change their entire fucking world.

———

Another twenty miles or so and they come to a mostly unmarked dirt road. Guy had said the cut-off wouldn't turn up on their GPS and he's right. There's just a hand-lettered sign, knee-high, fitted into the hard dirt on the shoulder: *THIS WAY.*

Lem nearly misses it and ends up making one of those hairpin Starsky and Hutch-type turns onto the dirt, fishtailing the Kia and leaving a swirl of road dust in his wake, but the car is righted soon enough and grooved into a set of well-worn tire tracks.

"You're good at this," Duck says, razzing.

"Fuck you," Lem says. "Fuck you very much." Then, "Says to look for some kind of planter, about two miles."

"Planter?" Duck says. "Like a peanut?" He laughs at his own stupid joke.

"Like, a half whiskey barrel or some shit," Lem says. "Like for plants."

"X marks the fuckin' spot," Duck says.

Lem follows Duck's thinking, but the way he sees it, this recon mission is the opposite of a treasure hunt. They're out here, middle of nowhere, looking for a place to bury their oversized, brightly-colored treasure—a treasure they don't yet have. A treasure they can't quite touch or calculate or understand. A treasure that may or may not point the way into the rest of their lives.

"You have our story straight?" Lem says to Duck.

"Straight enough," Duck says back, flat. "We're looking for some land, some storage sheds, whatever. Guy's looking to lease some land, some storage sheds, whatever."

"Again, fuck you very much," Lem says. "It might come up, what we're doing way out here. I don't know, he might try to get a conversation going."

"I can talk to people," Duck says.

"Not sure there's a whole lot of evidence," Lem says.

Duck considers this, sees Lem's point. "Okay," Duck says. "So?"

"We're in construction," Lem says. "Got some equipment and materials we needed to store."

"Some fucking story."

"How 'bout you just keep quiet then?" Lem says.

Before Duck can cut at Lem with a response, he's startled by a man, fifty-something, wearing overalls buckled only on one side. He just kind of appears alongside the car, tapping at the driver-side window with the knuckle of a ringed index finger. What Duck notices most of all, other than the sudden appearance, is that the bib of this guy's outfit is hanging unbuttoned from the right shoulder, revealing what's left of the artwork from a faded concert T-shirt announcing a years-ago Waylon and Willie appearance. At least, Duck assumes the T-shirt is from a Waylon and Willie show, because from where the denim has fallen from the man's barrel chest, he's only able to read the *Waylon & W* part of the logo, but he's guessing from the cartoonish, braided pony tail that's poking through that it must be Willie Nelson who rounded out that particular bill, unless there was once some Waylon Jennings and Wynona Judd tour that had somehow escaped his attention.

Also, best Duck can tell, the T-shirt used to fit.

"Gentlemen," the man says into the window, as Lem slides it down a crack. "Welcome to paradise." He reaches his arms wide, as though he means for his visitors to take in the sweeping vista behind him—only, the sweeping vista doesn't exactly pop how you might think, this part of the world, God's country, with imposing peaks and soaring backdrops and what have you. Down low, by that scenic overlook, Lem had thought his heart might stop, seeing what he was seeing. And then, with the way that slide just reached itself up from the earth in such a menacing, hard-to-figure way, he'd thought he should maybe have his eyes checked. But here, two miles up that dirt road, the backdrop has changed. Now it's almost claustrophobic, this view. Now all Lem and Duck can see is a patch of dirt and crabgrass stretching every which way, place looking like it's been neglected since Mitt Fucking Romney ran for president. Without even realizing it, Lem has inched the car along these grooved tire tracks and moved from Utah's wide-open spaces to an indistinguishable parcel that leaves him feeling hemmed in. Lem guesses this is a good thing, him not being able to see the sightseers' view, him feeling like this particular patch of land could be just about anywhere, because this means the tourists won't be eyeballing them when they haul that sculpture up here and start to tuck it away.

Lem steps out of the car, extends his hand. "Name's Clem," he says. "Thanks for taking the time. PC, right?"

"PC it is, Clem," the man says, shaking. "Good to meet. Thanks for making the trip."

"Not a bad ride," Lem says.

Lem looks to Duck. "Brought my partner, Chuck," he says. Again, not exactly swift on the alias front.

PC turns to shake Duck's hand as well and says, "Chuckie."

It pisses Duck off, this half-overalled, barrel-chested dude getting all personal with a name that doesn't even belong to Duck, but he shakes the man's fat hand just the same.

With these small pleasantries out of the way, PC moves to show his visitors around. Place is pretty much as advertised. Lem looks down across the valley toward the river and marvels at the rugged beauty of the landscape, the way the parcel sits in a kind of hollow up against the mountains, just a couple miles from what passes for a main road around here, tucked away from view. The outbuildings aren't much, but the barn seems to have been refurbished—tended to, at least. Once inside, he can see little rays of sunlight dancing through the walls but determines that the roof is airtight—there's not even a fleck of sunbeam peeking through as he cranes his neck. Ceiling height seems to be about twenty feet at the center of the barn, with sliding doors offering an opening of about fifteen feet on either side of the building. He's brought along a tape measure, but he can see from just eyeballing the place that there's plenty of room to store the Koons, plenty of room to get the thing in and out, especially with the way they'd have to break it down to fit it on the trucks.

"How much?" he says to PC. "Month to month?"

"Nine hundred," PC says.

"Full year?" Lem says.

"Nine grand."

"Cash?"

"We can do eight."

Lem thinks it's like the two of them are reading from a script. On his side, he's run through these questions, these numbers, knows what he's prepared to pay, how he's prepared to pay it. And on the other side, the dude with the overalls has run through what he expects to get out of the deal. Each of them, they've already run this conversation all the way through and now they're just going through the motions. It's like the middle-of-fucking-nowhere version of that scene in every movie with a high-stakes negotiation, where one asshole slips a piece of paper across a desk or a conference table with an offer, and the other asshole passes it right back with a response. It's like they're not even talking.

"Zoning?" Lem says—meaning, can he put in a couple beds, cook a meal.

"Just farmland," PC says. "Commercial. Don't think anyone will hassle you if you drag in a couple cots, though. Don't think anyone'll even notice."

"Plumbing?"

PC shakes his head, points to a small stand of aspens—says, "That's what them trees are for."

Lem steps back from the small huddle the three men have made and surveys the property. He looks at the barn, the outbuildings, the uneven terrain. He takes in the view, considers how the property seems to sit so far from the road, from civilization.

"Eight thousand seems fair," Lem finally says. One of the things he's learned from the negotiating books he reads is to repeat the lowest or most advantageous terms being discussed, to reintroduce the favorable numbers into the conversation in a way that helps to establish them as a kind of base. Next, he turns to Duck and says, "Chuckie?" Just, you know, to get his take, but also to bust his balls. He saw how Duck bristled when this guy stuck a nickname on his fake name.

Duck ignores the Chuckie part, goes off script and says, "What about cash up front?"

"Would have to talk to my father about that," PC says.

It surprises Lem, the way Duck pushes on this. As long as Lem's known him, he's never known Duck to push, to think or move aggressively. He never would have asked if the place was zoned residential, if there was a place to sleep or cook or shit. Duck's more of a take-things-as-they-come kind of guy. Lem, he's got more of a reach-for-what-you-want personality—only, he'll be the first to admit that he talks about reaching more than he actually reaches. Anyway, here's Duck, reaching, and here's Lem, impressed. And here's PC, sent by his father, reaching as well, because he wants to get some money coming in off this land. It's been a while, and he says as much. "Had a cattle farmer lease this place for a stretch," he says. "You can still see the pens, edges of the property." He looks up toward the base of the mountain, and lifts his chin in that direction, as if he means for his visitors to follow his gaze.

"How long ago?" Lem says, making conversation, but also checking to see if there might be some kind of leverage in the answer. That's another thing they tell you in those books, to look for clues in what people are saying to better understand their goals, what they hope to get out of a deal.

"Five, six years," PC says.

"And?" Lem says—meaning, you know, has there been anybody since.

"Zip," PC says. "We've stored some of our own equipment, is why we put in the new roof. The old man had some machinery, thought it might rust from the rain and snow. He don't get down here much. From Ogden. Thought he'd spend a couple bucks, wouldn't have to worry."

"How much?" Duck says—meaning, how much did he spend to fix the roof.

"Couple grand," PC says. "Mostly materials. Had his own crew do the work, so tough to put a hard number on it."

Lem sees where Duck is pushing with this, leaves him to it.

"Five grand," Duck says. "Cash. Up front. Enough to make your daddy whole on the roof and a little more besides."

"For the year?" PC says.

"Might be out sooner," Duck says, "but that's on us. We bolt early, we pay in full."

Lem watches as this fella with the overalls thinks this through. He looks at Duck, his expression blank, like he's playing poker and waiting for this guy to call his bet. If Duck had a hood, he'd throw it over his head and make like he wasn't there, that's how Lem pictures the situation. Like how they do it on television, *World Series of Poker*. He wonders what's got into Duck, where he's learned to push like this. He'd never figured him for a hard-charger, but here he is, hard-charging. All this time, Lem's been working this job over and over in his mind, like a puzzle, but he's never really thought about bringing Duck in on his thinking. Now, though, he's starting to see that Duck might have something to offer, other than an extra set of hands, a truck, and connections to some of the people and equipment they'll need to pull this thing off. He could be a real partner on this—you know, share in the weight and worry, whatever.

"Lemme think on that," PC says. "Lemme check with the boss."

At this point, there are a few small pleasantries still to be made, but the three men meander past them as if they don't mean anything. They've about run out of things to say, things to look at, so Lem moves to get back in the car and on the road. He's seen enough. Wants to let on that he's interested, without coming across as eager.

"You'll let us know your father's thoughts?" he says. "You have my information?"

"I have your information," PC says.

Duck doesn't cross to shake the man's hand in parting, but instead offers a polite nod as he leans back in the car.

"Consider us interested," he says, over the roof of the car. "Got to get down this mountain of yours and check out another spread, other side of Ogden. But yours seems fine."

As they double back on the unmarked, unpaved road, Lem adjusts the Kia's rear view to where he can see PC's large form begin to fade from view. The man gets smaller and smaller as they pull away. Lem can't be sure, but he believes the man has been waving at them the whole time, and that he means to keep waving until they disappear from view.

Pulling away, he's admiring how Duck came up with that bit about the other parcel the other side of Ogden, putting it out there they had options. A part of him wants to let Duck know how much he appreciates his instincts as a negotiator, but another part doesn't want Duck's head getting too big and giving Duck the idea that this isn't Lem's job to run.

"One thing, though," Lem says, as he turns onto the regular road on the wrong side of the *THIS WAY* sign. "Five thousand dollars? The fuck we gonna come up with that kind of money?"

7.

THE MORNING SUN WHEN IT'S IN YOUR FACE REALLY SHOWS YOUR AGE

MARJORIE KLOTT

THIS IS NOT the first time Marjorie Klott sits across from a reluctant high school junior who would rather be any place but in the guidance counselor's office discussing college plans.

Today's *victim*—yes, she's gone from thinking of her students as *clients* to feeling as if she is somehow encroaching on their busy little lives—is the daughter of a stay-at-home mom and a stray-from-home dad. This last is not the sort of detail that typically finds its way into a precollege counseling session, but Centerville, New York is the kind of small town where people talk, and in the halls of Centerville North High School the teachers and administrators talk as well. Lately, Marjorie listens more than she talks, but as the director of the school's guidance department *and* as the mother of a high school junior, she hears more than most, and what she's heard is that Chuck Tollerson may or may not have left his wife Becky for a young woman who may or may not have worked for the couple as an *au pair*, the uncertainty having to do with the precise nature of the young woman's work while she was in the Tollerson's employ and the quite possibly related fact that Chuck Tollerson had recently started dying what was left of his hair.

The Tollerson's daughter, Maven, had briefly been one of Joanna Klott's BFFs, but Marjorie has no specific memory of the girl ever sitting at the Klott kitchen table or rummaging for snacks in the cupboard with the rest of her daughter's friends. What's curious about the inaptly named Maven, Marjorie has now come to realize, is that she does not seem to have any discernible interests outside of the classroom and, judging from her transcript, she does not appear to be all that interested in what's going on inside the classroom. And yet here she sits, maven or no, in need of guidance.

"Have you given any thought to what you want to study in college?" Marjorie tries.

"Not really," Maven says.

"What do you see yourself doing in five years?" Marjorie tries again.

"I don't know. I'll be twenty-one, so I'll be able to go to bars and stuff . . ."

The girl's voice trails off in a way that suggests it is too much effort for her to complete the sentence, or to fully form the thought she might have meant to attach to it.

Marjorie can't think what to make of this girl, how to fill the time she has set aside for her in a meaningful way. There's only a week left in the school year, and the guidance office is making a push to see as many rising seniors as possible, to get them thinking ahead to their final year. "College," she says. "This is something you've talked about with your parents?"

Maven, inexpertly, shrugs.

The half hour Marjorie has allotted for Maven Tollerson cannot pass quickly enough, and when it finally appears to have done so, Marjorie resists the urge to collect the girl in a pitying hug. She's seen this type of cluelessness and aimlessness among her charges before, but here it seems to have been multiplied by the cluelessness and aimlessness of the girl's parents. Marjorie gets that she might be reading too much into this girl's home life, projecting, but here she is, reading too much into this girl's home life, projecting. She's trying to work with what she knows, what's been whispered among her colleagues. She tries to imagine what it was Joanna had once seen in this girl that had briefly placed the two of them in each other's orbit, but then she checks herself and realizes how her own daughter must appear to the teachers in this school, with her piercings and her indifference.

Marjorie stands, smooths the butt of her skirt, extends her hand. "So nice to see you again, Maven," she says.

"Same," Maven says, gathering her things, shaking Marjorie's hand. "Do you, like, need to see my parents or anything?"

"Only if you'd like," Marjorie offers. "If you think that'd be helpful."

"Cool," Maven says.

Marjorie can't think whether the girl means *cool* as in, "yes, absolutely, let's set it up!" or *cool* as in, "sure, fine, whatever." She doesn't have it in her to push, so she simply guides the girl to the door and says, "Cool." The word hangs at the threshold to Marjorie's office like it has someplace else to be, and after an uncertain beat, Maven turns on her scuffed Converse heels and returns herself to the hallways of Centerville North High School, home of the Fightin' Middies, where she is soon swallowed up by the various teenage dramas that fill her days—and, invariably, Marjorie Klott's as well.

Returning to her desk, Marjorie notices the clock on the wall, sees that Maven's half hour had only been half filled. She cannot imagine how the two of them might have passed the remaining time. She reaches for her cell phone, thinking she'll use these few found minutes before her next appointment to check her messages, her personal email, maybe take a look at social media. She never gets a chance to breathe during the school day, with her back-to-back appointments, so here she is, breathing.

She spends a little time on Snapchat and Instagram just to see what her kids have been up to—and, relatedly, to keep plugged in to what passes for discourse among her student charges. Nothing grabs her attention beyond the usual array of food pics and birthday greetings and inappropriate outfits. Soon, her attention turns to the personal emails that have surely piled up for her attention, so she logs on to the AOL account she shares with her husband Harrison: *HAIRYMARGE*. The name struck them both as playful the night they came up with it, lubricated by a half bottle of Grey Goose and looking ahead to a lifetime of shared intimacies, only now it grins back at her as a harsh, wistful reminder of a time in her life when anything seemed possible. She might have changed the name to something more age-appropriate, but her digital life has leaned in other, more relevant ways, and it is only in these rare moments of idle time at work that she even thinks to check their AOL email. Typically, the in-box is filled with promotional offers and solicitations, but she likes to give the thing a good scrub every once in a while, so that's what she means to do here. However, her eyes are drawn to the top of the queue by an email with an all-caps subject line: *YOU SHOULD BE ASHAMED OF YOURSELF!!!*

Marjorie Klott is well-aware of the dangers of opening exclamation-pointed emails from unfamiliar addresses, but the header has her attention and so she reads on:

Hello, Harry!!!

You do not know me and you're probably wondering why you're getting this email. But I know a little bit about you. A little bit more than you'd like me to know, I'm sure. (Heh heh!!!) I know you live on Briar Patch Lane. How about that? I know you like to watch people doing the nasty. Girl-on-girl. Bondage. Asian teens. Oh, I know all your little secrets, Harry. And I've got pictures, too! Videos, actually. You having a good time, when you think no one is watching. But someone is ALWAYS watching, Harry. I am ALWAYS watching.

Do you understand what I'm saying, Harry? Oh, I think you do, but just in case I'm not being clear I'll be specific. What I'm seeing is you, having your wee bit of fun. Everybody does it, right? You are no different than your neighbor. (I know—I watch your neighbor, too!!!) But I'm sure you don't want your neighbor spying on your wee bit of fun, do you, Harry? Your children? Your friends?

As she reads, a feeling of dread begins to form—first, in the deepest corners of Marjorie's mind, in those places where the stuff she doesn't like to think about gathers for her attention, but it's front and center in a flash. It is the kind of dread that hits her when she is whiplashed by surprise, a sudden feeling that's always reminded Marjorie of the stomach-drop on the downhill of a rollercoaster. For Marjorie, the unimaginable, imagined, comes with spasms of anxiety. For a brief moment she's unsettled—terrified, even—but then in the next moment her equilibrium is restored. There is chaos and then clarity. The spasms subside and she is back to only her baseline worries. As a young mother, she'd get that stomach-drop whenever Joanna coughed or sniffled, or whenever a car appeared suddenly in her rear-view, as if from nowhere. When the phone rang late at night. When she'd misjudge a step or catch an edge skiing. Here she is startled by an unseen worry, this plausible-seeming threat to her family's health and general well-being—but then, just as swiftly, she recognizes it as an online scam and the thing is stripped of its power.

Do you know anything about your computer, Harry? Do you know that once I'm able to control your system through my remote desktop function, I can see everything you're doing in front of your screen? It's true. And when I say everything, I mean EVERYTHING. (Oh, you naughty, naughty boy!!!)

To be clear, Marjorie knows all about Harry's online habits. It never occurs to him to clear the search history on the computer they also share, and she'll often flip the thing open to find a freeze-frame photo of some unknown someone or some group of unknown someones in scandalously compromising positions. From time to time—when the kids were visiting their grandparents, say—they'd even create a bit of search history together, another on a long string of shared intimacies, so it's not like Marjorie is entirely innocent in this area. Everybody looks at porn, masturbates to porn, fantasizes to porn—at least, in a rubbernecking sort of way.

Nevertheless, this email gets Marjorie thinking of the ways her husband has fallen short—in his own mind, mostly, but here, now, in hers as well. She wonders what it would be like to be married to one of those men who wouldn't push her to consider things like this, men of character and discipline and accomplishment who don't spend their days at their kitchen tables finding all these different ways to keep themselves from moving forward.

It's really so clever, what I have done. I've created a double-screen video, showing you on one side having your little adventures, and your favorite videos on the other side. Entertaining AF, as the kids like to say. As your kids like to say, I'm betting. There you are in all your glory, getting all worked up, and at the same time we can watch what you're watching. I could show you, if you'd like. I could show EVERYBODY.

But I don't want to do that to you, Harry. I'm not that sort of fellow. I'd rather get you to part with a little of your HARD-earned money. (See what I did there?) I'd rather hear from you that you'd like to keep our little secret just between us, so here's what I'd like you to do. I'd like you to send me a small amount of money. Only $399. That's not a lot, is it? The price of a round-trip airline ticket? This little bit, you won't even notice. But you can't just send me cash or give me your credit card information. No, you'll need to make the payment via Bitcoin. If you don't know how to do this, you can search "how to transact with Bitcoin" and you'll see a whole set of instructions. Very simple.

If I do not hear from you within twenty-four hours, I will send my favorite double-screen video to five of your contacts. That's right, I have set a special pixel in this email that sends me a signal on opening, so the clock is already ticking. (Don't you just love technology?) I will choose these lucky recipients at random, so you won't be able to sound the alarm or warn specific people not to open my emails unless you go ahead and warn EVERYBODY in your contact list. You wouldn't want to do that, now would you?

Marjorie supposes she has read enough of these emails to know when she is being scammed or spammed or shamed into acting irrationally, only here she is struck by the apparent command of the English language. The gently threatening tone. The teasing. The *plausibility*—that's what gets her most of all. Typically, these phishing emails read as if they'd been written by soulless bots, but this one strikes her as wholly other. This one is shot through with personality . . . and, pluck. What gets her, though, is the way the email leaves her questioning the life she has made with this man, the life they are sharing. She closes her eyes and pictures the face Harrison makes when he comes, hears the noises he makes and catches herself thinking what it would be like for everyone they know to see and hear the same. Their kids! Oh my fucking God, the kids!

In this way, Marjorie Klott is tossed from the apparent shock of being found out to the enduring faith she has placed in her husband, and in the back and forth she is made to see that the way her life appears from the outside looking in is not nearly how it appears from the inside looking out. Oh, she loves Harrison, their children, the home they've built, but in idle moments she sometimes wonders how all the pieces might have fit if he had been able to build on the promise of his first book, if he'd found something else to motivate him or make meaningful use of his abundant talents. It is not the threat of exposure that so alarms Marjorie Klott so much as it is the way she is made to reconsider her life as it might appear to someone who'd installed a porn-cam in their bedroom, their kitchen, wherever.

It hits so very close to home.

To be clear, Marjorie Klott knows enough to know the email is definitely some randomly generated bullshit con, crafted to appeal to people like her who are concerned about the ways they are vulnerable online but not enough to understand how or in what ways they are vulnerable online. Intellectually, she knows this. In her gut, even, she knows this. And yet the $399 extortion fee strikes her as genius—low enough to encourage doubters to hedge their bets and complete the transaction, and high enough to make it worth this bullshit con artist's while if he or she can push just a couple dozen targets to make the payment. There's a certain poetry to the extortion, Marjorie considers. It reminds her of that *Taxi* episode where Louie DePalma, played by Danny DeVito, pulls out what there is of his hair when he is offered a blank check to settle a matter with the father of Jim Ignatowksy, played by Christopher Lloyd. The sitcom conundrum is for Louie to maximize his potential windfall. Ask too much, and Jim's father might push back. Ask too little, and Jim's father might agree too quickly, leaving Louie to believe he should have aimed higher. Always, there is a dollar figure that will give pause, raise an eyebrow, but it won't kill the deal entirely. One dollar more, and the deal is dead.

For years, Marjorie used this *Taxi* storyline to illustrate to students that there is always a balance to be struck between the possible and the impossible, between what's at hand and what's just out of reach, only she's been at this guidance counseling thing long enough that the kids in her office no longer get the reference. She needs some new material. Her current students know Danny DeVito from that stupid cable show Joanna likes to watch, about those stupid friends in that stupid bar in Philadelphia, but the *Taxi* piece is now lost on them.

That's the math this Internet troll seems to be using here. The number is big enough to amount to something, in an incremental way, and small enough that a lot of folks, dubious or no, might be inclined to pay it, just to make the threat go away. It's like the guy said, just the price of an airline ticket. No biggie.

It's the same math Marjorie uses to balance the equations of her life. A more ambitious Harrison, and she wouldn't have her Harry around, so fully committed to the life they have made. So, you know, there's that.

An airline ticket. She's back to the troll's math and the way it connects to what's going on in the life of her family. She remembers that just last night Harrison was carping about how much he had to pay for his last-minute flight to Florida. She can't be sure, but he very likely purchased the ticket on the computer they share, and he very likely vented about it in range of his cell phone, or hers, or any of the devices that connect them inexorably to the outside world.

Marjorie puts away her phone and sits still, silent, her eyes drawn to a photo she keeps on her desk of Harrison and the kids at Hershey Park, taken in front of an old-timey kissing booth by the main entrance. The Hershey folks knew a thing or two about marketing via social media, because they were handing out buckets of Hershey Kisses candies, wrapped in different-colored foils, encouraging visitors to take and post photos in front of the booth. Stewie had the troubling but still a little bit fun idea that everyone should place the candies over their eyes, and pinch them tight in a squint, the way the ancient Greeks used to put coins over the eyes of their dead, and Marjorie remembers choosing to believe that this was merely an indication that he was paying attention in school and not any kind of concerning fascination with death.

Looking at the photo now, all these years later, Marjorie worries what it must be like for her husband to have to go through these motions with his father in Florida. She could hear the weight of sadness in Harrison's voice as he left for the airport this morning. He's not one to talk, or to share his emotions, but it comes out in the way he vents about the price of his airline ticket, or the incompetence of the staff at that place in Del Ray where it was hoped her father-in-law would receive the good and attentive care he needed. It comes out in the extra half beat he appends to their farewell embrace at the side of their bed—Marjorie in the extra-large *Mother of the Year Committee Announces Recall Vote* T-shirt her kids bought her for Mother's Day a couple years back, Harrison in the wrinkle-free Banana Republic blazer he wears when he travels. It is nothing, this half beat, an almost imperceptible shift in how things usually go, but at the same time it is everything—enough, certainly, for Marjorie to guess at what is left unsaid.

She fills in the blanks in her own thinking. Things have been so crazy-busy around the house these days, with Joanna leaning into her senior year and the twins becoming bar and bat mitzvah and Harrison being promoted to some kind of next level malingering, that Marjorie hasn't really stopped to reflect on her father-in-law's slow, sad fade. It's been going on for years, Hymie Klott's long battle with dementia, the longest of long goodbyes, and it is as if he's being painstakingly erased from the family picture she carries in her head. It is a picture based on an actual picture that hangs on the refrigerator in her kitchen, the edges curled in the places where the fridge magnets haven't been for a while—a shot from the twins' second birthday party, when Joanna was six and a half years old and all four of the kids' grandparents were still alive. There is her father-in-law, making a goofy face for Sydney, caught for all time in a moment of sweetness and silliness, a moment that feels like it happened a thousand years ago.

Always, that picture reminds Marjorie Klott of the marks we leave in this world and the messes we leave behind—and here, now, in this brief pocket of calm in her workday, side by side in her mind's eye with this picture she keeps on her desk in her cramped, cinder-block-walled office, she can't help but think of the ways she might need to cover the eyes of her children for the next while. She briefly worries she'll need more than a box of Hershey's Kisses to keep them from seeing images of their father, pants at his ankles, his face knotted up in what always looks to her like pain, until she realizes that what truly has her worried is the thought that Joanna, Sydney, and Stewie will at last see their father as he truly is. She's paralyzed by this thought, held by it, to where she is unable to move from her desk to answer the soft knock on her door—her colleague Bram. She knows it's Bram because of his trademark soft knock, which always sounds to Marjorie like a cat brushing up against the door, wanting to be let in. His manner of knocking bubbled up as a kind of running joke between them around the time Bram first came to the school and Marjorie said it was a wonder anyone ever let him inside.

"It's more like a suggestion of a knock than an actual knock," she once said to him, early on. "It's like you're thinking about getting around to it. Knocking."

"Possible it's because I went to Catholic school?" he had said. "Possible it's just residual passive aggression?"

"Really?" Marjorie had said. "You were raised by nuns?"

"No," Bram had said. "Just fucking with you."

They've been friends ever since—and now here he is, soft-knocking, pulling Marjorie for the moment from the dispiriting worries filling her head.

"That you, Bram?" she asks, as she stands and crosses to open her office door.

"That me," he says, as he steps inside. "Jesus, Marjorie. You look like you've just seen a ghost."

She guesses she does. She must. She catches her face in the wall-mounted mirror by her office door, refracted by the late-morning light angling through the small window over her desk. For a moment, she thinks she's looking at someone else—at her own mother, maybe. But she catches herself before blurting out what has her so agitated and pivots to a throwaway comment on the unmindfulness of today's high schoolers, an observation that at any other time would have left her looking a little pale.

"No," Bram counters, weighing Marjorie's explanation against how shaken she now appears. "Really. It's something else. What?"

"Nothing," she insists. "Really. Just had a frustrating session, that's all."

"Maven?" Bram says.

"Maven," Marjorie says. "You saw her leave?"

Bram nods. "What's in a name?" he says.

The school bell sounds in answer, announcing the end of the period, only it is not a bell so much as a bleat—better, a sick moan, like a foghorn on the last of its battery power. The noise fills Marjorie with another one of those flash-moments of dread, but then she recovers and realizes, *Oh, yeah, that.* Bram, of course, notices. He notices everything, this one.

"Skittish much?" he says.

"Funny," she says, in a way meant to indicate that it is not.

The bell sets loose a wave of noise and activity outside the guidance office, and Marjorie takes the time to register how it's like the spigots have been put on blast, unleashing a torrent of teenage angst and uncertainty into these hallways. If you're not careful, you could be swept along by it and dropped on some not-too-distant shore that will nevertheless feel to some of these kids like a deserted island, completely off the map of shared human experience. That's what high school is like, yes? She wishes she can remember how she filled her days when she was this age, if she was riddled with doubt and uncertainty like some of the students she sees in her office, if she seemed wise beyond her years or oblivious to the world around her. She wonders when it will happen for some of these kids that their days will be filled with purpose and meaning instead of the purposeless and meaningless nonsense that now passes for pressing matters—if it will happen at all.

8.

SOMEBODY HOLDS THE KEY

HARRISON KLOTT

IT WAS RAINING the last time Harrison Klott visited his father at the High Meadow Residences in Del Ray—one of those hard, sudden rains that shower down on South Florida as if it's in a hurry. Typically, the torrent only lasts ten minutes or so, but on this last visit it kept going and going. *Relentless* . . . that's the word that flitted in and out of Klott's otherwise idling mind as he sat in his car in the parking lot, also idling, trying to time his dash to the front doors before determining that the rain might outlast visiting hours and he had better just go for it. It ended up, he made a run for the entrance without a slicker or an umbrella or a plan for later, and when he got up to his father's room on the fourth floor he was so substantially soaked-through that even a substantially medicated Hyman Klott was moved to comment on his condition.

"Look at you!" Hyman Klott had said, when his son stepped into his room. "Just don't touch the wallpaper."

What was remarkable about this exchange, Harrison Klott noted at the time and continues to consider, was that Hyman Klott had not spoken a fully formed sentence in over two years, not within his son's earshot, and not in a way that any of his many caregivers had thought to mention. What was also remarkable was that there was no wallpaper. The room was painted in an industrial pastel that seemed to have been lifted from the pages of a years-ago issue of *Institutional Decorating Monthly*. And, what's especially remarkable on this sunny day in June as Harrison Klott arrives at the High Meadow reception area to find his father visiting agreeably with a woman Klott assumes must be Lurlene—she of the officious, staccato demeanor on the phone—who stands to greet Klott as if he is here on a social visit, is the way Klott the Elder looks up from his chair and smiles at his son and says, "It's not still raining is it, Harry?"

"No, dad," Harrison Klott says. "It finally stopped."

This is true. Far as Klott knows, it hasn't rained all week, and yet here he is, now, tasked with either packing up his father's few things and relocating him or attempting to deploy his diminishing charms to convince this woman that she should perhaps reconsider her position.

Either way, he doesn't like his chances.

"Mr. Klott," Lurlene says, seizing the initiative. "You'll be happy to know that your father and I have spent the day organizing his belongings and getting ready for your arrival."

It takes every last drop of Klott's *well-learned politesse*—a well-turned lyric that can't help but pop into his head every time he needs to remind himself to hold his tongue or bite his lip or otherwise manipulate his piehole to keep from saying whatever it is he means to say in the first place—not to turn to this woman and ask, snidely, why in the world he'd be happy to know this. Instead, he touches his pockets as if to indicate he might have misplaced his keys and says, stupidly, "You wouldn't happen to have a restroom on this floor?"

As if his keys might turn up on a trip to the Men's, or another of life's mysteries might make itself clear.

"Of course, Mr. Klott," Lurlene says. "Second door after the grand staircase."

As he heads off in the direction of the bathroom, it occurs to Harrison Klott that the High Meadow staircase by the front entryway isn't all that grand. Really, it's just a basic staircase, nothing like you'd expect to see in *Sunset Boulevard*, and more like what you'd find in the homes of some of his kids' friends back in Centerville—the ones with parents smart enough to work in finance or real estate development or software design. It sets him off, a little, that this woman stands so firmly on the company line that she feels the need to dress up the amenities of this facility even as she sends his father packing. It's like the *maître 'd* at a fine restaurant telling you there are no tables but that the cedar-planked salmon is excellent.

The bathroom itself also falls short in the *grand* scheme: a single-header, with a paper towel dispenser like the one from his middle school bathroom, from which he and his tween buddies would pull sheets of coarse brown paper towels to wet and toss ceilingward, where the wet suction would invariably hold them long enough for some unsuspecting someone to follow them into the boys' room and to step unwittingly to the urinal in time for a towel clump or two to plop hilariously onto his unsuspecting head, a prank young Harry and his fellows could never fully appreciate because it never worked out that they were on hand to witness the hilarity firsthand, since the merry pranksters were in the ill-conceived habit of ducking out of the bathroom before their next victims arrived.

There is a square of mirror over the lone sink in the High Meadow bathroom by the grand staircase, most of which is covered-up by a hand-lettered sign reminding employees to wash their hands and encouraging clients and visitors to do so as well. There's also a badly framed and somewhat yellowing poster of an already-yellowish Warhol triptych of Marilyn Monroe, which hangs opposite the mirror above the sink, so the effect when Klott leans in to splash some cold water on his face is of a funhouse hall of mirrors, his reflection reflected in the glass of the print, which is in turn reflected in the mirror, and back again in the frame, and on and on until just about forever, each image tinted by Warhol's shock of blond hair atop his Marilyns in a way that leaves Klott looking jaundiced.

He pauses for a beat to look at his primary reflection in the mirror and is struck by how much he looks like his father—how his father used to look, at least. Harrison Klott carries this image of his father that seems to be from a time in Klott's life that has shaped the way he looks out at the world, the way the world looks back in kind. In his mind's eye, Harrison Klott is ten, eleven, twelve years old. His father is about fifty. His mother is still alive. And it doesn't end here, with how he looks, how everyone else looks. It's how he thinks. His hopes and dreams are calibrated in many of the same ways they were when he was wetting those balled-up brown paper towels and tossing them to the ceiling.

Always, it feels to Harrison Klott as if his whole life is ahead of him, instead of in his wake, and so when he catches these brief glimpses of himself in a mirror or is prompted to contemplate where he is on this path and where he is headed, he is momentarily startled and has to remind himself of the many ways time has appeared to pass him by. Always, it comes as a surprise to him that he is no longer ten, eleven, twelve years old. That he is a deeply middle-aged man. That his mother is gone, and his father is fading. That Marjorie's face no longer lights up when he enters a room or says something he means to be clever. That his own children no longer look up to him as a kind of master of their universe and instead seem to grudgingly regard him as someone in their employ, whose job it is to drive them places and give them money and stand as counterweight to the idea that they can be or do or become anything they want as long as they work hard enough and keep focused. Sometimes, he doesn't even recognize himself, for the tiniest moment, but it is in these tiny moments, such as this one here, that Klott believes he exists in full. Here he is, in this square of bathroom mirror, in an assisted living facility in Del Ray, Florida, stressing over what to do with his father and at the same time worrying if he'll ever be able to commit his *haftorah* to memory and how long he's supposed to keep trying to coax a burp from little Joanna before he can put her back down in her crib and not worry that she'll aspirate or choke to death or whatever it is babies do when their first-time fathers are too fucking clueless or sleep-deprived to have even the first idea what they're doing.

He is ten, twenty, thirty, forty... and, now, fifty years old. He is all of these ages at once, every moment in his life all rolled into this one, wrapped in a tentacle of relationships and experiences that hold him in the ways they have always held him, and it startles him and amuses him and disappoints the crap out of him, what he has become.

He lets the water run from cold to hot and holds his hands beneath the stream until the temperature is uncomfortable, and then he rubs them briskly together until the temperature begins to feel comfortable, familiar. In this way, he tells himself he can get used to anything. It's an adjustment, that's all, and as he retraces his steps past the not so very grand staircase to the reception area, he realizes that what he must also get used to, together with idea that he has somehow become a card-carrying adult tasked with the care and feeding of a few too many humans other than himself, is the idea that he must now find another placement for his father.

"There's nothing to discuss?" he says to Lurlene, in a feeble attempt at negotiation.

"I'm afraid not, Mr. Klott," she says. "It's all been arranged."

No, he wants to say. No, it has not.

———

Later, in his father's fourth-floor bedroom, Harrison Klott sits in the straight-backed chair beside the bed. His father is on the bed, which has been stripped to reveal a troublingly stained mattress. Father and son are holding hands. It makes Klott a little uncomfortable to be holding his father's hand like this, but the old man reached for him at some point and now Klott doesn't have it in him to let go. His father's hand feels ancient—dry, fragile, fine. Klott worries that if he squeezes too hard it might crumble or disappear in a cloud of person-dust.

He cannot remember the last time he held his father's hand.

He looks about the room, which has been swept clean, and is struck by what his father's life has become. What there is left of it. There is a single small suitcase at the foot of the bed—an old Samsonite, brown, with a closure reaching over the top like an envelope. Klott remembers the suitcase from childhood, part of a matched set. "The good luggage," his parents always called it—a gift to themselves on their twenty-fifth wedding anniversary, looking ahead to a half lifetime of shared travel.

In the closet, a row of empty hangers frames his father's navy windbreaker, the one with his name stitched to the chest beneath the logo for his old softball team—the Del Ray American Giants, named for one of the original Negro League franchises. The name was not his father's doing, the old man was often quick to explain. That had been the work of the team's captain and player-manager, his father's friend Sy Kallenberg, a pesky hitter from the Bronx who had been something of a left-leaning socialist back in the day and never missed an opportunity to shine even meaningless light on the struggles of those who had been dismissed or discriminated against. Still, Klott's father wore his "Hymie" jacket with pride, and never missed an opportunity to tell one of the waitresses at his favorite coffee shop about the meaning of his team's *fakakta* name.

"American Giants," he used to say—his idea of a running joke. "The very best kind of giants, or the very best kind of Americans, you tell me."

Father and son sit in this way for the longest while, until Hyman Klott abruptly stands and crosses the room to the dresser at the foot of his bed. He moves slowly, painstakingly. It is an effort for the old man to walk, but he moves without apparent thought. Somehow, he is able to navigate these small confines without the aid of the four-footed cane he has taken to using.

Harrison Klott does not at first move to help, until he notices his father fighting with one of the dresser drawers, second drawer from the top, where Hyman Klott had always kept his watches and cufflinks and a diamond pinky ring that had belonged to his father that he only wore on special occasions.

"The top drawer is where they always look," he used to say, in explanation.

Together, the Klott men struggle to pull the empty second drawer from its base. It does not come easily, but Harrison Klott is finally able to shimmy the drawer from the dresser and rest it on the bed. The drawer is empty, of course, but Klott doesn't say anything, knowing full well that his father's watches and cufflinks and diamond pinky ring had been put away for safe keeping when they moved him from his apartment to the first of these assisted living facilities.

Then, Klott notices the strangest thing: his father, making what appears to be a burger-flipping motion with his right hand, over and over. When Klott can only stare back at his father with a look of bewilderment, the old man starts flipping burgers more forcefully, more urgently.

"What?" Klott says. "It's empty. Look." He lifts one edge of the drawer from the bed to give his father a better view inside.

Again, with the forceful flipping.

It's been months since Hyman Klott has spoken a word, according to the administrators and aids at High Meadow. That's how it goes sometimes with dementia, they've explained to Klott. The body is able to continue functioning in some ways, but the mind isn't always able to tell the body what it wants it to do. The wiring is off, frayed. But then there are times—like now, apparently—when his father is clearly trying to communicate through the fog of his dementia, and it's up to Klott to take his meaning.

"What?" he says. "I should turn it over." Asking, not asking.

Hyman Klott is unable to answer and keeps rotating his hands in this burger-flipping way.

And so, Harrison Klott flips the drawer onto its underside to reveal a small red packet taped to the bottom. The packet is about the size of a tea bag, and Klott recognizes it immediately for what it likely holds: a key. He peels the tape from the pressed wood at the bottom of the drawer and holds the freed packet up for his father.

"This what you're looking for?" he says.

His father doesn't answer, just points to the red packet excitedly, repeatedly with the index and middle fingers of his right hand, like he's hurrying to send a message in Morse code.

Klott studies the packet and sees it's from a Stow 'n Go storage facility, stamped with the usual fine print, only the usual fine print does not seem to indicate an address where the corresponding padlock might be located. You'd think, a piece of branded packaging like this, some corporate someone at Stow 'n Go might have thought to include a specific address, especially considering that they have locations all over South Florida, but there is only an insurance disclaimer and a PO box where you're supposed to send the key if it's been lost and you happen to have come upon this small red packet in some unsuspecting place—like, taped to the bottom of a dresser drawer.

For the moment, Klott is not too, too worried about locating his father's stuff, because he remembers driving with the old man to a storage facility shortly after the death of Klott's mother, long before his father's slide into senescence. And yet, on his side of this exchange, Hyman Klott appears too, too worried about this latest turn—agitated, even. He continues to point frantically at the red packet—tapping, tapping, tapping at the snap-closure as if to will the thing open.

Finally, abruptly, Hyman Klott gives up on the burger-flipping and the tapping and begins making a check-signing motion in the air with the same hand. It's a gesture Klott the Younger also remembers from childhood, a gesture he's by now made his own, a gesture that annoys the hell out of his own children every time they go out to eat and he indicates across the restaurant to the waiter that he's ready for the check.

"Might as well be snapping your fingers," Joanna once said, calling her father out.

"Here, boy!" Stewie had said, underlining the point.

Klott looks for a pen and a piece of paper to bring to his father, who is sometimes able to make himself understood by writing down what he means to say, but the room has been emptied of everything but the furniture and the lone suitcase. Scrambling, Kott touches his own pockets, to see if a pad and pen might have magically appeared, and then he moves to the closet and fists the pockets of his father's windbreaker, where he finds an old golf pencil riding one of the seams. He reaches for his wallet and pulls a receipt from the billfold and spreads it out on the dresser next to his father, upside down. Then he hands his father the pencil and says, "Here."

Hyman Klott takes the pencil and pinches it between his thumb and his Morse coding fingers and writes. Then he places the pencil on top of the receipt and sits down on the bed.

He has said what he needs to say.

Harrison Klott picks up the receipt to find the word *KEY* written in his father's childish scrawl, in block letters. That's all—just, *KEY*.

"Helpful, Dad," Harrison Klott says, joining his father on the bed. "Really fucking helpful."

———————

It turns out this Lurlene is not as bad as her officious manner might have suggested. Or as she would have Klott believe. Or maybe she is but has learned that if she sprinkles even the smallest kindness or consideration on the way she appears to dismiss the families of her clients, she can talk herself into believing she has done everything she can for these people. Anyway, she's taken the time to call ahead to three other residences in the area to check on placement options for Hyman Klott, and as Harrison Klott stops in the lobby with his father to make his final goodbyes, she hands him a sheet of paper with a list of names and numbers and addresses.

"I've also sent it to your email address," she says. "Me, I'm a paper person. It's just so much easier, don't you think?"

"Thank you," Klott says, glancing at the list. He sees that one of the names on the list has been highlighted, in purple.

Lurlene, noticing his noticing, points to the highlighted listing and says, "I've called ahead to this one. They know me over there."

Over there is the Sunshine Homes facility in Boynton Beach, part of a chain of assisted living and nursing home communities Klott had been told to avoid when he started in on these misadventures.

"And?" Klott says. "Is there a bed available?"

She nods. "Their client population is better suited for someone like your father," she says. "Their staff has a different orientation."

Klott does not know what this might mean, or how to set aside the less-than-sunny reviews he once read about the Sunshine Homes operation, but he is grateful for the extra effort. And the insight. And the kindness, however small. He doesn't want to leave this place in a huff. These people, Lurlene, they have been good to his father. He's a difficult man, Klott knows, although the dementia seems to have smoothed his difficult edges. Where he was once hard, he is now soft. Where he was once sharp, he is now dulled. But he remains stubborn, determined, set in his ways—probably not the best aspects of character to take with you into the memory unit of an assisted living facility.

"Thank you," Klott says, pocketing the paper.

The woman smiles, says she will have someone in bookkeeping get in touch to close out his father's account, says they can expect to be credited for the balance of the month, perhaps even for the full month if they are able to fill the bed in a timely manner. Then she touches Hyman Klott gently on the back, almost lovingly, and says, "You take good care, Hymie." She points to the chest of his windbreaker and says, "Our American giant."

Hyman Klott does not seem to notice her touch or her kindness. Klott cannot be sure his father knows he is leaving this place—and, if so, if he has the first idea why. The old man's expression is blank, his eyes facing straight ahead, his head nodding slightly. Klott had had to hold his father by the arm to get him to stand still in the lobby to make these goodbyes in the first place, and as soon as he let go, the old man continued walking, like a wind-up toy drawing down the last of its spring-action.

No one else from the High Meadow staff turns out for Hyman Klott's send-off, and as father and son step through the sliding doors and into the Florida heat, it is as if this brief period in their lives never happened. In a day or two, Klott knows, his father's room on the fourth floor will be filled with another someone slowly losing his or her grip on this world, the bruises on the shins of Mrs. Raccannelli up in Nine West will have healed, and Lurlene will be upending the lives of some other family in the name of efficiency or expediency or inconvenience.

It is the way of these things, these places.

Klott eases his father into the front seat of the car and buckles him in, then places the suitcase and cane in the hatchback.

"Let's blow this popsicle stand," Klott says once he's seated in the driver's seat—something his father used to say when Klott was a kid.

He studies his father for an acknowledgment, a flash of recognition . . . *something*. But the old man's face remains blank, without expression, and Klott is left to wonder what the hell it means to blow a popsicle stand. He wishes he could ask his father. He wishes he could see what his old man is seeing, know what he is thinking.

Before pulling away, Klott dials the Sunshine Homes facility and asks to be put through to the management office. He worries for a beat if he should maybe take the call off speaker, to spare his father any indignity in the conversation, but then he realizes his father wouldn't know if he was calling the pope. The receptionist asks for Klott's name before placing him on hold, and in about thirty seconds a sunny-throated woman comes on and greets him as if they've known each other for years instead of not at all.

"Your friends at High Meadow have told us all about your father," the woman says. "How soon can we expect you?"

Klott hadn't realized it was any kind of done deal, moving his father into Sunshine Homes or how it was that the people who had shown his father the door at High Meadow had become his friends, but it is as if the decision has been made for him and he doesn't have it in him to stand against it. The place is probably as good as any, he thinks, so he tells the woman on the phone they're on their way.

He knows these roads, a little bit, from his many visits over the years. He knows he can triangulate the short drive to Sunshine Homes with a stop at the storage facility, assuming the place Klott vaguely remembers visiting will connect in some way to his father's bottom-of-the-drawer mystery key. He figures it'll be easiest to gain access if the old man accompanies him, so he heads west on Atlantic Avenue toward Military Trail. He's pretty sure the storage facility is in one of the look-alike shopping malls that have come to dot the South Florida landscape like a contagion, each one anchored by a Target or an Applebee's, a Lowe's or a Winn-Dixie. Look-alike or no, he'll know it when he sees it.

And, sure enough he does—or, he thinks he does. Stupidly, he looks to his father for another one of those flashes of recognition that never seem to come, but the old man's face reveals nothing as the two men come upon a Stow 'n Go sign landscaped into the side of the road in a way that looks a little familiar.

Klott turns into the lot and parks the car in one of the handicapped spots in front of the storage facility. He doesn't have a tag or a sticker or whatever it is he might need to validate his parking, but he doesn't want his father to have to make the only marginally longer walk from a legitimate spot.

He switches off the ignition and turns to his father and says, "This the place?"

He gets back nothing.

"I'll take that as a maybe," Klott says, amusing himself, and as he helps his father from the car and along the few steps to the front entrance, he becomes more and more certain he has found the right location. There's a generic-seeming ATM machine cut into the concrete facing of the storefront with a *Free Money!* sticker fixed to the side panel that he remembers seeing on a previous visit—and, inside, an oversized mural of a colorfully crowded beach scene that once struck him as completely out of place and now appears as welcome corroboration.

Father and son take a seat in the small reception area, where they are greeted by a young female attendant who waves them to the counter. There are no other customers. The attendant is wearing a company polo shirt, her hair pulled back in a tight ponytail cinched with a scrunchy that's also been stamped with the Stow 'n Go logo. Klott shows the woman his father's key, and the bar code on the red packet. Then he reaches into his wallet for his father's license and hands it across the counter, thinking surely he is not the first adult child of a demented parent to have come to these offices looking to collect or inventory a parent's left-behind possessions.

"It's been a while," he says, as if in apology.

The young woman runs her fingers across her keyboard while staring intently at her screen in a way that suggests she might be summoning her grandmother's closely guarded gefilte fish recipe, keeping up a line of innocuous chatter as she types.

"Such a beautiful day," she says. Then, "Weather says rain this weekend." And finally, "Did you see the signs for the street fair off Jog Road? You didn't come in that way, did you? Just got a text from my mother, says traffic is a nightmare."

She piles these comments one on top of the other in such a way that Klott can't tell if he's meant to respond—the volleys keep coming before he has a chance to bat them back across the counter.

"Ah," the young woman finally says, presumably because she has at last found whatever she's been looking for on her computer. "Here you are, Mr. Klott." Then, to Klott the elder, in a much louder voice: "Here *you* are, Mr. Klott." As if the volume might help to lift the old man's apparent fog. Then, meaning to be helpful, she pivots her computer screen so that it faces Hyman Klott and says, "See?"

She turns the screen back to where it's facing in her direction and furrows her brow and nudges her glasses up the bridge of her noise to make like she's concentrating. She scratches out a few notes to herself on the pad by her keyboard. Then she looks up from her writing and says, "You're not kidding, it's been a while."

Klott waits for the rest of it.

"I'm afraid your father's account is no longer current," the young woman says.

"Are his things still here?" Klott says.

"Yes," she says. "And no. At Stow 'n Go, we hold on to abandoned items for three years from the end of our grace period." She says this part like she's committed it to memory, continuing, "Your father is not the first older person to forget to pay his invoice, I assure you."

Klott, hardly assured, explains that his father's been in an assisted living facility, and that he's no longer able to track or pay his bills. "Fuckin' Alzheimer's," he says.

"I understand," the young woman says. "My grandmother had it." She pauses a beat, smiles, and then says, "Fuckin' heartbreaking."

"Yes," Klott says. "Fuckin' heartbreaking."

And so, it is agreed, the situation is fuckin' heartbreaking, but the solution to this fuckin' heartbreak is not so readily apparent.

"What's the *no* part?" Klott says. "You said yes and no, his things are still here."

"Yes," she says. "That. After our grace period, which we believe is the most generous in the self-storage industry, we collect the items and place them in our off-site warehouse. We try to give our customers every opportunity to recover them. You can't replace a memory, right?"

Again with the rehearsed lines.

"How off-site is off-site?" Klott says.

"Not far," the young woman says. "Couple miles. Our main location. This is more of a satellite facility."

"And is there any way to tell what he's left behind?" Klott says. "If it's even worth the trouble? Maybe easiest to just donate whatever it is to Good Will."

The attendant taps again at her keyboard and studies her screen. "According to this, there's just a single suitcase," she says.

Klott looks to his father and says, "What's in the suitcase, Pop?"

Hyman Klott says nothing, gives away nothing.

Always, Hyman Klott says nothing, gives away nothing.

The young woman fills the silence with relevant details: she might be able to get Stow 'n Go corporate to waive the monthly fee for the unpaid term, she tells, considering the circumstances, but she will not be able to waive the seventy-nine-dollar reclamation fee, allowing Harrison Klott to collect his father's belongings. "I hope you understand," she says.

This seems fair enough, Klott thinks, only there's no way to know what his father has stashed in the suitcase, if it's even worth seventy-nine dollars, if the old man will ever miss what he's already missing. Klott cannot imagine a family heirloom or treasure or small keepsake that has not somehow been accounted for or written off, and yet he hands over his credit card and authorizes the charge before giving the matter a third thought—his second thoughts having been swiftly conjured and bundled together over the contents of the suitcase and just as swiftly abandoned.

The young woman processes the payment and hands Klott a brochure with his receipt and claim check. She circles an address on the back of the brochure and says, "About another two or three miles west on Atlantic. If you hit the turnpike, you've gone too far."

Klott thanks her for her patience, and for waiving the missed monthly fees.

The young woman shrugs off his thanks. "You gentlemen have a blessed day," she says. Then, louder to Hyman Klott: "All the best to *you*, Mr. Klott." Again, almost in a scream.

Klott wants to turn to her and explain that his father's hearing is fine, that this is not how dementia works, but he does not want to dampen the good feeling that is otherwise flowing from the other side of the Stow 'n Go counter and in so doing perhaps jeopardize the generous terms to which they've all just agreed. It takes some effort for Klott to restrain himself because the young woman has already offered that her own grandmother had once had Alzheimer's and should therefore probably know better, or different, but he doesn't want to set her off. He's learned that the older he gets, and the more invisible he becomes to the invariably young professionals he now must rely on to somehow accommodate him as he strives to meet his basic needs, the more he accepts that he must come at each interaction with his hand out and his mouth shut. Whatever sense of superiority he may have felt as he came of age, or after he'd published his novel, or when he first had children, has long since dissipated, to where any edge in any given situation most likely resides on the other side of the counter.

Cut to Stow 'n Go's main location, on a sprawling complex off Atlantic Avenue, where Klott once again pulls into a handicapped parking space out in front and patiently escorts his father inside. He presents the claim check from the satellite location and within minutes a bald, burly, Stow 'n Go-shirted man wheels a much-larger-than-necessary cart through the double doors leading to the facility's warehouse area. Atop the cart sits another worn brown suitcase—a twin to the bag the High Meadow staff had packed for Hyman Klott just a few hours earlier.

The good luggage!

Harrison Klott fishes in his pockets for a couple singles to give the bald, burly man for his troubles, but the smallest bill he has is a five. He hands it sheepishly to the man and says, "All I've got. Trade you for a couple singles?"

The man holds his palms open, as if to indicate he has no money—the charade of every hourly worker conditioned to expect a gratuity.

"Never mind," Klott says. "Keep it. And thanks."

The bald, burly man touches the brim of his Florida Marlins cap in thanks and pockets the five-dollar bill, and as he retreats through those same double doors, Klott calculates that if he had a dollar for every time he overtipped a baggage handler or a delivery person or a valet because he didn't have enough singles . . . well, he'd have a shitload of dollars.

He returns with his father to the car and reunites the suitcase with its partner in the hatchback, and as he sits back down behind the steering wheel, he takes the time to notice that his father seems fatigued by all this running around, a little more out of it than usual. At the same time, he wonders how to measure degrees of out-of-it-ness in someone in his father's condition, but it feels to him like the old man is less focused, less present. He wonders how such a thing is even possible, but here it is, here *they* are, at considerable remove from those moments just a couple hours earlier when his father was somehow able to communicate with a golf pencil.

As he doubles back on Atlantic Avenue toward Military Trail, Klott is struck by what is left of his father. There is the shell of the man who stood for years as a kind of model for his only child—not a role model, necessarily, but an example of what it meant to live a life of determination.

The old man had never really understood Harrison Klott's decision to pursue a career as a writer, was always on him to punch a clock in a more traditional field, to work his way up some corporate ladder, to seek a more certain path. Hyman Klott had served overseas as a shipping clerk during the Korean War and had returned to a warehouse job arranged for him by an Army buddy whose family was in the corrugated box business, and he wanted for his son what he had chosen for himself.

"Find a family business run by decent people," Klott the Elder used to tell his son, "and make them think of you as family."

This had been Hyman Klott's strategy for living, to insert himself fully where he did not fully belong, and yet what Harrison Klott remembers most vividly about his father during the prime of his career at Zwerling & Son Packaging was the way he always smelled of cardboard when he came home from work. It was one of the primary smells of Klott's growing up, almost like something from a horse stable, like his father had maybe stepped in shit and could not wash the scent from his shoes or his days. Klott remembers that his father kept a change of clothes in the mud room off the garage and that each night he would step out of the coveralls he was made to wear on the warehouse floor and into a fresh set of clothes Klott's mother would leave out for him. In the mornings, he would put the same coveralls back on as he left the house. Still, there was always the feint whiff of pressed, wet wood about Hyman Klott—a childhood smell his son never really minded but always associated with a life grooved into routine and lived in service of someone else's dream.

And so, Klott gets to thinking it is as if this shell of a man who had once been his father has been somehow boxed in this familiar-seeming way, his smells washed away by the years and his essence washed over by senility or madness or whatever they're calling this thing that has claimed Hyman Klott. Every once in a while, Klott swears he can see a glint or shimmer in his father's eye that makes him think his old man is still rattling about in there, but for the most part, there is just this package shaped to resemble father—this box, filling up the same space.

There's a circular driveway at the Sunshine Homes entrance, allowing

Klott to pull the car to the door to unload his father's few things. There's even a parking attendant, who tells Klott to leave the car while he goes to the office and gets his father settled.

Inside, they are met by a woman who introduces herself as Sunshine's relationship manager, with a sunny voice that seems to want to hang air quotes on her job title. Klott recognizes the sun in her voice from the sunshine that had earlier greeted him on the phone.

"I was starting to worry about you two," the relationship manager says in greeting. "But then I thought, it's such a beautiful day, maybe they stopped for a picnic."

Some picnic, Klott thinks—says, "Sorry if we've kept you waiting. We had some errands to do on the way."

"Not at all," she says, extending her hand for shaking. "I've already started on the paperwork, if you'd like to follow me to my office."

Klott, shaking, asks if he could maybe get his father situated in his room before they continue with the intake process. "I think it's taken a lot of out him," he says. "All this running around. His routines are all shot."

"Of course," the relationship manager says. "Let's get you settled."

She arranges for a wheelchair and an aide to escort Klott and his father to the memory unit on the third floor, where they will be met by a shift supervisor and introduced to the staff.

"Come see me when you catch your breath," the woman says to Klott.

Upstairs, Harrison Klott helps his father from the wheelchair to a faux-leather recliner by the window in his new room. He supposes he should see if the old man needs to use the bathroom, but the thought of helping him out of his pants and holding his dick as he pees feels like an intimacy Klott is unable to handle. It is enough that he was able to hold his father's hand, he thinks, and guesses an aide will come along soon enough to tend to any more basic needs.

As he moves the wheelchair to the far corner of the room, Klott is startled by the parking attendant, who appears in the doorway with the two suitcases from the car. He doesn't knock—he is just there, waiting for Klott to turn and notice him.

"Thought I'd save you the trouble," the attendant says.

Klott crosses to the door and collects the bags from the attendant. "Great," he says. "Thanks. Very kind of you."

The attendant nods. "Anything else I can get you?"

Klott shakes his head. "I think we're good," he says, and hands the attendant his last five-dollar bill. He worries that if he is shown any more kindnesses, they will cost him a ten or a twenty. The attendant nods again, and doffs his baseball cap, and closes the door behind him.

"Let's see what you've got in here, Pop," Klott says, lifting one of the brown suitcases onto the mattress, but when he opens it he realizes he's grabbed the original suitcase with his father's stuff from High Meadow.

"Must've driven you and Mom crazy," Klott says, as if to his father, who continues to look out the window at nothing much at all. "The exact same suitcases."

Klott closes the first suitcase and swaps it out with the second one and is staggered by what he finds inside.

Cash.

Lots and lots of cash.

Piles and piles of cash.

Just, cash. Everywhere, cash. Some of it neatly wrapped in stacks of twenties, fifties, hundreds. Some of it loosely arrayed, like the money was tossed in as an afterthought, in haste. Really, Klott has to steady himself on the bedframe to keep from toppling over, that's how thrown, how alarmed he is by the sight of all this cash. He's never seen so much money, all in one place—never even imagined so much money, all in one place.

Jesus. There could be ten thousand dollars in here, easy. One hundred thousand. One million.

"Dad?" he says, turning to the window. "What the fuck? What the actual fuck?"

9.

I DON'T NEED TO BE FORGIVEN

SHARI BRAVERMAN

SO, THE WAY IT WORKS in this particular book club is the host chooses the book and pairs it with a wine or a house cocktail. She's also expected to serve dinner and set a general tone for the evening. In the beginning, this meant days of planning and shopping and cooking, as members tried to one-up each other and prepare a feast matched in some way to the book under discussion—fried green tomatoes, say, with catfish and cornbread, when Fannie Flagg's *Fried Green Tomatoes at the Whistle Stop Cafe* was on the menu; or, *Champandongo*, a layered Mexican meat dish, with vegetables, nuts and mole, when they were reading Laura Esquivel's *Like Water For Chocolate*. Beryl Kasten had been the host for that one, and Shari Braverman remembers being surprised by the meal, for the way it suggested that Beryl had actually read the book, although she could have simply skimmed it and pinched one of the recipes. Beryl was famous among the group for not doing the reading—a high school English teacher, no less!—so when Shari got the email with the assignment, she figured Beryl would maybe serve a chocolate mousse or a chocolate fondue, thinking she wouldn't get much past the title for inspiration.

After a year or so and everyone had hosted a time or two, the extra efforts that went into these presentations began to fall away, to where now the hosts mostly order in. They're down to sushi and wraps and salads, although every now and then when a new place opens up in town, someone will branch out and order in Mediterranean or Indian. The women in this group, they like to be the first to post about a new restaurant or start a new trend. Once, a tea shop opened on Old Maine Road and Allison Tartel had the idea to serve an assortment of teas and finger sandwiches to underline a rereading of *Alice in Wonderland*, but all of that tea cut down on the alcohol consumption and several members thought that if they'd recently screened the animated Disney version with their kids, they could get away without reading the book. Still, Shari thought Allison deserved points for trying something new, and the group was generally pleased with the resulting photo opportunities, so the evening was counted a success, earning the host the nickname "Allison Wonderland" for the next while.

Now that it is Shari's turn to host—her first assignment, post Fred-suck—she's decided on an adultery-themed evening, to dishonor the ways her husband has so publicly dishonored her. She sends around an email, asking everyone to read *The Scarlet Letter* and promising "an evening of unadulterated conversation"—not quite sure the others will take her meaning. In the email, she includes a line from Hawthorne in the summary of the book the hosts are asked to share with the group: "No man, for any considerable period, can wear one face to himself and another to the multitude, without finally getting bewildered as to which may be the true"—adding, "Doesn't that just beat all?"

She imagines there have been some sidebar conversations over the appropriateness of her theme, since a number of the women are married to men who continue to be in touch with her not-yet-ex-husband Brian.

She knows these women well enough to know that what they say to her doesn't always align with what they say to each other. However, in the group text thread that includes Shari, the comments have all been positive, encouraging, validating—as in, "You go, girl!" and "Fuck him!" and "Excellent choice!"

(Shari's favorite—from Allison Wonderland, no less: "Get the boy a set of kneepads!")

For the meal, Shari's decided on a kielbasa and beet recipe from one of her mother's old cookbooks—not exactly on point, as far as the Hawthorne is concerned, but she figures the beets are the closest she can get to a scarlet hue without artificial food coloring, and that the kielbasa links can represent her neighbor Fred.

To lubricate the discussion, she's made a pitcher of scarletish screwdrivers, with ruby red grapefruit juice instead of orange juice, to get the evening started and set out a couple bottles of a dry Austrian Riesling to accompany the kielbasa. (Her hope here is that someone picks up on the wine's fruity notes.) For the screwdrivers, she's using a set of colorful plastic wine glasses she bought for the fortieth birthday party she threw herself a couple years back. For the Riesling, she's planning to use the good stemware she and Brian received for their wedding—because, you know, when the hell else is she going to use them?

As to the book itself . . . well, Shari is struck by the public shaming at the heart of Hawthorne's story, and she comes prepared to push the group to consider the resources and the aspects of character that might be available to someone like Hester Prynne in a more modern, more enlightened world, but the conversation never gets going in such a thoughtful direction and instead appears stuck on Shari's scandalous preparations. This makes sense, she's now realizing, as the evening gets underway—it's tough for these women not to groan or snicker at the sight of the limp, half-moon kielbasa links on Shari's grill top, once she announces that Fred was her inspiration. And yet a part of her thinks she should have dialed down on the indecency front and kept the Brian-skewering mostly to herself. Really, it starts to feel more like a bachelorette party than a book club, and as Beryl Kasten joins Shari to help mix a second pitcher of screwdrivers she says, "This is why we love you, Shari. What Brian has put you through, I can't even."

No, Shari guesses she can't.

The other women take turns sidling up to Shari and whispering how much they admire her, how much they feel for her and the kids, how they know in their heart of hearts that she will come out of this stronger for the experience.

Why is it, Shari takes the time to wonder as these well-meaning well-wishers fill her ears, as she's spun around her kitchen and passed from guest to guest like she's caught in a suburban square dance, that these sisterly shows of solidarity have lately come to include phrases like "heart of hearts" to indicate a particular depth of good feeling? Isn't it enough to just say, "Oh, man, this fuckin' sucks" and be done with it? She longs for the time when people looked at her with something other than pity or sympathy or whatever it is that now causes them to attach all these flowery phrases to their casual commentary.

Kaleema Said, a normally reserved Muslim woman who joined the group after befriending Shari at a mother-daughter art class she took with Jana, long after her other Jaxon-based friends had stopped having children, downs her second screwdriver and offers a toast that sends the evening off in a hardly flowery but perhaps inevitable direction.

"To Shari," she says. "Such a set of balls on our girl!"

Predictably, this starts the group conversation careening downhill, away from Hawthorne's Puritan Boston to the acid-tongued housewives of Centerville, in the fat middle of Long Island. And Shari, bless her angry, emboldened, trampled-upon heart, is at the front of the sled, steering— saying, "Balls weren't big enough for Brian, apparently."

She doesn't mean to, and she even thinks better of it as she does so, but she grabs her crotch as she says this—which, also predictably, sets off another round of roasting and merry-making of the kind that doesn't typically make an appearance at suburban book club gatherings, not this early in the evening—confirming that in this one way, at least, Shari

Braverman cannot walk any kind of high road when it comes to discussing her husband's affair, and the women in her book club are only too happy to be along for the journey.

It is, after all, her pain, not theirs.

It is, after all, her shame, not theirs.

"Always thought he was more of an ass man," says Suze Weiden, who'd worked briefly in PR before having children and is still able to score a dozen tickets each year to the local radio station's all-star holiday concert at Madison Square Garden, which she kindly shares with her middle school mom friends and their age-inappropriate daughters. Some -fest or -palooza or -topia with a name Shari can never remember, because her Jana is a little young for the two of them to be counted in.

"Bollocks!" says Allison Dartel, who never misses an opportunity to remind the group that she spent a semester in London while in college, studying art history.

The ribaldry is interrupted by the doorbell. This book group has been at it so long, and these women have been in and out of each other's homes so many times, that the sound of a doorbell is momentarily startling, out of place, because everyone just lets themselves in. But then, by turns, they realize it's the newest member of their group—a friend of Kaleema's from the city, Fiona Pluscht, who's been coming to these gatherings for a couple months and has already established a pattern of being the last to arrive. The other members have been generally accommodating of this, because Fiona does have the longest drive, and because their ranks have been thinning over the years as some of the group's original members have started snowbirding in Florida over the winters and they are in need of new blood.

"Now it's a party," says Kaleema, turning to Fiona.

Someone hands Fiona Pluscht a screwdriver, and soon there are another few toasts, and between sips and cheers and belly laughs Shari goes to greet her final guest.

"Good that you're here, Fi," she says, from inside a hug. "Traffic?"

"Not too bad," Fiona says. "I just never leave enough time. Sorry."

Shari waves to indicate it's not any kind of big deal, and the two women step back from each other and touch plastic wine glasses.

"To Hester Prynne," Shari says.

"To Hester Prynne," Fiona says.

Then, from the other side of the kitchen, another someone concurs: "To Hester Prynne."

And so, it is agreed, they shall all drink to the unassailable strength of Hester Prynne, and in this way the group signals itself that it is time to move to the living room to begin discussion of the book, but as they gather their things. Fiona Pluscht pivots abruptly to the spot on the kitchen counter where she'd placed a gift basket, wrapped in clear plastic and topped with a blood red ribbon. "I almost forgot," she says, reaching for the basket and walking it over to Shari. "This is for you."

"Oh, my. Fi. You shouldn't have," Shari says.

"It's nothing," Fiona says, handing over the gift. "So good of you to have me."

"No, really," Suze Weiden says, deadpan. "You shouldn't have. Makes us all look bad."

"Hear! Hear!" Allison Dartel says.

"Oh, stop," Shari says, setting down her glass to consider the gift. She unravels the ribbon and tears at the clear plastic to reveal a small stuffed toy, about the size of a beanie baby—an Alvin the Chipmunk doll, wearing a red sweater with a giant letter A across the chest.

She holds it out for the group to see. "Say hello to Alvin, girls," she says. Then, in a cartoon, chipmunky voice, as if she means for it to be coming from the doll: "Please drink responsibly, ladies."

There follows a good amount of laughter and hooting and glass raising.

Shari, on a roll, again as Alvin: "Always check your husband's collars for unwanted semen stains."

Fiona waits for another round of laughter and hooting and glass raising to die down, then points to the letter A on the doll's sweater. "Get it?" she says. "*The Scarlet Letter*. Hello?"

"This is so great," Shari says, doubling back to Fiona for a hug. "Never in a million years would I have made that connection." She holds the doll up for the group and says, "Look, ladies. An interloper!"

"It's from my husband's line," Fiona says. "They signed a licensing agreement with them. There was a movie, I think."

"Wait," Beryl Kasten says, making the connection. "Pluscht Toys. That's you?"

"My husband," Fiona says. "Family plush toy business. Third generation."

Shari, again as Alvin, in a cartoon voice: "Speak thou for me!"

This time, there is not quite so much laughter or hooting or glass raising, which tells Shari her line didn't exactly land. "It's from the book," she says. "Assholes."

At just this moment, just as Shari Braverman dismisses her friends for not having paid good and close attention to the assigned reading, just as the word "assholes" spills from her lips a little too loudly, little Jana Braverman steps into the living room to ask her mother for a snack.

"Language, Mommy," she says. "You know what we say."

"Aw, sweetie," Shari says, crossing to Jana and squeezing her close. Then, for the benefit of the room, in a voice as much hers as Alvin's: "Mommy's sorry. Mommy's been drinking. Mommy's bad."

"You said a bad word," Jana says.

"Yes, I did," Shari says. "I'm sorry."

She holds out the Alvin doll for her daughter. Jana doesn't know the Chipmunks—a touchstone that hasn't quite touched down in this house—but she is delighted to meet him. She even says as much, dipping into a slight, little kid curtsy and saying, "It's a pleasure to meet you."

"He's a present from my friend Fiona," Shari says, sending her gaze across the room to where Fiona Pluscht is standing. "His name is Alvin. He came to keep us company."

Jana follows her mother's gaze to Fiona, who returns a small curtsy of her own and says, "Delighted to meet you, Jana."

"Can I have him?" Jana says, turning back to her mother.

"How 'bout he stays with us for our meeting, and then he can come to your room and stay with you for a while?" Shari says.

Jana nods her head enthusiastically. She likes this idea.

Shari leans in close to her daughter for a private conversation and asks, "Where's your brother?"

Jana cups her hand at the side of her mouth, her face in profile to the group, and whisper-shouts: "Nintendo." However, she's placed her hand on the wrong side of her mouth, and her whisper-shout has got way more shout to it than whisper, so the effect is fairly adorable. The other women *oooh* and *aaah* as if they've never seen such a fairly adorable child.

Shari picks up Jana and carries her to the staircase. "How 'bout you hang out with your brother for a little," she says, "and Alvin and I will come upstairs in a few minutes to say goodnight?"

In answer, Jana throws her arms around Shari's neck and buries her face in her mother's hair. She likes this idea, too.

As her daughter scurries upstairs, Shari turns to the group and says, "Where were we?"

"Where we were," Beryl Kasten says, "is your daughter is just too fucking cute."

There is general agreement on this, and Shari doesn't have it in her to argue the point.

Shari had taken the time before the group arrived to move her dining room chairs into the living room and arrange them in a semicircle around her sectional sofa and ottoman to create a conversation pit, and as her friends move to claim their seats, she steps into the kitchen to reclaim her wine glass, where she's intercepted by Dottie Kledstat, the oldest member of the group.

Dottie touches Shari on the arm in a show of concern and says, "How's she doing? Your daughter?"

The concerning touch is accompanied by another one of those knowing, pitying looks Shari has come to dread, together with an extreme head tilt that leaves her momentarily uncertain of Dottie Kledstat's ability to keep her head atop her shoulders.

Shari shrugs. "You know, she's doing. *We're* doing."

"A child like that," Dottie says, as if she is one to know, "going through what you're all going through, she should be able to talk to someone. Is she talking to someone?"

Dottie, a retired school social worker, is often the first among this group to weigh in with unsolicited advice on parenting and related matters, and here Shari doesn't have the bandwidth to engage her on the care and feeding of her children. Probably, Shari wouldn't have the patience for such as this at any time, but now, three drinks into her evening and two shits beyond caring, she cannot be bothered.

"She's seven, Dottie," Shari says. "She's talking to me."

The two women are interrupted by Suze Weiden, who seems anxious to get the literary conversation started—or maybe she's been designated to rescue the host. Either way, Shari is happy to see her, at just this moment. "What are you two hens going on about?" Suze says, walking into the kitchen.

"Oh, the usual," Shari says. "The weight of the world. The weight of my worries. How me and my cute kiddies are holding up."

"And how *are* you and your cute kiddies holding up?" Suze says, with an exaggerated show of concern she half hopes doesn't register with Dottie Kledstat as mocking or accusatory. The other half hopes Dottie picks up on her tone and backs the fuck off.

Shari, sensing the evening is getting away from her and that the moment is becoming uncomfortable, reaches across the counter to the grill for one of the kielbasa links, which she fists and thrusts into her mouth and pretends to suck off. Here again, she does not mean to do this, and begins to think better of it as she does so, but once the thought alights in her head, she is powerless against it. "This is how we're holding up, ladies," she says in a mumble, her mouth full. "This is how we're fucking holding up."

Suze Weiden laughs, puts her hand on Shari's kielbasa-fist to keep it from thrusting, moves to quiet her friend before things get any weirder.

"Jesus," Shari says, taking a mental picture of herself and not liking what she sees. "Sorry."

"Hope you're not planning on serving that to any of your guests," Suze says.

"Well," Shari says, "now that you mention it . . ." She lets her voice trail off in a way that suggests she's pretending to think about it, while at the same time reaching in one of the cabinets for a small plate. Then she sets the fellated kielbasa on the plate and says, "Guess I got dibs on that one."

———————

Later, in Jana's bedroom, Shari sits with her daughter and the Alvin the Chipmunk doll on the canopied bed.

Bedtimes have been hard, with Brian out of the house. As raw and frank as she's been with the rest of the world—with Jaxon, even!—Shari can't think how to explain her father's absence to Jana. At seven, Jana's heard about divorce from her some of her first-grade pals, but Shari's not sure she understands it. They've read books together that were meant to help ease children into a conversation on what it means when parents decide they can no longer live together, and there's no avoiding the subject on the family-friendly sitcoms Jana watches with her brother on Nickelodeon and Disney, but none of these scenarios have seemed to register with Jana in a meaningful way. In her little head, a divorce is like a time-out, no more permanent than a squiggly drawing on her Etch A Sketch or a sleepover at her grandmother's.

It happens and then it unhappens and is gone.

"Where's Daddy?" Jana says, sweetly, for the millionth time.

"Daddy's at his new house," Shari says, patiently, for the millionth time.

"The place with the elevator?" Jana says.

Shari nods.

"That's not a house, Mommy," Jana says. "Houses don't have elevators."

"I'm sorry," Shari says, coaxing Jana's head to the pillow. "So what should we call it?"

"It's a condo, duh," Jana says.

"Okay, it's a condo, duh." Shari says.

"Is he sleeping, do you think?"

Shari says she doesn't think so. "It's early, still, for grown-ups." Then, "Duh."

Jana giggles in a way to show that she's too big for stupid little kid jokes. She knows she's supposed to laugh, and that her mother wants her to laugh, but she doesn't feel like laughing. It's more of a groan than a giggle.

"Do you want me to sing to you?" Shari says.

Jana nods, closes her eyes, and Shari begins to sing a nonsense song: "*Jana Banana/Jana Cabana/Jana Havana/Jana Bandana . . .*"

As she sings, softly, Shari runs her fingers gently through her daughter's hair and across her forehead. Since she was very little, Jana would fall asleep whenever her mother tippy-toed her fingers across her forehead, like she was playing at a toy piano. Shari used to think she had some kind of magic touch, the way the kid would drift off in just a couple minutes, and so she sings, and tippy-toes her fingers, and waits for it.

"*Jana Banana/Jana Cabana/Jana Havana/Jana Bandana . . .*"

Shari allows herself a small smile, remembering that the lyric was inspired by Jaxon, who used to call to his baby sister in this singsong way. To Jaxon, who had been just six or seven himself, his sister was Jana Banana almost from the moment she was born. They had a poster made by a local artist at a street fair, with the letters J-A-N-A spelled out with bananas and hung over the changing table in Jana's room. And then, Brian sat with Jaxon and they put a melody to the nickname, and all these other rhymes, and one day they looked up and this had become Jana's going-to-sleep song. Jaxon would sing it to her, in the back seat of the car—sometimes impatiently, when he wanted her to stop fussing so he could play his Game Boy.

For years, Shari would sing this homegrown lullaby and catch herself crying as she stood from Jana's bed, for the way the song seemed to wrap their household in sweetness and innocence and light. Now, as she sings, she closes her eyes and imagines Brian, turning this big brother silliness into a real song, when nobody could see into their shared future, when bedtimes were filled with hope and good cheer, and the words spill from her lips like they have been dipped in Strychnine. It kills her, to have to sing Brian's words, to have to sing his song, but she does it anyway.

"*Jana Banana/Jana Cabana/Jana Havana/Jana Bandana . . .*"

She sings for the family they used to be.

10.

SOMETIMES THE LIGHT'S ALL SHINING ON ME

HARRISON KLOTT

IT IS A DIFFICULT THING, Harrison Klott is realizing, to move about the planet with a heavy suitcase—a deceptively heavy suitcase, filled with tens and twenties and fifties and hundreds, and even a few singles and fivers. It's the kind of heavy that sneaks up on Klott and leaves him wondering how he's managed to get from where he was to where he is.

Klott's had the suitcase with him since he parked his father in his new room at Sunshine Homes, lugging it back to the lobby to complete the registration process, up again to the third floor memory unit to help his father get settled and sorted, down to the car where he belted it onto the now-empty front passenger seat, and finally to the Hilton Garden Inn by the airport in West Palm, where he's decided to stop for the night. He wouldn't even leave the bag with the valet in the lobby, said he'd carry it to his room himself, thank you very much, and it is only now, on these last legs of his lugging, facing down the ridiculously long corridor to his room, that he considers how it was that nobody thought to put wheels on suitcases until only recently. What was up with *that*? His poor parents, traveling through life without the benefit of roller bags, resisting the innovation for years and struggling with these after-market suitcase wheelers and jerry-rigged bungee cords that never seemed to hold *the good luggage* in place, as if this quite reasonable convenience was not meant for them . . . it's hard for Klott to get his head around how things were. Really, he can't imagine. It's hard enough to find a way to accommodate this one heavy suitcase on this one day. He's to where he's doing that fool move with his right leg, supporting the weight of the bag against his thigh and propelling it a little bit forward with every step, counting the every-other room numbers as he passes each door, and as he at last arrives at his room at the end of the hall, he lets the bag fall emphatically to the brightly carpeted floor and topple onto its side. He doesn't have it in him to set the thing right straightway and instead waves his key across the lock to open the door and leans inside, where he takes a quick look around before dragging the suitcase across the threshold.

Once inside, the door locked, the mouth harp-type security bolt folded into place, he steps over the bag and into the bathroom, where he splashes some cold water on his face, then wets a hand towel and wrings it out and drapes it around his head like he's at a deservedly unpopular barber shop. He doesn't have the patience to let the water run from hot to cold, so he shudders at the cool damp cloth and then starts to rub at it vigorously, mussing his hair and giving his face a good scrub and in this way shaking himself into focus.

In his head, he's asking the same question he put to his father when he first opened the bag: *what the fuck? . . . what the fuck? . . . what the fuck?* Over and over and over. As if expecting an answer. As if the mystery of all that cash might come clear. As if assessing the stuff of his dreams and cementing it to this new reality and looking for the new ways forward. It does not seem tangible to Klott, or plausible, all that money tucked away in his father's storage unit, all these years. He cannot even begin to understand where it might have come from, what it might mean, what he's now supposed to do with it.

He leaves the damp towel on the sink and walks to the window by the bed, where he opens the heavy curtains to reveal a view that is half parking lot, half HVAC system, half abutting strip mall. (Three halves in all!) He takes the time to notice that someone in Hilton's buildings and grounds department authorized the laying in of decorative wood chips, creating a kind of garden bed surrounding the vents and fans and exhaust piping—a corporate beautification effort that seems to have fallen short in Klott's estimation. His view is hardly softened by the mocha-colored wood chips, but Klott guesses the industrial landscaping must have seemed like a good idea to somebody, or some collective somebody, at some point.

Klott begins to step out of the clothes he's been wearing since he left for the airport this morning, but as he does so, he realizes he's left his own small carry-on in the hatchback of his car, and so for a moment he weighs doubling back along the ridiculously long corridor to the elevator and heading downstairs to the lot to collect it, but then decides against it and strips to his socks and boxer briefs—an unfortunate look Marjorie has taken to calling Harry's Hotel Casual. Always, he leaves on his socks, because he's skeeved out by hotel room carpets, the skeeving out having mostly to do with a report he once saw on *60 Minutes* or *Dateline* about the bedbug infestation problem at mid-tier short-stay hotels. The report featured a clip from an old Jerry Seinfeld routine, with a riff on how Jerry doesn't trust hotel bedspreads or comforters and has gotten into the habit of stripping the covering from the bed whenever he checks in to a new room, so Klott has taken up the habit as well, folding the top of the spread toward the foot of the bed and then halving and quartering the pile until he can carry it to a corner of the room and drop it to the floor in the trapped square of space between desk and window.

Next, he opens the double-doors to the closet in the narrow entryway, expecting to discover one of those sweet spa robes he sometimes finds in these mid-tier short-stay hotel chains—and, sure enough, there are two of them, on hooks festooned with hang-tags inviting him to wear the robes during his stay or to take them home and enjoy the luxury of the Hilton Garden Inn spa experience for the hardly reasonable price of $89.95 per, plus tax.

He grabs a robe and puts it on, then unfolds the luggage rack and sets it out by the side of the bed. Then he drags the suitcase from the door and leg-lifts it onto the rack, flips open the envelope clasp, unzips the zipper. As he opens the bag, he half expects to hear some crescendo-building music in the background, as in a movie, or maybe for a beam of light to shine down on all that cash and bathe the scene in a kind of halo, in a way that suggests the money has been heaven-sent. But there is no soundtrack or beam of light to accompany the moment, only the beating of his heart, which he now notices is racing, *ka-thumping*, as though he also half expects for the money to have all disappeared or been replaced by stacks of index cards.

Happily, mercifully, the money is all here, looking a little grimy and handled and well-circulated, but also glorious, like nothing Harrison Klott has ever encountered or considered. *Good God*, he thinks. *Good fucking God*. There could be a hundred thousand dollars in here, easy. A million dollars. The only way to know is to count it, and as Klott begins to do so, a part of him wants to press *fast forward* and get to the total, while another part wants to be good and thorough about it, to live purposefully in these next moments as the rest of his life takes on new shape, so he sets two large bath towels on the bed, to protect his clean sheets from the dirty money, and then he uses another towel as a kind of satchel to help ferry the money from the suitcase to the bed, where he sets the cash in two piles—one made up of the bundled bills and the other made of up the loose bills that had been stuffed on top.

He figures it'll take a couple hours to count both piles, and he's promised Marjorie he'd call once he checked in to his hotel, so he reaches for his phone and presses her number on his speed-dial. She picks up before the first full ring—telling him she's probably laying in bed, playing Words with Friends, her phone already in hand. He can close his eyes and picture her.

"That you?" Marjorie says.

"That me," Klott says.

"It's late," she says. "Was starting to worry."

"Well, here I am," he says. "At the lovely Hilton Garden Inn in West Palm Beach. The place to see and be seen."

"Should I be jealous?" she says.

"Not unless you have a craving for some sour cream and onion Pringles from the snack shelf in the lobby."

"Yum."

Silence, for a beat.

"Plus, those single-serve Ben & Jerry's you like," he says. "Cherry Garcia."

"Also, yum," Marjorie says—then, cutting to it, "How's Hymie?"

"Hymie's Hymie," Klott says. "Left him with a male nurse named Tiny at a place called Sunshine Homes. In Boca."

"Tiny?"

"As in, not so very. As in, irony."

"Sounds like a name for a prison guard," Marjorie says.

"Nobody knows the troubles he's seen?" Klott says, half-singing.

"Something like that," Marjorie says.

"Seemed nice enough," Klott says. "Place seemed nice enough. Not at all prisony. Don't know what I saw those other times that made me think it sucked."

"Those reviews," Marjorie says. She'd been down in Florida with Klott on the first frantic mission to place her father-in-law in an assisted living facility, his mind first starting to go. She remembers.

"You know how people are," he says, justifying his hurried decision. "One shitty or inconvenient or slightly concerning thing happens, you're fucked."

"Was more than one shitty review, Harry," Marjorie says—as ever, the voice of reason.

He nods, forgetting for a moment they're on the phone.

"Harry?"

"I know," he says. "But the woman at High Meadow, she had good things to say. Lurlene. Said he might be better off. Said they were better able to handle someone like him."

"Meaning?"

"Meaning, you know, difficult. Meaning, it's not like I have a whole lot of options." Then, half-singing again—"Nobody knows the troubles I've seen . . ."

Another silence, for another while.

"How's you?" Marjorie says.

"Me?" he says. "I'm fine. I'm me."

"You eat? Been a long day for you."

Klott hasn't eaten anything since the couple bags of almonds he had on the plane this morning, and an undercooked scone he'd picked up at the Starbucks with his coffee on the way to collect his father at High Meadow.

"They have food in Florida, you know," he says.

She lets the comment hang, pulls the conversation in a different direction. "Joanna's got the SATs tomorrow. Whole lotta stress going on."

"She's stressed or you're stressed?" Klott says.

"Yes."

"She'll do fine," Klott says. "She's smart as fuck, our girl."

"You know I hate that expression," Marjorie says.

"Sorry," he says. "Intelligent as fuck."

"Funny."

"Don't forget to tip your waitress," he says—another one of their routines.

He doesn't know how to tell Marjorie about the suitcase full of money. He can't think where to start. *Oh, by the way, Margie Bear, we're rich.* It can wait until he's home, he thinks, until he can tell the story with a couple hundred thousand visual aids, but for now it sits between them as a thing he should be saying, a thing to get past.

A monumental, big-ass thing.

He closes his eyes and pictures Marjorie again, still, mismatched ski socks on her feet, phone in hand, in bed, next to where he is meant to be.

"When's your flight?" Marjorie says.

His flight? Shit, he hadn't even thought about how to take all this money on an airplane. The suitcase is too big, too heavy for a carry-on, and there's no way he can trust JetBlue's baggage handlers to deliver it to him safely in New York.

"Harry?"

"Sorry," he says. "Early afternoon. One-something. Going to check on Hymie at the new place in the morning. If he's all good, I'll be home for dinner."

———————

That hurry Klott was in to get this money counted and sorted? He's still in the middle of it, but it's more of a painstaking hurry than a cascading hurry. It's the hurry he's in when he's driving with his foot is on the brakes, remembering the speed limit. He keeps starting in on a pile, and then losing his place and starting over. The system he comes up with is separating the loose cash into piles by denomination. Also, trying to determine his father's system, back when the old man started bundling the cash and socking it away. Not much of a system, he knows, but it's a step up from just plain counting, at least. Best Klott can tell, the bundled packets of money each contain one thousand dollars. Some of the packets contain only hundred-dollar bills, and some have fifties and twenties mixed in. He pulls a couple packets from the pile at random to confirm the amount—from the bottom, from the middle, from the sides—and except for a couple times when he counts out $980 or $950 or $1,040, it all checks out, and a second pass at each of those outlier piles shows those first passes had been miscounts.

Thirty minutes in, there are a surprising number of bills spread out atop these plush Hilton Garden Inn bath towels. Klott cannot imagine how his father had stuffed so many piles and all these other loose bills into this one suitcase, how he himself will ever be able to repack it all—like trying to return an air mattress to its carrying case after it's been deployed and deflated.

At some point, he switches on the television and scrolls his way to a music channel, wants to lose himself in the familiar rhythms of his growing up. He lands on a channel called Sounds of the Seventies: Badfinger . . . Seals & Croft . . . Kansas . . . Grand Funk Railroad . . . Familiar songs that have been filling his ears since just about forever.

After about an hour, Klott determines that there are 529 bundled packets of money. He keeps a tally on the notepad he finds on one of the night tables, making hash marks with the branded Hilton Hotels pen that had been placed alongside. Before he knows it, he's jumped to a second page. And a third. He does the math as he goes and grows rich in his head.

More than a half million dollars! And no telling just yet where all the loose cash will net out.

Jesus. Good fucking God.

Klott doesn't know whether to do a small dance or crawl under the bed, although this second option is undercut somewhat by his Seinfeld-stoked infestation worries, and so what he does instead is acknowledge that he's hungry. It's a way to put off facing what he now must face, but it's also a suddenly urgent need. He hadn't thought of food until Marjorie brought it up, but now that she has, he's all over the idea of eating something—only, when he calls Room Service he's told there'll be about an hour wait, so he decides to make a quick trip to the snack shelf in the lobby. He can't see holding out another whole hour without eating, figures the money will be safe in his room for a few minutes, but just to be sure he tosses the loose cash back into the suitcase and puts it in the closet, and drapes two additional bath towels over the piles of bundled cash on the bed. He recognizes the absurdity in believing he has somehow secured this windfall of cash, but he does these things anyway, talking himself into the idea that if anything happened, he'd always regret not laying down these extra towels.

Funny, he thinks, *the things you do when you're up against it. The things you justify or explain away.*

He dresses quickly, collars the *Do Not Disturb* sign to the doorknob, and scurries down the long corridor to the elevator in his socks. It's past eleven when he gets to the front desk. The lights have dimmed since he checked in earlier in the evening, the Muzak dialed down to a little less jaunty. It's as if another someone at Hilton corporate has determined that the lobby areas at all mid-tier short-stay hotel locations lapse into late-night mode after a certain hour, encouraging guests to be more chill as they ease into the wee hours.

There's a small cut-out area behind the desk with shelves of snacks you might find at a roadside gas station. The kiosk is set-up like a small pantry, with kitschy signs every here and there saying, *Kiss the cook!* and *Make mine a double!* and *Now that hits the spot!* There's also a fridge and freezer filled with drinks and ice cream and burritos and personal pizzas. And, a countertop microwave. Klott won't let himself stop long enough to consider his limited options, so he grabs an Amy's Kitchen Chicken 'n Beans burrito from the freezer and tosses it in the microwave. Then he fists a bottle of Sam Adams Winter Lager and a Mountain Dew from the fridge, two cups of Cherry Garcia from the freezer, a bag of caramel Bugles from the shelf, and an unusually bright red apple from the fruit basket by the microwave—not exactly a gourmet meal, but he's hoping at least one of these items will hit the spot.

By the time the guy at the front desk totals Klott's purchases to charge to his room, the microwave throws off a couple beeps to signal that his burrito is ready, so Klott paper-plates his burrito while the guy at the front desk bags the rest of his foodstuffs. Then he turns to the guy and says, "People actually eat this shit?"—Klott's way of acknowledging that he doesn't usually eat like this.

That he's somehow better than this.

The guy at the front desk shrugs, as if to say he has no opinions on the matter, and Klott returns the shrug, as if to say he is only wondering how it is that people's determination to eat smart can get kicked to the curb after ten o'clock in the evening at walk-thru convenience pantries at mid-tier short-stay hotel locations—or, how it is that in moments of startling plenty we can make the same choices we make in moments of quiet desperation.

Back in his room, back in his spa robe and boxer briefs, Klott sets his food on the narrow desk by the window, with an illuminated view of the hotel's HVAC system. The burrito is hot, but he is drawn to the Cherry Garcia. He peels the covering by its pull tab and licks the underside. He is transported by the memories the motion calls to mind—all those summer evenings as a kid chasing after the Good Humor man and ordering a black-and-white cup, the chocolate and vanilla meeting in a swirly line at the middle. Here, the ice cream has softened somewhat since he pulled it from the lobby freezer, so Klott is able to collect a heaping plastic spoonful without too much effort. He cleans the spoon in one bite—a bite filled with bits of chocolate and cherry. Klott wonders if this is just some random windfall or if Ben and Jerry and their flavor technicians have somehow figured out how to lay in an inordinate number of mix-ins at the top of each package to make a meaningful first and lasting impression.

He takes another scoop, and another, and each explosion of chocolate or cherry reminds him what a long, strange trip it's been—from being ten and eleven and twelve years old and dreaming of all that lay in wait to being thirty and forty and fifty years old and looking back at what he's missed . . . from Centerville to Boca this morning . . . from Boca to this Hilton Garden Inn hotel room this evening . . . from unzipping his father's suitcase and not knowing in any kind of full on way how its contents might change the arc of his life going forward.

Next thing he knows, he's scraping the last of the ice cream from the base and sides of the small container and starting in on the second cup—this time with his phone flat on its back on the desk in front of him as he scrolls idly through Facebook. End of the day, he likes to see what he's missed in the goings-on among this once-removed group of friends and acquaintances, and here it seems there's been the usual assortment of birthdays, promotions, staged engagements, and college graduations. As before, as ever, he does this without thinking, like these habits are a part of him. There's a rant from a girl he went to high school with about the closing of abortion clinics in Missouri . . . a link to a mash-up video of our so-called president struggling with what appears to be dry-mouth

at a series of hootenanny rallies . . . a crowd-sourcing campaign to raise
money to help pay for hospital expenses and round-the-clock at-home
care for a former high school English teacher in a losing battle with a
rare bone cancer. There are videos with more than a million views of frat
boys riding tricycles into swimming pools and little old ladies whacking
pizza delivery guys with their canes and cats working out with teeny, tiny
exercise equipment and being coaxed into yoga poses.

Oh, and there's the familiar face of Klott's virtual *inamorata*, Shari
Braverman—there she is!—who has thought to share some super-fun pics
from the wine-soaked book club gathering she appears to have hosted earlier
this evening. She's put together a photo album with the heading *Shame,
Shame, Shame*, featuring a bunch of women Klott recognizes from around
town—Marjorie's friends, the moms of his kids' friends, women he's seen
in the checkout line at Whole Foods. He opens the album so that each shot
fills the small screen on his phone, and he swipes contentedly through all
seventeen photos, pausing every here and there when some detail or pose
or caption catches his attention. When he swipes all the way through to
the last photo, he notices he's set down his spoon and reoccupied his right
hand beneath the elastic of his boxer briefs—gone to fiddling, as per usual.

The last photo is a shot of Shari Braverman holding a stuffed Alvin the
Chipmunk doll, with a caption that reads, *THE SCARLET SWEATER!!!*—
all caps, with three exclamation points.

From the comments, and the context, he gets that the book group had
been reading Hawthorne and that a good time was had by all. What he
also gets is how Shari Braverman seems so sure of herself among her group
of friends, so quick to laugh. She's like a force of nature, and Klott is drawn
to this force, lifted by it—moved, even. Typically, the pictures and posts
that fill his feed have to do with presenting a carefully cultivated image,
a public persona that may or may not have a thing to do with the actual
persona of the actual person doing the posting. With Shari Braverman,
though, Harrison Klott gets that what he sees is precisely what he would
get, if it somehow worked out that he was more closely connected to her
than he is on this platform.

The shine on her lips has not been carefully applied, he's decided. It just *is*.

With his free left hand, he enlarges the image on his screen and notices a familiar face come into focus—his friend Teddy's wife, Fiona. At first, Klott can't be sure it's Fi, he can't even remember the last time he saw her, but then he studies the comment thread and sees a message from Shari thanking Fi for the stuffed Alvin and it all comes clear.

He's thinking, *How did I not know about this?*

He's thinking, *Shit, I never booked those flights to Utah for Teddy's fly-fishing trip.*

Soon, these loosely connected thoughts align with his earlier worries about flying home with his father's suitcase full of cash, and as he continues to touch and rub and distract himself with his right hand he calls up the JetBlue app on his phone with his left. He wants to see about maybe canceling his flight tomorrow and applying the credit to a round-trip flight to Salt Lake City in September. He's wondering what the change fees might cost him—worried, even. But then he sees the open suitcase in the mirror above the desk, and all that cash heaped on the bed, and his worries shift from what it might cost to how he might adapt. He'll have to drive, he realizes. He'll have to work it out with the rental car company and return the car in New York. He'll have to find a place to stash the suitcase once he gets home. He'll have to reach out to Teddy and ask how well Fiona knows Shari Braverman and if maybe she might find a way to bring it up that they have this mutual friend in common.

He'll have to find a way to tell Marjorie he won't be back in time for dinner.

11.

WITHOUT LOVE, WHERE WOULD YOU BE NOW?

MARJORIE KLOTT

IT'S SIX-THIRTY on a Saturday morning and it takes a couple taps on Joanna Klott's bedroom door for her mother to rouse her—and a couple taps more to actually get her out of bed.

Marjorie Klott knows she is probably way too bouncy and loud and cheerful for this hour, but she's trying to fill the house with positivity and good energy, and to compensate for the ways she expects her daughter to be wanting in these areas. Okay, so maybe *wanting* is the wrong word for Marjorie to consider in relation to her daughter's moods this morning. What Joanna's most likely wanting, is to be left alone to do her thing—but that would leave Marjorie letting go of *her* thing, which she's not prepared to do just yet.

Already, Marjorie's been up for an hour, making Joanna her favorite breakfast: waffles, turkey bacon, strawberries, and whipped cream.

"Pass," Joanna says, when she finally shuffles downstairs and sees the spread her mother has set out on the kitchen table. She tosses a cinch sack onto the chair next to her as she sits down. Then, pretending at gratitude, she turns to her mother and says, "Maybe after. We can heat it up when I get home. Maybe for lunch or something."

Joanna's disappointed her mother, she knows—kept her from stepping into her role. She cares and she doesn't care. Joanna doesn't want to be a dick, but she doesn't want to buy in to whatever her mother is selling. Not today. Her mother's always saying that just because people expect something from you doesn't mean you have to meet those expectations if they take you away from what you expect of yourself—or, something like that. Joanna couldn't even tell you half the things her mother's always saying and can't imagine it's the same stuff she's always saying to the students she sees in her office.

"You need to eat, Jo," Marjorie says.

"I'll puke," Joanna says, reaching for the ear buds that almost always frame her face these days, putting it out there that she'd very much like to be done with this conversation.

"What about a banana, at least?" her mother says, holding one out as illustration.

Joanna shakes her head and thrusts out her right hand like she's stopping traffic, blocking the banana from view.

"We have those breakfast-bar thingies your brother likes," Marjorie says. "Blueberry."

"Mom, I'm good," Joanna says, putting her ear buds in place—the universal signal for letting a parent know you're done paying attention. Then, for emphasis: "Really."

Marjorie at last backs off and gives Joanna some room. It isn't always necessary to beat her over the head with a hammer to get her to respond to the many moods of her children, but sometimes it helps.

Mother and daughter are quiet for the next while. The rest of the house is quiet as well. Harrison is in Florida with Hymie, and the twins won't be up for another few hours. Joanna had insisted last night that she could get herself up and out of the house in time to make it to her SAT test this morning, maybe have one of her friends pick her up, but Marjorie cannot let these moments go unparented. She is determined to be available to her daughter in this sure, small way, even if her daughter doesn't seem to need her. Plus, Marjorie learned at the last conference she attended before the school board cut her travel budget that there's an alarmingly high incidence of fender-benders and other car accidents involving high school students driving themselves to their standardized testing sites, so she didn't want one of Joanna's friends driving Joanna to school on a morning when her head might be elsewhere. Marjorie was surprised when Joanna didn't push back on this, and now here they are, circling each other in the kitchen, not wanting to set each other off.

At one point, in the middle of this tentative silence, Marjorie notices that Joanna is somewhat less earringed than usual, her jeans hardly torn, which Marjorie takes as an indication of the weight her daughter is attaching to this exam, the seriousness of the morning. Maybe she's reading too much into her daughter's appearance, but a part of her wants to let Joanna know she's proud of her, to in some way acknowledge the evident maturity in how her daughter has dressed down for the occasion. And yet another part recognizes that to do so would likely end this momentary truce and so Marjorie says nothing. Anyway, she'd have to raise her voice to make herself heard above whatever music Joanna has just started pumping into her brain, and Marjorie doesn't want it to seem like she's shouting.

"That clock right?" Joanna says after a long silent while, pointing to the digital clock on the stove.

"Last I checked," Marjorie says.

"Well, can you?" Joanna says. "Check?"

Marjorie takes her phone from her back pocket and compares the time on her start screen to the time on the appliance. "Close enough," she says. Then she smiles, although it's possible that what comes across looks more like a wince, like she's in pain and trying not to show it.

"You got me up early," Joanna says—complaining, in a knee-jerk sort of way, but also resigned to it. "I could be sleeping."

"You need to get your motor running," Marjorie says, determined to sound sunny. "I thought you'd eat."

Joanna looks at the food on the plate in front of her. "I can see that," she says, determined to sound *not sunny*, inching the plate away from her toward the middle of the table.

"Can I pack you something, at least? You get a break. It says on the email from the College Board you get a break."

Joanna holds out the cinch sack and shakes it to let her mother know something's inside. "Red Bull and Kind Bars," she says, removing one of her ear buds. "Breakfast of champions."

These kids and their Red Bull, Marjorie thinks. It's like Gatorade to them. "What about extra pencils?" she says. "Extra batteries for your calculator?"

"Mom," Joanna says, admonishing. "Sit. Stay."

Marjorie holds out her hands in front of her and makes like they're paws, then sticks her tongue out and pretends to pant. "Sorry," she says. "I can't help myself."

"You should know better. You of all people."

"You're right," Marjorie says. "It's the ones who should know better who are the worst." Then she tells Joanna about the time one of the other guidance counselors at school—Tillie, or Mrs. Tillotson to Joanna and her friends—interrupted her own child during a Brown University alumni interview, reminding her to talk about how she learned to play the piano by ear. "Parents," she says. "We're all just a bunch of clueless idiots."

"Tell me about it," Joanna says, replacing the ear bud, ducking back into her own thoughts, trying to get her head around this test.

"So, we can just sit here and not eat or talk for another few minutes," Marjorie says, a little too loudly.

"Deal."

Almost as soon as they're in the car, Marjorie's phone starts to vibrate from her back pocket, and she reaches for it to see who could be texting her at this hour. They're still in the driveway, so she eases the car back into park and looks at her phone. "It's your father," she says—scrolling, trying not to shout. "Wants to know if you're up. Wants to wish you good luck."

She hands the phone to her daughter and continues backing out.

Joanna smiles. Of course, Joanna smiles. Whatever tension there is between Marjorie and Joanna is something wholly other between her husband and daughter. It's amazing, Marjorie often thinks, the way these two can be so at ease with each other. Even when they're slogging through some shit. Even when it's hard, with Harry it's easy. They go at it, same as Marjorie and Joanna go at it, but there's a bond, a connection Marjorie wishes she had with her children. A softness, maybe. Yes, Joanna is hard with her, and soft with her father. Harry doesn't agree with Marjorie on this, tells her it sometimes feels like Joanna is lost to him as well, like he can't read her moods through the antiestablishment vibe she puts on, but Marjorie's not sold. She sees that things are different, with Joanna and her father—lighter, more effortless.

She wants what they have.

Joanna seems relaxed enough with her here this morning—really, there's just been the usual friction over breakfast, no biggie—but Harry's so much better at this stuff. Harry could have gotten her to eat a little something, Marjorie thinks. Harry could have found his little ways to make her smile, lighten her mood. Like with this one stupid text, wasn't even meant for Joanna, not directly, and she brightens just hearing that he's checking in, asking about her.

Joanna calls her father back on her own phone before Marjorie can hit the call button on hers. She puts the call on Bluetooth.

"You're up early, old man," Joanna says when her father answers.

There, Marjorie thinks when she hears Joanna's playful tone. That's what she wants to hear when Joanna speaks to her, instead of being made to feel like she's bugging the shit out of her. To be addressed with affection instead of disaffection. To be on the receiving end of even a grudging show of warmth. To hear Joanna sound almost cheerful.

"Yep," Harrison Klott says. "Set my alarm because my grown-ass daughter is taking this grown-ass test and I wanted to see how she was doing.'

"She's doing okay," Joanna says. "Mom made breakfast."

"Ask her how much she ate," Marjorie says, leaning into the dashboard to where she imagines a microphone might be.

"I'm guessing not much," Klott says. "I'm guessing not even a bite."

"We can heat it up when she gets home," Marjorie says, trying not to put air quotes around Joanna's promise.

Klott tells Joanna the story of when he was in high school and had to take the SATs. He'd been up late the night before, at a Doobie Brothers concert. He'd had the tickets for months—Madison Square Garden, floor seats, fourteenth row—wasn't expecting any kind of conflict when the plans took shape. The test date snuck up on him, so he decided not to tell his parents about the exam. It ended up, he did well enough on the test that he didn't have to take it again, and as he tells the story, Marjorie isn't sure where he's going with it. What, he's letting Joanna know he practically blew off his own SATs, telling her it's no big deal?

She wants to say something to derail the story, but she worries that'd make her seem like a pill.

"Wait," Joanna says, jumping in. "The Doobie Brothers? Thought you were cool . . ."

"The Doobies were cool," Klott says. "The Doobies were the shit."

"Harry," Marjorie says. "Nobody cares about the Doobie Brothers. Back then either. Sorry to be the one to break it to you."

"And nobody says something's 'the shit' anymore," Joanna says. "That's, like, no longer the shit."

"I'll send you both a couple links," he says. "Essential listening. Part of the American songbook. You'll see." He pauses for a beat—then, "What's on your playlist this morning, Jo Jo?" He knows his kid didn't leave the house without her ear buds. He knows she's playing something to get her going. Something to tune her mother out. Something.

"Nothing you'd know," Joanna says.

"Try us," Marjorie says.

"I'm good, Mom," Joanna says.

"She's good, Mom," Harrison Klott says.

Marjorie Klott uncurls her fingers from the wheel, hands at ten and two, in a gesture meant to indicate surrender.

"It's a meditation podcast, actually," Joanna says—seeing that she's upset her mother by wanting to be left alone and so throwing her this small bone.

"Can you dance to it?" her father says—not seeing any such thing.

"Funny," Joanna says, rolling her eyes and lolling her head to the right so that it comes to rest against the passenger window.

"That came with an eye roll," Marjorie says to her husband, narrating. "Just so you know."

"That one of the new sections on the test?" Harrison Klott says. "Eye rolling?"

"Can we be done?" Joanna says. "You wish me luck. You love me. Got it."

"Call you later, Harry," Marjorie says.

"I wish you luck," he says. "I love you. Both of you."

He cuts the call, and the sound system switches to Joanna's meditation, her phone still connected to the car's Bluetooth. Marjorie is stunned, a little, to hear a soothing, gentle male voice coming through the car speakers in a thick Australian accent, telling them to picture themselves on a beach, the waves kissing their toes, the ocean air filling their lungs, the sun warming their bodies. She had thought Joanna had been bullshitting when she said she'd been listening to a meditation, and that surely she was playing one of those same-seeming rappers she's always listening to, telling her to fuck the police or pimp her ride or shake her sweet thang. But here is this voice that sounds like it's been drenched in butter and lime juice and thrown on the barbie, talking about the power to be found in a simple breath, and Marjorie cannot imagine when or how it happened that Joanna became the sort of person to reach for such as this.

"Wait, you were serious?" she says, turning to Joanna. "Thought you were just trying to shut us up."

Joanna holds out her hands and mimics her mother's motion from before, pretending to un-grip a steering wheel.

From the barbie: "You are the only you in your *you-niverse.*"

Marjorie bites back a smirk. She knows that if Joanna finds this kind of thing helpful, she should not dismiss it, but she wonders who writes this shit, how people find it anything but ridiculous.

Joanna says, "Alright, mother dear. Some of it is kinda lame."

"Kinda," Marjorie says. "But I'm sure some of it is, you know, not. Meditation can be a helpful tool."

"Was trying to get in some kind of zone."

"That's smart."

"Uh-huh."

"Don't let me keep you," Marjorie says.

"I'm good," Joanna says, taking out her ear buds. "The moment has passed."

"Sorry," Marjorie said. "You wanted to be in the zone. I've kept you from your zone. I should be shot."

"That's a little harsh," Joanna says as her mother turns onto the circular drive by the front entrance to the school. "Maybe just bound and gagged."

"Talk about a little harsh," Marjorie says.

"Drawn and quartered," Joanna says. "That still a thing?"

"Nice," Marjorie says, putting the car in park and reaching to the floor of the passenger seat to hand Joanna her cinch sack. "My baby, going in to take the SATs, dazzling us all with her deep knowledge of archaic punishments in the public square. How did that happen?"

Joanna shrugs. "It happened."

Marjorie touches her daughter's hair and counts it as a win that Joanna doesn't cringe or brush her hand away.

"I'll text you when I'm done," Joanna says, stepping from the car. "Might catch a ride with Prudence or Allie."

Marjorie wants to run around to Joanna's side of the car and collect her in a hug, maybe hold onto this moment for another few years, but instead she blows her daughter a kiss and says, "You are the only you in your *you-niverse!*"

Joanna half smiles, blows a kiss back, sees one of her friends getting out of the car in front of theirs and races over to her. Marjorie looks on and wonders if Joanna will look back for a final wave before heading inside.

———

She hits redial as she pulls from the school's circular drive.

"Hey," Harrison Klott says through the car speaker. He sounds far away.

"You go back to sleep?" she says.

"Had to get up anyway to answer the phone," he says—one of Harrison's favorite lines. (He stole it from Groucho Marx, Marjorie thinks. Or Yogi Berra. Or Coach from *Cheers*—one of those.)

"She's, like, an adult or something," Marjorie says. "Joanna."

"Not just yet."

"Close."

"Been thinking," Harrison says, changing the subject. "Might stay another day or two. Make sure he's good."

"Hymie?" Marjorie says.

"Don't know if he even knows what's going on," Harrison says. "But as long as I'm here, I should probably stop at this new place, check that he's settled. Maybe again in the morning."

"Makes sense," Marjorie says. "Long as you're there." She pauses for a too-long moment then says, "You doing okay?"

"I'm doing," Harrison says.

"It's sad," she says. "Hard. You want to think he's in there somewhere."

"He is," Harrison says. "He's . . ." He doesn't finish his thought.

"What?" Marjorie says. "He's what?"

"I don't know," Harrison says. "He's just, you know, Hymie. Looks the same, smells the same."

"The same but different," Marjorie says. "There and not there. Here and not here."

"Something like that," Harrison says. "Even has the same mannerisms. You know that thing he does when he eats? How he licks his lips before taking a bite?"

Marjorie says she can picture it, Hymie eating.

"How does that work?" Harrison says. "That he's still doing that?"

"Must be in the hardwiring," Marjorie says. Then, after Harrison doesn't say anything straightaway, she says, "We can talk about it more later. Or when you get home. Or not at all."

"I'm thinking maybe not at all," he says.

"Your call, husband," she says.

"What's up with Heckle and Jeckle, wife?" Harrison says, switching the subject again—this time to the twins. He's been tagging them with the various names of famous duos since Marjorie found out they were having twins. Their very first sonogram, they were Harry and Bess—and then, later on, he and Joanna would rest their heads on Marjorie's belly when she was pregnant and have these long conversations with Fred and Wilma, or Fred and Ginger, or Fred and Ethel. Once, briefly, after watching a documentary on the Lillehammer Olympics, they went by Torvill and Dean, the British ice dancers. Half the time, little Joanna would have no idea who these people were, but she would laugh and laugh—and then, when the babies were moving and kicking, she'd giggle whenever she felt a movement against her cheek. She'd giggle and say, "Stop it, Barney!" or, "Stop it, Baby Bop!"

Marjorie could never tell if the nicknaming was for her benefit, or Harrison's, or Joanna's, or the twins', but over the years she's come to recognize it as a kind of parlor game her husband likes to play and wonders if he keeps a stockpile of these celebrated pairs in his head.

"Asleep when I left," she says. "Stewie's got track practice later. A lazy day for Syd, I think."

"Tell them hey," Harrison says.

"Yep," she says. "And hey to you."

"Hey to you."

Without really realizing it, Marjorie has driven into the parking lot by a small pond near the school. She cannot recall even having the idea of stopping here on the way home and yet here she is, pulled alongside a beaten-up looking Subaru Brat—one of those half-truck-half-coupes she used to sometimes see with the two rear-facing exterior seats in the flatbed. She's thinking, *How did I even get here*? She's thinking, *Do they even make Subaru Brats anymore*? She's thinking, *What, it's 1990, all of a sudden*?

She gets out of her car and walks around to the back and reaches her arms skyward, as if she's been seated behind the wheel for three or four hours instead of just twenty minutes. She puts her hands on her hips and leans as far to one side as she can comfortably manage and holds the stretch for three or four breaths. Then she leans the other way and holds for three or four breaths more. Then she walks to the passenger side in the small lane she's left between her car and the Subaru, which she now notices is a faded baby blue, except for the driver door, which looks as if it has been recently replaced or repaired. It's the color of nothing much at all—an undercoat, waiting to be told what to be. Her car and the Subaru Brat are the only two cars in the parking lot, and now that she is outside and walking around, Marjorie cannot imagine why she parked so close to this one other car—the kind of close that at any other time might her to worry the other guy would nick the paint on her passenger si he swung his driver door all the way open.

It feels good to be outside—moving, stretching.

She looks around and is flooded with memories of the very m times she and Harry used to come to this pond with the kids to feed the ducks—a default family activity. Joanna started naming the duc before the twins were born, and later, whenever there was a new brace ducklings waddling in formation behind their mother along the shoreline they'd all take turns naming them and adopting them and talking about them like they were their friends. There was Nanny Poo Poo, and Stupid Head, and Guinevere, and Lickity Split, and Strega Nona, named for one of Sydney's favorite books.

Marjorie could never keep them all straight, but somehow the kids knew which was which, what was what. Or, they just pretended to know and decided on the day that the little guy doing something particularly cute was the one they remembered from last time. There was one duck, though, with a distinctive coat and a peculiar personality—a muted orange stripe along one of its wings, and a brighter orange blemish above its beak. One of the kids named it Orange Duck, and they would be endlessly entertained by the way it would trail its brothers and sisters on the pond, or veer off in its own direction as the group waddled onto the shore, or get stuck in a thicket of reeds while the others swam off after their mother.

This must be a thing, Marjorie's realizing, this nicknaming business. Here it is, barely eight o'clock in the morning, and she's already bumped into two enduring memories that turn on the ways her husband and children attach silly names to the objects of their affection—and, relatedly, the ways she has tagged along. She's never been the one to come up with these names, but she's quick to embrace them, and in this way she thinks she'd like Orange Duck, left behind on the shore while the rest of her family swims off in some other direction. It's all she can do to jump in the water after them and splash along behind.

Once, when she was reading *The Story of Ping* to the twins, a book that had been one of Marjorie's favorites when she was a girl, she got it in her head that Ping was very much like Orange Duck, with the way he was always getting lost or playing catch-up or making do on his own. She tried to get the kids to see the similarities, and to maybe think up some Ping-type misadventures for Orange Duck, to encourage their imaginations and maybe attach some of the feelings from the story to the feelings they might have for this sweet, orange-highlighted creature—only, they resisted the idea, or lacked the ability to think in this way at that time in their little kid lives.

But then, they came home one day after a visit to the pond with their father and announced that they were going to write a book about Orange Duck.

"Daddy said there can be pictures," Stewie said, with more enthusiasm than Marjorie was accustomed to seeing in her young son.

"It's a book for children," Sydney said, explaining it to her mother like she might not understand. "We get to make up the story, and Daddy will help us with the words."

It was all so very exciting, Marjorie remembers, but the project never got beyond a couple fits and starts. No one could agree if the Orange Duck in the story was a boy or a girl, and after a while Harrison gave up on brokering a solution and the twins turned their attention in another direction.

Marjorie can't remember the last time she's been to this park. She thinks back and tries to recall if she'd had any inkling that the very last time she visited with the kids would be the very last time they would be here as a family. Perhaps there had been a falling off in the frequency of their visits, or perhaps there was one autumn when the season turned and they tromped across the crisp, golden leaves on the footpath rimming the pond a final time, tossing stale bread and fresh birdseed to their little friends. Some of the ducks would come right up to Sydney and eat from her hands! Stewie could never stand still long enough for the ducks to feel comfortable around him, and Joanna, even then, was a little too cool for the room and would hang back and watch her brother and sister empty the last of the bread bag onto the ground and shriek with delight as the ducks jostled for position and ate their fill. And then—who knows—maybe by the time that next spring came around Marjorie's family had leaned in some other direction, and the kids had become busy with their own individual activities, and these trips to the park were no longer a part of their routine.

It saddens Marjorie, to think how these visits have fallen away. She wonders, too, at the absurd amount of duck shit, sprinkled all over the footpath, the parking lot, the worn grass by the every-here-and-there benches and picnic tables. She wonders if it had always been like this, a minefield of duck shit, all around. It's almost impossible for Marjorie to take a step in any direction without veering off course, this way and that. If she looks up for even a moment as she walks, she'll be scraping greenish-white duck shit from her sneakers with a toothpick when she gets home. This, too, makes her sad. It's not the duck shit so much as the ways she cannot help but notice it now, the ways she clearly did not notice it then. Surely, there was an absurd amount of duck shit eight or nine or ten years ago, or whenever it was that she and Harrison were coming here regularly with their children. Right? It's not like there's been some change in the diets or digestive systems of these creatures that has changed the landscape in this way.

She finds her way through the droppings to a spot on a bench close to the water and tries to remember when she moved from a person who didn't pay attention to such things to someone who could not look past such things.

FALL

12.

ALL IN ALL IS ALL WE ARE

SHARI BRAVERMAN

"SHABBAT SHALOM, BITCHES!"

Here is Shari Braverman in the B'nai Centerville coat room, greeting her friends Suze Weiden and Allison Dartel with a little too much enthusiasm—for the occasion, for this hour of the morning, and for this small, enclosed space.

"Look at you," Suze says, stepping back from the mother of the bar mitzvah boy to take in a full view. "That dress."

Shari does a mock model's twirl. "It's from before," she says—as in, before her life turned to the kind of shit other people step around when they see it on the sidewalk. "Been waiting to wear it."

What she's been waiting to wear is a flared circle star dress from Stella McCartney, with a scalloped neck and long sleeves—a flowing, tasteful mix of beige, brown, and off-white. She saw it on a mannequin in a Fifth Avenue boutique about a year ago and it felt to her like she had to have it. Cost almost three thousand dollars, way more than she was used to spending on a dress for no apparent reason, but then the Fred-suck happened, and the dress stayed in the closet and now the apparent reason is Jaxon's *simcha*. She guesses the dress is probably not appropriate for synagogue and certainly not for the mother of the bar mitzvah boy, but it's understated enough, long enough, stylish enough.

"You go, girl," Allison says, as if in applause. "Bohemian chic!"

"Yep," Shari says—no longer twirling or feeling quite as amped as just a beat or two before. "I go, girl."

It's nine o'clock on a Saturday morning, and there are a couple hundred little details jockeying for space in Shari Braverman's brain, eighty-seven of them calling for her immediate attention. There's the email she just received from the guy catering the *kiddush* luncheon to follow this morning's service, letting her know he has been unable to "source" any gluten-free bagels and wondering if it would be okay to swap out Pepperidge Farms bagel flats instead. (It would not.) There's her former-but-technically-*still* mother-in-law, Gwennie, who let it be known through Shari's former-but-technically-*still*-sister-in-law, Audrey, that she's no longer crazy about the idea of sharing an *aliyah* with Brian, now that she has had a chance to read the mood of the room and determine that almost all of the invited guests have been informed of her son's "transgression," as she has taken to calling it, and that she does not wish for her sliver of spotlight as the grandmother of the bar mitzvah boy to be diminished. (Shari's thinking her mother-in-law can step to the *bima* with Brian's siblings instead.) There's Jaxon's over-stimulated friends, who seem to think it's entirely appropriate to drool and titter and point in the direction of poor Alana Seidenfeld, who for her part seems to have sprouted an impressive rack while she was away at summer camp, and who has shown up in the B'nai Centerville lobby in her version of the same size double-zero body-con dress all the other thirteen-year-old girls are wearing, smiling gamely behind the pink rubber bands of her braces, oblivious to the fact that the tight dress is no longer fitting and that she might now be sporting a little too much body for this particular con. (Perhaps Shari can corral Stewie Klott's father, on parent usher duty, to escort Jaxon's friends into the sanctuary and separate them into small groups of two or three before the drooling and tittering get any worse.) There's the easel she'd planned on bringing as a prop for the family study they are meant to lead during the service, offering the Braverman take on this week's Torah portion, which may or may not have something to do with standing tall in the face of apparent adversity. (She recalls seeing an easel in one of the Hebrew School classrooms and makes a note to ask the building custodian if he could maybe track it down for her.)

"What?" Suze says, after a too-long beat, as if snapping her friend to attention. "You look stressed."

"I'm stressed," Shari says. "I look stressed because I am stressed. This is stressful."

"Aw, sweetie," Suze says, collecting Shari in a half hug. "You look sen*saysh*. The social hall, the balloons, all sen*saysh*. Little Jana, sen*saysh*. The whole damn thing, sen*saysh*."

Allison says, for good measure: "Sen*saysh*."

Shari, stepping from her half hug, half scowls at her pals. "Fuck you very much," she says. "Both of you. You're like a Greek chorus."

The women slip sensationally from the coatroom into the synagogue's main entry hall, where they are absorbed by a lobby full of appropriately dressed guests and congregants. Shari is made to run a gauntlet of well-wishers as she heads off in search of the custodian. She hates that she can't remember the guy's name—he's been so helpful during the run-up to this event, and she doesn't want to come across as one of those entitled congregants who can't even be bothered to remember a name. *Leo*, she thinks. *Or maybe Charlie. Sam. Something.*

It turns out, she runs into Stewie Klott's father first. At the moment, she can't remember his name either, but she knows they are connected on Facebook, and that they have therefore entered into a contemporary social contract that forbids them from reintroducing themselves.

"Thank you so much for helping out this morning," she says when their eyes meet as she makes her way through the scrum.

"Happy to be here," he says.

Shari shrugs and does a knowing half roll of her eyes to indicate that she'd be more inclined to believe Stewie Klott's father if he held an index finger to his temple and pretended to shoot himself. "There's a lot that goes on, day of," she says, hoping the emphasis on the *of* might explain her harried demeanor. "You'll see."

"Mazel tov, by the way," Stewie's father says.

"Thank you, by the way," Shari says. "Shabbat shalom, by the way. L'shana tova, by the way."

"Not just yet, by the way," he says. "Rosh Hashana's, what, next week?"

"Tomorrow night," Shari says. "Whole place is in High Holiday mode. The new rabbi, the cantor, the office staff. It's, like, nobody has the bandwidth for a simple bar mitzvah."

"Tell me about it," Stewie Klott's father says.

I just did, Shari wants to say. She's all out of small talk, so she shares her pressing concern over Alana Seidenfeld's tight-fitting dress, and the dozen or so pubescent boys who can't seem to keep their eyes in their sockets in her presence. "Maybe you could separate them or something," she says. "You know these kids, right? Tell them whatever you have to tell them. Please please please."

"Done," he says.

Shari smiles and heads off in search of the custodian, but she only takes a couple steps before she's intercepted by the new rabbi—Barbara Kaltinick, a Birkenstock-wearing, granola-crunching woman of indeterminate middle age who seems to regret being born twenty years too late to have worn flowers in her hair without irony and who seems to want to rally the congregation to call her Rabs Babs. This last is not going well, as far as Shari Braverman can determine, because among Shari's crowd the rabbi is known as "New Rabbi," a moniker she is unlikely to shake any time soon.

"Look at you," New Rabbi says, touching Shari's arm with practiced precision, to affirm her sincerity.

"Shabbat shalom," Shari says.

"Hard to believe the day is actually here," the rabbi says, in a way that signals she has had a hand it is arrival. "Jaxon has worked so hard. He's been through so much." Again, with the arm-touching—the rabbinical version of the extreme head tilt in the show of sympathy department, Shari is guessing.

"Thank you, Rabbi, yes," Shari says. "Here we are."

"And you," the rabbi says—then, with the weight of concern, "You."

Yes, Shari wants to say: "Me. *Me.* Good to know that I am here, standing next to you on the morning of my son's bar mitzvah, and that he has been through so much and that so, presumably, have I." Instead, she says nothing and leaves it to New Rabbi to fill the awkward silence that soon hangs between them like the odor lines you sometimes see in cartoons or comic strips to indicate an overpowering smell.

Rabs Babs is up to the task. "And Brian," she says, "How is he holding up?"

This time, what Shari wants to say is exactly what she says: "Fuck Brian." And, "I can't believe you're actually asking me about Brian. 'How is he holding up?' You're kidding, right?"

Shari's outrage is delivered *sotto voce*—a good thing, as far as Rabbi Barbara Kaltinick is concerned. The last thing either woman wants is a scene—the rabbi, because the optics on pissing off the mother of the bar mitzvah boy on the last sabbath before the high holidays would probably be less than ideal; Shari, because she wants this day to be about Jaxon.

"I've overstepped," the rabbi says, mustering some *sotto voce* of her own. "I apologize. I don't wish to get in the middle of a marital tension."

"A marital tension?" Shari says, in a tone meant to indicate air quotes. "Is that the euphemism of choice in rabbi school these days?"

"Again, I apologize," the rabbi says. "It's just, you know, Brian is a congregant too. I don't wish to take sides."

"Sides?" Shari says, still in a near-whisper. "Sides?"

"Neutral," the rabbi says. "I mean to be neutral. Like Switzerland."

Shari can only assume this woman has missed a memo and has not been made aware of the circumstances surrounding her estrangement from the bar mitzvah boy's father. New Rabbi is, after all, new.

"You do know he was sucking off our neighbor, Fred?" Shari says, making the situation clear. "In the garage. Middle of the afternoon."

From the look on her face, Shari can tell that this is news to Rabbi Barbara Kaltinick. She can also tell from the rabbi's crinkled up expression that she has now conjured an image of her congregant giving another man a blowjob, while at the same time trying to chase that image from her mind. Shari can't be sure, but she believes she sees the rabbi give a little head shake, almost like a shudder, to help with the chasing.

There follows another awkward silence, which Shari supposes is to be expected.

"How's that for marital tension?" Shari says—her way of lightening the mood.

Already, in her short time at B'nai Centerville, Rabs Babs has developed a reputation as someone rarely at a loss for words. She can go on and on, Shari and her friends have taken turns observing, only here she seems to have run out of things to say.

"Fred . . ." the rabbi finally says, as if trying to place the name.

"Don't worry, Rabbi," Shari says. "He's not one of ours."

———

Mercifully, Jaxon's *parsha* is one of the shortest in the Torah—*Nitzavim*, which begins with a call from Moses to the Jewish people to enter a covenant with God or be visited by a series of curses.

The mercy is two-fold: Jaxon has only had to commit a few short verses to memory, which in turn means the congregation now must only listen to just a few short verses of him chanting in a discordant whine that could have been inspired by that "Time to Change" episode of *The Brady Bunch*, where Peter gamely sang his way through a sudden onset of puberty.

Following the reading, Shari steps to the *bima* with Jana to join Jaxon around a small table that had been set up prior to the service, alongside the borrowed easel that had been kindly retrieved by the custodian whose name Shari had somehow neglected to learn during the transaction. Once they are seated, Jana waves adorably to her father to join them, and as Brian makes his way from the third row where he is seated with his sister's family, Shari can hear a shared gasp coming from those seated in the sanctuary. At least, she *thinks* she can hear a gasp, but gasps by their nature can be difficult to distinguish from other noise-making inhalations and so she instead decides that what she is hearing is the trace evidence of a shared surprise—or, perhaps, the sound of air being let out of the room in a communal sigh of relief.

The tradition at B'nai Centerville is for the family of the *b'nai mitzvah* to lead the congregation in study following the reading of each week's Torah portion. Typically, the family *D'var Torah* is offered as a skit or a roundtable discussion, with input from brothers and sisters and parents and grandparents. What this means is that there is often an extra layer of pressure on participating families to entertain their invited guests. What this also means, when the parents of the bar mitzvah boy are going through an ugly separation occasioned by a very public same-sex infidelity, is that there are another few folds in that extra layer of pressure, and here Shari Braverman can only imagine how the congregation might have sighed if Brian had not been called to the *bima* to participate in this part of the service.

He is Jaxon's father, after all. This is his family, after all.

As much as possible, Shari has left it to Jaxon to outline the themes of this week's Torah portion. Her take, in case anyone asks, is that the reading is all about defiance, about standing in the face of adversity, about finding the strength and the strength of character to make and stand by your own decisions, although this has lately been her take on pretty much any piece of popular culture. Whatever book she tries to read, whatever movie she tries to watch, whatever old album she pulls from Brian's vinyl collection and tries to listen to, it all gets filtered through the lens of somebody wronged or damaged or disregarded. Like, just yesterday, she had Nirvana on the turntable, "All Apologies," and Kurt Cobain was wailing about being married and buried like they were two sides of the same coin, and it felt to her like he was singing about her life. The day before that, she was zoning out in front of the television with Jana, who had lately discovered *The Wizards of Waverly Place*, and Shari caught herself feeling the same way about an episode where the cute little wizard family was facing the loss of their sandwich shop, and it was as if these Disney sitcom people were telling her to stand and be counted.

Jaxon's take is almost the exact opposite, focusing on what it means to accept what is given to you, and Shari supposes this has more to do with Jaxon's father than anything to be found in these few chapters of Deuteronomy. It's funny, she thinks, how the same passage can speak in different ways to different people in different circumstances. She talked about this with Jaxon one night over dinner, when it was just the three of them, and sweet little Jana sat quietly in her usual spot at the kitchen table, listening to her mother and brother interpret the *parsha* in this fidgety way she has that suggested she wasn't really listening at all. And yet when her mother and brother had talked themselves out, she stood from the table and said, "Duh! You get what you get and you don't get upset!"

At the time, this struck Shari as just about the funniest thing she had ever heard, and she grabbed Jana by the arm as she passed her chair and pulled her in for a squeeze—saying, "Smarty Pants! My little Smarty Pants!"

In the end, they worked it out that their study would be focused on a family dinner table conversation about consequences and acceptance. Jaxon and Jana would be the parents in their presentation, and Shari and Brian would be the children. They set it up like a scene from a play—an upside-down scene from a life they were no longer living. Since Brian wasn't there to lobby for a less humiliating role, Shari suggested he play an infant in this scenario, and that his only lines be *goo-goo-gaga*-type noises. This struck Jaxon and Jana as just about the funniest thing *they'd* ever heard, and so it was decided, and when Jaxon pitched it excitedly to Brian the following weekend, his father didn't have it in him to argue against it.

So here they are now, this broken family, gathered in front of a couple hundred friends and family members and assorted members of their synagogue community, sharing a single wireless microphone and going through these motions as if all is right in their little world, even as Shari has made it a special point to let everyone know in what ways all has gone wrong. She sits across the table from Brian, in front of all these other people, and tries to think when it was that his heart began to close to her. She wonders if it was something she'd said or done, or if the life they had built together had been a kind of Band-Aid all along, a way to cover a bruise on his soul that could never quite heal.

"I don't get why I just can't do what I want to do," Shari says into the *mic* in a child's voice, making a scripted appeal to the "parents" in their little Torah study play.

She hands the microphone across the table to Jaxon.

"There are consequences to your actions," he says, behind the fake mustache Shari had remembered to bring, to signal his supposed maturity. (He drops his voice to signal the same.)

Jana, wearing a string of fake pearls to advertise *her* age, stands and crosses with the microphone to the easel. She says, "Can you tell us, children, what can happen when you make a choice that is only good for you and not for your family or for your friends?"

"You can hurt someone's feelings?" Shari offers.

"Very good," Jana says—and then she takes a marker her mother had strung from the large blank pad resting on the borrowed easel and writes *HURT FEELINGS* in an adorable scrawl. It takes a while for her to spell it all out, and she starts to run out of room as she writes, so what is also adorable is the way she squeezes in a tiny little *N* and *G* and an even tinier *S* at the end. When she finishes, she lets the marker drop back against the pad and jumps up and down for a little.

"Can you think of anything else?" Jaxon says.

He holds the *mic* out in front of his father.

"Goo goo," Brian says, to nervous laughter from the congregation. Shari had brought one of Jana's old rattles for him to shake as a prop, but he leaves it on the table in front of him.

"A punishment," Shari says.

"Very good," Jana says—flipping the page on the large note pad and writing, *PUNISHMENT*.

"What about if you see you've done something wrong and you apologize?" Jaxon says.

"Ga ga," Brian says, this time to genuine belly laughter.

"Like a do-over!" Shari says excitedly.

"Excellent," Jana says. "Like a do-over." She flips the pad and writes, *DOOVER*, forgetting the hyphen so the directive looks more like the name of an off-brand vacuum cleaner.

After another few entries, Jaxon walks to where his sister is standing by the easel and turns to the congregation. He asks everyone to remember all the bad things that can happen when you go against your community, turning back the pages of the large note pad and flipping through each panel once more. Then he asks people to remember the good things that can happen when you realize you have made a mistake and ask to be forgiven and reads through the next set of responses.

Finally, he says, "This is what we have learned by studying this Torah portion. The name of it is *Nitzavim* and it means to stand firmly. It tells us how important it is to make your own decisions and learn from your mistakes."

Then Jana takes the microphone from her brother and says, "This concludes our little play," and does a small curtsy.

━━━━━━

Following the service, Jaxon is descended upon by a dozen or so pals who had been scattered about the sanctuary. They take turns clapping him on the back or hooking him in a headlock or mussing his hair with their knuckles, knocking his *yarmulke* to the floor. He seems happy, relieved. Shari looks on and smiles at the way her son moves effortlessly among his peers. She thinks this probably comes from Brian, who was always more outgoing. It's only lately that Shari has started putting herself out there with people, making more of an effort on social media, finding consolation in the company of others, grabbing at every opportunity to shame Brian for the way he has shamed their marriage.

She's gone from shy to shocking in the space of a blow job.

Shari allows herself a beat to take in Jaxon's ease with his friends as the congregation makes its way to the social hall for the kiddush luncheon that may or may not feature gluten-free bagels, and marvels at the turns her life has taken. From the moment Jaxon was born, she and Brian had looked ahead to this day. It was a talked-about thing, a looked-forward-to thing . . . and yet, now that it is upon them, this *thing* is nothing like she'd imagined. The day has been folded and mix-mastered into a thing to get past, and Shari wonders if Jaxon can see that she's checked out—going through the motions, just.

She is called to attention by a tap on her shoulder. She turns and sees her new friend Fiona Pluscht, who drove out from the city with her husband Theo for this morning's service. Shari had seen them come in and was touched that they'd made the effort, since the reception wasn't until later tonight. Most people, they come for the party, especially when they're coming from long distance, but here is Fiona to share in the fullness of this moment.

"You came?" Shari says.

"I came," Fiona says—then, indicating her husband, she adds, "*We* came. You know Theo, don't you? Maybe you don't. Maybe you've never met."

"Don't think I've had the pleasure," Teddy says, extending his hand. "Mazel Tov."

"Good to finally meet," Shari says. "I'm a big fan of Fi's."

Teddy lets the comment slide. "Your son did a beautiful job," he says. "My bar mitzvah, I had my *haftorah* portion written out on a small index card. In transliteration. I couldn't even memorize it. Your kid, it's like he was actually reading."

"Don't know about that," Shari says.

"You look amazing," Fiona says, cutting in. "That dress."

Shari does another one of those fake twirls to show that she is in receipt of the compliment and that she doesn't think she deserves it.

"And little Jana, up on that stage," Fiona says. "So precious."

"Thank you," Shari says. "We aim to please. Speaking of which, there's food. Bagels, lox, coffee."

"Whitefish salad?" Teddy says. "Tell me there's whitefish salad."

"I believe there's whitefish salad," Shari says. "Your lucky day."

Fiona touches Shari on the arm and indicates with a nod of her head that there's a small cluster of people gathering in the aisle to greet her. "I'll leave you to your guests," Fiona says.

Teddy Pluscht reaches for Shari's hand again and when she takes it he pulls her toward him as if he's about to share a secret. "Was that Harry Klott I saw *shushing* those kids?" he says.

Harry, Shari thinks. *Harrison Klott*. Right. She's happy for the chance to remember his name.

"It was," she says. "Is. His kid's next up, after the holidays."

"Friend of yours?" Teddy says.

"Our kids are in the same Hebrew school class," Shari says. "He's here on usher duty. You're supposed to 'volunteer' the weekend before your *simcha*." She makes a single set of air quotes with the free hand Teddy Pluscht is not still holding.

"Harry is one of Theo's oldest friends," Fiona says, filling in the blanks before they can materialize in Shari's head.

"College roommates," Teddy says.

"Wow," Shari says. "I did not know that. I totally did not know that."

"They're going fly-fishing next weekend," Fiona says. "A group of them."

"You fish?" Shari says, realizing she's keeping her guests waiting but she's intrigued by this out-of-nowhere connection.

"I drink like a fish," Teddy says. "That count?"

Shari makes an effort to smile, wondering how it is that women she likes and admires always seem to wind up with loud, handsy men who seem to think it's admirable to talk about how much they drink.

"Come on," Fiona says, tugging at the sleeve of her husband's jacket. "Let's leave this poor woman to her guests. She doesn't even know you."

"She does now," Teddy says. "It's like we're related."

13.

ANY WAY THE WIND BLOWS

HARRISON KLOTT

HE'D FORGOTTEN about the money.

Well, okay, this is not entirely true, but in the months since he returned from Florida with his father's battered suitcase full of cash, the windfall has moved from a front-and-center worry to that place in a corner of Harrison Klott's mind where his all-consuming thoughts go to die.

How does that happen? he wonders. *When does that happen? Why?*

It's like that old pair of blue suede Puma Clydes he's had in his closet since he claimed them from a neighbor's yard sale when he was a kid, near mint. He knows the sneakers are in there somewhere, and it gives him a measure of satisfaction to know they're in there somewhere, and he's even packed them up and moved them with him a bunch of times, but he can go weeks, months, even years without thinking about them.

They are a part of him, inventoried with his other assets and qualities and backstories, but they are no longer a part of his day-to-day—until, for a moment, they are.

With the money, same thing. It's there and it's not there, all at once. It's changed him and it hasn't changed him. Basically, the money went from all he thought about to something that just *was*, almost as if he has momentarily misplaced the idea of it, and now that he's been uncomfortably middle-seated on a Wednesday afternoon Delta flight from JFK to Salt Lake City he takes the time to consider the shift. Really, he wants to understand what the money has meant to him these past couple months, what it might mean to him going forward, if it means anything at all. He went from obsessing over where to put his father's cash (it ended up, he hid several piles of it around the house—in drop ceilings and crawl spaces and top closet shelves—and he placed another sizeable chunk in a safe deposit box that had been mostly empty), whether or not to tell Marjorie about it (he never could find the right time to bring it up, or the right words to justify not coming clean immediately), or how determined he was to learn what the hell was up with his father that he had been able to squirrel so much of it away in the first place (he meant to, but then it started to seem like too much trouble).

Like today—*right fucking now*—the money is in and out of his head so often it's like there's been a breezeway drilled into his skull. Before heading out for the airport, the house already emptied by the morning rush to school, he'd checked his hiding places a final time or two, and as he left, he couldn't shake the thought that Marjorie might discover a pile of cash when he wasn't around to explain it away, but then he got stuck in a long conversation with his Lyft driver, Dawar, and the money was gone from this thinking. Klott remembers having been distracted by the strong notes of cherry and oak that filled the car and that he took time to wonder if the pleasing scent was coming from the driver's soap or shampoo, or if perhaps there'd been an air freshener fitted to one of the vents on the dash. Also, he was caught up in whether Dawar's brother, whose name also happened to be Dawar, was wrong to have come to the United States to complete his medical school studies if he was never planning to practice medicine. It was not as if the chance to purchase a turn-key car wash in Astoria was the opportunity of a lifetime, this Dawar had said. It was not as if their father had not sacrificed everything to pay for this other Dawar's education. It was only that what was once just out of reach and was now at hand no longer held its initial promise or appeal.

"A doctor," this Dawar had said. "A doctor for the skin. Dermatology, this was his field. You know it, yes?"

Harrison Klott could see the driver's eyes in the rearview mirror, and he could see the driver eyeing him as well, so he merely nodded in response.

"Yes, yes, you know it," this Dawar had said, excitedly, as if the two of them were now in agreement. "He would have been very successful. It is very important field of medicine."

In just this moment, Harrison Klott was not thinking of his father's money. He was thinking only of the midday traffic, of making polite conversation with this good-smelling man in this good-smelling car, of what he might purchase to eat on the plane. It was the mundane, as ever, that occupied his abiding attention. But then, as he navigated his way through the airport, he was reminded every here and there of this unlikely dividend—specifically, of the *weight* of this unlikely dividend. He could not think where his father might have gotten his hands on all that cash. He did not want to think about it. He could not think how to tell Marjorie, or how to justify all these weeks of *not* telling Marjorie. He did not want to think about this either. The consequential stresses of the money kept finding him through the same breezeway. In the security line, for example, he remembered how worried he'd been at the idea of flying from West Palm Beach to New York with a suitcase full of cash, how he'd chosen to make the long drive instead. At the Hudson News kiosk in his terminal, sizing up an overpriced package of designer trail mix, he bristled at the price: $8.95, for a four-ounce bag. And then, bristling still, he thought of all that drop-ceilinged and safe-deposit-boxed money and the trail mix suddenly felt like less of an indulgence and more like a basic need. He didn't buy the trail mix, of course, and settled instead for a correspondingly overpriced Kind bar, but he felt for the moment that his circumstances had changed.

They have and they haven't. His life, really, is much the same as before. His worldview, also mostly unchanged. This is the line of thinking he's planning to share with Marjorie, in the scripted conversations he has not yet gotten around to having with her. It is not "life-changing" money, after all. It is not what people in Centerville sometimes call "fuck you" money—meaning, it holds the power to let you do whatever you want, say whatever you want, live however you want. It isn't even enough to pay for his kids' college educations, if all three of them decide to attend one of the elite private schools Marjorie has been identifying for them since gestation. It is, however, significant. *Impactful*—that's the word he'd use to describe the discovery of all that money, if he ever got around to talking about it. He'd set aside five hundred thousand in his tucked-away spaces and kept the rest in circulation—bundled in his sock drawer. Half a million dollars! His idea had been to segregate that big round number from the rest of pile, and to use the "change" to start paying for certain household expenses in cash: money for the cleaning lady, money for takeout, money for impulse purchases for Marjorie or the kids. At the supermarket, he'd buy a nicer cut of ground beef, or the slivered, roasted almonds that had always struck him as just a little too expensive, but when he paid for these things with his father's loose cash, he didn't really notice the transaction. It was a windfall on top of a windfall, a tsunami of seamless commerce. For a while, when he and Marjorie would go out to dinner with another couple, he became that guy at the table who asked his opposite number if he minded putting the entire tab on his credit card and allowing Klott to reimburse him with cash. His friends were always happy for the chance to generate a bigger receipt and a correspondingly bigger tax deduction, if they were in the habit of writing off their restaurant tabs.

It's like he was working his own little money-laundering scheme, and from time to time Klott would unbundle the wads of cash in his sock drawer and take an accounting. He'd started out with over sixty thousand dollars, and it had quickly become a secret thrill to peel off a couple bills to pay the landscaper or the guy who repaired his electric garage doors and make it so the transaction didn't touch the Klott household in any meaningful way, or to grease his kids' palms with a sudden show of largesse and allow them to think their father wasn't quite the tightwad he'd been playing at all along. He'd even pinched a small stack of bills as he left for the airport, thinking the cash would come in handy on this trip to Utah.

Klott is flanked in his middle seat by an overweight young man on the aisle wearing a red University of Utah hoodie and a pair of cargo shorts, and a woman of indeterminate middle age by the window wearing a beige cable-knit sweater reading a worn paperback edition of Sidney Sheldon's *Tell Me Your Dreams*. Regrettably, he neglected to pluck his earbuds from the carry-on he'd stuffed into the overhead bin before takeoff, and for the first half hour of the flight he worries how to comfortably ask the overweight college student to move so he could stand in the aisle and rummage around in his bag for the earbuds—or, relatedly, over whether to spring for the airline's two-dollar headset charge, a purchase he is disinclined to make on principle, no matter how much cash there is burning a hole in his drop ceiling. During this time, he has amused himself by scrolling through the television offerings on the Delta entertainment platform without the benefit of sound. He's made a game of it, landing on a PBS Kids channel featuring a full season of *Arthur*, an animated series about an anthropomorphic aardvark to which Joanna had been unreasonably devoted as a small child. Best he can tell, Klott has come upon an episode centered on the title character's sister, D.W., who seems to have gotten lost. The game comes in trying to reverse engineer a story from the images on the small screen, and in real time, Klott tries to keep pace with the animated action and supply dialogue of his own.

It amuses him, this game, until D.W. enters an old-timey general store and Klott thinks to have her ask the anthropomorphic moose behind the counter if she could please have a licorice whip, because he has it in his head that licorice whips are the kinds of treats often enjoyed in general stores populated by anthropomorphic cartoon characters.

"Do you have strawberry, mister?" he has his D.W. character say.

"That'll be fifteen cents, little lady," he has the moose say, and it is at this point that Klott runs out of steam in his story because the action on the screen takes a sudden turn with the appearance of a mother and her infant child at the store's threshold, and the moose's attention is diverted by a tantrum the baby now appears to be throwing.

Klott is unable to keep up with the shift in the action, and he briefly wonders if this bit of difficulty might explain the fallings short in his own story-telling career, if maybe one of the reasons he's never gotten around to completing (or, even, to unequivocally *starting*) his second novel is because he doesn't have anything to say. Or maybe it's that he has too much to say and no way to keep up with all of it. Also, he realizes he has likely been mouthing the lines of dialogue he has been supplying these cartoon characters, and for a moment he is frozen with embarrassment, ashamed of how he must appear to this chunky Ute in the aisle seat, or to this woman by the window who probably doesn't know Sidney Sheldon was the guy who created *I Dream of Jeannie*.

Klott gives up on his game and stares dully at the screen in front of him. He presses his finger to the screen to change the channel. He lands eventually on CNBC, and at the base of the screen, where the moving stock prices crawl against the darkened border, he can occasionally make out a smudge of fingerprints, and he briefly wonders if the prints are his own or if they might have belonged to a previous passenger assigned to this same middle seat. At some point, his hands drift to his lap and he begins to press against himself as he watches the business headlines—ready position, yet again. He's wrapped himself in one of those unnatural-fiber Delta blankets, so it's not as if he's jerking off right there in the middle of the plane. Hardly. In fact, it's not as if he's jerking off at all, just stealing another moment to apply another pleasing bit of friction while his mind wanders to another string of disconnected musings. There is nothing sexual about the way he touches himself. There is only distraction—and the feeling, perhaps, that even though he is soaring across the country at thirty thousand feet, at speeds approaching six hundred miles an hour, cocooned in a ton of aluminum alongside a couple hundred fellow passengers, including the two companions at his elbows, he is essentially alone . . . alone with his thoughts of Barbara Eden, wearing a midriff and eager to do her master's bidding . . . alone with his thoughts of the lovely and no longer so elusive Shari Braverman, who had only this weekend spoken softly and perhaps even conspiratorially into his ear at her son's bar mitzvah . . . alone with his thoughts of his father's cash that may or may not have redirected the course of his life . . . but not so very alone that the stiffness in his lap isn't startling, disconcerting.

It is at just this moment—startled, disconcerted—that Harrison Klott makes eye contact with the woman in the cable-knit sweater, who looks up from her reading and intercepts his gaze as he stares dumbly out the window.

"Too bright for you?" she says, reaching for the shade and sliding it an inch or two up and then an inch or two down, as if to let Klott know he has options. Middle-seated or no, she wants him to feel as if he has a say in the amount of daylight spilling into their row.

There is nothing to indicate that the woman has seen where Klott has placed his hands or considered the pleasing bit of friction he might have been enjoying as a result.

"No," he says. "Thank you. I'm good." He was not expecting to be caught in a conversation with this woman, or to step from the peculiar détente that allows three people to sit in such close proximity for such an extended period without having to make direct eye contact.

The woman slides the shade back to where it was in the first place and says, "You sure?"

He says, "However you like it, is good."

She smiles and turns back to her book, but the brief exchange leaves Klott feeling found-out, anxious. Indication or no, he worries the woman has seen him pressing against himself through the Delta blanket, and so is determined to smooth over any awkwardness with some additional small talk.

"Sidney Sheldon, huh?" he says, indicating the book.

The woman looks up from her reading and flips the book over with her wrist so that the spine is visible and she might consider the name of the author yet again. "He was very popular, for a while," she says. "In the airport bookstores, there were always a few of his on the shelves."

"Not anymore?" Klott says.

"He's dead, I think," she says. "So, probably, no. Not anymore."

"And?" he says, meaning to push his seatmate on the enduring appeal of commercial fiction a couple decades past its sell-by date. From her tone, and her willingness to participate in these benign pleasantries, Klott is guessing she does not think he's some kind of perv.

"You know, it's funny," the woman says, looking again at the spine of her book and leaning the conversation in some other way instead. "I think I read this one already. Maybe when it first came out. Has that ever happened to you with a book? You're reading and reading and it's like you know what's coming? Like you've met these people before?"

Klott allows that this is not something he has ever experienced as a reader, but what he doesn't share is that it's also not something he has ever experienced as a writer, and for a moment he wonders what it must be like to be so deeply inside a story that you know in your bones how it's going to turn out.

———

Teddy Pluscht has never met a spreadsheet he didn't like.

For this Park City trip, Harrison Klott's college roommate has organized his guests' flights and ground transportation as if the fate of the planet hangs on the minimization of the group's carbon footprint. According to the itinerary Teddy has circulated to the group, Klott is meant to collect Teddy's friend Marco, a reality show producer whose short-hop flight from Los Angeles is due to arrive in Salt Lake City about an hour behind Klott's flight from New York. Klott doesn't get why he has to wait an hour to pick this guy up so they can carpool to Park City, but he doesn't have it in him to go against Teddy Pluscht—the kind of social force of nature accustomed to getting his way. The thing to do, Klott figures, is to fill the time by heading to the Alamo counter and getting started on his car rental. He'd called ahead earlier in the week to reserve an economy car, but Teddy instructed him to upgrade to a luxury SUV.

"Some of these fishing spots are an hour away," Teddy had said. "There're nine of us, this trip. Let's see if we can all squeeze into two cars."

Here again, Klott didn't have it in him to argue, even though the difference was a couple hundred dollars a day.

"I'll put it on the spreadsheet," Teddy had said, anticipating Klott's concern about the money.

As he rides the escalator down from the arrivals terminal to the baggage claim area, Klott is struck by the large welcoming party on the lower level of the Salt Lake City International Airport. There are about fifty or sixty people looking up at him expectantly, holding balloons and homemade signs. They are not looking at him exactly, but in his general direction. On closer inspection, there appear to be several welcoming parties bunched together by the base of the escalator—parents and grandparents, children, and grandchildren. They are gathered, it further appears, to celebrate the homecomings of their sons and daughters and brothers and sisters, returning from their missions on behalf of the Church of Jesus Christ of Latter-day Saints. It's like a Mormon bar mitzvah, Klott thinks, only instead of a catered luncheon or an over-the-top black-tie affair, it's a rite of passage marked by these joyous airport greetings.

Klott is struck by one sign in particular, held aloft by a crew-cutted boy of about six or seven wearing an oversized Utah Jazz jersey that nearly reaches to the floor: "Welcome home, Elder Wood."

He wonders for a beat if perhaps the sign is meant for him and his aging hard-on.

As he trudges to the rental car counter he wonders if he should double back and take a picture, so that he might share the joke with someone at some other time . . . with Marjorie, even. The geometry is conspiring against him, however, because with each step he moves exponentially further from that fleeting moment when a snap photo might have been hardly noticed and perhaps appropriate and inextricably closer to calling all kinds of unwanted attention to himself if he returns to the scene to photograph a small child.

By the time he claims his car and starts circling the terminal, he is distracted from his math by his phone, humming with a text from a number it doesn't recognize: *Here.*

That's all. Just, *here.*

It strikes Klott as the sort of dickish message you send if you are the dickish, Hollywood-adjacent friend of Teddy Pluscht, deplaned and ready to be whisked to your mountain bacchanal.

Klott texts back: *Same.*

That's all. Just, *Same*—the sort of dickish response you send if you mean to indicate that you are put off by having to wait a full hour before continuing on to the same mountain bacchanal.

He pulls to the curb by the first passenger pickup area and waits for a response, and when none is forthcoming, he decides to follow up with a phone call, even though Joanna and the twins and Jess and Avery and every other youngish person in his acquaintance tells him nobody just picks up the phone and calls anybody—it's, like, no longer a thing.

"Bro!" Marco answers before Klott hears a ring. "Where you at?"

"Acura SUV," Klott says. "Red. Outside in the pickup line."

"Cool, cool," Marco says.

He is easy to spot, this Marco person. He is fit, dressed in a crisp lime polo shirt tucked neatly into a pair of khakis, a silver Tumi backpack slung over one shoulder with a matching silver Tumi roller in tow. A pair of Maui Jim sunglasses with lenses that seem to want to echo the lime tint of his shirt rest atop his forehead. He looks to Klott as if he has stepped from the pages of a men's fashion spread on traveling in style—more like a caricature of how a reality show producer might look than an actual reality show producer.

"Bro!" Marco says again, as he tosses his bags in the back seat—then, sliding himself into the front passenger seat, he extends his hand for a shake and says, "Good to meet."

Klott accepts the handshake and decides not to remind this Marco person that they were on Teddy's Miami trip together, or that the two of them were actually seated next to each other at dinner one night at the Malibu beach house when this Marco person had driven up to join them for the day.

"Easy flight?" Klott asks.

"Easy peasy," Marco says, settling in and putting it out there that he'll likely be repeating himself or speaking in singsong rhyme all weekend long.

Within minutes, Klott gets that this Marco person is developing a new dating show for Netflix. He gets this first from Marco's end of a couple possibly urgent phone calls he makes like he has to answer, and then from the pitch he shares with Klott to fill in some of the blanks. Pauly Shore, the former MTV veejay who is apparently still holding to some kind of career, has just signed to host. The high concept for the show strikes Klott as particularly low: it's a dating show for the disabled—or, as this Marco person is quick to clarify behind air quotes, "the differently-abled." Maybe on one episode they'll match a blind person with a deaf person, or a one-legged person with a one-armed person. Maybe they'll send two wheelchair-bound people out to dinner, followed by a romantic roll on the boardwalk.

"It's not about what these people *can't* do," he says, "it's about what they *can* do."

Klott guesses this is a line from the pitch.

"The title?" Marco says. "You sitting down?"

Clearly, Klott wants to say. *Clearly, I am sitting down. Right here in the car. Next to you. Same guy you don't remember meeting in Miami or having dinner with in Malibu.*

This Marco person begins beating on the dashboard in front of him, as in a drumroll. "Wait for it!" he says—then, "Afflicted to Love."

Klott cannot think what to say in response, and Teddy's friend mistakes his silence for confusion.

"Like the Robert Palmer song," Marco says, in explanation. "Hello?" Then, in further explanation, he starts singing: "Might as well face it, you're addicted to love. Might as well face it, you're addicted to love."

When he's done singing, he says, "We're getting the rights. With any luck, he'll redo the lyrics, maybe cut a new version for the open. Robert Fucking Palmer. That'd be huge."

"Huge," Klott says.

This Marco person bangs on the dashboard another time or two, for emphasis.

"Wait," Klott says, when the drumbeat dies down. "A blind person and a deaf person on a date. How would that work, exactly?"

This Marco person plucks his sunglasses from his forehead and begins to chew on the arm, as if he to indicate he is considering such as this for the first time—then, as if taking in Klott for the first time as well, he says, "You're Theo's writer friend."

"I'm Theo's writer friend," Klott says. "Used to be, anyway. It's Harrison."

"Fuck, bro'. Harrison. My bad," Marco says. "Good to see you."

"Good to be seen," Klott says, and the two drive on in silence for the next while.

This Marco person takes the time to check his phone and laugh theatrically at a couple inside jokes he is disinclined to share, while Klott takes the time to wonder how it is that the urban sprawl of Salt Lake City can be bracketed in such a breathtaking way by these jagged, snow-capped mountains. It's like the city is being cradled, and for the moment he is happy to be held by what he sees. In this same moment, he catches himself thinking again of his father's money and what it all might mean, and his place in the cosmos and what this might mean as well, but his attention is soon enough returned to his passenger.

"You hungry?" Marco says suddenly. "I could eat. Can you eat?"

 "I can eat," Klott says. "I can always eat."

"There's this place on the way," Marco says. "Best breakfast in Utah."

"Tell me where," Klott says.

"No Worries," Marco says. "When we're out for Sundance, it's our go-to. A hidden gem."

If someone had established twenty minutes as the over-under on the amount of time it would take this Marco person to mention he was a Sundance Film Festival regular, Klott would have taken the under. As it happens, he might have lost the bet, but he counts it a victory just the same as he waits for the rest of it. Here it is: just this past January, Marco came to Sundance looking for a distributor for a reality show about bad haircuts. The idea for the show, which was called *Bad Haircuts*, was to start each segment with an actual photo of an actual bad haircut, and then to dramatize the events leading up to the haircut and the often hilarious and frequently embarrassing fallout from the bad haircut.

It does not seem to Klott like a good idea for a show. Also, the handicapped dating show does not seem like a good idea for a show. He's guessing this must be some kind of prerequisite.

"Don't tell me," he says. "It was called '*Clipped!*' With an exclamation point."

"Actually, no," Marco says, not amused. "'*Bad Haircuts.*' Kind of a no-brainer."

"*Special Needs!*" Klott says, adding an exclamation point of his own.

This Marco person has no idea what Klott's talking about, doesn't follow. He crinkles up his face and shrugs to indicate that Klott has lost him.

"For your other show," Klott says. "The handicapped dating show. Possible title."

With his side-eye, Klott can see this Marco person start to smile and then nod his head up and down—repeatedly, rhythmically, like Wayne and Garth and company in *Wayne's World*, rocking out to "Bohemian Rhapsody" in the car.

"Writer Man, for the win!" Marco says, with an enthusiasm to match his rhythmic head-nodding. "*Special Needs!*" Then he holds out his left hand, palm facing, and says, "Up top!"

Klott completes the high five by lifting his elbow to meet the palm of this Marco person and wonders if his half-hearted show of reciprocal excitement might even come across as merely quarter hearted.

And then, showing off, he says, "*Cerebral Pauly!*"

Here again, this Marco person doesn't follow.

"Nickname," Klott says, by way of explanation. "For Pauly Shore. You can put it on T-shirts, stir up some controversy."

"Oh, that's bad," Marco says, laughing in a way he means to signify that he doesn't mean to be laughing.

"That doesn't leave the car," Klott says, ashamed of his own joke. "That title, too. Between us girls. Shouldn't be joking about this shit."

"No worries," Marco says, swallowing up what's left of his laughing.

Klott hears this as some kind of assurance that his secrets are safe.

"No Worries," Marco says again. "Next exit."

It is here, in this moment, that Klott begins to recognize a disconnect between him and Teddy's Hollywood producer friend. The way this Marco person keeps chanting "No worries," like a mantra, like Frank Costanza declaring "Serenity now!" on *Seinfeld*, it's starting to creep Klott out, more than a little.

"Where we headed?" he says, trying to move Teddy's friend off his refrain.

"No Worries," Marco says.

There it is again, Klott thinks. Fuck! Last thing he needs is for this guy to go batshit crazy on him.

"The hidden gem?" Klott says, trying again. "Your go-to?"

"No Worries?"

It comes out as in a question, and Klott at last realizes that the batshit craziness must be a miscommunication. It must be that they have slipped into "Who's on First?" territory and that this Marco person hasn't simply been reassuring him that he's got the directions covered or that he's got his back.

"That's the name of the place?" Klott says, making sure. "No Worries?"

"What?" Marco says. "Writer Man's got a corner on the market for clever titles and restaurant names?"

Klott pulls off at the Parley's Summit exit and follows this Marco person's directions to a large Sinclair gas station sign by the side of the road—the kind of up-high road sign you can see for miles. There's a small café attached to the convenience store in the gas station parking lot—a nothing special storefront with no sign to indicate they've arrived at the right place.

"Fuck, 'bro!" Marco says, slapping the dashboard again. He is visibly distressed. "What, the place just disappeared?" He reaches for his phone and starts searching frantically for news on the whereabouts of his hidden gem.

"This the place?" Klott says.

"Was," Marco says, looking at his phone. "Google says they've closed. Lost their lease, so they moved, but now they're closed."

Klott doesn't know how to answer. "This place looks decent," he says, nodding in the direction of the restaurant where the hidden gem used to be. "Could still get something to eat."

"You're kidding me, right?" Marco says. "Tell me you're fucking kidding."

It is unclear to Klott whether this is just something to say when you are disappointed by an unexpected turn, or if this Marco person actually believes Klott is committing some sort of sacrilege by suggesting they dine at this new place instead.

"Fuck it," Marco finally says. "Let's just go."

Klott steers the SUV through the empty gas pump lane and turns the car back onto the access road to the highway.

"Some worries," he says, pulling out—not expecting his comment to land in any kind of meaningful way.

———

The first thing Harrison Klott notices as he pulls past the short stone wall guarding the sprawling home where he'll be staying for the next couple days is the splash of industrial red against the brown dirt of the mountain bike trails. The contrast is stunning, startling—the rich cherry reds of a fleet of high-end vehicles and the fire engine red of what appears to be an enormous balloon sculpture looking like it might flit and float across the clear, late summer sky.

"At least we match," Klott says as he steps from the also red rental SUV—another comment he does not expect to land.

Klott cannot imagine the money it would take to afford a home like this, in a place like this, at a time like this. Perhaps, back when Park City was an old mining town, before this mountainside had been developed into a world-class ski resort, his father's cash might have been enough to purchase the undeveloped land beneath his feet, but in today's dollars he guesses he'd barely have enough to cover the Tesla, the Land Rover and the Ford truck parked in the driveway. *This is not how the other half lives*, he thinks as he collects his bag from the trunk and looks around. This is not even how one percent of the other half lives.

This is not even real.

There are three other cars parked along the side of the house—two Honda SUVs, black and silver, and a mocha Hyundai compact that looks to have been dipped in milk chocolate. Klott figures these for the weekend rentals and thinks, *So much for squeezing into just two cars.*

Teddy Pluscht races out the metal-and-glass front door like he's been waiting at the window for Klott and this Marco person to arrive.

"Gentlemen!" Teddy says, as he crosses the circular drive to the car. "Welcome to fucking paradise."

He holds out his arms to call attention to the majestic scenery and the colossal manse that sits among it as if it belongs no place else, as if he is in some way responsible for this moment. He even twirls a time or two, making like Julie Andrews trilling how the hills are alive with the sound of music and the color of money. When he reaches his guests, he links thumbs with this Marco person in what used to be called a soul shake and pulls him in for a chest-bump hug. Then he turns to Klott and punches him gently in the arm and says, "Long time no see, Harry."

"Wait," Marco says. "'Harry' is on the table?"

"Only if 'Marky' is on the table," Klott says—then, turning to his old roommate, "And Teddy."

"Fuck you very much, Harry," Teddy says.

"We the first?" Marco says, turning to the house. "Dibs on the good bedrooms!"

"The last," Teddy says. "Somebody didn't read his itinerary. You're sleeping in the servants' quarters."

Marco puts his friend in a headlock and says, "The fuck would I read that itinerary, Theo?" Then, indicating Klott: "I copied Writer Man's phone number. All I needed to know."

"Dick," Teddy says.

"Actually, it's Marco," Marco says, and it is unclear to Klott if this is meant as a joke or a correction.

The three men walk inside and Klott is struck by the height of the ceilings, the size of the Robert Indiana canvas in the entryway, the incongruity of the Kaws figurine standing to one side of the canvas and looking to Klott like an encephalitic Mickey Mouse, and the Calder mobile hanging just above it that could just as reasonably be hanging over a baby's crib. What's striking is the way these contemporary works seem to have nothing to do with each other—it's like they don't even belong in the same room, let alone the same sightline.

Also in Klott's sightline as he enters the home is a vast open fireplace that dominates the great room, topped by a chimney designed to look like a stalactite dripping from the top of a cave. And, there's an indoor pool that snakes around the main entrance hall in a lazy river sort of way, with a footbridge reaching from the entrance hall to a sitting area rimming the fireplace, where Teddy's pals are gathered, sipping brightly colored drinks from delicate champagne flutes. There's another footbridge on the opposite side of the sitting area, which Klott now sees sits in the middle of the indoor pool.

On arrival, the place gives off a Playboy mansion grotto-type vibe, but as Klott adjusts to the scene he remembers that Hef was partial to knotty pine and crushed velvet and sees that this place has more of a distressed leather aesthetic. Also, there's not a whiff of chlorine.

There are six or seven fresh drinks on a stainless silver serving tray, resting precariously on an oversized leather ottoman, and Teddy steps from the footbridge onto this fireplace island to retrieve it and present it to his late arrivals.

"We're starting with an Aperol spritz," he says to Klott and this Marco person. "Can you believe, they were almost out of Aperol? I got the last six bottles."

Klott takes a glass from Teddy's tray and wonders how many bottles of Aperol a liquor store is meant to stock in a mountain resort town at the beginning of shoulder season.

He raises his glass to the room and says, "Good to see everyone."

The others raise their glasses and exchange shouts of welcome and good cheer.

Klott recognizes most of the group. There's Simon, the Manhattan divorce attorney, who made the mistake of confiding to Klott on a chairlift in Vermont that he's known among a certain clique of Upper East Side divorcees as "Si of Relief," for the ways he's helped them through their ugly splits—ways that perhaps blurred the lines between the personal and the professional, if you knew what he was saying.

There's Angus, from Goldman, who retired at forty-two to a life of golf and sailing and wine collecting, and an angel investor named Anselmo (originally from Mexico City, Klott thinks), who'd been in early on Napster and Uber, but not quite early enough to match portfolios with Teddy's brother-in-law.

And then there are the two plastic surgeons from Great Neck, Eddie and Steve—brothers in private practice who have lately been attracting patients from the plastic surgery group run by Klott's one and only client—together with a tech from their office named Alexander, who in a former life had been a competitive fly fisherman.

(This is Alexander's first trip with this group—owing, certainly, to his competitive fly fishing, but Teddy has confided that in addition to his experience as an outdoorsman, the dude has also brought with him a killer supply of weed, which Klott has been instructed to call "flower" for the run of the weekend.)

Klott and this Marco person have arrived during the group's idea of show-and-tell—a favorite pastime of the plastic surgery brothers, who, like every other plastic surgeon in their acquaintance, are in the habit of taking before and after pictures of their patients. In fairness to Eddie and Steve, and the doctor-patient confidentiality they may or may not be upholding, they hadn't intended to share these (mostly) boob-job pics with the (mostly) boobs on Theo's weekend trips. It happened innocently enough—or, at least, stupidly enough to explain away their alarming lack of professionalism. See, there had been a colleague accompanying them on the trip to Vermont, the very first of these outings, and at one point over the weekend the three doctors became absorbed in a hardly appropriate but perhaps justifiable professional discussion on technique and instrumentation, calling on the visual aids in their phone galleries to illustrate or argue a point. Klott had been seated across the table with Teddy and the Si of Relief guy, lost in a conversation of their own on the relative merits of the 1986 Mets versus the 1998 Yankees, when it became clear to the three of them that what their drunken doctor pals were passing off as a professional consultation was really just the swapping of boob-job pics.

There had followed, Klott remembers, some good-natured jostling for the doctors' phones, one of which eventually wound up in Teddy's hands, which in turn had led to a curious standoff, with Angus refusing to let the three doctors share in the bottles of wine he had set out for the evening unless they let the rest of the group ogle some of the boob-job pics—a compelling argument, because on that night Angus was pouring a 1982 Petrus, and a 2005 Domaine Ramonet *Le Montrachet*, which the plastic surgeons knew enough to appreciate.

(Also, after dinner, two bottles of a 1990 Trimbach *Close Ste. Hune*, which even Harrison Klott knew as one of the world's most drinkable Rieslings—"drinkable" having always struck him as a decidedly low bar in the language of wine criticism.)

In truth, the doctors did not so very much mind sharing their handiwork with the group, which they had come to convince themselves wasn't any kind of violation of the Hippocratic Oath or indication of their loose medical ethics, and to look upon these moments of drunken prurience as an opportunity to share their artistry with their friends—in much the same way they were in the habit of sharing it with each other and with their colleagues. Plus, you know, there was Angus's wine. Always, there is Angus's wine—so it's not like these plastic surgery brothers will be denying this group any time soon. Over the years, however, as the plastic surgeons expanded their practice to include pioneering work in the field of vaginal rejuvenation, the elasticity of the brothers' ethics began to resemble the elasticity of the *labia minora* of their monied and collagened patients, and so these before and after pics have now moved downstairs.

"Show him the one you just showed me," Teddy says to Eddie, who had been holding court as Klott and this Marco person arrived on the scene. "The clitoral hood reduction."

Surely, on the picturesque drive from Salt Lake City, cradled by these Wasatch mountains, dumbfounded by the sudden appearance of each home he'd passed on the winding road to this address, each one more stately or ostentatious than the last, and looking ahead to a too-long weekend of fishing and golfing and carousing that promises to exceed his capacity for all three, Klott could not have imagined there would be a photo of a clitoral hood reduction waiting for him at the top of the climb . . . but here it is . . . here *he* is.

Eddie passes his phone to his brother Steve, who passes it to Anselmo, who sneaks a second look at the screen before passing it on to Klott.

"Someone you know?" Teddy says, as Klott looks at the phone, in a way meant to indicate that the rejuvenated vagina does indeed belong to someone he knows.

Klott means to rise to the occasion. He means to make a careful study of the proffered photo—and, in this way, to fit himself in. He sets down his champagne flute and enlarges the image on the screen with a reverse pinch, and as he does so, he is struck by the incongruity of this moment. Consider: he has spent the first part of his day flying halfway across the country and driving to this magnificent home to meet with these dubiously accomplished and somewhat less magnificent people, only to have been handed a cell phone with a picture of a presumably rejuvenated vagina he is now meant to recognize or comment upon. It is, he now sees, a lovely vagina, framed by a perfectly manicured bush, its soft, close-cropped hairs running artfully in the same direction, as if they had been windswept by the gentlest breeze. He is struck most of all by the almost imperceptible bits of moisture at the vaginal opening, which calls to mind the wetness and sheen that might attach to a sweaty glass of iced tea. To his hardly experienced eyes, what he's looking at just might be the mother of all vaginas—a blue ribbon vagina!—and even though Klott supposes it must be possible to look on at such as this in a clinical manner, he cannot imagine a set of circumstances or a well-established code of conduct that would keep him from staring with anything resembling dispassion.

"Arianna Grande?" he says, handing the phone back to Anselmo, trying to mask his distraction with a joke. "Angela Merkel?"

"It's your Cheese Doodle pal," Teddy says, with the same glee he'd announced to Klott back in college that he'd made out with the TA in his Macro class.

"No names, Theo," Eddie says to his host. "Loose lips and all that."

Klott is too stunned by Teddy's revelation (and, Eddie's rejuvenation) to acknowledge the wordplay, but he imagines it is not original to this moment.

Teddy throws up his hands, as in surrender. "No names," he says. "All adults here."

"Hardly," Angus says, to general laughter, which Klott takes the time to think remarkable considering that his Angela Merkel line and Eddie's *loose lips* line didn't even rate a titter, and as the focus of the room splinters into three or four separate conversations, he steps to Teddy for a sidebar.

"And you know this how?" he says. Before letting his mind wander to *who knows where* and *God only knows* he wants to be sure there's no mistaking the connection.

It has been only a few seconds since Teddy's grand reveal, but already he has moved on to where he doesn't get the reference. "Know what?" he says.

"Shari Braverman," Klott says. "Fiona's friend. Mother of the bar mitzvah boy."

Teddy smiles—the kind of shit-eating grin that puts it out there that he's gotten away with something. "I saw the way you were looking at her," he says.

"When?" Klott says. "Where?"

"Last week. In synagogue."

Klott has nothing to say. It surprises him, that Teddy would have picked up on his extra-curricular interest. It surprises him, too, that he is so shaken by a picture of this woman's lovely vagina. It feels like a violation—not only of Shari Braverman, but of the intimacy they now share. Okay, so maybe it's not an intimacy so much as a proximity, their kids being friends and all. Their back-to-back *simchas*. Him coming to her aid in a moment of need. The two of them cross-pollenating with so many of the same people on Facebook.

Later, alone in his room on the third floor, Harrison Klott will unpack his few things and open his laptop and go immediately to Shari Braverman's Facebook page, where he will expect to find dozens of fresh photos from her son's bar mitzvah, and where he will expect to lose himself yet again in the alluring stuff of this woman's life—a life, he will realize, that has nothing at all to do with him, but that will now be accented in his memory by the cell phone photo circulated by the plastic surgery brothers. There she will be, smiling confidently in that stunning beige and brown dress she was wearing just this past weekend, and there he will be, holed up in this grand mountain home, surrounded by these people who cannot be bothered to remember his name, who have accomplished more in their inconsequential lives than he has in his, who have made the kind of collective noise that calls attention to their being here. He will close his eyes and imagine that there was nothing beneath the sheer fabric of Shari Braverman's dress but Shari Braverman herself, and that the gently windswept hairs of her very lovely vagina will have been blowing ever so sweetly, ever so subtly in the same direction.

Toward him.

14.

LET'S MOVE BEFORE THEY RAISE THE PARKING RATE

LEM DEVLIN

THESE OTHER CARS, they could be a problem.

Past couple weeks, Lem's been running worst-case scenarios. What if *this* thing happens? . . . what if *that* thing happens? . . . what if this other thing I don't even know to think about starts to happen? Anything might trip them up, send them home. This is what's in his head. There was the weather—the biggest variable. Had this Thursday on the calendar all along, with the idea they could slide to Friday if there was rain. The rain itself, it's not a problem. Arty has them out on his Fine Artemis jobs all the time, middle of a downpour. It's how it looks, him and his guys out there, moving this giant-ass sculpture in the rain. Raises questions, you know. Last thing they want is to raise questions.

There was somebody in the house—another scenario. If it was the owner, Lem could talk his way around it, say there'd been a screw-up. Might get Arty to thinking, might cost Lem his job, but that's where it would end. No way Arty'd call the cops on one of his own and put it out there his crew couldn't be trusted.

Lem couldn't sleep, had so many worst-case scenarios running through his brain, so he'd left from his place in Sugar House around six this morning, figured he'd get an early start. Get the job going. Stopped for coffee on the way—some drive-thru place, with breakfast burritos. He'd dropped the coffee in the one empty cup-holder and peeled back the tinfoil on his burrito, tried to eat and drink as he drove but finally pulled over. Hard enough to eat these things sitting at a table, with two free hands. Ran through his notes on his legal pad a final time, before balling up his burrito wrapper and continuing on to the house.

The plan is for Duck to meet the rest of the crew at the Walmart parking lot in Kimball Junction at seven-thirty. Made sense for it to be Duck on the rendezvous because most of the guys were his contacts: Cool Mo, with the crane; Vern, with the custom crates and some padding from his gig in New Mexico; Benjy, this guy Vern works with, along to help out; and Lem's buddy Roland, who used to work with him at Fine Artemis and knows a ton of shit about these outdoor installations.

Lem had left Duck with some collared polo shirts for everyone to wear—red, with the words *Moveable Feast* stitched on the chest. That's the fake name Lem had come up with for their fake moving company. He got it from the title of a book—a book he's never read, but it's one of those titles, it hangs in the air like something he's supposed to know.

Duck didn't get it when Lem showed him the shirts—said, "What, we're a catering company?"

The deal is they're supposed to stay off their phones this morning. All this shit in the news, how the cops can track your cell phone activity—your movements, even—they don't want to put themselves out there like that. Either they'll meet up at the house or they won't. Things will go as planned or they won't, so no way to know if Duck and the rest of the guys are on the way. No way for Lem to know if Duck remembered the shirts.

(He'd been on him all week to remember the shirts.) No way for Lem to call everyone off, if he's spooked about the other cars.

Lem pulls his truck alongside the stone wall at the perimeter of the property and settles into the scene. He's been reading one of these Tony Robbins-type books, tells him it's a good idea before an important meeting to arrive early and become familiar with your surroundings. The idea is to get comfortable, establish home field advantage. That's how they put it, like it's a turf war and they're telling you to give yourself an edge by making like you're on your own turf, on your own terms. It's not an important meeting, exactly, but it's a big deal, Lem getting with Duck and them to lift this enormous balloon sculpture off the side of this mountain, so he takes a deep breath and tries to ease into where he is, where he'll be for the next while. Coffee's gone cold, but he sips at it anyway. He steps from the cab and walks around, makes like he belongs.

These four other cars parked in the driveway, Lem wasn't expecting them. But he tells himself the thing to do is move around with confidence. Like somebody's looking. Like he's supposed to be here. He's got a dummy work order printed up, snapped to his clipboard. Been on enough of these jobs to know how to play it. If it starts to look like it's going down the wrong way, he can always cut out—say there must have been some mistake, some miscommunication, whatever. He had to guess, the guy who owns the house isn't driving one of these rentals. The guy's friends, they aren't driving one of these rentals. A crappy little Hyundai—are you shittin' him? Must be, he's got some people staying here, is all.

Anyway, the house is quiet. The mountainside is quiet. Sometimes, you can hear the whir of the bikers, zipping down these trails, shifting gears, kicking up dirt or rocks or whatever. You can hear the snap and crackle of leaves as these armored assholes careen past the canopies of low-hanging branches on the hard dirt, the crunch of twigs as they make the sharp, curlicue turns cut into the mountain. But on this morning, at this early hour . . . nothing. Lem guesses it's too early for mountain bikers, this late in the season. It's actually a little cold, now that he's out here, pacing. He can see his breath—and as long as he's exhaling, hard, he balls his hands into a fist, one over the other and blows into the hole in the space between his thumb and forefinger.

It's not *that* cold, but it is something to do.

He can hear the lurch of a big rig, downshifting, and he turns to see Cool Mo's crane making the last of its climb, followed by Duck and Roland in Duck's pickup and then Vern and Benjy in the flatbed with the New Mexico plates. Duck inches his truck around Cool Mo's crane and arranges it so the crane and the flatbed are nose to toe, like they talked about. The reach on the crane is over a hundred feet, but this makes it easy to settle the crates on the flatbed and do what they have to do.

Roland steps from Duck's pickup to stretch his legs, and Lem sees he's wearing his red *Moveable Feast* shirt, tucked into his jeans. It looks good, Lem takes the time to think. Professional. He slips into Roland's seat to get with Duck, go over a couple things. As he closes the passenger door behind him, he notices the truck's front bench seat has been duct taped—like, seriously duct taped, where the nylon fabric covering has been slashed or frayed. Ride must be ten, twelve years old, it's seen some shit, and here is this duct tape covering up what it's seen. This is how it is with Duck, Lem knows. How he gets his name. Fucker uses his duct tape on everything. The sleeves of his winter jackets, the toes of his boots, the fake leather of his tool bag . . . whatever's broke or ripped or worn through, he tapes that shit up and moves on.

"Home Depot called," he says to Duck. "They need all their fucking duct tape back."

"What's with them cars?" Duck says, turning over his shoulder toward the rentals parked by the side of the house.

"Fuck if I know," Lem says.

Duck considers this a moment. "We call it off?"

Lem: "Not yet." Then, "Maybe. I don't know."

Duck waves his hand in a way that's meant to say he doesn't give a shit. Or maybe he's saying he does give a shit but they're so far along he doesn't want to double back.

"We good, you think?" Lem says.

"Whatever," Duck says. "Least we all have these fuckin' shirts."

─────────────

Turns out there's no doorbell—at least, no *regular* doorbell. Instead, there's a heavy, braided rope, hanging from the archway over the front door, and as Lem looks up and follows the rope through the opening in the arch he sees it leads to a kind of bell tower, and an actual fucking bell, so he tugs on it, like he's the fucking Hunchback of Notre Dame—another book he's never read but should probably know.

One thing that's never come up, all his years moving fine art for Arthur Hammond, is how hard you're supposed to pull or tug on a heavy, braided rope attached to a bell tower if you want to signal to someone inside the house that you're at the front door and ready to start in on a job but worried the noise might wake the moose and the deer and any other beasts might be hanging around in these woods, sleeping in. He tugs gently on the rope, but this only gets the rope to slap soundlessly against the bowl, so he puts a little more into it to get the clapper going, and next thing he knows there are some pretty significant bleats and peals sounding from the tower, and it feels to Lem like it's too much—like he's calling in his ranch hands for supper.

He hears a muffled shout from inside the house, quickly followed by the sight of a blurry male figure approaching the door through the double-pane glass. The blurry male figure pulls the door open and says, "You rang," in a dark, throaty voice he means to sound like Lurch from *The Addams Family*.

Lem doesn't get the reference, just thinks the guy's got a dark, throaty voice and is maybe a little off. Lem holds out the doctored ID badge he's hung from a *Utah Man* lanyard around his neck—a giveaway from the last time he went to see the Utes at Rice-Eccles Stadium.

He says, "I'm here for the Koons."

That's the line he's rehearsed into the ground, in case he needed it— the line to set this whole thing in motion, if it needed some kind of push.

I'm here for the Koons—the line they'll put on T-shirts if this job makes news and they turn it into a movie.

The guy who opened the door looks at Lem's badge, and then he follows Lem's eyes to the sculpture.

"That balloon dog thingy?" the guy says.

"That balloon dog thingy," Lem says, trying to sound patient and agreeable and not at all concerned that he's stepped into one of his worst-case scenarios.

"Hmph," the guy says, thinking this over. Whatever his relationship might be to the owner of the house, this person had not expected to be awakened at eight o'clock in the morning by the bleats of an actual bell from an actual bell tower and confronted with the possible removal of a giant balloon dog sculpture, so he has some questions—like, "Where you taking it?" And, "Why?"

From the way this guy is speaking and moving, Lem figures he's hungover.

"Winter storage," Lem says, trying to remember the script he'd written out on one of his legal pads. "Balloon dogs, they don't do well in the cold and snow."

In the planning, he'd thought it would be good to throw in a small joke—you know, make it seem like it was the most natural thing in the world, him and his crew showing up like this, to haul off this giant sculpture. And now here, in the execution, the line seems to have the desired effect, because the guy who opened the door says, "Been wondering what the hell was up with that balloon dog. I'm like, what is art, right?"

"See a lot of crazy shit on this job," Lem says. "But this guy, Koons. Pop art or some shit. People say he's some kind of genius."

"I'll check him out," the guy says, a little drunkenly. "Definitely."

"Great," Lem says. Then, after a beat, "Cool to get started?"

"Yeah," the guy says. "Cool. Just give me a sec. Buddy of mine, it's his sister's place. Should probably wake him and let him know."

"Definitely. You should probably wake him," Lem says. "Okay for us to start setting up while you get him? Gonna take a while."

"No prob," the guy says, and as he disappears back into the house, Lem walks over to Duck and them and flashes a thumbs-up signal, so

Vern and Benjy start unloading the packing crates, while Cool Mo waves Roland over to the flatbed to help him set up his hooks and ties and chains. Duck leans against the rear of his pickup, unwilling to move just yet. He can see the guy in the house has left the front door open and that Lem is hanging back and waiting on his return, so he himself is in no great hurry.

Wasted motion and him, they don't really get along.

In just a couple minutes, the guy from the front door returns with another guy, and as the two of them step outside Lem sees they're both wearing flannel pajama bottoms and T-shirts, like they're in a club and this is their uniform. The one from before has a shirt on that says *DON'T BLAME ME, I VOTED FOR JILL STEIN*. The new guy has a shirt on that says *MY OTHER WIFE IS A UTAH NINE!*

After a beat, Lem checks himself for being so quick to jump on these guys for dressing alike, realizing he's got his crew in these red polo shirts.

As the new guy approaches, Lem once again holds out his doctored ID badge—this time extending his hand. "Name's Clem," he says. "Sorry to bother you so early."

Like he'd practiced it.

"Theo," the new guy says, accepting Lem's handshake. "Don't worry about the time. We should be up already. Going fishing, a bunch of us. Meant to get an early start."

"Where at?" Lem says, making conversation.

"Somewhere on the Weber," the new guy says. "S'posed to be out there already but tell that to whatever the hell we drank last night."

Lem laughs politely. "Hope you like trout," he says. "Rainbow, tiger, brookies . . . hear they're running good."

The new guy appears to have run out of small talk and nods in the direction of the Koons—says, "I know he has this thing moved every year, but he didn't say you were coming."

"Standing work order," Lem says, holding out his clipboard prop to support his claim. "Down in the fall, up again in the spring. Storm coming in next week. Trying to get to what we can before the weather turns to shit."

When the new guy doesn't reach for the clipboard, Lem returns it to the crook of his arm, leaving both hands free. The new guy steps from the house toward the Koons. He scratches his head and says, "Looks like something my kid would make. Am I right?"

"Well, it's big," Lem says. "Heavy. But yeah, I get what you mean. It's very simple."

The guy in the Jill Stein shirt has been tapping on his phone, and he walks it over to his buddy to illustrate whatever it is he's about to say. "Your brother-in-law doesn't fuck around, Theo," he says. "Says he's in, like, the Whitney. Koons. The Guggenheim. Some serious shit."

"Yep," the new guy says, taking his friend's phone and giving it a quick glance. "Some serious shit. That's our boy." Then, to Lem, "We need to be here, while you do your thing? Trout ain't gonna catch themselves."

Lem laughs his most professional laugh, like he wants the customer to think he's the funniest fuck in these mountains—like this guy is even his customer. "We're good," he says. "Just your signature." He points to the clipboard under his opposite arm.

"I'll sign on the way out," the new guy says. "Half hour. You still be here?"

"Gonna take a while," Lem says.

———

How it works is Roland runs the dismantling and packing, and Cool Mo deals with the rigging. Everyone else, they're the muscle—the eyes, and the muscle. The muscle, because there's a lot to move, tie up, position into place. The eyes, because these rich assholes from inside the house keep spilling outside to supervise. It's like they've never seen someone dismantle an industrial sculpture and pack it carefully into crates. A couple times, Lem has to stop them from taking pictures with their phones, because that would just be another worst-case scenario he hadn't even considered— pictures on Instagram or Snapchat or some shit of him and his crew, hijacking the Koons. How he stops them is with some line about how the artist doesn't want anybody to see his work in pieces—disconnected parts, all over the fucking place.

"It's like a code of ethics," he says to this guy who'd come to the door, Theo, who's stepped out of his pajama pants and into a pair of many-pocketed khaki shorts. "Not really fair to the artist, unless the pictures show his full vision. Gotta respect the full vision, right?"

"You say so, brother," says Theo, holding up his empty hands to show he's not taking any pictures—how the rich, monied fucks in this old mining town show they're unarmed.

Lem has crated this piece before, but Vern goes at it in a different way. He's taken Lem's specs and built these custom crates, with foam inserts cut to accommodate these balloon dog parts. Plus, he's brought a bunch of drop cloths to protect the hi-gloss of the piece.

Roland tells Lem this is the first thing collectors look for, when they're considering a Koons—the pristine finish.

"Can't be no blemishes," he says. "No gashes. His work, the colors pop in this perfect way. Like a new toy out of the box. That's like his signature, Jeffrey Koons. The high gloss."

Vern had said he'd handle the crates, but Lem had no idea the extra effort he'd put into the job. He's looking on and thinking he'll have to throw Vern some kind of bonus, him going out of his way like this. Above and beyond. Really, it's looking like these foam inserts will fit like they'd been molded around each piece, snug as shit. And the crates, once they're loaded onto the flatbed, won't be no way to tell if they're hauling furniture or food or office supplies.

It's a pain-in-the-ass job, unbolting the piece, strapping each balloon dog "link" to Cool Mo's crane, placing it carefully into its nest inside each crate—like surgery, almost. Lem gets the surgery comparison from these two guys hovering near the flatbed, going on about the precision of this operation. From the way they're talking, Lem gets that they're doctors. Also, that they want him to know they're doctors, or maybe it's just that this is how they see the world, every problem a thing to be solved with surgical precision—solved, and then analyzed and talked into the ground. People are like that, he thinks. Whatever they do for a job, however they spend their days, it becomes their personality. Like with

Duck, always drinking the same beer, always acting like the world is out to fuck him over. Him with his duct tape, patching over what's wrong instead of fixing what's wrong. It's why he's always bouncing from one gig to the next. Making repairs, you know? Taking care of what he needs for the time being but never trusting himself or anyone else to take care of what he needs for the long haul. All he knows is what he knows. Lem thinks maybe he's cut in a lot of the same ways. It's why he's out here, grabbing at this balloon dog sculpture. Except with him there's another piece to it. There's this piece that pisses him off, how some people step in shit and it follows them around and turns to gold. These rich assholes with their priceless art, he's in and out of their homes, in and out of their lives, busting his butt just to sort and organize the shit they've stepped in so it doesn't get in their way.

He wants what comes easy, what other people have without even thinking about it—what they can't handle, even.

There's this one dude, he comes out of the house with Starbucks iced coffees—you know, those blended Frappuccino drinks Lem sees in the refrigerator aisle at the 7-Eleven, running four or five dollars for a small bottle. The ones he can never justify buying. And here's this one dude, this friend of a friend of whoever owns the house, and he's bringing out six coffee drinks and making like Lem and his crew would be doing him some kind of favor, taking them off his hands.

"Thought you and your buddies might be thirsty," this dude says, approaching Lem with these bottles. He's got four of them pressed to his chest with his right forearm, and one more in each hand. "Mocha," he says. "Might have vanilla inside, if mocha's no good."

"Thanks, man," Lem says, taking the two bottles from the dude's hands and setting them on the stone wall, then reaching for the other four and doing the same. "Mocha's good."

"Nice," the dude says. "We've got, like, way too many of these puppies."

Lem wonders what it must be like, to spread thirty dollars worth of designer coffee along this mountainside like no big thing, to have way too much of the stuff to know what to do with. This must be what it means to be blessed, he thinks. To be so fucking flush, you don't put a price on the simple kindnesses you put out into the world.

Dude seems to want to talk. The others, they're tossing gear into those rentals on the side of the house—coolers and towels and changes of clothes. No fishing gear, though. Lem notices this and thinks, Fuck, why would these guys need fishing gear? Probably meeting up with some outfitter who'll take all their money and set them up with waders and lures and those throwback trout baskets like you see in the movies and maybe even a chef with a stove to cook up whatever they manage to catch. This dude with the coffee, though, he's in no kind of hurry. He turns to Lem and says, "You know about art?"

Lem considers the question. He doesn't hear any condescension in it. Doesn't come off like he's being judged—like, how is it that a working stiff like yourself, a presumably uneducated person like yourself, a guy who works with your hands like yourself has come to handle these magnificent sculptures? Someone else, they might get to thinking this dude is holding something over on them, but this isn't like that, how Lem sees it. He's usually a good judge of character, and here it feels to him like this dude is just being curious, friendly.

"Some," Lem says. "I'm around it, a lot. Can't help but pick up on some shit."

"This Koons piece," the dude says, indicating a section of the balloon dog sculpture swinging from Cool Mo's crane, Roland and Duck helping to guide it into its foam nest in one of Vern's crates. "I don't get it. It's a fucking balloon dog. A couple tons of metal shaped to look like a fucking balloon dog."

"Think that's the point," Lem says, setting down his clipboard and reaching for the one of the Frappuccinos while they're still cold. He rests on the wide bumper of his truck and takes a sip and says, "Art should take you somewhere, right? Should remind you of something."

"And this is supposed to remind us of what? Our childhoods?" the dude says, jumping in to finish Lem's thought. "The circus? We see a balloon toy and we're supposed to be filled with innocence and wonder?"

"Maybe," Lem says. "I don't know."

"But where's the art?" the dude says. "It's just a replica of something else. It's nothing. A ton of nothing. Made to look exactly like this inconsequential thing. This ephemeral, childlike thing. Looks like it could just fly away and disappear in the clouds. I don't get it."

"Don't think you're supposed to get it," Lem says. "Think that's the guy's point. Koons. He wants you to see it and remember how it felt to be a kid. When you believed in magic. When anything was possible. Right? You'd see some clown, some magician, whatever, blowing up those long-ass balloons and turning 'em into animals or silly hats or some shit, and it was like magic. It was like, poof, look at this impossible thing I just made possible."

"Nice," the dude with the coffee says again. Lem can see he's lost in contemplation, thinking about whatever Lem has just shared, giving it some real weight. He's leaned his elbows on the edges of Lem's truck bed, and Lem thinks it makes an odd picture, the two of them, sitting and leaning against his truck in this way, talking about art, the meaning of life, the loss of innocence, whatever. He's in the middle of this elaborate theft, right out in the open, talking art and life with one of the guys he's essentially stealing from, but Lem doesn't see this part. What he sees are two guys shooting the shit, trying to make sense out of what makes no sense at all.

15.

NOTHING LEFT TO LOSE

HARRISON KLOTT

TELL HARRISON KLOTT how he'll never think the same thinks as Teddy Pluscht and his variously rich fishing buddies who are only variously interested in fishing. Tell him how there's no way Teddy could have reasonably expected everyone to squeeze into the two biggest cars in their spreadsheeted rental fleet, when they can just take their own rides and caravan to the river instead. Tell him how it happens that he's stuck once again making teeny-tiny small talk with this Marco person, who by virtue of yesterday's ride from the airport has decided the shotgun seat in Klott's rented SUV has got his name on it.

The good news here, far as Klott can tell, is that this Marco person wants to navigate. He enters the address for the fishing spot into his Waze app as they snake along the meandering drive to the main road for what's supposed to be a half-hour ride and says, "In case we lose those fuckers." Then, after a beat, he says, "I was thinking. About before. That should be a show."

Klott can't follow. "What?" he says.

"Those guys just now," Marco says. "The art movers. That's a show, right there."

Klott doesn't see it. "What, like *This Old House*, but with these enormous sculptures? Taking them apart and putting them back together?"

"Bro, no," Marco says. "Like *Lifestyles of the Rich and Famous*, only the people aren't famous, it's the art."

"So, you see how people live, how they spend their money, the place they make in their lives for these great works of art?" Klott says. "Like that?"

"Bingo!" Marco says. "That's a fucking show. Tell me I'm right."

Klott guesses he is. (What the hell does he know?) "You'll probably be needing another one of my titles," he says. Like this is now a recognized area of strength.

"Writer Man!" Marco says.

"Give me a sec," Klott says, suddenly feeling an odd bit of pressure to help someone who says things like "Bingo!" and "Writer Man!" develop his pitch. "It'll come to me."

"Let it gestate, bro," Marco says. "Marinate, gestate, which one is it?"

"Pick 'em," Klott says. "Could also go with percolate. More of a coffee vibe."

"Think on it, bro," Marco says. "Percolate!"

Klott makes a show of doing so. The way he does this is to wear a look of concentration and place two fingers of his right hand to his right temple, which seems to provide the necessary cover until they are on to some other topic: Ryan Seacrest's bandwidth . . . Brett Kavanagh's confirmation hearings . . . the latest royal wedding, bundled with the observation that Meghan Markle used to be a fun girl, which this Marco person seems to have on good authority.

Somewhere in there, Marco fills this welcome silence with another thought Klott can't quite follow. "This is good," Marco says.

"What?" Klott says. "What's good?"

"This," Marco says, waving his arm in front of him like a bus driver turning a tilted steering wheel.. "This back-and-forth we've got going, you and me. How I work. It's good for you to see my process."

Klott hadn't realized he was meant to be learning how this Marco person works or that his insights on second-tier reality television might be useful. He cannot think what to say in response, so he offers a weak smile and says nothing. In the abutting silence, he imagines a sequence of events that might cause him to presume that the person sitting next to him on a longish car ride would need to know how he drafts a press release or an Instagram post on keloid removal for his one and only client.

Finally, a couple miles from the cutoff to their designated fishing spot on the Weber River, at a lull in the mostly one-sided conversation, Klott says, "*The Beholders*." He puts it out there like it just fell from the sky through the crack in his open window, like it's a sure winner of a television show title, like this Marco person will even get it.

Almost immediately, Klott can see that his title doesn't land.

"W.T.F., bro?" Marco says. He actually spells out the letters, doesn't say "What the fuck?" or even "Whatthafuh?" like a normal person, the way Jess and Avery sometimes say "L.O.L." instead of actually laughing.

"*The Beholders*," Klott says again, "as in, 'Beauty is in the eye of. . . ' As in, 'Art is in the eye of. . . ' As in, these people with all the money and the big, fancy homes, they're the ones who get to decide what is beautiful and what is art. They're the beholders. They're the ones doing the beholding, deciding what's valuable, what isn't. What's precious, what isn't. What means something to them, and what the fuck it might mean. What is art anyway if there's no one to collect it or behold it or tell us if it's any fucking good?"

"*The Beholders*?" Marco says, emphasis on the question mark. He shakes his head, like he's clearing his brain of Klott's bad idea for a title. "You've never worked in television, right?"

"Can't all be pearls," Klott says, removing his right hand from the steering wheel and waving it over the gear shift, palm down, like he's stirring a pot. "My process, bro," he says.

As he says this, they're pulling up to a trailhead parking area alongside the river. Klott sees they're the last to arrive, and that Teddy and his cohort are already having a look around.

"Theo!" Marco says, as he crosses the small footpath from the parking area to a riverbed of polished granite that looks to Klott like it's been trucked in from a garden supply store. "This place is s-i-i-i-ick!" He draws out the last word with far too many syllables.

What's s-i-i-i-ick about it, Klott sees, is the high-end catering tent pitched by the side of the river, presumably on the group's shared dime. There are chafing dishes and bar-height tables with linen tablecloths and a tightly-pony-tailed server whose nametag identifies her as Brandi. She approaches Klott with a tray of designer Bloody Marys garnished with strips of bacon.

From the chatter, Klott gets that the caterer will stay on all afternoon, to clean the day's catch and prepare a giant fish fry, but for now there's fresh fruit, granola, muffins, eggs, home fries, and a tray of avocado toast slices on what appears to be sourdough bread.

"How many breakfasts we are supposed to eat?" says Anselmo, considering the spread.

"Actually, it's more of a brunch," Teddy says. "Bloody Marys and avo toast. Fuel for our weary souls."

Klott wonders how it is that his college roommate and semi-lifelong pal has become the sort of person who so easily restyles his name and the names of trendy breakfast dishes in ways that help him feel like he matters, someone who spends other people's money with abandon and passes it off as a show of generosity. In addition to the catering crew, Teddy has also spent the group's money on a river guide, who is dressed in waders and consulting with Alexander on lures and strategies for this stretch of river. They're standing alongside a rack of wading suits and an assortment of rods and tackle boxes. Klott sets down his drink and walks over to them, figures if he's flown halfway across the country to go fly fishing he might as well get down to it.

Meanwhile, the rest of the group is content to eat and drink and leave the fish alone. They make a curious picture, Klott thinks, these entitled, successful men, and he wonders at his place among them. He wonders, too, at the irony of Teddy's friends half-heartedly fishing for cutthroat, which is what he's overheard the river guide say are biting. He thinks how it's not enough to be smart or to have a way with words if you're not also motivated, relentless, determined. How it's possible to be a blowhard and a dumbass and still manage to get and keep ahead if you're driven in the right way.

Cutthroat . . . what it all comes down to, Klott thinks.

There's a clinking of glasses over the by catering tent, so Klott walks over with Alexander and the river guide for what he imagines will be a pronouncement or toast or kickoff ceremony of some kind. *Leave it to Teddy to let no circumstance go unpomped,* he thinks, and as he rejoins the group, he sees Teddy handing out custom, beige-brimmed trucker hats, with his hardly clever *A Water-Hazard Runs Through It* slogan stitched to the front, encircling a stock animation mash-up of a fly-fisherman casting his line into the cup on some eighteenth green. These, too, he passes around like they came out of his own pocket.

Teddy's arranged for Brandi to take a picture of the beige-hatted group with his phone, and soon all the guys are handing her their phones for their version of same.

Klott, not wanting to appear any more *less than* or *other* than he does by default, reaches for his own phone to add to Brandi's collection, but the pocket where he thinks he's left it is empty. He touches all of his pockets, not yet frantically, and sees that they are empty as well. He must have left it back at the house but makes a note to double back to the car as soon as they finish with the photo op to see if he possibly left it in the console, and as their cheerful server takes five or six versions of the same picture, he wonders if anybody other than Ashton Kutcher or Jessica Simpson or an actual trucker has ever looked good in a trucker hat.

Funny how the day goes when you let it run where it may—like a river, Klott might think, if he still had that way with words.

Klott can't remember the last time he went so long without looking at his cell phone. Like everyone else he knows, he's gotten in the bad habit of checking his phone constantly—for emails or texts, or news bulletins, or to see if his wife or his kids or the vaginally-rejuvenated Shari Braverman might have posted anything to distract him from his routines. Here he is, balanced on two slick boulders in the middle of a slow-rolling river that may or may not stand as some kind of metaphor, trying to figure out this casting thing. There's an art to it, he can see from the way Alexander and the river guide are balanced on rocks of their own, doing their thing. Alexander is particularly graceful, the way he thrusts his arms forward and tips them gently back, inviting his fishing line to dance in the crisp mountain air.

Klott himself is struggling with the lure the guide has advised him to use—a bead head pheasant tail nymph, to which the cutthroat are said to be partial. It feels too heavy at the end of Klott's line for him to achieve anything like the grace of Alexander's casting—like trying to get the timing right on one of those paddleball toys he played with as a kid, when the rubber ball misses the wooden paddle and the weight of the ball is too much for the elastic string. Still, he gets it right from time to time, and he is able to lose himself in the sweet monotony of the effort, in the sounds of the whitewater against the river rocks.

The time fairly flies—or, stands the fuck still. Really, it might have been a minute or two since he stepped onto these boulders, or an hour or two. He is in that place in his head where he is not thinking of any one thing but at the same time is thinking of every last thing, and with each thought and nonthought he is brought back to where he is and what he is meant to be doing. In his peripheral vision, he can see the others wading through the shallows, looking for a new spot, and at one point he sees the guide fighting his line and following it into the deepest part of the river, pulled into the current to where the rushing waters nearly reach to his shoulders.

It is a lonely business, this fly-fishing, but as Klott scans the river, he sees there is fellowship in it as well. Some in his group have paired off, in twos and threes. Now and then a voice cries out in triumph, when someone pulls a silvery, slithery fish from the water, but there are long stretches of calm and quiet where Klott hears nothing but the slosh of the river, and it is inside these long stretches that he returns his attention to his father's money and what it might mean. He cannot imagine and he can only imagine, both. The mere presence of all that cash strikes him as so completely out of a character for his father that it seems incongruous. Too, that Hyman Klott had the presence of mind, through the fog of his dementia, to lead his son to the money is almost as unlikely as the fact that he was able to squirrel it all away in the first place.

Klott knows he should say something to Marjorie. It feels, more and more, like a secret he's keeping from her, a secret that keeps getting bigger and bigger. Also, he'd like to get her take, see what she thinks—where the money might have come from, what they should do about it. He decides to come clean. Right now. He doesn't know what he'll say, exactly, but he knows he must say something. On the banks of the Weber River, wearing a ridiculous set of olive-drab waders, thrusting a pheasant tail nymph into the air and hoping to control its flight, he determines that this is what he will do, and he touches again at the pocket where his phone is meant to be.

Fuck, he thinks, remembering. *Fuck, fuck, fuck, fuck, fuck.*

Six fucks in all.

He steps from the two slick boulders into the rushing knee-high water and wades to the nearest member of the group. Simon. As Klott approaches he sees that Simon is struggling with the tie on one of the lures from the guide's collection, which has been presented to the group at their fishing spots like a pass-around tray of hors d'oeuvres.

"How they biting?" Klott says—his idea of talking the talk.

"Meh," Simon says, opening the little catch-basket they've each received from the guide to reveal two oily fish, one of them still wriggling. "Kinda small."

"Too small and you have to throw them back," Klott says, sharing his extensive knowledge of Utah's Division of Wildlife Resources guidelines.

"Too late for this little guy," Simon says, picking up the dead fish. "I'll find the guide and see if the other one makes the cut."

"It's like a rollercoaster," Klott says. "You must be this tall to ride this ride."

"You must be this tall to land in Theo's fish fry," Simon says.

The two men laugh—Simon at this own joke and Klott at Teddy's elaborate show.

"You?" Simon says, pointing to Klott's basket. "I've shown you mine, you show me yours."

Klott opens his empty basket—says, "Bupkus."

"Well, at least you haven't broken the law. I'll use my one phone call to get one of my associates to bust me out of fish jail."

"Speaking of one phone call," Klott says, grateful for the opening. "You got a phone I can borrow? Think I left mine at the house."

"Got two," Simon says, setting down his line and fishing for the phones in the upper pockets of his outdoorsman's vest. "Business and personal." He holds them both out for Klott's inspection and says, "Choose your weapon."

Klott reaches for a phone and thinks it's no wonder they call this guy "Si of Relief," because he appears to him as salvation. At just this moment, in just this wilderness, troubled by just these troubles, the borrowed cellphone is like a lifeline. Klott tells himself the weight he's been carrying about his father's money will be lifted as soon as he gets Marjorie on the line and downloads what he knows and what he's done into their shared history.

The call goes to Marjorie's voice mail, and Klott kicks himself for not realizing the call would go to Marjorie's voice mail. She's gotten in the habit lately of only answering calls from numbers she recognizes. He doesn't leave a message, sends a text instead, tells her it's him, tells her he left his phone at the house, tells her he misses her and to call him back on this number when she gets the message. Then he hands the phone back to Simon and says, "Bupkus. She's not picking up."

Simon says, "Keep it. Try again in a bit. I've got my work phone."

The FOMO is strong within him, Klott thinks—only among this group it's more like the opposite of FOMO. What he's afraid of is not missing out but being roped into a conversation about wine with Angus, or a debate on the benefits of rhinoplasty with one of the plastic surgery brothers, and so when he looks around at the small social clusters forming and reforming at Teddy's pop-up campsite, he wonders what the hell everyone else is talking about with each other and if it's any less agonizing or insufferable than what the hell he is being made to listen to.

What he's got, he thinks, is a case of the FOBS—fear of being stuck.

Or, FOBAT—fear of becoming a tool.

Or, FOBSOALCRWTMP—fear of being stuck on another long car ride with this Marco person.

Still, it's hard not admire the way these men bounce so effortlessly from one conversation to another, the way they appear to be so comfortable with themselves and with each other. Klott can't think what it would take for him to move about with such ease. To feel like he belongs. To *actually* belong. These guys, they don't see each other outside of Teddy's circle. They are not a group of friends so much as a random collection of Teddy's friends. And yet they joke and roughhouse and bullshit with each other like fraternity brothers. Even Alexander, the newbie, seems to have this group figured out, and now that everyone has seen his artistry on the river, he's become the center of attention.

Teddy steps to the bar-height table where Klott has positioned himself and claps his old friend on the back. "Not bad, huh?" Teddy says, fishing for a compliment.

"Not bad," Klott says, tugging on Teddy's line.

Teddy pierces a morsel of perfectly seared fish from his plate and holds his fork out in front of him and says, "This guy right here, he put up a good fight."

"One of yours?" Klott says. "How can you tell?"

Teddy puts the morsel of fish in his mouth and makes a grand show of savoring it. "Because it tastes like victory," he says, chewing.

Klott takes a bite of his own. "This one tastes like complacency. Must be one of mine."

As if in cue, the tightly ponytailed Brandi approaches with a tray of Old Fashioneds, which Klott guesses might be helpful in washing down the truth of his last comment. She places a glass in front of Teddy and Klott, and hands a third glass to Simon, who has bounced over to join them.

"Got to hand it to you, Theo," Simon says. "Quite a day." He raises his glass and the other two join him.

"To Theo," Klott says. "The life of the fucking party."

The three men drink to that.

"You make that call?" Simon says, turning to Klott.

Klott had forgotten he'd been trying to reach Marjorie, had forgotten the kindness Simon had shown earlier in lending him his cell phone. He pulls Simon's phone from his pocket and sets it out on the table. "It wants me to put in your security code," he says. "I should check and see if my wife got my text, maybe try her again."

Simon shares his security code—7-4-4-4—which he tells Klott is easy to remember because it spells S-I-G-H. Then the two men take turns explaining to Teddy that Klott thinks he left his phone at the house and that he's been trying to reach his wife.

"You can check, you know," Teddy says to Klott. "See where your phone is." He explains how you can now locate your phone as long as it's powered on, and as long as the GPS function has been activated.

"You don't have to, like, opt in or anything?" Klott says.

"Not anymore," Teddy says. "The Russian bots are free to just have at it."

Teddy shows them on Simon's phone how to load the app and enter Klott's data and in the time it takes for Brandi to circle the campsite and return with fresh drinks, they have set up an account and begun a search. Soon, Simon's phone chimes and the screen fills with an animated fireworks display and the message "Success!" in bubble letters.

"Looks like your phone went for a ride, Harry," Teddy says.

"How is that possible?" Klott says. "It should be at the house."

"Says here it's in a town called Enterprise," Teddy says, looking at Simon's phone. "Says it's another twenty-something miles in the other direction, away from Park City."

"No way," Klott says.

"Way," Teddy says, handing over the phone so Klott can see for himself.

As he considers the results on the app Klott gets a flash-memory from this morning: him talking art and balloons and life in general with that guy running the job on that sculpture. He was leaning over the bed of the guy's truck, he now remembers, shooting the shit, and at one point he rested his coffee in the flat bed and his phone must have fallen from his pocket or maybe he set it down at some point and forgot to pick it back up.

"Fuck," he says. "The art movers. From before. Was out there talking to the foreman, or whoever. Was leaning over his truck bed."

"Mystery solved," Simon says. "Wherever that sculpture is, that's where your phone is." He tells Klott he should take his phone and let the app lead him there. "You're halfway there," he says. "Might as well."

"What the hell, right?" Teddy says.

"What the hell," Klott says.

16.

ALL WILL BE REVEALED

LEM DEVLIN

DUCK AND ROLAND are the last to leave. Temperature has dropped, what, twenty degrees since the heat of the day when they started to unload.

The sweat on his brow, his collar, the back of his shirt has suddenly cooled and Lem feels a chill as Duck climbs into the cab and turns the ignition. He steps toward Duck's pickup and motions for his friend to roll down his window. Duck nods in receipt of the gesture but guns the engine just to fuck with Lem and then begins to back up anyway, and it's only when he's righted the vehicle and is set to drive off that he steps on the brakes and does as Lem asks.

"What?" Duck says, waiting for it.

Lem rests his forearms on the trim assembly and looks Duck in the eye and says, "You'll hear from me."

Duck meets Lem's gaze with his own. "I'll hear from you." Then
he steps on the gas and pulls out, spitting more dirt and rocks than the
moment calls for. They're like exclamation points, the dirt and rocks, a
way to signal his disinterest. His tires spin wildly in search of traction.

Lem watches the truck disappear down the mountain, and as the road
dust swirls and fades against the orange sky, he thinks of all he and Duck
have accomplished on the back of this one arrogant, angry idea: to take
back a measure of certainty in their lives by taking this one larger-than-life
object that was never meant to speak to people like them. To grab at what
he feels he deserves. To rescue what people think is this great work of art
and put it back into the universe, where it can swirl or fade or do whatever
it's meant to do. He feels like a little kid, letting go the string on his stupid
red balloon and watching it lift from his grasp and into the clouds, into
infinity. Really, since the idea hit, moving this same fucking piece back and
forth, from storage to display, display to storage, moving all these fucking
pieces, no one around to even babysit their prized possessions as they're
carted away, it's been as much about releasing this balloon dog into the
atmosphere as it is about making a pile of money. Don't get him wrong,
the money is the thing, the good fortune he's been reaching for since he
quit community college and started working full time, but now there's
this whole other piece to the job that also speaks to Lem.

In his head, it's like performance art, what he and his boys are doing.
Like poetry.

He can still hear the irritated groan of Duck's engine as it disappears
down the mountain, but it soon weakens and is replaced by a hard
silence—the sweet sound of nothing left to do but sit and wait. This is
what he's good at, Lem thinks. This is what he's used to. Sitting. Waiting.
Wondering what it's like, how other people live, how to move himself from
here to there. All his life, Lem has been on the outside of things, but it
was only with this job at Fine Artemis that he was made to fully consider
what he could never have. It was in his face, and all around. The pay was
decent, the work steady, but with it came the constant reminder that Lem
and the other haulers didn't breathe the same air as the clients they served.

Even Arty, with his fancy degree in art restoration or whatever, running his own business, he wasn't good enough or rich enough or polished enough to live in the homes they worked. The art that hung on those walls would never hang in his. So, Lem grabbed at this one stupid, beautiful, graceless idea. This *uncivilized* idea. Wasn't just a high-end art theft, how he saw it. Wasn't just an opportunity. No, it was also a statement, a protest—his way of saying, "Hey, this shit is fucked." Ten million dollars for a giant-ass balloon dog, maybe more, probably more, and the dude who buys it isn't even around to look at it.

What the fuck is that?

He crosses to the cooler in the bed of his truck, where he's laid in a bunch of beer, including a sixer of Salt Flats Tankslapper—a Salt Lake City IPA. Calls itself a double-rye ale—says so right there on the label. He's never tried this one, but he's been drinking his way through the local breweries and this one had a high-end price point and an interesting label, so he's had it in mind for a special occasion. His idea, one of these days, is to take the money from this balloon dog and maybe get into the beer business. That's the pie-in-the-sky on the back of this job. That's the heart-of-hearts, hopes-and-dreams end of this transaction, for Lem. He doesn't know shit about brewing, but he can taste what's special, can even tell you what makes it special.

Art, beer . . . whatever. He knows what people like, what people will pay for.

Lem thinks about this type of thing, you know. It's not just this one job. He's always looking out for what comes next. Looking to make his way out of no way at all.

He twists one of the cans from the plastic collar holding it to the others. The ice in the cooler has only half melted, so the beer is still cold. This pleases Lem, that he has planned ahead in this way, and he walks with his beer to a tree stump alongside the door to the refurbished barn, where the crates have been stored. Would've been a bitch, guiding those crates from the crane and into the barn, but Vern and Benjy had thought to bring a double-wide hand truck, so that helped. Will be another bitch to move these same fucking crates at the other end of this deal, but he's thinking that won't be his problem. Let whoever buys it off him worry about that.

The door to the barn is still open, and this pleases Lem, too, that he can set himself down and look on at what he's pulled off. What he's all set to pull off. There it is, this massive sculpture, boxed like a couple presents waiting to be opened on Christmas morning. No way to know what's inside unless you know what's inside. No way to imagine.

He flips the top on the IPA and listens for the release of air. A beer like this, it's meant to be poured into an icy mug, with a thumbnail of head. Lem's read the tasting notes on the Salt Flats website and knows there's supposed to be an oak barrel aroma to it, but the aroma doesn't reach him through the small opening in the aluminum can, just the satisfying release of air to let him know what's coming.

Fuck it, he thinks, drawing the can to his lips for a deep pull. What he gets back is hoppy. Spicey. Bitter on the first swallow, but then it goes all citrusy on him—like the beer is telling him, "Oh, by the way, life can be shit, but if you fight your way through it, there'll be some sweetness on the other side."

This is the beer talking, telling him what's what.

He gifts himself another pull, and then another. He sets down the can on a flat steppingstone wedged into the berm by the barn door, and as he does, he hears the crunch of tires rolling up the dirt road to his new hideaway. At first, he thinks maybe Duck forgot something, doubled back. It's been, what, twenty minutes since he left—fucker must be pissed, wasting all that time.

Lem stands to see if can spot Duck as he approaches but is startled instead by a red SUV coming around the final switchback on the climb to the farm. An Acura. Maybe the same Acura from the job this morning back in Park City.

This is not good, Lem thinks. This is not what's supposed to happen.

———————

The Acura pulls up alongside Lem's truck. The driver gets out, stretches, sees Lem standing by the barn. Lem marks the guy from the house, the guy with the designer cold brews. He can't think of a single fucking scenario that would bring this guy all the way out here, all the way up this mountain, all this time later. What, he followed them, was hanging down by the cutoff, waiting for Duck and Roland to call it a day?

"A movable feast!" the guy calls out to him, putting two and two together but still waiting on four. His voice is cheerful, hopeful.

Lem makes like he doesn't know who this guy is or what he wants, but he wanders over to him anyway, beer in hand, cuts his approach in half. "From this morning," the guy says, extending his hand. "Harrison Klott." He appears to be out of breath, and Lem can't imagine why he might be out of breath. He's only stepped thirty, forty yards from the car. Must be the altitude, Lem thinks.

Must be the not knowing what's about to go down.

Lem shakes the guy's hand like he's been expecting him. "Right," he says. "The mochaccino guy."

Harrison Klott spins on his flip-flops, catches his breath, seems to take in the setting for the first time. He is dressed, Lem notices, like he is from someplace else: cargo shorts, Hawaiianish shirt, fucked-up trucker hat . . . oh, and those flip-flops. "This your place?" Klott says. "Some fucking view."

"Yep," Lem says. "Some fucking view."

He's got no idea what this guy's doing here, what he knows, what he doesn't know.

"Didn't catch your name," the guy says, making conversation.

"Clem," Lem says, sticking to his thin cover. "Good to meet you, Harrison Klott."

"Why am I here, right?" Klott says.

"My next question," Lem says.

"My phone," Klott says, touching the many pockets of his cargo shorts to show it's gone missing. "I think it fell from my shirt pocket when we were hanging by your truck, bullshitting. This morning. At the house. Think it might have hitched a ride with you."

Lem remembers the moment by his truck. "Still," he says, "why are you here? *How?*"

He thinks back to the conversation he had with Duck, one of their first meetings to talk through the job. Duck had asked if they should carry. "Shit goes down, you should have a gun," Duck had said, sounding reasonable, and Lem had pushed back, also reasonable, saying a gun would change the whole operation, maybe make things worse for them if they had to use it. He doesn't even own a gun, Lem—has never even considered it.

"Right," Klott says. "That." He pulls a phone from his shorts. "Borrowed this from another guy from our group. Simon. There's a tracking app, let's you find your phone."

Lem's heard of this, starts to think he's good. Sucks that this guy is here, but it's not a worst-case scenario. It's just a scenario. Lem's heart slows from racing to a steady jog. "Fuckin' Steve Jobs," he says.

"An app for everything, right?" Klott says. "Find My Phone. Find My Soulmate. Find My Purpose."

"Telling me," Lem says, behind a fake laugh.

"Right?" Klott says. "Whatever's missing, Apple can find it."

Lem doesn't know what to say to this, so he nods in the direction of his truck and starts walking, expecting this guy to follow. The dump bed is mostly empty, except for a bunched-up drop cloth, a rusted crowbar, some other loose tools, a length of rope, the cooler. The two men lean in for a look, from opposite sides of the truck—and there, wedged between the cooler and the sidewall, on its edge, is this guy's phone, minding its own.

"How 'bout that?" Klott says, reaching for it.

"How 'bout that?" Lem says. He means to be friendly, but he wants this guy gone. "That it?"

Klott points to the Tankslapper in Lem's hand. "Could use one of those."

Lem still wants this guy gone, but he doesn't know how to play it, thinks friendly is the way to go. He's thinking, *One beer.* He's thinking,

Make it like no big thing, this rich asshole driving up to where you've just hidden this world-famous sculpture by this world-famous artist.

He opens the cooler and twists another Tankslapper from its collar, and then another one for himself. "Drink local," he says, handing one of the cans to his visitor—thinking, Duck would just shit, me having a beer, all the way up here, with one of those guys from the house.

Klott looks at the label—says, "Full strength?"

"Full strength," Lem says, flipping the top and raising his can in salute. "Fuckin' Utah, right?"

"Fuckin' Utah," Klott says, returning the toast. He sips, looks at his phone. "Good thing it was charged."

Lem agrees that this is a good thing, although it is not even close to a good thing. It's a thing, is all. A thing in the way of his thing.

"Your friends know where you are?" Lem says, trying not to sound like he's pumping this guy with questions.

"They know I'm off looking for my phone," Klott says.

"Where they at?" Lem says.

"Some bend in the Weber," Klott says. He looks off in the direction of the river. "Not too far."

Lem gives this scenario some thought. Dude accidently drops his phone in Lem's truck dump, dude is already halfway here when he figures it out, dude borrows some other dude's phone and uses a locator app to take him the rest of the way. The rest of them dudes, they know he's off looking for his phone. This is how it breaks down. Doesn't feel to Lem like he's been found out, only that he has to change things up, you know. This guy here, this Harrison Klott, he's not a threat. He's just a speed bump. A hiccup. Whatever.

"Catch anything?" Lem says, trying to pull another bit of intel. He figures, he gets this guy talking, he finds out if anyone in his group had anything to say about Lem and his crew showing up at the house this morning and hauling off the sculpture. If it was a talked-about something or just something to notice. He figures, somebody must be talking to the dude who owns the house. He figures, a crew showing up unannounced to remove a famous sculpture, it's the kind of thing someone might mention.

"Nothing," Klott says. "The other guys, though, they did alright. Enough to cook up a little feast on the riverbed."

Another something that tells Lem he's good. For now, he's good. Nobody's looking for him, for the balloon dog. Any reason for him to be concerned, these assholes wouldn't be out on the river, cooking up their little feast. There'd be this whole Starsky and Hutch operation happening, local cops on the scene, maybe a couple feds from the bureau's art theft team.

Harrison Klott takes another sip of his beer and steps back from Lem, as if to take a look around. "Nice place," he says, walking toward the barn.

"Used to be a cow farm," Lem says, hoping to turn this guy's attention to the small pasture in the opposite direction. "What I'm told."

"And now?" Klott says, still moving toward the barn.

Lem thinks he should maybe quicken his pace and find a way to get out in front of this guy—*actually* out in front, like maybe a couple steps ahead of him, maybe turn him in some other direction. You know, find another something to point out. "Not sure yet," he says. He points down the mountain, the way this guy drove up. "We're a ways off the road. Not exactly a commercial hot spot."

Klott raises his beer to that. "Can say that again." He tells Lem about the *THIS WAY* sign he passed, on his way up the mountain from the main road, tells him how it must be a bitch to get a pizza delivered.

By this point, the two men have wandered to where the barn door opening is in full view, and Lem can see two of the crates from where he stands. The crates are distinctive, he now sees, with the letters *SALAMANDER* stenciled to the sides in bright orange paint, in big block letters. Lem's got no idea where Vern picked up these crates, or what *SALAMANDER* might mean—only that it's not the sort of stamp a person is likely to forget, a situation like this, and he goes from thinking he's in the clear with this guy to thinking he's fucked. He can see the guy spotting the crates, connecting them to the crates from this morning. He can see him looking at this spread, middle of fucking nowhere, trying to figure why a guy who owns a house like that in Park City would arrange to have a piece of art like this fucking balloon dog sculpture stored in a place like this. It makes no sense, and in a flash, Lem can see that it makes no sense and that he needs to find a way to control the narrative. That's the phrase he's always hearing on the cable news shows, telling him you can shape what people think by telling them what to think, but before Lem can come up with something the guy beats him to it.

"A moveable feast?" Harrison Klott finally says. "Hemingway?"

"Hemingway, yeah, but also from the bible, I think," Lem says. "Like, a holiday or celebration that falls on a different day each year. Like Easter."

"Like how you fix on a goal or a prize and it keeps moving on you?" Klott says.

Lem hadn't thought of it in just this way but wants to keep this guy talking. "Could be," he says, waiting for the rest of it.

"Like how a balloon can just float up into the sky and disappear?" Klott says.

With these words, Lem knows. He knows this guy knows. And Lem knows that what this guy knows can fuck him over.

———————

Another beer.

This is the way to play it, Lem thinks. See what this guy Klott has figured out, what he thinks he's in a position to do about what he's figured out. He opens the cooler and sees there are three more Tankslappers, plus a couple sixers of Coors Light he'd laid in for Duck and the crew. He holds up a sixer of one and the half sixer of the other and says, "IPA or piss?"

"That IPA was pretty good," Klott says. "Different."

Lem twists off two more and leaves the third with what's left of its plastic collar, drops the other beers in the cooler. "So?" he says, handing one of the pulled cans to Klott. He wonders what Duck would say, him handing this guy a beer instead of drawing a gun on him.

"So," Klott says.

The two men just stare at each other for a couple beats. There is nothing to say and everything to say, all at once. It's like a stalemate, Lem thinks—only, they're not out of moves.

Klott goes first. "The balls on you," he says, like he can't believe it, what he's pulled off.

Lem's not sure if this guy means this as a compliment or what. He thinks, *No, man. The balls on* you, *calling me on whatever it is you're calling me on.* He lets the comment hang, to see if this guy sticks anything on the end of it.

He does, soon enough: "Right out in the open like that."

"House was supposed to be empty," Lem says. "It's always empty." It's like he's talking himself through how it went down, how it might have gone different.

"But the cars?" Klott says. "In the drive? You knew the house wasn't empty."

"Still had some outs. Could've always called it off if we thought there was trouble."

Klott appears to consider this. "I get it," he says.

Lem doesn't know what this guy gets. "What?" he says.

"Why," Klott says. "I get the why. What I don't get is the how?"

"You saw the fucking how. Had to stop you and your friends from taking pictures."

"No," Klott says. "The how you plan to move this piece. Not like you can hide this thing away for a couple years and then slip it to some crooked art dealer."

"You'd be surprised," Lem says. "There's a big market for this guy, Koons."

Klott says he knows all about Koons—says what he didn't know he learned when he Googled the guy, soon as he pulled up to the house yesterday and saw the sculpture. "It's whimsy," he says. "His work. What he's selling is whimsy. Innocence. The people who buy into Koons aren't chasing him on the black market, I don't think. It's all too ephemeral for that."

There's that word again. *Ephemeral.* From this morning. It's like it showed up on this guy's word-a-day calendar and he's determined to keep working it into the conversation. "Not sure what ephemeral has to do with it," Lem says. Last thing he expected at the end of this long day was to be sitting on a mountaintop, sipping beers with some rich asshole from the house, debating the fleeting nature of a Jeff Koons sculpture and considering whether or not it's too simple or childlike to fence.

"Maybe," Lem says. He downs the last of his beer, wonders if maybe he and Duck should have focused on some other artist with a little more substance. A little more tradition. This balloon dog, it's like there's nothing to it. Like it's meant to just float away.

He walks with his empty to the back of his truck and drops the tailgate. His heart is back to racing again, with what this guy knows, what he might do with what he knows. He reaches for the cooler and grabs one of Duck's Coors Lights, and as he does so he wonders what the fuck is wrong with him, leaving the last good beer for this guy from the house. He wonders if that's even what he's doing, or if he maybe just wants to switch it up, is overthinking things. He wonders how Duck would play it, if it was Duck in this spot, and he goes from thinking his play is to take this guy's temperature to thinking he needs to take this guy out.

He's not a fighter, Lem. Hasn't used his fists since he's been in the States. He's cut another way, doesn't think he has it in him to hurt someone, the way Duck would do without even thinking about it. The way Duck would have him do here. But at the same time, Lem's not ready to go down on the back of this. He's not ready to give up on what this job might mean. He's put too much time into it, spent too much of his own fucking money—paying Vern and them, leasing this farm. His savings, basically, all tied up in where this sculpture might take him.

His every waking thought, tied to this fucking balloon.

There's another two or three hours of daylight, Lem knows. Another two or three hours to take back control of this job. Whatever advantage he might have had, whatever next moves he might have been lining up, they all slipped away the moment this guy from the house drove up in his SUV, so he gets it in his head that he needs to take it all back. His advantage, authority, whatever.

He needs to control the narrative.

He reaches for the crowbar from the passenger side of the dump bed, where it had been half hidden by the drop cloth. He moves suddenly, swiftly, like this had been his plan all along. He holds the crowbar in his right hand and is momentarily surprised by the weight of it. It surprises him, too, how his personality shifts the moment he grabs the crowbar. He goes from feeling like this moment has gotten away from him to believing he is once again in charge and that this magical sculpture, all boxed-up in the barn, will somehow lift him from what his life has become and set him down onto some other path.

Lem Devlin slaps the crowbar into his left hand a couple times like he's some teamster thug in a bad movie. He crosses to Harrison Klott and says, "I can't let you leave."

He hopes his meaning is clear, but of course it is not. How could his meaning be clear if he doesn't even know what the fuck he means? Still, he makes his voice hard. He flattens the expression on his face, hoping he looks like someone you don't want to fuck with. He is not sure he recognizes himself in how he sounds, how he probably looks, but he wants to own the situation. He wants this guy to fear him, to question why he thought it was so fucking important to head out looking for his phone in the first place.

"I'll take that last IPA, if you don't mind," Klott says, not exactly cowering in the face of Lem's show of strength. "Looks like I'll be here a while."

———————

Lem doesn't have it in him to hurt this guy from the house. If it comes to that, Lem has Klott by about sixty pounds, and a couple inches, so even without a crowbar it wouldn't be a fair fight, but both men seem to know it won't come to that.

What it will come to, though, remains unclear.

Lem grabs the length of rope and motions for Klott to grab the cooler and the two men walk with their supplies to the flat stepping-stone by the barn door.

"Maybe give me your phone," Lem says, as he sets down the rope and leans the crowbar against the barn. He says it like a suggestion but it's not a suggestion. "I'll give it back when I figure out what I'm gonna do."

Klott hands him his phone and says, "After you pry me open with that crowbar?"

Lem can't tell if this guy is funny or foolish or nervous and just wanting to talk. He'd like it if the guy would shut the fuck up, but he also doesn't have it in him to be intimidating or to come up with some other way to get this guy to shut the fuck up. He's got this theory that things have a way of working out, like how the television sometimes fixes itself when it goes out, only here he's not sure how that theory might hold. It's on him, to work things out. It's on him, to figure out what to do about this guy from the house, showing up, creating a problem.

"I need to think," Lem says.

"I get that," Klott says. "You need to think."

Here again, Lem is unable to read this guy, can't tell if he's being condescending or understanding. In the self-help books he reads, they're always talking about defense mechanisms and shit, about how people deal with their fears and anxieties by exaggerating certain parts of their personalities—a way of covering up, you know.

"I need to think, and you need to be quiet," Lem says to Klott. He hears himself talking and it sounds like he's scolding a child.

Klott nods and sets the cooler on the stepping-stone, helps himself to a Coors Light.

"Thing is," Lem says, "it helps to think out loud."

Klott pops the top on his beer and says, "Don't mind me."

The way this is going, Lem can't see a whole lot of positive outcomes. The two men are, what, three or four beers into this hostage-type situation, and Lem is starting to see the crazy in letting Harrison Klott return to the house in Park City, and alongside of that there's the crazy in keeping him here. Also, he's thinking there's no way he can move this Koons sculpture any time soon, for anything close to what it's worth. Already, he's made some calls and gotten some pushback, not a whole lot of enthusiasm. All along, he's been thinking he'll have time to figure out this last part, moving the piece to a black-market collector or a rogue museum, but now that this guy has showed up, there's a clock on the job. He's thinking maybe he should call Duck, get his take, maybe get him to come back out here, but then he checks himself, realizes getting Duck all worked up might just pile crazy on top of crazy. He's the one running this thing, doesn't want Duck thinking different.

When Lem says it helps if he thinks out loud, what he really means is it helps if he can yell or curse every time a hopeless thought or a deepening worry enters his brain. He doesn't talk himself through this situation, and all the related situations that have now pulled up next to it, but as each new outcome or next step occurs to him, he lets out a frustrated cry of "Fuck!" or "Motherfucker!" Like the answer to every question he asks himself is wrong.

"Sometimes it helps to take a step back," Klott says, meaning to talk to his captor like a human being instead of a bad guy on tilt.

"A step back from what?" Lem says.

"Whatever you've got going on," Klott says. "Whatever you're not telling me."

"You mean, like, go for a walk for something?" Lem says. "Clear my head?"

"I could go with you," Klott says. "So you don't have to worry about me running off and calling the cops or anything." He waits a beat and then says, "You can bring your crowbar."

"You trying to be funny?" Lem says. He is not in the mood for funny.

"I'm trying to be helpful," Klott says. "Whatever shit you're in, I'm in it too. If you're fucked, I'm fucked. If I'm fucked, you're fucked. Around and around we go."

"Fuckin' A," Lem says.

There's a footpath running from the barn to the pasture and Lem points to it with the crowbar and says, "Let's go. Clear my head, like you said."

The path snakes through high grass to a stand of aspens. Beyond the trees, up another small rise, Lem can see into the valley below: a rundown shed, a small lake, a dirt road that seems to stop in the middle of the hill, like it's run out of where to go. Lem's never walked the property, out to here. It's like they're the last two people on earth, him and his hostage. No signs of life, far as he can see, down to that abandoned shed and the dirt road to nowhere.

He stops, waits for Klott to reach him. Guy seems to be having trouble with the altitude, and it doesn't help that he's lugged a couple questions up here with him.

"It's worth what?" Klott says. "The Koons. In a legit sale."

"Ten," Lem says. "Maybe twelve. Somewhere in there."

"Million?" Klott says, making sure.

"Million."

"Jesus," Klott says. "For a giant balloon dog."

"People love this shit," Lem says.

"Not exactly a simple canvas you can roll up in a tube and stick in a closet," Klott says.

"I know some people," Lem says. He hears this back, too, and it sounds to Lem like the kind of line you'd hear in that bad teamsters movie, the kind of line he'd say to bring a guy like Duck into it, not the kind of line that leaves him liking his chances of actually finding a buyer for this piece.

I know some people.

Lem hears it back and thinks, *It's just one guy. Just one guy I haven't called yet who may or may not be in the market for a Koons.* Just one guy who may or may not give Lem his price. Just one guy who may or may not have the patience to wait this one out or the cash to make it worth Lem's while or the stomach for the kind of attention there'll be on this piece once it goes missing. He tries to clear his head and see what this thing looks like, for real, instead of what it looks like in his wildest dreams. To see what it looks like to a guy like Harrison Klott—in it, like him, only not in the same ways.

"They'll be wondering where I am," Klott says, telling Lem what he knows. "The guys at the house. They don't hear from me, might start to worry. Maybe ping my phone." He doesn't mention about the phone he borrowed to find his way here. The phone he left on his car charger.

Lem thinks again of the clock on this job. It's not just ticking on the Koons, on how long he has to wait to sell it. It's ticking on this guy who's just found him out. He goes missing, those rich assholes back at the house will think something's up. They'll start asking questions. It'll come up about the art removal. It'll come up about the crew with the collared shirts, the guy with the clipboard who appeared to be in charge. It'll come up through the phone he borrowed, to find his way here.

"This doesn't end well, does it?" Klott says.

17.

IT DIED WITH AN AWFUL SOUND

SHARI BRAVERMAN

TO BE HONEST, Shari Braverman never really gave a shit about religion. It was there, all around, except where it might have softened her, moved her, lifted her to places she could not imagine. In the Braverman household growing up, being Jewish was more of a given than a deeply held set of beliefs. It was who you were and not what you were—better, it was your identity and not your soul. It was expected that Shari and her two brothers go to Sunday School, that the boys attend Hebrew School and become bar mitzvah, that Shari continue on to Confirmation, but she cannot recall a single time either one of her parents asked her what she was learning or what she thought about what she was learning.

It just *was*.

To be sure, Shari felt a deep connection to her Jewish ancestors, to the *idea* of being Jewish. It was in her bones. Over time, she came to embrace the rituals: gathering with family for a Passover seder, lighting the Chanukah candles, reciting the Mourner's Kaddish for those no longer here. What struck her as she went through these motions was the idea that she was continuing the string, feasting and celebrating and mourning the way Jewish women had feasted and celebrated and mourned for centuries. In this way, her beliefs had more to do with the connective tissue of faith than with faith itself, with holding up her end of the deal. And so, when Jaxon was born she immediately looked ahead to the moment of *his* bar mitzvah. It would be a marker on their shared journey, a thing to be anticipated and held dear—and what was expected.

Brian was cut in a lot of the same ways. He was proudly Jewish, perhaps even staunchly Jewish, but he could barely read Hebrew or attach any sort of meaning to the traditions. His thing was that this what you did because this was what Jews had always done. Together, as brand-new parents, the two of them would look on at Jaxon's tiny sleeping form, swaddled in that custom baby blanket Shari's mother had made with the repeating orange and blue Jax curls that some genius in the Braverman promotional department later had the idea to market in the company's online store, together with an orange and pink version, and fast-forward to that time in their lives when their son would chant from the Torah and be counted in among his Jewish community . . . among *their* Jewish community.

Here, now, in the wake of Jaxon's *simcha*, after watching her son lead the synagogue community in prayer—after hosting a luncheon for two hundred people and being made to consider the ever more solemn angles on the pitying head tilts that continued to come her way— after inadvertently locking arms during the *hora* with her former-but-technically-*still* mother-in-law, Gwennie, and smiling gamely as she was spun about on the dance floor like a tea cup on that Mad Tea Party ride at Disney World her kids inexplicably loved—after being hit on (or, more accurately, *touched upon*) by so many single and not-yet-single and not-at-all single men who seemed to think their shows of concern or friendship were best expressed by brushing up against her or placing a hand gently on her back or collecting her forearm in both their hands and holding it there for a too-long moment—after standing off to the side as the party was dying down and hoping not to be seen as Brian huddled with Jaxon and noticing that both of them appeared to be crying—after all of *that*, she can't shake thinking there is something else going on with her. Something beyond her anger at Brian. Something more than her relief at surviving the bar mitzvah. Something bigger than the fear of what lies ahead.

Here, now, she is reminded of that "Smoke on the Water" song she used to struggle to play on the guitar—part of the background music to her own middle school years. For the longest time, it was the only song she could make out, one string at a time, and she never could fight her way past the opening riff, but those few notes had always signaled a fury still to come, a sleeping energy ready to be awakened, and as she sits at her kitchen table nursing her third cup of Nespresso after depositing her kids at their separate bus stops down the street, she wonders at the meaning behind the lyric. She calls it up on her phone, sees that *smoke on the water* is an old Southern expression to indicate an unseen trouble about to burst forth. Folks would gather by a lake or a river or whatever and sip at their moonshine or bathtub gin or whatever and marvel at the mist or fog or whatever that hung above the surface of the water and suggested dark times ahead—as in, "Best to watch out, there's smoke on the water tonight."

Here, now, in these Days of Awe that stretch between Rosh Hashanah and Yom Kippur like a hammock upon which Shari Braverman is pushed to reflect on the meaning of her life and the lives she touches, she begins to see that what first strikes her as a portent of gloom and doom is really just the opposite. What she's feeling, for the first time in months, is that there is no other shoe about to drop, no axe about to fall, no rug about to be pulled from beneath her feet, no husband about to be found on his knees in service of another man. No, what's she's feeling is hopeful, purposeful . . . peaceful, even. It startles her, to be feeling this way, after feeling so long as if her world was spinning like one of those mad teacups, out of control—so startling that the absence of dread registers itself as a kind of dread.

How is it, she wonders, that the momentary state of not being alarmed is itself alarming? In considering all of this, Shari Braverman is pushed yet again to consider the Torah portion that for all she knows has already started disappearing from Jaxon's short-term memory. For weeks, he'd been trudging through the house, chanting the prayers and blessings from the service and the lines from *Nitzavim*, etching the Hebrew and the melody into his brain. It got to where Shari and little Jana could cue him if he missed a word or stumbled over how it should sound. It was the song of their summer, and now that the summer has passed and taken the ceremony with it, the melody lingers. Shari cannot remember being moved or even all that interested by the reading in translation as she sat with Jaxon to help him interpret the material for their little presentation, but now that this moment has washed over her it appears to have left its mark. In being pushed to consider what it means to stand in the face of adversity, she has turned inward to consider the ways she has been strengthened by the recent turns her life has taken.

The strengthened piece doesn't exactly surprise her. She's been playing at strength all along, from the moment she came upon Brian in the garage with their neighbor. The story she told herself was in the story she told everybody else. Her husband was a shit. He'd made her life a lie. He didn't just cheat on her—he cheated her out of everything they'd built together. And so, she railed at him, consigned him to the blackest part of her heart. In the beginning, it energized her to dismiss Brian in this way. It was necessary, deserved. By reducing him she found she could pump herself up, maybe fill some of the spaces where her piece of shit husband was meant to be. She'd made it so her hatred was a kind of superpower—only now, strangely, she sees that the power has left her or is no longer needed. She notices this in the flash-memory of that moment between Brian and Jaxon as they parted on Saturday night. For the first time, she allowed herself to see Brian's actions not as an indiscretion or an invalidation but as a moment of personal discovery. She started to think of the weight her husband had surely carried for most of his life, the shame he must have felt at the life he was living, the life he was denying himself by denying himself.

She is not prepared to admit this at any other time but in this here and now, at her kitchen table, nursing her third Nespresso, her house quiet enough for the littlest voices inside her head to make themselves heard. She will not share this softening in her view of Brian with her friends, her family, her children, or even with Brian. Not just yet. For now, she can only recognize it and set it aside and try to remember what it was like to look out at the world when she didn't have to worry how the world looked back at her.

———

It's a new school year and Jana has asked her mother to stop meeting her at the bus stop. Dropping her off in the morning is fine, because all the other mothers are there, many of them dressed for work and planning to walk the few blocks to the train station after depositing their charges onto the bus and into the maw of the Centerville public school system. After school is a whole other dance. The super little kids are met at the bus by their caregivers, while the somewhat little kids like Jana are allowed to walk home by themselves, often splintering into little playgroups or stopping along the way to share secrets or silliness.

Shari wonders if Jana is simply spreading her wings and being independent, or if she is embarrassed that her mommy doesn't go to work.

It is what it is, she thinks—one of her least favorite phrases when people give it voice, but as an attitude it seems to hit all the right notes.

Meanwhile, it's only the first week of school and Shari can't imagine getting used to the idea of her baby girl walking home by herself from the bus stop. She's asked her neighbor, whose oldest is just starting kindergarten, to keep an eye on Jana as she makes her way back to the house, but she knows at some point she will have to let her daughter move about the neighborhood if she ever hopes for her to move about the planet, and already Shari has gotten in the early-in-the-school-year habit of busying herself in the kitchen and trying not to look at the clock or listen for the bus at drop-off time.

Jana bursts through the kitchen door smelling of sunshine and paint. She drops her backpack on the floor and says, "Are we Believe-in-God people?"

This is not a question Shari is prepared to answer, so she puts it back on Jana to buy herself some time. She says, "Believe-in-God people?"

Jana says, "This boy in my class, Marcel, he said Jewish people don't believe in God."

"Marcel?" Shari says, buying herself a couple beats more. "I don't know Marcel. Is he new?"

"He's from Curacao," Jana says, swallowing a vowel or two. "He showed me where it is on a map. There's a map in our classroom this year. It's giant. You can pull it down and roll it back up like a window-thingy. It's an island. Curacao. Where he's from. He said in his religion you're supposed to believe in all religions. Even the ones that don't believe in God. He said he lives in an apartment over a candy store. He's funny."

Shari thinks she knows which candy store Jana means, but it had never occurred to her that there were apartments above the store, or that there might be little classmates for her children living in those apartments above the store, and now that it has she cannot imagine why this has never occurred to her because there are clearly two or three stories of windows above the storefronts on Main Street—with window treatments and flower pots and George Forman grills on the fire escapes and every reason to think someone might be living inside.

"Where he's from, it sounds like it hurts when you say a curse," Jana says. "Ow, a curse! Curse, ow!" She laughs and laughs.

"That's a good way to remember the name, Jana Banana," Shari says.

Jana collects her backpack from the floor by the kitchen door and walks with it to the kitchen table. She pulls her *Frozen* lunchbox from the backpack and says, "I didn't finish my lunch. The other kids have GoGurts. Marcel let me have one of his. People from Curacao are good at sharing, I think. Strawberry-Blueberry. Do you know GoGurts? They're just delicious."

Shari has always loved it when Jana gets going on how her day has gone. She laughs and laughs, and talks and talks, and bounces all over the place with a kind of tossed-about ferocity, like a pinball.

"But you hate yogurt," Shari says. "I'm always trying to get you to eat yogurt."

Indeed, the last time Shari had tried to get her daughter to eat yogurt, Jana had said, "Back off, woman."

"It's not yogurt," Mommy. "It's GoGurt. Duh! It has flavors."

Shari is beginning to think they have moved on from spirituality and religion and have nestled comfortably onto what she should be packing Jana for lunch, but she has another think coming—another expression she hates when she hears it out loud but doesn't mind so much when it pops into her own head.

"So?" Jana says, waiting for it.

"So what?" Shari says, stiff-arming the conversation a final, feeble time.

"Believe-in-God people?" Jana says. "Hello?" She puts a finger to her temple, as if to tell her mother she should be paying better attention.

"We're believe-in-what-you-want-to-believe people," Shari says. "Kind of like your friend Marcel."

"We, like you and Daddy and me and Jaxon?" Jana says. "Or we, like all the people who are Jewish?"

"I don't know what your Daddy believes anymore," Shari says, wanting to take back her words the moment they leave her mouth. "About God. We should ask him."

"But if we're in the same religion we're supposed to believe the same things," Jana says. "It's like a rule. Jaxon had his bar mitzvah and now he's a grownup and has to decide. That's the rule. I don't have to decide yet because I'm just a kid, but Jaxon has to decide. If he believes in God."

Shari patiently explains how there shouldn't be any rules when it comes to religion or to believing in God. In the Jewish religion, especially. She tells her daughter that some Jewish people believe in Heaven and some don't. That some Jewish people believe in God and some don't. She tells her that people can grow up in the same house and believe different things. People can be married to each other and believe different things. People can even say the same prayer and have it mean different things. She tells Jana how she likes to believe that God is in the many kindnesses we show to each other.

"Some people, they believe God lives inside each of us," she says. "God is how we take care of each other."

"He's not, like, a person?" Jana says.

Shari tells Jana that when Jaxon was younger, he used to think God looked like The Man in the Yellow Hat from *Curious George*, and that he lived up in the clouds and looked down on us from beneath his yellow hat and decided if we were being good or bad or if he should help us.

"That's funny," Jana says. "And stupid."

Then Shari tells Jana that when she herself was a little girl she heard this line in a gospel song or some hymn that said, "God is good."

"That was the decider for Mommy," Shari says. "Just that one little line. I heard it in the song and decided that when people pray to God, what they're really doing is hoping for good things to happen for the people they care about."

"But what if I just want good things for me?" Jana says. "What if I pray to God and ask Him for a canopy princess bed? Or an Xbox because Jaxon doesn't share?"

"You don't even play video games, Jana," Shari says, stuck on what's important.

"Because Jaxon doesn't share," Jana says. "Duh!"

Shari smiles. "Well, in that case, I think it's okay to want good things to happen for you and your family, as long as you also pray a little bit for good things to happen for the world."

Jana says she likes this explanation and is going to tell Marcel about it tomorrow. She says, "Tomorrow I will tell him Jewish people are allowed to believe in God and that his religion is wrong. About that part. It's good that they say you can believe whatever you want, but it's not good to say what you can believe if you're Jewish." Then, in an island patois Shari can only imagine has come from Marcel himself, echoing a line he's picked up at home, Jana says, "That boy, he be crazy, mon."

Later, the kids in bed, a repeat of Trevor Noah on the TV, Shari Braverman gets to thinking again of the change in her feelings about Brian. She wouldn't call it a softening, necessarily, but where her anger had been on blast it now appears to be on mute. It's there, but she would like it if it no longer drives her, defines her. She could use a reset. And now, alongside what remains of the anger, there's room in her feelings for empathy—or, at least, an opportunity to consider how empathy might look on her going forward.

She wonders if this shift has to do in some way with Saturday. With going through the motions of celebrating after everything that's happened. With being the center of attention of her friends and family, her community. With chanting the blessings that have been etched into the history of the Jewish people in the same way this week's Torah portion had been briefly etched into Jaxon's short-term memory. With being in the presence of God and the goodness of people. With seeing Brian tearing up with his son . . . with *their* son.

With knowing that the life she'd imagined might be just out of reach and yet still close enough to touch.

She grabs her phone and thinks about calling Brian. It's late, but she knows he's awake —probably watching the same rerun of *The Daily Show* in the furnished garden apartment he'd taken the next town over. She doesn't know what she wants to say to him, or even if she wants to hear his ridiculous, humiliated voice, but before she realizes what she's doing and has a chance to right herself she sends him a text.

Hey, she writes.

That's all. Just, *hey*.

Hey, she gets back after a couple beats.

That's all. Just, *hey*.

Funny how with everything that has passed between them, with everything left unsaid, there is only this.

You up? she writes—thinking, *Dumbass! He just responded to your text.*

He's up. What she meant to ask, what she guesses she's afraid to ask, is if he is alone.

Remember how you used to say watching a Trevor Noah repeat was like reading an old newspaper? he writes.

She remembers. *Even if you didn't see it the first time, it feels stale,* she writes.

There follows a too-long silence, and Shari imagines that Brian must be looking at his screen as well, wondering what Shari might want from him, what he might have done to piss her off now.

Just wanted to circle back to you about Saturday, she finally writes. *About Jaxon.*

He was something, huh? he writes.

Yes.

Proud of him.

Yes. Proud of us too. That we got through it. Without making a scene.

Must have been hard for you, Brian writes, and Shari gets that he knows the extent of her hurt and fury and that she doesn't have it in her to sit on those feelings.

Not so very, she writes. Then, *It was Jaxon's day.*

Yes, he writes. *So very.*

Another pause.

Shari can't think what to write, how to let this crude form of communication stand in for what the two of them have not said to each other, what they might never say to each other. She wants to tell Brian that the kids are doing mostly okay. She wants to tell him that she's doing mostly okay. She wants him to know there's a part of her that wishes he is doing mostly okay. Not a big part just yet, but a part—the same part that admired, at least a little bit, the way he was able to stand before everyone in his family and all their friends and confront their knowing. Also, she wants to bring him up to speed, to tell him everything that's happened since he moved out and she's been refusing to talk to him. She wants to let him know she's had plastic surgery, that procedure she's always talked about, doesn't want him to hear it from one of their mutual friends. How this seemed like the right time to pretty herself up, *down there*. How for the first while she couldn't shake thinking there was something wrong with her, something broken, something *less than* or not quite enough or whatever.

Her good girlfriends, the ones who are still married, they talk to their husbands. Shari gets that—she was the same way. She wants to tell Brian that it sucks, him wasting his life with a partner who didn't mean the same things to him as he meant to her, her wasting her life with a partner who wasn't free to be himself. She wants to bitch and cry that their kids don't get to continue with their childhoods with a father under their roof, and to admit to him that she's scared, more than a little, at the idea of being alone.

But she does not write any of these things. Whatever sleeping energy there is still to be awakened will not be roused any time soon. Whatever drumroll she might have kickstarted by reaching out to Brian in the first place has quieted, to where Shari has gone from having everything to say to having nothing to say—to not knowing where to even begin.

You still there? Brian finally writes.

Still here, she writes.

18.

'CAUSE I'M ALREADY STANDING ON THE GROUND

MARJORIE KLOTT

SHE CAN'T SLEEP.

This alone is not so unusual, these days. What's unusual, for Marjorie Klott, is that she can't sleep because of a certain sense of a certain dread—a dread she cannot name or identify, but she can feel it welling up within her and making itself known.

There.

There it is.

Right now.

Most nights, it takes Marjorie an extra-long while to drift off, owing mostly to impatience and a racing imagination, together with the idea that the world is spinning wildly out of control. And then there's the idea that she's on this rock, too—spinning, spinning, spinning—so even when she is quiet and at rest it feels to her as if she is moving. Her equilibrium is off. Even when she's bone-tired, it feels to Marjorie Klott as if her thoughts might run on forever, all the way to what the future might hold. There's no letup. She gets stuck, say, on what life will be like for her twins, as they move out into the world without the tether of each other—or, on Joanna, struggling to find her voice. She thinks what it will be like alone in this house with Harrison, the kids off in pursuit of lives of their own, the two of them left to grow old at each other's side, to consider the life they have built, to think back on how things might have been different.

With Harrison in the bed next to her, she can lose herself in the rhythm of his breathing. He falls asleep the moment he closes his eyes, and when they were first married Marjorie would sometimes poke at her sleeping husband to see what kind of reaction she might coax from his sleeping form. She made it into a kind of game—a game Harrison almost never knew they were playing. She would tug gently on his pillow, to where his head would loll back and forth until he might become startled, and she would work it so her gentle tugging wasn't quite enough to wake him but just enough to get him to reposition himself in response to it. He was like a new toy to her in those days, a thing to be played with, and cherished, and sweetly tormented, and she would lie awake and watch him sleep and marvel at whatever blessings had aligned themselves in just this way to place this man in this bed beside her.

Over time, she learned to match her breathing to Harrison's and to will herself to join him in sleep, as if he had gone off ahead to scout some new territory and was now sending for her, and in the comfort of their shared routine she is able on most nights to discover quiet in her disquiet and find sleep.

Tonight's unknowable dread doesn't feel to Marjorie like it has to do with Harrison being away. It doesn't have to do with Stewie and Sydney getting ready to finish middle school, or Joanna getting ready to finish high school, or life itself running away from her. She's not stressed about the twins' *simcha* next weekend, or the changes she can already see taking place at work, with the new department head hired by the district to address an alarming spike in drug abuse and depression among students, and to coordinate the logjam of requests for accommodations in testing and placement. No, she's gotten pretty good at shutting out her daylight worries and clearing her head for what she has come to regard as her nighttime angst. The economy, the health of the planet, the cheapening of our institutions and the all-over coarsening of human behavior—the things she can't change are the things that keep her up, only on this night she has no idea what's got her bent with worry. But there is something in particular. Something out of place in the place the world has made for her and her family.

Lately, when she can't sleep, she's gotten in the habit of listening to podcasts—on her noise-cancelling headphones, when Harrison's asleep next to her, and on her phone's speaker when she or Harrison have wandered restlessly to the living room couch or to the spare bedroom in the attic. Tonight, she scrolls through recent episodes of Marc Maron's *What the Fuck* podcast, to see if there's anyone on his guest list who catches her attention. She likes how Maron says whatever pops into his brain, without filter—a quality she guesses would be problematic in someone other than a stand-up-comedian-turned-podcast host. She clicks on an episode featuring an interview with the guitarist Joe Walsh, from a couple weeks back. She used to know Joe Walsh from the ways he reshaped her favorite band, The Eagles, when he joined them and drove them from a peaceful, easy feeling to a life in the fast lane. Lately she knows him from the occasional reports that pop up online that leave her thinking he's batshit crazy.

More and more, she finds herself reaching for batshit crazy: Gary Busey, Kanye West, Britney Spears, Charlie Sheen—it's the folks with nothing to say and a platform on which to not say it who have something to tell her in the middle of the night. In between the lines of their rants and ramblings, she listens for clues, to hear where or how they went off the rails, where or how they might right themselves and continue on their journey. Always, she believes, there is a kind of leash, tying these good and lost and striving people to the children they once were, to the hopes and dreams that were once in their grasps, and that it is on her to discover it.

Joe Walsh is not helping. Marc Maron is not helping. The two men talk over each other like they're fighting for the mic. Joe Walsh sounds like he just got out of bed or is just off a bender, his voice rum-soaked and raspy, his thoughts all over the place and nowhere at all, and Marc Maron sounds like one of her students at school, a little too excited that one of the popular kids has taken the time to talk to him. The conversation is circular, disjointed, pointless, and were it somewhat less so, Marjorie Klott might never have reached for her phone at just this moment to search for another something to distract from her own racing imagination. The reaching is key, because at this late hour her phone retreats into DO NOT DISTURB mode—meaning, it won't ring or vibrate or alert her in any way if a call or text comes in from someone other than Harrison or the kids or her parents or her sister. And yet because the phone is in her hands at this precise moment, because she is looking at the screen, she sees the pulsing handset icon, sees that the call is from Harrison's friend Teddy, sees that there have been two or three missed calls from Teddy earlier in the evening—calls she never received because of the late hour —and in the half beats between the moment she recognizes Teddy's call to the moment she answers it she has time to consider the looming dread that had been making itself known to her and attach it to what she's about to hear.

"Teddy," she says. "What's wrong?"

"Sorry to call so late, Marjorie," Teddy says. He sounds calm. "Nothing to worry about. Our boy is fine."

"'Nothing to worry about?' Fuck, Teddy, it's two o'clock in the morning."

She's yelling, but she's not angry. She hears those words—*our boy is fine*—and she fights the reflex to burst into tears.

"I know," he says. "That's why I'm calling. Been trying you all night. Thought you'd see the missed calls and get all freaked out."

"Kinda freaking me out anyway," she says.

"Right," he says. "Sorry. Harry's fine. Everything's fine."

"Tell me what's not fine," Marjorie says.

Teddy goes into it, in a meandering way—like he's Joe Walsh being interviewed by Marc Maron and can only surround his point without entirely making it. What Marjorie gets is that Harrison left the group to go looking for his phone, while they were still out fishing. Late afternoon. When the group got back to the house, they started in on dinner . . . and, drinking. (Angus really outdid himself this year on the wine front, Teddy finds room in his circular storytelling to share with Marjorie—sent a couple cases to the house and traveled with a roller filled with another twelve bottles—while Marjorie finds room in her listening to wonder who Angus is and when Teddy will get around to tell her what's going on.) At some point, early eveningish, the guys back at the house started to wonder what happened to Harrison. It was getting dark. They hadn't heard from him. He wasn't answering his phone. And the phone he borrowed from Teddy's divorce attorney friend, he wasn't answering that one either.

"That's why I called earlier," Teddy says. "A couple hours past dark, must've been about nine. Wanted to see if you'd heard from him."

"That's eleven here," Marjorie says. "Why I didn't get those calls. Could've called the house, you know."

"Didn't think of that," Teddy says. "Sorry."

He goes on to tell how the group kept trying Harrison's phone and the divorce attorney's phone. How they kept trying to locate the two phones. How Teddy kept trying Marjorie. Finally, around ten-thirty, Teddy got a text from the divorce attorney's phone—Harrison, letting him know he'd found his phone and that he'd fallen into talking with the art storage guy from this morning, had a couple beers, didn't think it was smart for him to be driving home on these mountain roads, half in the bag. Saying the service was lousy.

"The art storage guy?" Marjorie says.

"Right," Teddy says. "Long story."

"Tell me."

"Robin's got this great Jeffrey Koons sculpture, sitting out in front of the house," he says. "This giant balloon dog sculpture. Massive. Bright red. Koons, you've probably seen his work. Pop-art stuff, really something. Not my thing, but magnificent. It's set up so it sways a little bit in the wind, almost like a mobile but not really."

"There a short version of this long story?" Marjorie says.

"Right," Teddy says. "Sorry. Anyway, they have this sculpture moved at the end of the summer, and these art storage guys came first thing this morning to crate it up and haul it away. With a crane and everything. Our boy was out there chatting it up with the crew, must've dropped his phone in the back of one of the flatbeds. Fell out of his pocket or something. Wasn't until we were out on the river that he realized he didn't have it. It ended up, he borrowed my buddy's phone and was able to track it to the storage facility."

"There you go," Marjorie says, almost patronizing. "Long story short. Wasn't so hard."

Teddy doesn't notice her tone, keeps talking, tells Marjorie what a great day they had on the water, tells her about the fish they caught, the caterer he brought in, the wine they've been drinking, all that. Tells her Harrison doesn't know what he's missing.

"So, basically, you called to worry me and then you called back a bunch of times to tell me not to worry?" Marjorie says, at the first opening in Teddy's account.

"Basically."

"And Harry sounded okay to you? Had a place to stay? All good?"

"Was just a text," Teddy says. "But yeah, he's fine."

Marjorie has put the call on speaker so she can scroll through her history to see if she'd maybe missed a call from Harrison—notices a series of texts from a number she doesn't recognize, telling her it's him on a borrowed phone, telling her he misses her. Nothing about having too much to drink and not being able to drive back to Park City—just, he misses her, and to call him back on the borrowed line.

"Anything else?" Marjorie says. "It's late."

"That's it," Teddy says, still on speaker. "Sorry to freak you out but didn't want you to freak out, know what I mean?"

Marjorie guesses she does.

Joanna leans into her parents' bedroom as her mother cuts the call.

"I heard voices," she says. "Daddy okay?"

"Just Uncle Teddy," Marjorie says. "Telling me Daddy lost his phone. He's fine."

"He calls in the middle of the night to tell you Daddy's fine?"

"Long story," Marjorie says—but unlike Teddy, she has no plans to tell it. Instead, she clicks on the unknown number from Harrison's texts and hears her call go straight to voicemail.

"Who are you calling?" Joanna says.

"Trying Daddy," Marjorie says. "I just want to hear his voice." In trying not to freak her out, Teddy has got her thinking there might have been something to those late-afternoon texts, Harrison telling her he misses her, telling her to call. *It's not like him*, she thinks. *He calls when there's something to say.*

"Thought you said he's fine," Joanna says.

"Yes," Marjorie says. "He's fine. We should go back to sleep."

What she wants to say is that when you get a call in the middle of the night, the thing to do is line up the people you love for a headcount, make sure everyone is where they should be, doing what they should be doing. More and more, this is how she looks at her life, now that these small people she and Harrison somehow raised are getting bigger, more independent. She takes attendance. It's her thing, a baseline condition, and what she wants to tell Joanna is that someday she will know what it's like to knit yourself to a partner, to your children, in such a way that when you pull on the thread of one, you pull on the threads of the others.

What she wants for her children is to know that the voice of reason doesn't always tell you what you want to hear.

"I'm up," Joanna says.

"Me too," they hear from Stewie, who has somehow skulked into his parents' bedroom without being noticed. "You people are loud."

"Sorry, Stew-pot," Marjorie says, folding down the covers on Harrison's side of the bed and patting his pillow, as in an invitation. "Movie night?"

Stewie doesn't have to be asked twice. He dive-bombs from the foot of the bed onto his father's half of the mattress, like he is six or seven instead of thirteen and about to be counted as an adult member of his synagogue community.

"It's, like, three in the morning," Joanna says—not exactly declining her mother's invitation so much as placing it in context.

Marjorie scooches to Stewie and leaves room on her side for Joanna. Then she reaches for the remote control, which she believes has been kicked beneath the covers at or around the bed's equator.

Stewie finds the remote and hands it to his mother. "Something good," he says. "The movies you pick always suck. They're always in black and white."

"What's wrong with black and white?" Marjorie says. "It makes you pay attention to the story."

"B-o-o-o-r-i-n-g," Stewie says in a singsong.

He bounces out of bed to wake Sydney, and Marjorie is touched at his impulse to make room in this moment for his twin sister.

Joanna heads downstairs to make popcorn, leaving Marjorie to scroll through the offerings on TCM and Netflix, thinking maybe the kids might like *East of Eden*, thinking maybe they might see something of themselves in what she remembers as a story about acceptance and fitting in, thinking maybe Joanna and Sydney and even Stewie might thrill in the discovery of James Dean, thinking maybe she hit on the idea of the movie from the way her head had just been filled with The Eagles and that everything is connected, her thoughts all ajumble and at the same time aligned in this perfect way, this picture-perfect way that makes it so the fullness of this wee-hours moment with her children is just about everything.

19.

THE SAME CIGARETTES AS ME

HARRISON KLOTT

IT IS, HE BELIEVES, an elegant solution.

His father's money was never real to him, was never truly his, so when it occurs to Harrison Klott to dangle it in exchange for his release and for the release of the Koons into his care, it does not feel to him like he's giving anything away.

"Your name's not really Clem," he says to the art storage guy who's been holding him at this mountain farm for the past few hours while their situations come into focus.

Lem Devlin shakes his head.

"We go through a bank, they'll need a real name to make a wire transfer," Klott says.

"I get that," Lem says.

"We don't go through a bank, it gets tricky," Klott says. "Cash is in New York."

Lem gets that, too. "Not agreeing to anything," he says. "Just hearing you out."

They talk about it some more. For a couple hours now, they've been talking about it, and Klott is no closer to believing this is a good idea than he was when he first gave it voice, if it's even workable, and on the other side of the conversation the art storage guy who's name isn't really Clem is no closer to believing the half million is enough to make the job worth his while or that the money itself won't leave him even more exposed than he already is.

The setting sun has lit this remote spread with the embers of the day, and as Klott sits across from his captor by the open door to the refurbished barn, he cannot remember losing the full light. At another time, in another circumstance, he might be struck by the landscape, by the way the leaves on the hillside have started to burst into umber and rust—but at this time, in this circumstance, what hits him is that it's become hard to see. In one moment, the sun hung full overhead, and in the next it had dipped behind the Wasatch peaks across the way, and now the two men are almost in shadow and it feels to Klott as if he is lost, without tether.

He thinks back to how his elegant solution took shape. They were an hour or so into this unlikely standoff, this guy threatening him with a crowbar but not really threatening him with a crowbar, holding him hostage but not really holding him hostage. He's no expert on criminal behavior, but he could see this guy Clem had no exit strategy—if he'd had one going in, it disappeared the moment Klott stumbled onto the scene. Klott could also see that the more he pressed on what the sculpture might be worth, on how or where this guy Clem planned to find a buyer, on why he hadn't lined one up beforehand, the more this guy Clem seemed to realize he'd be sitting on this piece for a long-ass while. Probably, it took seeing his situation through another set of eyes for the timeline to become clear. Best case, he'd have this enormous, iconic sculpture by this world-famous artist, and no way to sell it or display it or realize any return on his investment. Worst case, he'd have these rich assholes from the house in Park City wondering what the hell had happened to their friend and to the balloon dog that had been lifted from their front yard while they all stood and watched.

Either way, he was beat—stuck.

Somewhere in there, Klott hit on the idea of a trade. That's how he was thinking of it at the time—something he had and didn't quite know what to do with in exchange for this other something this guy Clem had and didn't quite know what to do with. Wasn't thinking whether he'd hold onto the sculpture, or sell it himself, or return it to Teddy's brother-in-law. Wasn't thinking that far ahead. He was only thinking his father's money could maybe buy his way out of this.

He'd just put it out there—said, "I've got five hundred thousand, cash, back in New York."

The guy said, "Yeah, so?"

Klott said, "So, it will cover your costs and leave you a decent payday."

He surprised himself, a little, with the forceful way he shared his thinking, and with the concomitant idea that he might not be so quick to call the cops or return the sculpture to Teddy's brother-in-law if this guy bit on the offer. Oh, he was not wired in the kinds of ways that would leave him holding onto the Koons indefinitely, but a part of him relished the thought that it might be in his control for just a short while. Shit, he could keep the thing for a week and still be a kind of hero to Teddy and his group at the other end of the deal—and during that time he could fool himself into believing he was the sort of person who deserved to own a magnificent sculpture by a famous artist, valued at more than he could ever hope to earn over the rest of his life.

He could sit here, at the top of this mountain, breathing the same air as these other assholes, imagining his life had gone in some other way. It would not be real, but it would be something—satisfaction, of a kind.

The guy said, "Five hundred thousand? What, this is a negotiation?" Like he couldn't believe such a lowball number. Like it was an insult—to him, to Koons . . . to the art world, even.

Klott said, "Not a negotiation. It's just what I have." Then he told the story about his father's condition, his suitcase, and Klott's windfall of cash.

"No idea where it came from?" the guy said. "The money?"

Klott shook his head, said the best he's come up with is Jai Alai. Said his old man was a regular, loved to bet a boxed quinella, had a system—thinking out loud, working the same puzzle he's been working for the past six months, letting someone else try on his theory.

Despite himself, despite these circumstances, Klott found it easy to talk to this curious art thief. Despite the crowbar, he wasn't menacing. Despite his apparent upper hand, he wasn't superior. He asked questions and pursued lines of thought that had nothing to do with getting what he wanted—a quality Klott found refreshing.

"That's a whole lotta of bets, coming in," the guy said.

"Went every day," Klott said, "for a whole lotta years. Said it was mostly about the math, where you are in the lineup. Said, over time, it's the guys in the second, third, or fourth positions who finish in the money."

The two men sat in silence for the next while, and Klott's thoughts ran to how his life might look if he ended up with the balloon dog. It surprised him, a little, that he thought the sculpture might lift him in some way from the life he had made, the person he had become.

Lem seemed to guess what Klott was thinking. He said, "What—a guy like you deserves to have this world-class work of art, from this world-class artist?"

Klott smiled. "Define *have*," he said.

"*Hold*, maybe, is more like it," Lem said. "For the moment."

"Is that so bad?" Klott said. "Me wanting what's just out of reach? I should be shot, right?"

"Was thinking a crowbar to the skull."

"Funny."

"Not fucking funny."

"No," Klott said. "Nothing funny except that my friend's brother-in-law paid whatever he paid for that balloon dog."

"The fuck is wrong with people, right?"

"People in general or people with money?" Klott said.

"People in general. How we treat each other."

"Said the man with the crowbar."

The guy shot past the joke and kept going, like he was riffing on something he'd been busting to say—not to Klott, necessarily, but to the universe. "Like, you know, what we decide to call art," he said, letting his opinions run from simmer to boil. "What money can buy. What it can't buy. How it changes us, how it doesn't. How some of us, we work and work and never get ahead, we're just chasing, and some of us, we roll out of bed and the world comes to us."

With that, they were back on the value of the Koons, on how this guy had set it up so this job would make some kind of statement, maybe clarify his thinking on where and how he fits in this world. Yeah, it was meant to be easy money, retire to Fiji money, get out from under money, and the balloon dog was just asking to be taken, but that was only a part of it. Mostly, it was a *fuck you* to the people who make all the money. Whatever else this guy was expecting to get out of this deal, he wasn't prepared to give up on any of it just yet. "Thing is worth ten million, easy," he said.

"That was before," Klott said—again surprising himself with how he was playing it cool.

"Before what?" the guy said.

"Before I showed up."

"Fuckin' tell me about it."

They went back and forth on this and it became clear to Klott that this guy didn't want to hurt him, had never meant to hurt him, didn't have it in him to hurt him, and was only trying to hold the door open until he could see a way out. What sealed it for Klott was how, after a long silence, the guy lifted a beer to him in salute and said, "Sorry to hear about your dad, man. Fuckin' Alzheimer's."

By this point, the sun had dropped behind the nearest peak and their shadows had grown long, the light dimmed to where Klott couldn't make out the expression on this guy's face, the look in his eyes, but he was struck by the comment. A guy who says something like that, Klott thought, a situation like this, the bad way it's gone, he's not about to beat you with a crowbar, and from there it was as if a switch had flipped and the two of them were now working together on this. It went from good guy versus bad guy to a couple guys just sitting around bullshitting over beers, figuring their way through a shared mess.

Klott wasn't sure his captor saw the situation in the same way, but at least now there was this set of hopeful outcomes they could line up against all these other outcomes. First thing Klott was able to do with this apparent shift in their relationship was to get this guy to see the danger in keeping him here on this mountain, his asshole buddies expecting him back in Park City, the day slouching away from them and into tomorrow. Or, maybe not danger so much as foolishness. This was how he put it, trying to sound reassuring: "Nobody's looking for the Koons. Not yet. But I've been here a while already. It's late. They don't hear from me, they might start to worry."

They, meaning his friends at the house—the people this guy seemed to want to stick it to by stealing the sculpture, the people Klott seemed to want to impress by rescuing the sculpture . . . by keeping it, even.

Klott heard himself as he said this, and he could not even convince himself of his own argument, because on all these trips with Teddy's friends, all these years, it's never felt to him like he belongs among this group, and so a part of him believed it was entirely possible for him to stay the night on this mountain and that it wouldn't be until Simon the divorce attorney realized he didn't have his personal phone with him at the breakfast table tomorrow or until this Marco person needed a title for some other bullshit reality show concept he wanted to "develop" that anyone would notice he was missing.

Still, he was able to keep these self-doubts to himself, and to get this guy Clem to see that Klott should probably come up with some story, let his buddies know he was okay. They weren't agreeing on anything, and there was no clear path forward, no clean way to move a half million dollars from this kind of long distance, but they could send a text and buy some time.

"You can send it yourself on my phone," Klott said, still thinking he was some kind of hostage. "The text. Make sure I'm not trying to signal them or anything."

He explained how there was an active text thread with the whole group, and how it made sense to attach this text to the thread, make it seem like no big thing.

It was at this point that Klott's captor stood and crossed the threshold into the barn to hit the lights—a pair of outdoor floods, mounted above the barn door and pointing this way and that—and in the harsh light their situation became even more apparent.

The story they came up with was a version of the truth: Klott had come looking for his phone, had got to talking with this guy he'd met back at the house that morning, had a couple beers, and was in no shape to drive. This guy Clem wrote the text himself but showed it to Klott before he hit *SEND*, to make sure it sounded like him, and within just a couple minutes there was a string of hardly clever texts in response about how Harrison Klott never could hold his liquor, how they were going to have to ground him for missing curfew, how he'll have to pass the oatmeal test before they let him back in the house.

"The fuck's an oatmeal test?" this guy Clem asked, as Klott's text thread filled.

Klott explained how that one must have been from his friend Teddy, the guy whose brother-in-law owned the house, said it was a running gag from back in school that they got from a book by James Crumley, the crime novelist. "We used to read the shit out of him," he said, and then he explained how there was a character in one of Crumley's books whose wife or girlfriend suspected him of chronic infidelity and was in the habit of making him drop his pants when he'd come home late from a night on the town so she could toss a fistful of dried oatmeal at his junk. "If the oatmeal stuck, he was in trouble," Klott said.

"Don't remember that one," this guy Clem said.

"You read Crumley?" Klott said, trying to mask his astonishment.

"What, a working man can't read?"

"Never said that. It's just, most working men don't usually read Crumley . . . I'm guessing."

"Fair enough," Lem said.

Klott went on to tell how the oatmeal test became a thing, all through college, whenever one of his fraternity brothers rolled into the house after a late night—only, they used baby powder instead of oatmeal. "The oatmeal was a bitch to clean up," he explained, and as this guy Clem powered down the phone in case anyone thought to track its location, Klott got to thinking how easy it was to fall into conversation with this apparently good-hearted and decidedly well-read art bandit, who apparently understood the truthfulness of a Jeff Koons sculpture alongside the ruthlessness of a James Crumley novel—and, hoping they were not so fucked, the two of them, that they couldn't find a way to pass the oatmeal tests that lay in wait.

———————

They are silent for a while. There is nothing to talk about and everything to talk about, but underneath all of that talking and not talking they get their heads around the idea that there is no way out or around or through whatever they're facing unless they find a way to trust each other. Klott is prepared to trust that this guy wouldn't hurt him or his family—he has no choice!—but he doesn't know how to tell him his friend's brother-in-law probably has a giant insurance policy to cover the Koons. He starts to explain how the loss of this famous balloon dog sculpture will be more of an inconvenience than a devastation to these people, but then he gets to thinking that if he piles on all these explanations and justifications, it might sound like he's lobbying, saving his own ass—or worse, like he's trying to buy the piece out from under him.

Klott works the situation in his head to where it truly does start to feel like a negotiation, only the terms under discussion have nothing to do with what the Koons is worth or what he can pay for it. What's being negotiated, he's realizing, is how they might lift each other from where they are to where they hope to be.

An opportunity for Klott to stand and be counted—in his own mind, at least—among the angel investors and divorce attorneys and plush toy magnates of the world . . . *that's* what's on the table.

A way for the other guy to cut his losses and make it so his grand theft is not a total bust . . . *that*, too.

"Name's Lem," Klott's captor says, letting it be known that he's prepared to trust Klott on this—with his name, anyway. He holds out his hand. "Lem Devlin."

"So, not Clem?" Klott says, shaking his hand.

"Not Clem."

"Jesus, you really outdid yourself with that alias." He hopes to come across as smart-alecky, playful. He's not afraid of this guy, this Lem, but Klott guesses he must be spooked by his situation, so his play is to make like he belongs.

Lem laughs and says, "Fuck you."

"Yes," Klott says. "Fuck me. I am well and truly fucked." Then, "Don't think I ever met a Lem."

"Short for Lemuel," Lem says. "Like Lemuel Gulliver."

"That's his full name?" Klott says. "From *Gulliver's Travels*?"

Lem nods. "That's where my mother got the name." He explains that she's a school librarian in New Mexico, where he's from. *Was* a school librarian, before she retired. Says she meant for him to feel like he was a giant, a mountain among men, destined to live a big, full life.

"A school librarian, huh?" Klott says, like he's never heard of such a thing.

"What, working class people don't read? Working class people are just a drain on the upper class?"

"No, you're just international art thieves."

"Touché, motherfucker," Lem says, laughing again. "*Tou fucking shay.* Put me in my place."

His tone is softer, easier than it's been since Klott arrived, and Klott thinks it might be the beers—that, or the bad-guy-turned-not-so-bad-guy is getting comfortable with the idea of a half million dollars for the day's work and the planning that went into it. When he laughs, his body seems to shake with alarm.

"Ha," Klott says. "And my place is on the side of this mountain with an impulsive art bandit who reads Crumley and Swift."

(He leaves off the Hemingway, from the shirt.)

What's supposed to happen next would be so much clearer if Klott had his father's cash with him here in Utah instead of tucked into the drop ceilings and crawl spaces of his house in the fat middle of Long Island. This presents a problem. He'd mentioned the idea of a wire transfer early on, but he's not sure how that can work and still keep Lem out of trouble. Earlier this year, he and Marjorie had opened a line of credit at Wells Fargo, after their financial advisor said it would be a good thing for them to have at the ready as they prepared to send their oldest off to college. Klott's thinking at the time was that it didn't cost anything to apply, and that money was cheap to borrow, so they filled out an application. The money would be there if they needed it. Far as he knows, the line is big enough to cover the half million.

"We do a wire transfer, there's a paper trail," Klott says, telling Lem what he already knows. "There's taxes, questions."

"And cash?" Lem says.

"The cash is two thousand miles away."

"Fuck."

It also presents the problem of Klott having to tell Marjorie about the money. If he draws on their margin account, she'll get an alert, so if he doesn't get to her first with an alert of his own, he'll catch all kinds of shit. He ends his trip early, shows up announced to harvest all that cash, he'll have to explain himself. Already, he's been thinking he needs to tell Marjorie about his father's money—already, he's reached out to her on Simon's phone to do just that.

"There someone you need to talk to?" Klott says—thinking, maybe he gets this guy talking about the fallout that might be waiting for him on his end he can get him to see the fallout on Klott's end. "You have a partner on this deal? Someone needs to know, the shit we're in?"

"There's one guy," Lem says. "Wanted me to carry a gun, in case the job went bad."

"Sucks for me," Klott says, still trying to play it cool and smart-alecky, even in the face of this bad-guy partner inclined to do him in for being in the wrong place at the wrong time.

"Sucks all around," Lem says—then, "What about you, Harrison Klott? Someone you need to call, freeing up all that money? Wife or something?"

"Or something," Klott says.

━━━━━━━━

Lem can't believe it when Klott tells him he hasn't told his wife about the money. "You are so fucked," he says.

"I am so fucked," Klott says.

"What, it never came up?"

"'Oh, by the way, here's a half million in cash,'" Klott says in a voice meant to sound like he's in an Improv class and the reality of his father's cash is the setup. "Could never find the right time," he says. "The right way."

"You just come out and say it."

Klott snorts, swallows a laugh and says, "You married?"

Lem shakes his head.

"A half million dollars, out of nowhere, it's hard to explain. But then, you don't say something right away, it's even harder. You dig yourself a hole," Klott says. "That's, like, Marriage 101. The longer it goes, the deeper the hole."

He stands, stretches, looks at his watch.

"Been a long day," Lem says, noticing. "We callin' it?"

It hadn't occurred to Klott he'd be staying the night, but now that it has, it seems obvious. Nothing has been resolved. There are still a number of ways this thing can turn. There is no place for him to go. They can stay up all night, talking it through, or they can sleep on it.

"There a spare bedroom?" he says.

"What, this is the Holiday Fucking Inn?" Lem says. "Under the stars, amigo."

This is concerning to Harrison Klott—a man who has not slept under the stars since summer camp, and then only under the guidance of a trip counselor who knew his way around the Adirondack wilderness. Here, in these mountains, there are moose, elk, deer. Surely, there are racoons. Probably, there are mountain lions. Bears.

Lem looks over at Klott's Acura and says, "Those seats recline?"

"Far as I know," Klott says.

The two men walk to the rented SUV to see if the seats lay flat or close enough to flat to allow for even a fitful sleep. Klott sits himself in the driver's seat and leans back.

Lem stands by the driver side door and says, "Open the sunroof at least. Get some fresh mountain air." Like he's playing host.

Klott had left the key fob in the console when he pulled onto this pasture earlier in the evening, so he steps on the brake to ignite the battery and slide the roof open. Then he lays back and tries to get comfortable.

"You good?" Lem says.

"Good enough," Klott says.

Lem turns to walk back to the barn, where he means to lay out on one of the drop cloths from the bed of his truck.

Klott calls out to him: "Forget something?"

Lem retraces his steps to the Acura and sees Klott reaching out to him with the Acura key fob.

"In case I decide to make a run for it," Klott says.

Lem collects the key fob and turns it over a time or two in his hand before fisting it into the pocket of his jeans—says, "Motherfucker."

Klott wonders why he said anything about the key fob, why he didn't drive off as Lem stepped away from the car. Why it didn't even occur to him. He wonders what Marjorie would think. She's always talking about the fight-or-flight instinct, about the ways her students respond to moments of stress or danger, and here he's showing a giant case of neither. It's like his strategy is to play this thing out, see if it can't maybe change the spin on his days. Like he's in it already, with no way out that doesn't involve this Lem person.

"Can I give you a phone charger?" Klott says—thinking there'll be another opportunity in the morning to disentangle himself from this mess. "Is there a power outlet in the barn? I should probably charge my phone."

"Yours or the other guy's?"

"Mine," Klott says, handing Lem the phone charger. "Should work on both, if you have time. Maybe switch them out, middle of the night, if you get up to take a leak."

Lem nods. "That it?" he says. "Cup of warm milk and some cookies?"

"That's it."

Klott watches as Lem walks back to the barn and is held by the way he's silhouetted by the twin flood lights against the clear night sky. He's not a big man, Lem, but the effect leaves him looking larger than life, all-powerful . . . perhaps even ethereal. To Klott, Lem's disappearing form appears before him as an apparition, a man-mountain among these jagged peaks, ruling over this remote patch of land like his life depends on it, in a way that leaves Klott thinking he's not really here at all.

━━━━━━

Here's where they are, what can happen next: Lem can let Klott return to his buddies in Park City and trust that he keeps his mouth shut; Lem can accompany Klott on a cross-country drive to New York in the rented Acura to collect the cash; Klott can persuade Marjorie to harvest the cash from his hiding places around the house and drive the money out to Utah; Klott can wire the money from his Wells Fargo margin account to any number of accounts in Guadalajara, where it turns out Lem has a childhood buddy who owns a legit steel manufacturing business through a number of less-than-legit shell accounts.

One more thing: Lem can tie Klott to one of the aspens rimming the property with the length of rope from his truck bed and leave him to the bears or mountain lions or maybe wait for his partner with the gun to drive up from Salt Lake or wherever and put a bullet in him.

These are the main scenarios bumping into each other inside Klott's brain as he sits and fidgets in the driver seat of his Acura rental. There's no way he can sleep, with everything going on. It's like he's ten years old and has been shaken awake by that same trip counselor from summer camp, rousing his charges in the middle of the night to tell them their supplies are being ransacked by a family of racoons and not to worry because they'll be gone at first light. Not to worry? How the fuck is Klott supposed to not worry? He's backdoored his way into a heist of a ten-million-dollar sculpture by a world-renowned artist, being run up close by a well-read thief who for a time had seemed to want to beat him with a crowbar and by another guy behind-the-scenes who would surely want him dead if he knew the deal.

He doesn't belong in the middle of any of this, Klott... and yet, here he is.

He wishes he was back home, struggling over the new winter menu for his one and only client, helping Stewie and Sydney study their Torah readings for next week, getting Joanna to maybe start thinking of topics for her college admissions essay. He wishes he was in bed, with Marjorie sleeping next to him, her whistling breaths reaching him from across her pillow like something from his own mouth.

Klott can't say where Lem is leaning. The guy doesn't have a tell. He laughs easily, jokes easily, but there was no reading him in the dim light last night. If it was up to him, Klott would vote for any outcome that doesn't involve a crowbar or a gun or violence of any kind. Next, it shouldn't involve wiring the money from his margin account, because it will forever tie him to this episode and to Lem and his partners on this deal. Whatever happens, here on in, he'll be a part of it. Klott doesn't care about his father's money or having to pay taxes on his father's money once he uses it to pay off the margin loan. It's that he'll never be free and clear of this fucking balloon dog, of these men who tried to steal it. The rest of his life, he'll be looking over his shoulder, worried for his family. Clearly, it's best for him if he pays Lem in cash, but there's no way he can ask Marjorie to take a couple days off work to drive all the way out here. No way she'd understand the mess he's in. Now that he's thinking in this way, he realizes that Teddy is the only other person he could tap to run this kind of errand for him, and he's already out here, probably dead asleep between his brother-in-law's Egyptian-cotton sheets, 1200 thread count, completely unaware that this magnificent sculpture has gone missing on his watch or that his college roommate has been press-ganged into complicity, and he wonders how it is that he's shot past fifty and there are only two people in his life he could ask to drop what they're doing and drive cross-country to save his ass, no questions asked, and that he's unable to call on either one of them.

The way Klott sees it, the best course is some kind of road trip to New York, him and Lem driving straight through. They could probably make it there by tomorrow night with a couple pit stops. Klott figures he can fix it with the rental car company, drop the car in New York, but that doesn't get Lem back to Salt Lake City or Guadalajara or wherever he means to go from here.

This is why he's never pursued a life of crime, Klott thinks—too many moving parts, too many variables to consider.

To be sure, there's really nothing for Klott to consider. This is not his job to run, so he doesn't get a vote. He's just the innocent bystander trying to clamber from whatever hole he's in. He's put it out there, about the money, about the hoops they'd each have to jump through to get the money, so now it's up to Lemuel Devlin to decide his next move.

By the time Lem emerges from his drop cloth bedroll at first light, Klott can see from his purposeful stride as he walks toward the car that he has been playing out these same options in his head, knows what's involved, knows what's at stake, and has come up with a strategy. He taps on the driver side window of the Acura. "Rise and shine, motherfucker."

Klott motions for Lem to step back from the car so he can open the door. "I'm up." He unfolds himself from the seat.

Lem hands him his phone, presumably charged. "We got some calls to make," he says.

"Who we calling?" Klott says.

"The ball and chain."

Lem tells Klott he's decided to take his $500,000 offer, seeing how the job has turned to shit and that it was probably shit to begin with. He seems resigned to it. He says the two days it would take to drive to collect the cash are two days too many, and that the wire transfer is the way to go. He says he spoke to his buddy in Monterrey and there should be no problem with him collecting the money in a way that doesn't tie anyone to the Koons. He'd been thinking of heading to Mexico to join him, maybe start in on something new.

Klott wants to understand his captor's thinking, how the day will go, here on in. "And you want me to say what, exactly? To my wife?"

"Up to you, man," Lem says. "Need you to get right with her before we send the wire, you know."

"What about the money you were hoping to make on the Koons?"

"Like you said, not a negotiation. This is what you have. I can't string you up for what you don't have."

"And your partner? The guy who wanted you to carry a gun?"

Lem says to let him worry about that, says the money sounds richer when you turn it into pesos. "Five hundred thousand is, like, ninety-five million pesos," he says. "Money goes a long way down there."

"You'll leave Utah?" Klott says.

"For now," Lem says. "Till I run out of pesos." He laughs, in the joyful, full-body way Klott has quickly come to appreciate. "Fuck Utah."

Klott considers this a moment, how a shift in perspective can make a half million look like almost a hundred million, and then indicates his presumably charged phone and says, "Don't suppose you'll let me make this call in private."

"Sorry, Harrison Klott," Lem says. "Not in my best interests. Put it on speaker."

"I can tell her everything?" Klott says. Just to be clear.

"You can tell her what you need to tell her."

The sun is just up. Klott presses Marjorie's number on his speed dial, can't think how the call will go.

"You found your phone," Marjorie says, picking up.

"I found my phone," Klott says.

"It's early," she says. "Everything alright?"

"Everything's alright," he says. "Thought I'd catch you, before school."

"Teddy called last night. Late. Freaked me out."

"Jesus, Margie Bear. Sorry."

"Saw a bunch of your texts, from earlier. Freaked me out, too."

"Didn't mean to worry you," Klott says. "Teddy was looking for me?"

"He was. Then he called to say he wasn't. Said you met up with some guy who had your phone, said you had a couple drinks, didn't want to drive."

Klott holds the phone out for Lem, like he's saying, "See," like the device itself now validates their decision last night to send that group text.

"Just trying to be smart," he says—to Marjorie and Lem both, he supposes.

"What else?" she says. "There's something else."

"The something else is something I've been meaning to tell you," he says, and then he goes into it. The part about his father leading him to the key to the storage facility, the part about chasing down his old man's suitcase, driving the money from Florida to New York, hiding it all over the house, and not knowing what to do with it or what to make of it or how to even talk about it—mostly, the part about knowing how each day he didn't talk about it with Marjorie made it harder to have the conversation he knew he needed to have.

"Jesus, Harry," Marjorie says, when Klott pauses to catch his breath.

"I know, right?" he says. "I'm so sorry."

"Hymie?"

"It's like one of those obituaries you read in the paper," Klott says. "Some shoeshine man hoards his tips for fifty years, leaves a couple hundred thousand in coins and singles for the local children's hospital."

"Jesus, Harry, he's not dead yet."

"No," Klott says. "But you know what I mean."

"And those texts from yesterday?" she says. "You're telling me now because . . ." Like she's leading him to what he needs to say.

"Right, that," he says. "Don't you have, like, your morning staff meeting at nine?"

"Fuck my morning staff meeting at nine. Tell me what's going on, Harry."

He tells her what's going on, tells her he's in trouble but he's okay, tells her about the Koons, the bad guy who threatened him with a crowbar, the other bad guy who wants to threaten him with a gun. He tells her how the first bad guy turned out to be not so bad after all, how the two of them got to drinking and talking and started to see they were inside the same jam, and how Klott came up with this idea about his father's money.

"You idiots just stood around and watched them dismantle this giant sculpture?" she says, trying to process.

"It wasn't like that," Klott says. "But, yeah."

"And now you're, like, buying it back? With the five hundred thousand dollars I didn't even know we had?"

"It's not like that, either. But, yeah."

"And why shouldn't I call the police?" she says. "Tell Teddy and them?"

Klott flashes Lem a look that tell him not to worry, he's on this.

"Because you're on speaker phone," Klott says. "Because my guy gets it in his head that this is what's in your head, I'm fucked."

Silence for a few beats.

"And you're okay?" she says, pressing, the worry in her voice coming through the tinny speaker of Klott's phone. "You're not in danger? Nobody's threatening you with a crowbar?"

"There's no immediate crowbar threat. I'm okay. We'll be okay. I'll use my father's money to pay off the margin loan when I get back. It'll be like that money never happened. The kids will have their *simcha* next week and we'll find a way to pay for Joanna's college and it'll be like this whole thing never happened."

Klott has run out of things to say. It feels to him like he's covered everything.

"He's listening in, the guy who stole the balloon dog?" Marjorie says, after another small silence.

Klott turns to Lem, who smiles not quite menacingly, and waves, not quite cheerfully.

"He is," Klott says.

"The one with the crowbar? He have a name?"

Klott looks once again to Lem, who's shaking head. "No name," Klott says. "Just, Bad Guy Number One."

"No jokes, Klott," Marjorie says. "This is a lot."

"I know," Klott says. "And there's more, probably. Stuff I'm forgetting. But we can't talk about this. Not to anyone. This guy is trusting me. Trusting you."

"That safe word we used, when the twins were little?" Marjorie says. "Remember?"

Klott remembers. They were up all night, one after the other. Every night. For the first couple months. They were like zombies, him and Marjorie, tag-teaming, trying to take care of Joanna and these restless twins. Trying to work, keep the household going. And somewhere in the middle of all that craziness they came up with this signal, the two of them, meant to remind them that they were in this together. That everything was going to be okay. One of them would say the word "scaffolding" and the other would know that all was right with their little world.

Klott remembers the word but doesn't remember where it came from, or which one of them had come up with it. Probably, it came from a book one of them was trying to read, or a children's book they were trying to read to Joanna before her bedtime. Probably, it had to do with the ways they were meant to lift each other up or stand on each other's shoulders. Probably, it was meant to remind them that whatever shit-hot mess they were in was only temporary, and that they just needed to keep lifting each other up while the life they were building was still under construction.

"I remember," he says.

"And?" Marjorie says.

"Scaffolding," he says.

"Scaffolding," she says. She sounds pissed but not pissed—like it's an everyday thing, to be alarmed in the middle of the night because your husband has maybe gone missing, only to find out in the morning that he's not really missing but has somehow agreed to transfer a half million dollars you didn't even know you had to an art thief who has apparently overestimated his ability to fence a famous sculpture of a red balloon dog that is supposedly worth over ten million dollars.

Yes, this is a lot. And certainly, there is so very much more to be discussed, but Klott gets from the way Lem now reaches for the phone that it's time to move on, so Klott quickly explains to Marjorie that she might get a call from their guy at Wells Fargo, Moshe, needing her to confirm the transfer.

"Tell him it's for a personal loan," he says. "There are some documents we'll need to sign, 'cause the money's going to Mexico, but for now just say that. A personal loan."

"Scaffolding," she says again. "A personal loan. Got it."

"Love you," Klott says.

"Love you," Marjorie says.

Lem cuts the call.

"Maybe we should have a safe word, Harry," he says, turning to Klott. "Me, you, and Margie Bear."

Lem has it all worked out. He's been on the phone all night, his buddy walking him through it. He says, "You call your guy at Wells Fargo. Tell him you have a friend in Mexico looking to start a business. In Guadalajara. Tell him you and your wife have agreed to front him a personal loan. We can get him paperwork, a promissory note, whatever he needs."

"You talk to your partner?" Klott says. "Dude with the gun."

"Not yet," Lem says. "But he'll be fine. I worked it out. Fifty grand or so for expenses. Pay the crew, the equipment rental, the lease on this place. The rest we'll split." He says there are too many eyes on this job, on this sculpture, for it to work in a bigger way, says there are no guarantees. They're already out of pocket and even if they get away with the theft,

they could end up stuck with this fucking balloon dog—all the arguments
Klott had been lining up in his head in favor of some kind of Plan B.

He returns Klott's phone and says, "Time to call Moshe."

Klott does his part, tells his financial advisor he needs him to act on
this, tells him Marjorie is expecting a call if he needs confirmation, gives
him the wiring instructions. Tells him, "I know this is unusual, but I need
you to do this for me. For us. As quickly as possible. No questions asked."

"Some questions asked," Moshe says, firm. "I can't lose my job over
this, Harry."

"You won't lose your job," Klott says. "It's all straight. You've known
me how long?"

Moshe lets the question hang, explains how a US to Mexico transfer
requires documentation. "There a Wells Fargo office where you are?" he
asks.

"Possible to do an e-sign?" Klott says. "I'm in the middle of nowhere.
Fishing trip. Can you draft something and send it to me for signature?"

Moshe says he'll need his friend's signature as well.

Klott looks to Lem who offers a slight nod.

"Not a problem," Klott says. Then, "Look, Mosh, I really appreciate
this. Marjorie really appreciates it. Our friends in Mexico, they're
tremendous people. This is a real opportunity for them. I'll fill you in
next time you buy me dinner."

"What makes you think it's my turn to buy dinner?" Moshe says, the
firmness in his voice starting to soften.

"I'm the client."

"Yes," Moshe says. "You're the client. On a fishing trip. In the middle
of nowhere. Needs five hundred thousand dollars, ASAP." He says the
acronym like he's reading it instead of spelling it out: "A-sap." He wonders
if this is now a thing, people under forty pronouncing acronyms.

Lem makes a swirling motion with the index finger of his right hand,
telling Klott to wrap things up, and when he ends the Wells Fargo call,
they move on to the guys at the house, fix it so they're not expecting Klott
to meet up with them until later, maybe see if anyone's still talking about

the sculpture—you know, asking questions. Lem's idea is for Klott to play out the same story from last night, say he's hung over, feeling like shit. In no shape to join them on today's fishing trip.

"Golf, actually," Klott says. "Fishing again tomorrow."

"Must be nice," Lem says. "Staying in that house. Fishing. Playing golf. Probably hitting the wine cellar."

"Not exactly my thing, the rest of the year," Klott says. "I'm just along for the ride."

"Some ride," Lem says. "Golf. You have a tee time?"

Klott says he thinks the group is scheduled for ten o'clock at a course called Soldiers Hollow, outside of Park City, maybe a couple towns over.

"I know where it is," Lem says. "Midway. That's the other direction from here." He looks at his watch. "Still early, but they should be up."

Klott gets Teddy on the phone and says, "Hey, man. Afraid I'm out for golf."

"Say it ain't so," Teddy says, in a voice that sounds only a little bit sorry and mostly like he's performing for the rest of the group. "You get lucky last night? That it?"

"Hardly," Klott says, and he goes into his story.

"Helps with our foursomes, at least," Teddy says—meaning, they were nine and now they are eight. "I called Marjorie last night. Think I scared the crap out of her."

"So I hear," Klott says. "Feel like shit, though. Switched from beers to bourbon at some point, and it's like I've been hit with a crowbar."

He sees Lem giving him the finger over the crowbar line.

"Lightweight," Teddy says.

"That's me," Klott says. "What's going on at the house? I miss anything?"

"Only if you were interested in our friend Brandi, from the river yesterday."

"Meaning?"

"Meaning she's in the pool. In just her panties. As we speak."

"The caterer?" Klott says. "With the ponytail?"

"Cute, right?" Teddy says, and he explains how Alexander and Marco had each invited the girl back to the house after the fish fry, how each had no idea the other was making the same move, how when she showed up later there was a kind of pissing contest between the two of them, fighting for her attention. "Never a dull moment," he says.

"Telling me," Klott says. Then—"So who won? The pissing contest?"

"Both, I think," Teddy says. "They decided to share."

"Animals," Klott says. "She's somebody's daughter."

"Look at you," Teddy says. "All holier than thou, off on your little bender with your new friend, the art dealer."

"Moving and storage," Klott says. "More like a consultant."

"That was something, huh?" Teddy says, meaning how Lem and his guys showed up with their crane and their trucks and disassembled the sculpture.

"That was something."

Lem makes another swirling motion with his finger and Klott gets that he has heard what he wanted to hear, that there's nothing in Teddy's account or in his tone to suggest anyone has any suspicions about the removal of the balloon dog, that this piece of the puzzle has been solved for the moment. Klott signs off and tells Teddy he'll meet the group back at the house for dinner and gets to thinking how it is he's come to spend so much time with these people, and what it was that left him thinking he was better off here with them in Utah than he would have been at home, with his wife and children and his father's money.

"Sorry," he says to Lem, returning the phone. "My friends, they can be assholes."

"Telling me."

20.

TURN AND FACE THE STRANGE

LEM DEVLIN

NOTHING TO DO BUT WAIT.

It's a little past eight-thirty in the morning by the time they set these wheels spinning, and it occurs to Lem he could use a cup of coffee. He tells Klott they're going for a ride.

"We'll take my truck," he says. "You're buying."

"Since when does the hostage buy?" Klott says.

"Since you followed me up here and blew up my spot," Lem says—a half joke he means to signal to Klott that it's on him for the way his plans have been upended.

Lem hears himself and wonders at the easy way he is with this guy from the house. It's like they've known each other for years instead of hours, like they're cut in the same ways instead of the one holding the other against his will. Also, Lem wonders at his own meaning, a line like that, suggesting that this job has gone wrong for reasons that have nothing to do with him. His mother, the school librarian, was always telling him the first step to making his feelings known is to know them himself, but he never had time for that shit. She'd tell him he was being passive-aggressive, and he'd have to look it up later, to see what she meant. He'd shuffle his feet and not ask for what he wanted or not say what he was thinking, and she'd challenge him to live up to his name and reach for what he deserved, and here he is now, making it seem like this guy from the house has maybe fucked up this deal, instead of that the deal was maybe fucked up to begin with.

"We don't have to do this trade," Klott says, responding only to the aggressive part of his captor's demeanor. "The half million, you think you can do better."

"This because I asked you to pick up the coffee?" Lem says—another half joke he means to add to the first to make it whole.

Klott waves the idea away and says, "Because I don't want you thinking I'm getting away with something."

"You get to go home to Margie Bear," Lem says. "That's what you're getting away with."

"Exactly," Klott says. "Your balloon dog wouldn't even fit in my backyard."

"*My* balloon dog?"

"Your balloon dog."

"What, I should keep it then?"

"You keep it, it ties you to the theft. You keep it, it ties you to me. The guys at the house, they'll figure it out. Probably soon."

"Tick fucking tock," Lem says. "You keep it, then what?"

"Then I guess we'll see," Klott says. "Get it back to my friend's brother-in-law, eventually."

"Eventually, as in after you see for yourself if you can sell it?"

"Dude," Klott says. "It's not like that."

It sets Lem off, a little, when middle-aged men with money and privilege try to sound like one of those teenage assholes from those excellent adventure movies. "Dude," he says back. "Provenance."

"Meaning?"

"Provenance," Lem says again, like he's in a spelling bee and is about to use it in a sentence. "How you trace ownership of a piece. Authenticity, you know. Truth."

Klott waits for the rest of the riff as the two men cross to Lem's truck.

It comes soon enough: "Easy to prove authenticity with a Koons, what I've learned. Not a whole lot of people set up to do what he does on this scale. The finish he gets, the way his colors pop and shine, people say it's unmatched."

"So?"

"So, ownership is a bitch. His massive pieces, they sell for massive bucks, there's a paper trail. Someone moves a Koons, it makes news."

"You and your partner, you knew all of this," Klott says.

"Guess I did," Lem says. "But I didn't think of it in just this way. Didn't think it would matter."

"But it matters?" Klott says, his voice lifting as if he's asking a question, even though he already knows the answer."

"Fuckin' A, it matters," Lem says. "People don't want to touch this fucking dog, it turns out. And now there's you, stepping in our dogshit."

"Fuckin' provenance," Klott says.

"Fuckin' provenance," Lem says, his voice trailing off.

The two men race down the mountain in silence, until Lem makes for a convenience store at the bottom of the dirt road, a couple hundred yards past the hand-lettered *THIS WAY* sign. The place calls itself *Eleven Eleven*, and from the signage and the design Lem gets that it was once a 7-Eleven.

"Eleven-eleven," Klott says, noticing the sign, now wanting to talk. "You know what that means?"

"What, motherfucker broke his franchise agreement and was too lazy to repaint and come up with a whole new name?" Lem says.

Klott laughs. "That, maybe. But also, it's the time, twice a day, when angels are near."

Lem considers this for a beat—then says, "That's some New Age bullshit right there. Didn't think you were one of those assholes."

"What kind of asshole you think I was?"

Lem smiles. "Just, regular. A regular asshole."

He slips the truck into one of the angled parking spaces in front of the store and leans his weight into the driver door to open it. Klott opens the passenger door and makes to follow his captor, but Lem calls him back into the cab from across the front seat. "Not you, motherfucker," he says, not unkindly. "You stay in the truck. Just tell me how you like your coffee."

"Black."

"Thought you regular assholes all drink that *mocha latte surprise*-type shit."

"Black is fine," Klott says—then, dutifully, he reaches into his pocket for a twenty-dollar bill and holds it out to Lem.

"Five hundred thousand and twenty," Lem says, grabbing the bill. "Price keeps going up."

———

Lem pumps two coffees from one of the thermos dispensers lined up on a counter in the center of the store, the whole time keeping an eye on the front passenger seat of his truck. He's not thinking the guy from the house will bolt on him, necessarily, but he doesn't want him walking around the parking lot, doesn't want to be seen with him in a public setting. Most convenience stores, there are security cameras and shit. Last thing Lem needs is surveillance footage tying him to his eyewitness.

From the way the truck is angled into its spot, Lem's got a full-on view of Klott through the store window, and he is struck by how this guy is able to sit there, completely still, not even looking around to see if he can maybe make a mad dash or maybe engage in conversation with another customer and signal he's in trouble. No, he's just sitting there, eyes dead ahead, given over to whatever may or may not happen next. To what's already up and happened. If Lem had to bet, he'd put his money on this guy not even thinking of stepping away from whatever it is he's stepped into.

Lem thinks again of the way his mother used to dismiss his behavior, thinks maybe there's some of that same personality shit going on with Harrison Klott. The guy is passive about not wanting to upset the situation, not wanting to make any move to free himself—like, last night when he called Lem back to the car to give him the key fob. And he's aggressive about buying his way out with his half million, saying how the Koons and the lease on the farm should be part of the deal. He sets it up so he gets what he wants without pushing his way to what he wants.

There's a jerky display by the cash register, so Lem grabs a couple vacuum-packed sticks to add to his order—says, "This stuff any good?"

The clerk behind the counter says, "We sell a bunch."

"A four-star review," Lem says, amusing himself. "Should put it on the package."

He catches Klott's attention as he leaves the store and motions for him to roll down his window. Then he hands over one of the coffees and holds out the jerky sticks and says, "Elk or turkey?"

Klott chooses the turkey. "Breakfast of champions."

Lem motions for him to roll his window back up and steps away from the truck, indicates with his phone in his outstretched hand that he has to make a call. He steps beneath the small overhang and sets his coffee on the narrow ledge framing the picture window that dominates the storefront. He leans back and presses Duck's number from his contact list.

"We rich yet?" Duck says, when the call goes through.

"Not exactly," Lem says.

"Tell me."

Lem tells him. About the trouble he's already seeing, trying to move the Koons. About the guy from the house who tracked his phone to the farm. About the five hundred thousand.

"You mean, like a ransom?" Duck says.

"Like a ransom," Lem says, "only we walk away from the Koons, from the lease, the whole deal."

"So, a consolation prize?"

"Call it what you want."

"What's he need with the art, this guy?"

"Says he needs to know I'm gone. Says it makes it so I won't come looking for him."

"Makes no sense," Duck says. "Sculpture or not, you can come looking for him."

Lem says he takes Duck's point, but it's about seeing this job from another perspective. Seeing how it could be months, years before he'd be able to move this piece. Seeing how there will now be all these other eyes on them—on him. Seeing how this is what makes this guy comfortable, you know.

"We can take care of this guy, you know," Duck says—saying what needs to be said without really saying it.

"We're not taking care of this guy, Duck," Lem says, hard, flat. "We're in the fine art consignment business."

"The fuck is that?"

"We're middlemen. Facilitators. The job goes bad, we don't make people disappear."

The phone goes silent for a while, and at first Lem thinks this means Duck is considering the turns this job has taken, thinking how he would have handled it, but then he starts to think maybe Duck has cut the call. "You still there?" Lem says.

"Still here."

"So?"

"So, this is why we have guns. Like we talked about."

Lem thinks, *No, man, this is why we don't have guns.* He sips at his coffee, which tastes like plastic and unfiltered water. It is not even close to hot. "We're out, what, forty thousand, tops?" Lem says. "The lease, the crane, something for our guys."

"Was thinking a little extra for our guys," Duck says. "All those eyes on them."

"Whatever. Still leaves us close to a quarter million each. Cash."

"Not cash, like you said. Wired."

"To my buddy in Guadalajara. As good as cash."

"And it comes back to me how, in the States?"

Lem chews on this. "Maybe go visit your share. Maybe spend it down there. Maybe the two of us, we get something going down there."

"That's not what we talked about," Duck says.

"No," Lem says. "The whole deal's not like we talked about. But things have changed."

"Fuck that," Duck says. "What's changed is you're spooked, this guy finding our barn."

Lem tells Duck how the job was cursed from the beginning, all those fuckers at the house watching Vern and Cool Mo and them crate and haul the sculpture, how it's looking more and more like they'll be sitting on this balloon dog long enough for it to start losing air. "Could end up with nothing," he says.

"No way to know, right?" Duck says. "A sculpture that looks like nothing, meant to look like nothing. Could end up worth nothing or everything or something in between."

Lem doesn't have it in him to push back on Duck, to let him know how it's the artist's job to connect his work to how we live, to the ways we think about how we live. Some people, you can't talk to them about this shit. They have their own ideas.

"We do this right, Duck, we get a taste," Lem says. "Not what we wanted, but a taste. Like you said, something in between. This is our something in between."

"In between is like somewhere in the middle," Duck says. "No way a half million is in the fucking middle."

"Still," Lem says.

"Not my call," Duck says, after a beat, like he's resigned to it. "Puts us on the wrong end of something in between, but not my call."

"No," Lem says. "My call. In consultation with you. But this is where we are."

He cuts the call before Duck can respond, tugs at the wrapping on his elk jerky with his teeth and walks the few feet from the overhang to the truck. He leaves his coffee cup on the sill. He approaches the truck on the passenger side, sees that Klott has cracked his window and says, "You been listening?"

"Quack, quack," Klott says.

"Motherfucker."

———————

The rest of the day goes the way Lem's buddy the steel manufacturing magnate said it would. There's a bullshit personal loan document someone in his friend's office needs to sign from Wells Fargo, using whatever bullshit name his friend had provided; a promissory note, issued by the bank in Mexico, from the same bullshit name back to Harrison and Marjorie Klott; a confirming call that comes in on Klott's phone from someone on the Wells Fargo compliance desk needing Klott's verbal authorization for the wire transfer; and a confirming text from Klott's wife, letting them know she has been contacted and has given her verbal authorization.

At one point, in the middle of all these calls, all of this waiting, Lem notices the time and says, "Check your watch, Harrison Klott."

Klott checks his watch and sees it's just past eleven o'clock. He says, "And?"

"Eleven-eleven," Lem says. "Like you said. Time for your fucking angels."

"Time for good things to happen," Klott says.

"A-fucking-men."

It amazes Lem, a little bit, that each piece of the transaction can be accomplished electronically, together with the very many assurances that the wire will not be traced back to him. It is as if Klott and his wife are taking a match to a $500,000 bill and watching it turn to ash, as the people charged with the safekeeping of their money look on and as Lem and his friend wait for the burned cash to reform itself on the other side of border, as if by magic.

"This is legit?" Lem says to his buddy in Guadalajara during their back-and-forth, after the angels had maybe come and gone.

"Legit, no," his friend says. "Clean, yes."

By midafternoon, the late summer sun is high in the mountain sky and Harrison Klott and Lem Devlin have run out of things to talk about. Whatever common ground they might have found last night, whatever connection these two men might have felt to each other earlier this morning, seems to have fallen away as the disappointing payoff to this big-time theft began to line itself up on the other end of all these cell calls and emails. And so, they will sit here, joined in this unlikely way by this unlikely set of circumstances, comfortable in each other's company but without a whole lot left to say to each other, until one of them gets an alert telling him ninety-five million pesos have been gently deposited into one of the steel company's shell accounts and that he is good to go.

21.

HARRISON KLOTT

IT HAPPENS FAST.

Not just today, with the wiring of funds to Mexico. With feeling threatened and not threatened. It goes back months, years—a lifetime, even. It goes from publishing his first novel to not being able to write or to stop thinking about not being able to write his second. It goes from the moment he discovered his father's cash, to the moment just before he flew to Florida to move his old man into a new facility, when he and Marjorie were worrying over how to pay for college. It goes from having these three little kids, a couple of them at once, to seeing them flower into something resembling adulthood.

Blink and everything changes, Klott thinks.

Breathe and there's no way to retrace the steps from where you were to where you are.

This, the whiplashing of his prospects, the directionless getting and spending and accommodating, the sudden lurching from one way of being and looking out at the world to another, leaves Harrison Klott feeling turned around, not himself. He tries to remember a time when he and Marjorie had some kind of plan, when he himself thought he had it all figured out. It used to be there was a thread knitting one day to the next, a predictable pattern he could anticipate or understand. Even yesterday, before breakfast, before the fake movers arrived to dismantle the Koons and haul it away, Klott had a sense of how the day would go. Yes, time was racing away from him—more and more, racing and racing—but it was careening along a certain course, and he could at least tell himself he was *somewhat* in control of his days. He could see the path ahead. He would fish and drink and slog his way through whatever male-bonding activities his friend Teddy had lined up for the group, and he would try not to think what the misadventure was costing him before eventually retiring to bed and waking up the next morning to do these things all over again with this same group of same-seeming people, this time on a golf course where the hitch in his swing and his creeping disinterest would only add to his feelings of not belonging.

It was all so *right there*, right in front of him . . . until, at last, it wasn't.

Just now, as the bad-guy-turned-not-so-bad-guy Lem Devlin received an alert that Hymie Klott's cash had been somehow wired and laundered and deposited into an indiscernibly marked account in Mexico, Harrison Klott could not guess how the rest of his day might go. And now that his captor has fled the scene and headed off in search of his ill-gotten pesos, Klott is left to wonder what to make of the whole deal. Already, it is two o'clock in the afternoon, less than seven hours after he'd come clean to Marjorie and directed the transfer, and he cannot recognize the man he was this morning alongside the man he is this afternoon.

This morning, he was a man who'd been unable to find a way to tell his wife of the sudden windfall of his father's cash.

This morning, he was a man being held on this mountaintop farm by a high-end art thief who may or may not have known what he was doing, who may or may not have been making a statement on the imperceptible value of art and the inconceivable barometers of success, and who may or may not have had it in him to beat him with a crowbar.

This morning, he was a man in stasis, walled into complacency, holding to the memory of what it was to have a boundless future unfurling in front of him instead of a series of anti-climaxes in his wake.

This morning, he was a would-be writer with nothing to would-be write about.

And then he blinked. And everything changed.

———

This afternoon's version of Harrison Klott, lifted by the transfer of a half million dollars in exchange for his freedom and momentary custody of a momentarily iconic sculpture, is not moving any time soon. He is sitting, perhaps contentedly, on the flat stepping-stone by the barn door where some hours earlier he had sat with Lem Devlin. Just inside the door, puzzled into one large crate and two smaller crates, are the bits and pieces of Jeff Koons's *Balloon Dog #17 (Red)*—a massive metal sculpture valued at over ten million dollars and yet very nearly worthless to the man who had conspired to pinch it from its base outside a luxurious mountain home.

The pure, brilliant red of Koons's enamel finish appears to Klott through the narrow slats of the large crate like slivers of hope against the despairing browns of pine and dirt floor and barnwood. The splashes of color seem to want to burst forth and fill the barn with wonder. Klott closes his eyes to the scene and then opens them, to see if the picture has changed. He begins to think the piece might be kinetic, even when disassembled and crated, to where he opens and closes his eyes to see if maybe the thing has moved or taken on new shape or been lifted magically—wondrously!—from the ground. He does this again and again. Then he squints, half opening his eyes so that what registers is the mood of the trapped, broken sculpture . . . the bursts of red . . . the tone . . . the essence. What he finds, on opening his eyes a final time and readjusting to the scene, reminds him of *The Red Balloon—Le Ballon Rouge*—a mostly silent short film he remembers from childhood that follows a small boy playing in the grim streets of post-war Paris who comes upon a red balloon with a will of its own.

It surprises Klott, a little, that the movie has stayed with him since his fifth grade French teacher, Mademoiselle Bernheim, killed a Friday afternoon class by screening the film for her charges while she finished her taxes by the dim light of her desk lamp. The story of the film comes to him again as if he is in its middle.

Ah, yes . . . here it is. Remember?

Klott remembers that instead of moving with the breeze or drifting into the sky against the pull of its string, the balloon in the movie seemed to exhibit a playful personality, drawing the boy on a string through war-torn Paris, eventually alighting upon a blue balloon being held by a small girl. He remembers the balloon taking on its owner's personality— spurring him to action, even.

In life, the boy and girl might have met by chance, by fate, but in the life of the movie they meet by the determination of their balloons.

This is like that, he thinks.

I am like that.

I am the small boy with the red balloon. And, this balloon, my *balloon, is telling me what to do.*

Klott, alone with his thoughts and the industrial sculpture that has now come to him on the back of his father's cash, takes his phone from his shirt pocket—the very pocket from which it had fallen the day before into the truck bed of the man who masterminded the theft of the Koons. As he does so, it occurs to Klott that *mastermind* is perhaps too generous a term to describe the clumsy machinations of Lemuel Devlin, who in the end was persuaded to accept less than ten cents on the dollar for his time and effort in rescuing the Koons from its glorious perch.

He navigates to the Rotten Tomatoes website, to see how his memory of the French film matches up with the audience reviews, and he is struck by the way the bright red of the balloon has come to be seen as a symbol of hope and light and innocence among viewers, while the dismal greys of post-war Paris signal despair and darkness and disappointment.

Yes, he thinks. *Yes, yes, yes.*

Yes, his balloon seems to say to him, from between the slats of the large crate and the two smaller crates. This *is* like that. Yes. It very much is. The connection to the movie and to the past couple days gets him thinking how easy it should be to write such a simple story, almost like a fable, and leaves him wondering how it is that he has been unable all these years to find the words to tell such a basic tale of his own. There was a time, early on, when Klott imagined he would spend his days telling modest stories laced with these kinds of universal truths, a time that has been erased in his mind by an intervening period during which he has come to realize he doesn't have all that much to say—or, not unrelatedly, that the world is not all that much interested in what he has to say.

From Rotten Tomatoes, a couple taps against his phone's touchscreen take Klott to Facebook—as ever, his default landing spot when his mind switches to idle. He moves like he is being pulled along by a string tied to a giant red balloon dog, soaring into the heavens. He opens the platform's search bar and enters the name Brandi, with an *i*, together with the key words *Utah* and *catering* and *fly-fishing*. This is how it is with him: Teddy casually mentions that this tightly ponytailed server was enticed back to the house by two of his rich asshole friends, and that she is frolicking in the indoor pool encircling the house's ridiculous main floor sitting area wearing only her panties, and the takeaway for Klott is that there are almost certainly pictures of this young woman waiting to be discovered. He gets this idea and the next thing he knows he's acting on it in his own halting way—one hand on his phone, one down his pants. He cannot help himself, doesn't even think to help himself. He's not fluent in Snapchat or Instagram, where he is more likely to find a social media account assiduously maintained by a twentysomething Utahan inclined to accept the separately creepy invitations of two middle-aged men to join them at the same time at the same location for a vaguely impersonal bacchanal, now made exponentially creepy by the shared pursuit and the other rich assholes who were most likely looking on, sipping at another couple bottles of Angus's most-drinkable 1990 Trimbach, or some other impossibly wonderful grape from some other wondrous harvest, and so he lands here, on comfortable ground.

Predictably, Klott finds a Facebook page under the banner *Brandi at Your Service*, with freshly posted photos from yesterday's riverside brunch and fish fry, together with another set of pics from last night that leave Klott to only imagine what had gone on back at the house while he was here by this spectacularly framed pasture with the hardly masterful mastermind of an art heist gone bad.

Best he can tell, Brandi at Your Service is trying to start her own catering company, while working for a chef who seems to have cornered the market in the presumably high-end and decidedly rugged-seeming farm-to-table and river-to-plate food service category in and around Park City. One of Brandi's specialties, he's noticing, is her willingness to stand in as a human crudité board, judging by the many shots of her upon some table or other, decidedly underdressed and festooned with meats and cheeses and dips. In one, someone seems to have placed a dollop of hummus on her naval area, alongside a handful of what appear to be crusted ciabatta bread cubes. The image gets Klott going for a moment, until he starts to wonder if there might be some compelling way to describe this spread on the new winter menu he's been working on for his one and only client.

Soon, his thoughts run to Shari Braverman, who has by now surely posted additional photos from her son's bar mitzvah—and who, it happily turns out, surely has.

Here she is, the camera drawn to the stunning dress she was wearing at synagogue last week, her hair looking like Jennifer Aniston's in seasons five, six, and eight of *Friends*, her lips shimmering like they always do in her pictures, like he'd failed to notice when he was standing next to her.

Here she is again: a shot of her dancing with her son, a shot of her in the middle of a cluster of women Klott recognizes from around town, from his kids' network of intersecting friends, a shot of her making a toast at the luncheon.

And here, in the final shot of a Facebook album she's titled *Jaxon's*

Big Day!, there's a shot of Klott himself alongside the radiant, *Friends*-like, and vaginally-rejuvenated Shari Braverman, snapped at the very moment she leaned into him conspiratorially in the B'nai Centerville lobby and asked for his help on a delicate matter. The picture takes him back to that moment, to where he now remembers that he could actually feel the wet heat of Shari Braverman's breath across his neck as she spoke softly into his ear, as if they had known each other intimately instead of hardly at all.

It strikes Klott that what had been a casual request in the moment now appears before him on Facebook as a kind of familiarity, and he presses against himself with his free hand, hard at the memory of an exchange that did not register in quite this way while it was taking place. He thrills, a little, that she has chosen to include this image in her album of images—a nothing moment, Klott would have thought, now elevated to *something* by its appearance here, on his app, on his phone, in his other hand.

He sets his phone on his thigh and thinks he should probably comment on the picture. This is what people do, right? This is how interactions happen, how connections get made. He tries not to obsess about it, doesn't think he has it in him to *not* obsess about it, but then he surprises himself and starts typing, his fingers hunting and pecking across his touchscreen without being told what to do. He writes, *Mazel tov! Such a meaningful ceremony. Jaxon did a terrific job.*

There, he thinks. *Wasn't so hard.*

He doesn't post it just yet, gives himself a moment to consider what he's just written—then he adds, *Don't know if you've pulled usher duty for our service next week, but if so, Marjorie and I would love you to join us for our kiddush luncheon afterward. Looking forward to our day of. L'shana tova and all that.*

Again, he stops typing and reads back what he's written—and this time, satisfied, he hits *POST*.

He watches as the comment thread fills with what he's written, as his deepening connection takes its place beneath all these other deepening connections stacking up for Shari Braverman's attention.

Next, he clicks on his notifications, where he sees that Marjorie has mentioned him in a post. The time stamp is from 2:34 a.m., and he recognizes that with the way his phone automatically adjusts for the time difference this means she was awake and looking to let the world know she was awake at 4:34 a.m. on the East Coast, well before they spoke earlier this morning. He imagines it was those calls from Teddy that had her so agitated, those texts from him—why she was awake, at least. Agitated or no, she had enough of her wits to make one of those photo collages, two pictures in one frame. In one, from a million years ago, the five of them stand by the duck pond near their house—with Stewie riding Klott's shoulders, Sydney strapped into Marjorie's forward-facing Baby Bjorn carrier, and Joanna clinging to her mother's hip. In the other, one of Marjorie's clumsily crafted selfies, his three grownish children are splayed across his bed, wearing T-shirts and bar mitzvah giveaway pajama bottoms, a bowl of popcorn tilted on its side atop the bedcovers, with half of Marjorie in frame as she took the picture.

The caption: *Who knows where the time goes?*

Marjorie has somehow attached a song-link to her post, so that when Klott clicks on the split photo it is accompanied by the song of the same name, which had been one of the theme songs of Marjorie's growing up. This, Klott knows, is the kind of detail you carry about someone after your lives are conjoined, intertwined. The experiences of one are soon enough the experiences of the other—and in Marjorie's experience, in what has by now become Klott's shared experience, there was a counselor at *her* sleepaway camp who played "Who Knows Where The Times Goes?" every year at the end-of-summer campfire, and whenever Marjorie would get together with her camp friends they would make an effort to play it, or sing it, or make some sort of reference to it, usually ending in a bout of wistfulness or breathlessness. Here, Marjorie has chosen the original Sandy Denny version to accent her post, instead of the more popular Judy Collins version—a small detail that nevertheless has also got Klott all excited, for the way it reminds him he has been gifted with a wife who reaches for the source material instead of the reasonable facsimiles.

He listens to the song and imagines himself into the scene in his bedroom, into the movie night he has apparently missed. He wonders what they were watching, who made the popcorn, how it happened that they were all awake at four in the morning on a school night, and how it is that the moments of sweetness and light and connectedness that once smiled upon him in full now seem to elude him, or happen without him . . . or, sometimes, without him even noticing.

He begins to type a response to Marjorie's post in the comments thread, which is already gushing with stale Facebook sentiment: *Aw!* and *Feeling all the feels!* and *Adorbs!* and heart emojis in assorted colors and groupings. He tries to think of something fresh to add to the thread, something to maybe push Marjorie's friends and colleagues to think how great it is that she has managed to marry a man so in touch with his feels, but he is distracted by the appearance of three pulsing dots at the top of his Facebook screen. For a brief moment, he cannot think who might be composing a message to him on this platform, but then he realizes the three dots correspond to a second set of dots pulsing beneath his comment on Shari Braverman's thread.

Ah, yes, he realizes. I have made a comment and now someone else is making a comment, and Facebook is simply letting me know. This is how social media works, that's all. But then he sees a message telling him that Shari Braverman is typing a response to his comment—specifically to his comment . . . to *him*—and Klott catches himself staring at his screen, waiting for it to fill what with she has to say.

For the moment, *in* the moment, he forgets about a killer response to Marjorie's sweet post and can only stare at Shari Braverman's three pulsing dots . . . until the three dots stop pulsing and disappear from Klott's screen. He thinks maybe he has imagined them. Then they reappear on his screen and he's back to wondering what they will have to tell them. And there he sits for the next while, in the mid-afternoon sun, alongside this ostensibly refurbished barn which, for the moment, houses an ostensible work of industrial genius, worth more money than Klott will ever understand— which, also for the moment, now seems to belong to him, purchased along with his freedom with a reasonable facsimile of the five hundred thousand in cash from his father's old suitcase.

He is caught in the tight crawl spaces between everything that's come before and everything that might come next, everything he had thought he could anticipate and now can only imagine, with no idea where the time goes from here—where the rest of the day might take him, even.

ACKNOWLEDGMENTS

FOR EARLY READS, editorial and emotional support, art world insights, happy distractions, artistic inspiration and commiseration, and the general care and feeding of what passes for my career, I wish to thank: Mel Berger, Dan Strone, John Silbersack, Jeff Stern, Dallas Hudgens, Lauren Cerand, Jeff Waxman, Timothy Devine, Kevin Burke, Hilary Liftin, Tobias Carroll, Amy Ferris, Laura Zigman, Darin Strauss, Erin Somers, Annie Hartnett, Lydia Kiesling, Ellen Meister, Ronna Wineberg, Ted Flanagan, David Buss, Jonathan Paisner, Eric Kahan, Steve Ludmer, Robert Brinkman, Moshe Banin, Daymond John, Steve Aoki, John Kasich, Ron Darling, Paul Bogaards, Dona Chernoff, Michael Homer, Jonathan Och, Anne Sherwood Pundyk, Jay Alders, Peter Samberg, Jenny Bent, Kirsten Neuhaus, and Madeleine Morel. Also, a shout-out to Daniel Ford and my fellow hosts on the Writers Bone Podcast Network, for helping to celebrate the written word. A hat tip as well to the kind souls and kindred spirits who gather on the first Wednesday of each month to discuss what it means to write in collaboration. (You "ghosts" know who you are.) Special thanks to John Koehler, Joe Coccaro, Becky Hilliker, Skyler Kratofil, Tyler Smiley, and the outstanding team at Koehler Books for finding enough things to like about *Balloon Dog* to want to take it on, and for setting it aloft with such grace and good cheer, and to Sarah Miniaci for beating the drums on its behalf.

Mostly, I am grateful to my family, for supporting me, tolerating me, and indulging me in this endeavor, as in so many others. Curiously, my adultish children are in the habit these days of justifying the fact that they've read very few of my very many books by telling me they're saving them to read after I die— a way to keep my voice alive in their minds when I'm gone, or so they say. Well, here's another one for them to add to the *to read* pile. May it be a good long while before they get around to it.

Daniel Paisner
Park City, Utah—March 2022

Lightning Source UK Ltd.
Milton Keynes UK
UKHW010040291122
413021UK00003B/47

9 781646 636990